THE SHAMAN'S WAR
BOOK 3 OF THE SHAMANIC MYSTERIES

Norman W. Wilson PhD

THE SHAMAN'S WAR
BOOK 3 OF THE SHAMANIC MYSTERIES

ACKNOWLEDGMENTS

First and foremost, a very special thanks to my wife, Suzanne for her continued support, encouragement, and dedication to my writing efforts. She is my chief cheerleader.

A vote of appreciation to Stuart Holland, my editor, and publishers who made all this possible

DEDICATION

This book is dedicated to all those seekers who have fought their own wars in their struggle to ONENESS.

CHAPTER 1
SAYING GOODBYE TO SAY HELLO

The individual is responsible for living his own life and for finding himself. If he persists in shifting this responsibility to somebody else, he fails to find the meaning of his own existence.
Thomas Merton

Running-water knew where he was to go—Mesa Verde, an eight-thousand-foot high plateau in Colorado. It had been there he had first met the new shaman, and it would be there they would meet again.

He took great pains to dress in Native clothing, just enough to heighten his handsome features. Leather moccasins were the right added touch. He left the SUV parked at the hotel. The park was closed. With a backpack slung over his broad shoulders, he set out for the deep canyon. He felt the few last tourists staring at him as he easily jogged along the upper ridge. He paused just long enough to give the young women an extra treat. He enjoyed his sensuality and didn't mind showing it.

He knew how to find the place. The shaman had told him there would cairns marking the directions he should follow.

Running-water's long legs and surefootedness made the trek along the rim of the canyon a good warm up. His days at the university track team paid off as he broke into an easy trot, passing what the white man called Spruce Tree House and on toward Cliff Palace. The smell of pinon pines and tamarisks filled his lungs with their freshness. He felt good being an Indian. *Hell, I don't need Native American attached to my heritage. I am that I am!* For the first time in his young life, he felt sure of who he was, of what he was, and he liked the whole damn feeling. True, much of what had transpired in his life was because of his association with the man he was about to meet.

Cautiously, he climbed down an old wooden ladder into the canyon's basin. As he jumped from the last rung of the ladder, he wondered if Adam would look the same. A canon wren called out as he jogged by a bunch of thistles. *Surely, he must be different after the hellish battle with the witch, Moon-Woman. Am I not changed?*

His mood changed as did the color of the sandstone cliffs. It flowed up from the earth itself— a renewed sense of sacredness about the ground on which he now jogged. Becoming more respectful, he slowed his pace. What a difference between now and then. He had first met Adam at the Spirit of Place Conference.

Man, I was so young then. My primary interest was in getting laid. Not that I am not interested in that now. It's . . . well . . . I'm more experienced now.

A smile spread its way across his full lips.

The rapid-fire chirping from a nearby Mountain Bluebird sounded an alarm.

"No need to worry, my feathered friend, you are in no danger."

In the old days, he would have thrown a stone at the bird. He remembered how he had thrown himself into Adam's presence. That memory caused a sudden burning in his face. He was rash, arrogant even to think the white man who traveled with the most respected and feared of all shaman, would give him a story. It amazed him even more that he and this same man are so connected, so harmonized. It is an enigma.

A slight breeze caught his long blue-black hair. The coolness against his face felt good after his sudden bout with self-embarrassment. He stopped and looked up at the marvel that was the palace of the Ancient Ones.

"It must have at least two-hundred rooms," he whispered, "and in one Adam waits."

"Right on time."

"Man you nearly scared the shit out of me. Where'd you come from?" Running water said, grabbing the man who had fashioned his destiny. He released Adam immediately, embarrassed by his sudden display of emotion.

"Up there," Adam said, looking up at a ridge high above them.

"Yeah, right. You jumped down from up there."

"Used a rope," Adam said as he pointed to a rope hanging down along the cliff's wall.

Most people would not have noticed the rope and the few that did would think it was a vine. Running-water silently scolded himself for not seeing it.

"We'll have to climb back up," Adam said interrupting Running-water's thoughts. "It's just some added security. Come."

Running-water shook his head at Adam's speed and agility climbing the rope. Despite his disbelief, he reminded himself it had been a good year since he had seen Adam. *A man can change a lot in a year.*

The strain of the hand-over-hand rope climb made itself know to Running-water by the sharp pains in his arms. He hadn't done any rope climbing since his high school days. He sat down on the ledge to catch his breath and Looked out at the vast sky spreading itself before him. The colors, jewel-like and ablaze, were bouncing off the sandstone rim that arched high above his head—a rainbow sunset. Distant junipers dutifully reflected the sunlight.

"Beautiful, isn't it?"

"Awesome. It makes a guy humble."

"And grateful," Adam replied.

"Adam, have you ever wondered by the Ancient Ones [1] left? It's so totally fantastic here, "Running-water said as he got up to help Adam with their evening meal.

"It's one of the great mysteries. We have much to talk about, my brother, decisions to be made, and preparations to put in place," Adam said. His voice was low and quiet.

It felt natural to Running-water to have Adam call his "my brother" and he accepted it as having come from a fellow Indian. *What differences does it make if Adam is white? He is an adopted Indian. He has learned Indian ways, and particularly those of a shaman. He sure looks like an Indian and would if it weren't for his azure blue eyes.*

"Yes, I know the ways of the shaman and my powers have grown. And you, friend, have forgotten I can read your thoughts."

"You're right about that one. I had forgotten," Running-water said.

"We still have to find the sixth and seventh person on the list left by my father, Esaugetuh. Hopefully, one of them will lead us to him or at least provide some indication as to what happened to him."

Running-water detected the subdued sadness in Adam's voice.

"You miss him, don't you?"

"All too often, my brother, we let go of the things most important to us. Yes, I miss him and I have missed you."

"And I you, " Running-water replied as tears gathered and he looked away.

He remembered that terrible moment when he thought the soul-snatcher, Moon-Woman had destroyed Adam. *My god, I owe him so much. He fought her to save me, to give my life back.*

"Quiet your mind. You have no debts with me," Adam replied, interrupting Running-water's thoughts.

All Running-water nodded as he wiped the tears away.

Darkness enveloped the huge cave in which the Palace had been built. Adam had laid a small protected fire and had started their evening meal, reminiscent of the many times Esaugetuh had cooked his meals.

Using a metate and mano [2] to grind acorns and corn into flour, Adam then patted it into flat round cakes and placed them in a pot of boiling water. Yucca was baking under the coals, and its stalks laced together were laid over the top of the kettle of boiling water, allowing the steam to cook them. He had set aside some of the boiling water to steep sweet birch twigs for tea. The small pot was just inside the fire ring to keep the tea hot. He chuckled as he checked the baking Yucca root.

"What are you laughing about?" Running-water broke the silence between them.

"The other name for the Yucca plant is Adam's Needle." His broad smile spread itself out. Even in the dim light of the small cooking fire, Adam's azure blue eyes glowed.

"Got it. By the way, where does a guy take a shower around here?" Too late, he realized it was a dumb question.

"There's a bucket to your right. A tin of powder is next to the bucket. Wet your hands, use the powder to create a lather. Lather up and then use the rest of the water to rinse yourself. Best I can do, " Adam replied.

Running-water stepped out of his moccasins. With two moves he had his shirt and pants off. Next, he dropped his shorts. Once his hands were wet, he took a small quantity of the powder. The amount of suds it generated amazed him.

"Hey, Adam, what's this powder? Man, it sure kicks up a great lather."

"Dried Yucca Plant."

The firelight played along Running-water's sinews as he continued to lather up. His man-parts began to grow in size as he lathered himself. Embarrassed, he doused himself with the bucket of water. Its coldness reduced his member to normal. *Damn, I bet I just used up all the water. Every time I am bare-butt naked in the wilds I get an erection.*

Stepping into the light of the fire, Running-water said, "Adam, I didn't bring a towel since you said to travel light. And I was stupid just now and used up all the water. I'm sorry, man."

The fire will dry you and don't dress until you are completely dry. You'll chafe and infections are difficult to cure here. Wrap up in this blanket. Don't worry about the water. There will be more," Adam said pointing to a moisture catcher he had built.

Little was said while they ate. Once finished, Adam offered a brandy, the aged kind they both had learned to appreciate, the same brand favored by Esaugetuh. It was a pleasant surprise for Running-water but not to be outdone, he reached behind him, pulled around his backpack and opened it. He pulled out a black velvet cloth and with great care untied it, removed two pieces of his flute and put them together. He then fished around in the black velvet and brought out the mouthpiece.

The song he played called up memories of a past people. Mysterious, melodic, and sorrowful; a soul-sound played for the past and present lives, calling out the universal spirit—a cry for eternal wisdom, compassion, and understanding among all peoples.

So haunting was the melody even the magnificent cliffs that housed them blushed with their own memories of times gone by—memories of the first creation, of seen and unseen generations of cosmic tadpoles.

As Adam looked at Running-water he nodded. They locked their gaze, both realizing and understanding their connectivity—twin souls connected in universal brotherhood. Words were not necessary. Each man knew of the other's brotherly love; each accepting the sacred trust existing between them. Both had met the ultimate test—the willingness to die for the other—both had risen to the call. Both had survived! For the moment, peace belonged to them.

Running-water nodded back.

Bird song and sunrise announced the promise of a beautiful day. Adam offered up the left-over bread topped with fresh berries. In the daylight, Running-water saw a new and lean Adam, bronzed and hair now long and dark. *Most would think he was an Indian. Of course, the azure blue eyes give him away.*

Adam's voice broke into his thoughts.

"What have you found out about the sixth person on our list?"

"There's been a problem because I wasn't sure if the name referred to a woman or a man."

"So, nothing," Adam said.

"Quite to the contrary. Sydney Thompson is a woman," Running-water replied.

"Sounds British. Is she?"

"Canadian. She lives in Toronto. So now, do we go to Canada? And maybe on to Montreal to open Esaugetuh's safety deposit box? It's been a while since we knew of its existence. There might be important information there, something that might give us a hint as to where he is."

Ignoring the questions Adam said, "Do you have anything specific on this Karuna House I supposedly own?"

"It's in Toronto also. It's a large estate housing a charitable society. Its location in Toronto tells me it's pricy."

"Hmm. Interesting that our sixth person just happens to live in Toronto where I just happen to own a mansion and I believe a private sanitarium. So what did you find out about this Sydney Thompson?" Adam asked.

"She's hot. I mean hot!"

"Cut the crap."

"I can't help it, Adam. I'm in heat or haven't you noticed?" "Running said laughing as he

17

humped the air in ithyphallic motions. "She owns a bar, lives upstairs. She occasionally dates a TJ Russell, a bouncer she hires on heavy weekends. I have photos if you want to take a look."

"Sure. Have you made contact? And what's the name of the bar? " Adam paused, let out a low whistle. "You are right about one thing."

"What's that?"

"She's hot."

"Yeah, I thought you'd agree. And no, I haven't made contact. The bar's called "Sid's". You want me to call her."

"No, not yet," Adam replied. His voice trailed off.

Since his arrival at the cliff-dwelling, Running-water felt Ada was distracted, even detached from his surroundings. He looked at Adam just sitting there with a blank expression on his face, eyes half shut. *I wonder where he goes when he's like this? He just sits there staring at the sky or across the canyon searching for something.*

Coming out of his other worldliness, Adam said, "You want to know about the battle with Moon-Woman?"

"Well, yes—yes I do." The question surprised him. "I've wondered about it. You've not indicated you wanted to talk about it."

He shifted his body, leaning forward, he looked directly at Adam.

"How did you defeat her? My god, Adam, I have never been so terrorized in my life as I watched you battle her." A wave of nausea flooded him.

"It's difficult to explain exactly what happened. Because of the shamanistic powers transferred to me from Esaugetuh, I can tune into certain universal experiences that others cannot. Feedback loops exist whenever two entities interact, and the information exchanged has a decided effect of both individuals. As information exchange continues, there is a continued increased complexity. Listen, do you hear it?"

There was a long pause.

"No," Running-water said. "I don't hear anything."

"That's it. I had to present myself to Moon-Woman as non-emotive. The total silence of my being was essential. I had to still my soul, so she could not find a target. The lightning she was generating was her own hatred, a hatred for what she had become."

"Man, I remember the lightning she was generating. The total sky was on fire. I even felt the hair on my arms being singed. It scared the shit out of me. I was so sure you had been fried," Running-water said.

"It was powerful," Adam continued. "Traditional thinkers tell us that the one component of existence that is beyond change is the soul. They are wrong, dead wrong!"

"Why?"

"Just because the soul is energy and the second law of thermodynamics says energy can't be destroyed doesn't mean that it can't be transformed. The soul can be transformed. It is either transformed into pure love or pure hatred. When one is surrounded by abject hatred and love is gone, there is nothing left, " Adam said.

"You mentioned a feedback-loop. How did that impact Moon-Woman?

"It brought her no emotional response from me, and as she struggled to combat that, the complexity of our exchange increased to such a degree she became neutralized. At that point, I had to recharge my emotional level. That's why I called out to you. I need your strength, energy and your love. Total love and unconditional. You gave that to me and I defeated her."

"I don't really understand," Running-water said.

"Moon-Woman was the twin of Marrie Copa, your grandmother. When they were young and courted by Jedediah Woods, your grandfather, they played the old switch game. He slept with both women and never knew it. Moon-Woman could not conceive. Denied the one thing she wanted, she grew bitter. She was barren. She transfixed that hate to Marrie and then to you when she learned of your existence."

"You think I've inherited her barrenness?" Running-water asked.

Roaring with laughter, Adam said, "I hardly think so."

"What's so damn funny," Running-water snapped.

"Only women are barren. I thought we covered this before," Adam said struggling to contain his laughter.

"Yeah, I know. I guess I'll always wonder until a woman has my kid. Sorry I interrupted."

Adam got up, moved to the back of the cave. There he picked up two chunks of dried cactus. Returning to the fire pit, he placed one at the edge of the fire, waited until it caught fire, and then he moved it closer to the center. Satisfied, he settled back on the blanket next to Running-water's.

"If I had met Moon-Woman with hatred, and believe me, I felt plenty, I would have been consumed by her. The loop would have returned my hatred tenfold. I had to clear any ill will I felt toward her. To do that I had to think of only one thing," Adam said.

"Which was," Running-water asked as he sipped the rest of his brandy.

"The consummate ultimate truth."

"You are talking way beyond me. First, it was silence, then non-hatred, and now it's ultimate truth. Boil it down, my brother, so this Indian can get it."

"Love, my brother, love. It's the heart of all creations, of the cosmos, of our very existence. I thought only of love, unconditional love, and it drew her in because it was the one thing she really didn't have."

"And?"

"Since my experience in a parallel universe, I have realized that we and all other things that exist or ever have existed are inexorably linked. Every breath we have inhaled has been exhaled at some point by some human, animal, or another life form. Their expelled atoms are a part of us. And because they are, all other knowledge exists within each of us—the sum total that has gone on before and all that will become, " Adam replied.

Continuing, Adam said, "That means every molecule, every atom, and all of their subparts exist in each of us. If love and only love existed in my heart, then that was all Moon-Woman could experience. We experienced the same information, the same energy, even our thoughts are units of energy. I transferred that energy to her."

"Okay, so what happened to her? Where is she?"

"Because so much of her life force was used up in hatred, there was enough left to save her. At least, that what I believe. I think she simply disintegrated," Adam said.

"Man, I just don't get it. To begin with, I thought she was in an institution in Pennsylvania. "

"I am told the authorities found a pile of ashes in her cell. They call it spontaneous human combustion. I believe her spirit died."

"And not her soul?" Running-water asked.

"The soul cannot be destroyed, but one's spirit can."

"So, where's her soul? Won't it come back and try to kill you again?"

"I can only guess. And it is my understanding that the soul returns to its original source. In this case back to the Akashic Field where it will be transformed."

"Whew! I am sure glad it's over. She nearly nailed you," Running-water said.

"No, my brother, she nearly killed you. I was her conduit to you."

A sharp flash of lightning scissored the sky. Its appearance reminded Adam of the hours he spent with Esaugetuh. While they used to sit and talk, lightning always seemed to be a part of their relationship. *Actually, I think lightning baptized me. Every time I asked Esaugetuh questions that irritated him or got to personal, lightning blasted out of nowhere. Even on a clear day or night as it did just now. I wonder what omen it holds.*

"Hey, you've left me again. Where are you, Adam?" Running-water said, giving Adam a gentle poke.

"I was thinking about Esaugetuh and the sessions we used to have. He was always teaching me a lesson. Mostly, about what he called the Attributes of Selfhood. Good, God! I've nearly forgotten them."

Adam closed his eyes trying to remember. *When you live something or at least try, it's difficult to put it to labels.*

"The park will soon be open. Won't we be seen by the Rangers as well as the hordes of tourists?"

"What? Oh, yes. I'll take care of that. Move your gear to the back about ten feet," Adam replied indicating a V-notch behind them. "Ease your way up through the crevice. You'll find a small cavern there."

Adam followed, stopped part way, turned around, and moved a large rock back into the opening before continuing the climb.

It was an ideal spot. They would be out of view and there was ample room for two adults. At the moment it was comfortably cool but by nightfall, it would be cold.

"Adam, why are we here? Are you in danger?" Running-water said. His voice barely a whisper.

There was something about this place that quieted him. Maybe it was out of respect for the civilization that once was. Whatever it was, he felt it deep within his soul.

Adam sensed Running-waters inner thoughts because they were so strong. Turning to him, he said, "Is it not fitting we should come back to the place of the Ancient Ones to capture a sense of their essence, to reestablish a connection to Esaugetuh since I believe him to be a direct descendant of the Ancient Ones?"

"I suppose you are right, but . . . "

"This woman to whom Esaugetuh gave a building and a bar to manage may provide another piece of the puzzle," Adam said, ignoring Running-water's comment.

"He gave her the business to run. You still own it. Hmm, do you know something you're not telling me?

"No. It's just that I have questions. Why, for example, would Esaugetuh give her a bar to run? What's her issue?"

"Her issue? What do you mean?"

"Her problem. Each of the other people on our list had problems. There have been monetary, physical health, emotional health, or interpersonal relationship issues. I believe Esaugetuh felt we are a diminished society and he expects us to do something about it. If we examine the list, we'll find the people on it are a social experiment, " Adam said.

"Explain."

"I think Esaugetuh believed the human race is separated, detached, or diminished because it has denied the value of Self. We are no more than faded holograms separated from our original source."

"Sorry, Adam. I'm not following you."

"Let me put it this way. If a light bulb continually burns, its brightness over time gradually dims; it diminishes. Isn't our world like that? Disease, wars, greed, exploitation, mass murders, terrorism, and political correction. There is a total disregard for human life. Road rage deaths are indicative of our inability to control our emotions. Children are toting guns into their schools. Children are killing their parents and grandparents. And certainly, the continuous pollution of the environment and the lack of respect for wildlife demonstrates our separation from the natural world. Not only are we poisoning our physical world, but we are also poisoning our emotional world."

"Man, you are sure on a downward spiral. Makes me almost sorry I asked," Running-water said as he let out a low whistle.

"I am very serious. Thirteen percent of Americans are on antidepressants. Each year in the United States there are over 700,000 attempted suicides. Diminished is a good word for the current state of affairs. A former President of the United States touted the idea of a thousand points of light. It failed to ignite the involvement of the citizens. It was a political agenda and not a spiritual one. Our goal, society's goal, must be to find our way back to our wholeness—to rediscover the value of Self. And if this is true, doesn't it establish the necessity for reincarnation in its highest sense?"

"So, you're saying these five people from our list of seven lost their sense of Self Value?"

"Not self-value; the value of Self. There's a difference. Self-value implies self-centeredness, that is, an over appraisal of one's worth, a selfishness. Value of the Self, on the other hand, is recognition of the source of one's being, a spiritual recognition of one's *deity in posse*."

"One's what? Man, you sure are off on a run. You sure you're okay?" Running-water said. His voice was subdued showing concern.

"I am fine. I have much time to think about all of this. If there is a lesson to be learned from Moon-Woman, we must define it. To answer your question, *Deity in posse* simply means the potentiality of the divine. If you accept the notion human beings are a creation, and I don't give a crapshoot if it was instantaneous or evolutionary, then who or whatever was responsible for this creation, must be a part of us. In that respect, the Hindus have it right."

"Okay, so in what way did you bring about a reincarnation, a recognition of the value of Self in the five people on our list of seven? Remember, three of them are dead," Running-water said.

"Hmm. Maybe if I hadn't looked for them, Marrie Copa, Christopher Saint-Michaels, and Jedediah Woods would still be alive. Their deaths haunt me. I know of nothing they did to harm me or anyone else."

Running-water watched the change taking place in Adam. A cloud of non-being, shroud-like, enveloped him. Eyes now blank, Adam stared off into empty space.

Why did these three people have to die, Adam thought. *Each experienced a horrible death. A bunch of drug-smugglers gunned down Christopher Saint-Michaels. Marie Copa was starved to death by her twin sister, Moon-Woman, and Jedediah Woods was electrocuted by a high-voltage wire. Why?*

A tear rolled down his bronzed check as Adam continued an unwilling remembrance.

Pulitzer author, Thornton Wilder asked the same question of why. He also provided the answer. When I read his book, The Bridge of San Luis Rey his answer didn't mean much then. Today, however, it says it all. He wrote, "There is a land of the living

27

and a land of the dead and the bridge is love, the only survival, the only meaning. [3]

"Adam," Running-water said.

"Huh?"

"You can't blame yourself for their deaths. If you really look at it, you brought a renewal of life to each of them. To Saint-Michaels, you brought a realization of his humanity. You gave Marrie Copa a reason for living and for Jedediah, my grandfather, you helped him realize his bitterness eroded far too many of the precious years of his isolated life. Did you not show them the ultimate truth, as you have called it, is love? You gave to each of them without condition and for a brief time, they realized the reality of their lives. No greater gift can a man give than that. Do not fret, my brother," Running-water said.

Running-water realized there was a bluish glow slowly emanating from Adam, enfolding him. Gradually Adam became nearly transparent. Somewhere in the deep enfolded recesses of memory, he recalled seeing Adam become a glowing blue light. Until now, he had always believed it to be part of his delirium as he lay desperately ill in the hospital, waiting to die. *I haven't been imagining things. I am seeing a physical transformation taking place, the emergence of a new power, a magnificent power waiting to be set free. Good, God! Why am I even here? What am I supposed to be doing?'*

"All in good time, my brother."

Running-water wasn't sure, but for a moment he thought the voice came from outer space.

"Our relationship," Adam continued as he returned to his normal appearance, "is much more than mere mutualism."

"Mutualism? Sounds like some form of torture."

"Well, for starters—organisms live together in a relationship, each dependent upon the other. The cougar and the deer have a predatory relationship. That is, the cougar depends upon the deer for its food and survival. The deer, on the other hand, needs the cougar to keep the population down, thus preventing starvation. Children depend upon their mothers in an almost parasitic relationship. The overall degree of such dependency rests upon the mutual need each participant displays.""

"So, what you're saying is that you and I are dependent upon one another. Which one of us is the cougar, the deer, the parent, or the child? " Running-water said.

"As I said our relationship is more than mutualism. Ours is like the yucca plant, which has a relationship with another organism, the Yucca Moth. Their relationship is more like the kind you and I have."

Reaching over, he poked Running-water.

"And how is that?"

"The yucca plant can't reproduce seeds without the Yucca Moth. Normally, the yucca plant produces only small rosettes and they remain by the parent plant, mere copies of the parent, and because they are copies, there is little possibility or potential for genetic variation."

"What's the point?" Running-water said.

"The Yucca Moth is dependent on the plant for its sustenance. Its caterpillars eat the seeds and as they move about, expel the seeds; thus, spreading the plant."

"How are we like that? Damn it, Adam why don't you just say what you mean? I sure as hell don't need a botany lesson."

Ignoring Running-water's impatience, Adam got up and paced around their small living space. Turning toward Running-water, his voice very quiet, he said, "You are not developing your potential. You are not becoming what you are to become because you remain with me. And that's why I asked you to meet me here, the home of your ancestors. I thought the spirit of place would help you understand that you must go your own way, be your own person."

"You can't kiss me off just like that. I won't let you. Damn it, Adam, what's gotten into you? We are soul mates, inseparable. You said so yourself."

"You must go and leave me to do what I must do. We will meet again, but for now, we must say goodbye."

"And if I won't leave?"

"Then I will make you go. I want you to continue to handle my legal and business affairs. You are to remain as my attorney. However, days as my shield and protector are over. You, my brother, have a destiny of your own to fulfill."

A helicopter came into view, hovered over their hiding place. A ladder tumbled down to the waiting men.

"Climb," Adam said.

Grabbing his backpack, slinging it over his broad shoulders, Running-water fastened himself into the harness, wiped tears from his eyes, and gave a thumbs up to the helicopter.

Adam watched the slow ascent, wiped the tears from his own eyes. The chopper rose up, dipped a goodbye, and disappeared from sight. Even though it was no longer visible, he continued to stare after the chopper.

Instead of using the yucca metaphor, I should have told him I had read the unhappiness in his soul, the sorrow that lingered there, and that I knew his deepest desire. He sure can't father children if he remains with me. Maybe I could have been gentler, showed more appreciation for all that he has done for me. I do know that if he stayed, his destiny would be denied.

CHAPTER 2
THE MASTER

If ultimate reality can create, dissolve, and recreate, then human beings participate in that creation.

Esaugetuh

Adam's private jet landed at Toronto's Pearson International without incident. This time, Dutch, his pilot remained with the plane and navigator; Brett Montana went with him. Because Running-water was no longer with him, it was now standard procedure for one of these two men to remain on board the plane while the other went with Adam.

Usually, there would be a rental car waiting for them, but not this time. A stretch limo with a uniformed chauffeur standing by the side of the car waited for them.

A shiny brass nametag across the right breast pocket of his dark-blue jacket announced he was Bradford. He was a handsome figure of a man, broad-shouldered and muscular. His perfect white teeth flashed a smile as he opened the door for Adam and Brett, then touched the brim of his hat with two fingers once his two passengers seated themselves.

Adam sensed that beneath this man's polite manner was a deadly seething power. Bradford asked no questions, so not directions; nor did Adam give any.

Seven heavily armed guards stood at attention at various stations along the poorly lighted narrow drive. Each had a security dog. At each station, as they passed by, Brett felt the hair on the nape of his neck curl. His hand instinctively touched his jacket, finding comfort in his holstered automatic. He knew that where Adam was concerned there was always the possibility of great danger. He wondered if it had been that with the original Adam. Or had God protected him from predators? *Whatever the case, I am ready. Glad I trained as a Navy SEAL. I guess he dismissed Running-water. Wonder when my turn will come.*

"I did not dismiss Running-water. He remains as my attorney and manager of my affairs," Adam said, interjecting himself into Brett's thoughts.

"You always mind-read?"

"No, only when the thoughts reach out to me. And yours did."

"Why did you send him away?" Brett insisted as the limo snaked its way around the huge mansion.

"So he could marry and create babies."

Brett roared at the prospect of a woman hooking up with Running-water long enough to marry him. Adam just smiled. Such a woman had already entered Running-water's life.

Besides being a dark night, the limousine's heavily tinted windows made it nearly impossible to see anything. Brett pushed a button and lowered his window. He squinted as he struggled to see the house. Despite its massiveness, it was barely visible. The limo's headlights glanced off the front of the building. It appeared to be red stone. A lone light shone on the front portico. *Surely not enough to illuminate the place*, Brett thought.

No interior lights were visible. *Strange,* Brett thought*, if you want security you'd want lots of lights.*

Bradford eased the limo around a corner and headed into an underground garage. Brett felt his muscles tighten. Memories of another underground facility and dead bodies caused his breathing to accelerate. He shook his head and then glanced sideways at Adam. He detected no uneasiness from him.

"Easy does it," Brett said.

"Easy does it?" Adam replied.

"Yeah, don't you feel it? Sense it? There's an uneasiness here, a tension. Look at that wall. Looks like it was just stuck there. Wonder why?" Brett's tense voice said it all.

Before Adam could answer, Bradford had their doors open and was signaling they should follow him. They climbed their way up a long narrow set of poorly lighted stairs. Eventually, they entered a large reception hall, a throwback to the Nineteenth Century with its marble floor, oriental scatter rugs and chandelier.

Turning to Adam, Bradford said, "Wait here. The Master will see you shortly."

"What did you say?" Adam's voice was so cold it surprised Brett.

Immediately, Brett stepped in front of Adam, gun drawn and said, " You always speak to your employer with such contempt?"

"Please excuse Bradford. I am The Master," the voice came from a dark robed figure at the end of the room. Continuing, the figure said, "There's no need for weapons here."

"I am Adam. Show yourself."

"You heard him. Show yourself and put your hands behind your head," Brett growled.

The robed figure disappeared.

"Damn it, Adam. How do you keep getting into these weird places?" Bred said as he un-holstered his other gun.

"Easy. I think we are about to have a show."

Groans and sorrowful cries filled the reception room. The cries echoes bounced off the walls. It was something right out of Disney's *Haunted Mansion*. A barrage of laser lights flashed followed by the rumble of thunder. All went quiet. Then from nowhere yet from everywhere came a phantom voice.

"Do not, and I repeat, do not, trifle with The Master."

"Hmm. Looks like I need to put on a little side-show myself," Adam said winking at Brett.

Cupping his hands together, Adam formed a PSI ball and sent it flying down the center of the room to the spot where The Master had stood. It hovered there, and at Adam's command, it made a sudden right turn. Adam three a second PSI ball and then a third. The last brought The Master to his knees at Adam's feet, begging for mercy.

A dozen red-bobbed figures gathered along an upper balcony. They remained motionless but soon began to hum in unison. Gradually, they increased the pitch, which took on a life of its own—fevered and hypnotic.

"Silence!" Adam's voice boomed with such force the chandelier shook. It's crystal droplets tinkled creating a sharp contrast to the relentless humming.

"Come down here immediately. And get rid of those silly red robes. This is not a monastery."

Adam's voice was a vibrating roar in their ears. A couple of the men cried out in pain.

"Stop. Please stop."

Ignoring their pleas, Adam responded, "Now!"

Looking down from their balcony, they saw their leader on his knees. The bluish glow emanating from Adam frightened them, and they clung to one another. Slowly, the twelve men descended the stairs and formed a semi-circle around The Master. Herd-like, they pressed close to one another as they focused on the guns in Brett's hands. When they shyly glanced at his eyes, they saw death.

Looking at the man still on his knees, Adam said, "Why the pretense, this childish charade of fake moons and lightning? You know who I am and why I am here."

"I . . . I don't know who you are. You and that man with the guns," The Master lied. *Just who does he think he is, coming here like he's some high muckety-muck? I'll have to watch him so he doesn't spoil everything.*

"This is the Esaugetuh Benevolent Society is it not? Named for my father," Adam said, his voice cold. He had read The Master's thoughts. *I'll wait and see how far this character goes with this charade.*

"Yes," the red-robed men said in unison.

Coming up off of his hurting knees, The Master forced a smile and said, "We thought HE was arriving. He had said he would be back. I assumed the person the chauffeur went to get was Esaugetuh." *I am so clever.*

"Why would you assume that? My attorney notified you that I was the one coming here."

"Oh, my," The Master feigned. "I just caught the name Esaugetuh and assumed HE was coming. I can see now, I am mistaken."

"My bodyguard and I are hungry. Have hot foot sent to my father's apartment. I believe it's on the third floor. Make sure there's enough food for four people. Bradford, you will join us."

With a nod from The Master, one of the red-robed men escorted Adam and Brett to an elevator. It was one of those birdcages and like the gate at the front of the house, it complained. It was slower than the proverbial 'slow board to China.'

Finally, it creaked to a halt at the third floor.

The Victorian motif continued from the first flower mahogany paneled walls with gilded scone shaped lights on every third panel. The panels between the scone lights were floor-to-ceiling plate glass mirrors giving a distinct impression that the room had originally been a ballroom.

At the right of the entrance and off to one side was a large marble fireplace. Its location broke the rectangularity of the room. In front of the fireplace, several red leather chairs formed a zone of intimacy. Tables with eagle-claw brass feet created a discrete separation between the chairs. On these were Tiffany lamps. A matching red leather three seat sofa with beautifully sculptured wooden arms and legs sat a few feet from the chairs. With a carved wooden credenza and its twin Tiffany lamps, a private conversation area was created.

At the opposite end of the room, Adam noticed a set of large folding wooden doors. A questioning frown formed on his brow.

One of the red-robed men broke his silence and responded to Adam's quizzical look.

"Sleeping quarters are behind those doors."

"Thank you," Adam said as he nodded at the man.

Within a few minutes Bradford and the man who called himself The Master arrived. The red-robed man bowed and left the room. The elevator creaked his leaving. Bradford and The Master had carts full of steaming food.

"Come, join us," Adam said as he signaled that all of them should sit down. "Bradford, you sit here, please."

The Master looked at Bradford with total scorn. It was almost a snarl as his lower lip curled and then turned into a half-assed condescending smile.

Ignoring The Master's disapproval, Bradford nodded his acknowledgment of the invitation and stepped over to the fireplace, pushed a button and gas flames lapped their way around artificial logs, an obvious recent change to the fireplace.

Adam lifted the lids of each food cart, sniffing the aromas as he did so. Slices of roast turkey in a light gravy occupied one pot. The others contained steaming vegetables. The remaining dish contained slices of roast beef au jus. The next cart contained assorted breads, butter, and preserves. The last cart contained a variety of deserts.

Picking up a warm plate, Adam dished up food from each of the pots and handed it to Brett. He fixed the second plate. The Master held out his hand to accept it, but Adam gave it to Bradford. The Master's lower jaw went into a dive. He glared at Bradford. The Master got the third plate and then Adam took a small portion of food for himself and then sat down.

The aroma of hot spiced tea floated up from beneath the first cart and reminded Adam of another time when he has been served tea. A frown creased his face. *Marrie Copa, Running-water's grandmother, would still be alive had I not left her alone. The tea she served me was the worst tea in the world and like so many others in my life, she offered me what she had. It's different here.*

The lack of prayer from The Master surprised Adam since Esaugetuh had always expressed his thanks for the food provided. *It seems to me that Esaugetuh would have had the members of his Society give thanks.*

"Unto thee," Adam said remembering those were the words of the Late Jedediah Woods.

No one spoke during their eating. Brett was the only one who was eating with any enthusiasm. He picked at his food, taking a small sample of each item on his plate. He stood up, nearly knocking his food over.

"Where's the head?" Brett said.

"If you men the lieux d'aisances," "The Master said with a slight sneer. "Go through the doors at the rear of this room. Second door on the right."

Once he was on the john Brett began muttering to himself. *I don't get it! I'm sure Dutch knew nothing about this Society of Benevolence. Hell, none of us knew it existed. Adam sure doesn't share any confidences with us anymore.*

He flushed the toilet and then washed his hands. He looked in the mirror over the green marble sink. *Hmm, wonder if this Bradford is my replacement. He sure is strange. Gives me the creeps.*

Brett returned to the group and turning to Bradford he said, "Bradford do you fly?"

"Yes, but I don't get away very often."

"No, I was an AMPV man. You were a Navy SEAL?" Bradford asked.

"Yeah, how'd you know that?"

"Easy, you're wearing the insignia on your holster," Bradford said.

"Man, how'd you end up with—"

"Brett," Adam interrupted, "would you and Bradford explore that question in another area of the room while I have a private chat with The Master."

"It would please this humble person," The Master replied as he gave Bradford and Brett a dismissive nod.

Brett felt a flush come to his cheeks, turned to respond but clinched his teeth shut instead. *That son-of-a-bitch. Who does he think he is dismissing me like some servant? I out to fix him so h has a permanent high-pitched voice.*

Adam's voice interrupted his thoughts. "Thanks, Brett. I'll catch up with a bit later."

Adam sensed the building anger in his navigator and sometimes bodyguard. He gave him a thumbs-up. Turning to The Master, Adam said, "Tell me how else are you called?"

"I am called Joseph."

"Well, Joseph, tell me what is the purpose of The Esaugetuh Society of Benevolence?"

"To spread the word of benevolence, of course," Joseph replied. *I would have thought he would have asked about me.*

"And how does the Society define benevolence?"

"Compassion," Joseph said as he fiddled with the sleeve of his robe.

"And how does the Society define compassion?"

"Well, I—"

"Good God, man! Don't you know? You don't, do you? And you are The Master. Come now, surely you must know what the Society does to spread the idea of benevolence, to provide role models for others to follow."

"I don't understand," Joseph mumbled. He felt confused, threatened by the line of questioning. *Wasn't the Society formed to take care of The Brothers and myself? Surely, this upstart knows that. So, what's his game?"*

"What does the Esaugetuh Society of Benevolence do to spread its idea of compassion? Do you hold seminars, teach-ins, lecture series, or offer free publications?"

"We don't do any of that stuff. We are simply The Brotherhood. We look out for each other," Joseph said.

"And who pays for this brotherly love?" Adam's tone sharpened.

"He paid for us to live here, Esaugetuh did."

"And you have no duty toward others?"

"Well, yes," Joseph said barely above a whisper. "We treat one another with compassion."

Adam struggled to control the anger he felt building as he said, "You are living a selfish and non-productive existence. One that has no meaning or purpose. You haven't the slightest idea what benevolence means or what compassion is. "

"But," Joseph tried to protest.

"All of that is about to change. From now on, there will be a new direction with a new purpose for the Esaugetuh Society of Benevolence. Suppose you begin, Joseph, by telling me how you can show compassion," Adam said leaning across his leather chair and looking directly at Joseph.

"I don't understand. What do you mean?"

"Suppose a man came to the gate of this mansion and asked for food."

"We don't get those types here," Joseph replied, his lips curled showing the contempt he felt.

"Well, suppose, just for the moment, that such a person did come to the gate. What would The Brothers do? What would their response be?" Adam persisted.

"The guards would chase him away."

"And that's how you define The Brothers' purpose. Why don't you want people here?"

"We do chase people away. We don't want people coming here because it disturbs the tranquility we have here. People would disrupt our meditation," Joseph replied. His voice rose as he assumed his defensive tone and added a touch if indignation for effect.

"And how does that show benevolence or compassion as you have defined it?" Adam said, warming to the interrogation.

"It, it doesn't," Joseph replied. His lower lip quivered.

"I see. During your meditations on what do you meditate?"

"Nothing. The whole point of meditation is to empty one's mind," Joseph said. Pleased with his answer, he let a small smile appear at the corner of his mouth.

"And what is the purpose of this emptying?"

"To connect with our inner selves."

"So in reality, you sit around, meditate, eat, sleep, relieve yourselves, and then repeat the cycle day after day. And all of this is in the hope of getting in touch with your inner selves. And for what purpose do you want to get in touch with your inner self?

"Unbelievable! Didn't my father, Esaugetuh, The Master of Breath, talk to you about the Five Attributes of Selfhood?"

"I don't remember," Joseph replied. Beads of perspiration formed on this shaved head. Instinctively, he wiped his brow and head with the back of his long sleeve.

"The First Attribute of Selfhood has definite application here. Mindfulness, Joseph, involves being aware of all existence, not just your own."

Adam had softened his tone. He leaned back in the red leather chair and waited.

"Explain," Joseph finally said.

"It means being aware of all existence—not just as a passer-by but as one who is involved in the act of awareness. It also means you must respect that existence."

"So, how does one do that, become aware of existence?"

"First of all, you need to look at all existence as an act of creative beauty. Have reverence for those acts necessary for you to sustain yourself. Earlier, I noted you didn't show any appreciate for the food you were about to eat. I would think that would be one of the behaviors of The Brothers," Adam said as he stood up to stretch.

"You're right. Absolutely right. I showed no appreciation for the food provided for me and no respect for the man who made it possible for us to live," Joseph said as he stretched his neck to look up at the man towering over him. He forced tears to come to his eyes. "Next time Adam, we'll pray to him our thanks."

"Come now, Joseph. I can't believe you would pray to my father, Esaugetuh. You know very well I meant to that which is Divine. You must look at everyone as something unique. Once you begin to involve yourself in what makes that person unique you will suspend all judgment. You will stop saying I don't like this or that about a person. With suspension, value is witnessed."

Wiping his eyes with the back of his hand, Joseph said, "But I don't see how all that brings about a realization of our inner selves." He sniffed for dramatic effect, inwardly pleased by his question.

"When you suspend judgment, value shows in yourself because you see it reflected in others. It comes back to you. If you do not value your Self, then you cannot value others beyond their functionality."

"Functionality?" Joseph said, screwing his face into feigned astonishment as he sat back down.

As Adam lowered his six-foot frame into the red leather chair he reached over, pick up his cup and took a sip of the still slightly warm tea. For just a moment he savored its spicy flavor.

"When Brett and I entered the reception hall you identified your as to what your function is in The Brotherhood, not who you are. Have you noticed when someone is introduced, he is introduced, for example, as Fire Chief Jon Kin? That immediately identifies function and denies personhood. And that brings me to Bradford. You view him only as a chauffeur, as a servant, and not as a unique human being with deity in posse," Adam said.

"My goodness, Adam, how you do carry on. Deity in posse? What's that? "

"Simply this. If you believe you are the creation of the divine, and I don't care what you call him or her, then you must have within you some of that divinity. Deity in posse implies the potential for divines. And isn't all life a series of potentialities?"

"Whew!" Joseph said. "My goodness." He leaned forward just a bit to show enthusiasm.

"Take Brett, for example. He is not my servant even though he works for me. He is, first, my trusted friend. He is my equal, and I respect his opinions and views. That's why I sent him off with Bradford. Bradford has a world to reveal and you,

Joseph must walk lightly when it comes to him."
Adam said, stretching his long legs out in front of
the fire.

"Goodness, " Joseph said barely above a
whisper. *We'll see who walks lightly.*

At that moment Brett sauntered back into the
area of the fireplace, pulled a chair around and sat
down.

"Bradford said he had an early day ahead of
him. It seems he's not only the chauffeur but all the
cook and housekeeper. Hope I'm not intruding."

"No, not at all, we are through here," Adam
said. Turning to Joseph, he continued, " Go and tell
Bradford to come back here. We'll see you in the
morning, Joseph.

"Whatever you wish. Good night," Joseph said.
His face flushed at the dismissal.

Adam waited until Joseph had entered the
elevator and has started the downward trip before
speaking to Brett. "What's your impression our
Bradford?"

"He's a loaded cannon. More likely a
smoldering volcano. What's your interest in him?"
Brett noted Adam's use of the words 'our Bradford.'

"Running-water is busy with my business
affairs and I need to bring someone else into our
immediate group. Someone who is strong, multi-
skilled, and capable."

The clickety whir of the elevator interrupted.
The clank of its metal gate announced Bradford's
arrival. Standing up, Adam warmly greeted him and
indicated he should take a seat next to Brett in front

of the fireplace. Bradford did as he was directed. He sat down, remaining rigid and very alert.

"There's some brandy on the food cart. Would you join Brett and me in an after-dinner drink?" Adam said as he pulled the cart toward him.

Surprised by the familial behavior of Adam, Bradford nearly fell out of his chair. Stammering, he managed to get out a "Yes. Yes, sir. Thank you."

Adam poured the brandy into three snifters. He offered the first one to Brett, next to Bradford, keeping the third for himself. He waited for them to taste the nutty flavor of the aged brandy. Once they had, Adam took a sip, rolling it around on his tongue, savoring its richness. Comfortable, they enjoyed the silence of the stilled moment. The flames from the fireplace cast dancing shadows across their faces.

Breaking the warmed silence, Adam said, "I would like to visit a particular bar, and I would like you to join Brett and me."

"You want me to drive you?"

"Yes, and I am also asking you to join us. I noticed an SUV in the garage. We can take that rather than the limo."

"I'm not sure I should. I should be to bed because I get up in a couple of hours to start breakfast for The Brothers. They like to eat by six," Bradford replied.

"The Brothers can cook their own meals. I'd like you to work exclusively for me as my chauffeur and as an additional bodyguard. What do you say, will you join us?" Adam said.

"The pay's good, great fringe benefits," Brett chimed in.

Bradford sat, dumbfounded. Since he had been at the Society, he had been the cook, servant, and chauffeur but never a member of The Brothers. In spite of his resentment, he had remained because the job was reasonably secure.

Stiffening his back and sitting up very straight, Bradford asked, "Will my pay remain the same and will I have a place here to stay?"

"No. I will double your current pay, provide health benefits, and give you a two-week paid vacation, and a bonus at the year's end. For your living quarters, you will move into the bedroom suite on the second floor. I want the first-floor apartment converted into a security office. Furthermore, The Brothers do not need a separate apartment for The Master. He will now bunk in with the others. Any questions?"

Bradford took a deep breath. Shook his head in disbelief. Unsure of the protocol, he stood up, extended his hand to Adam and said, "Count me in. What's the name of the bar you want to go to?"

"Glad to have you aboard. The bar is called Sid's." Adam replied.

CHAPTER 3
SIDNEY

Do not judge or you too will be judged. With the measure you use, it will be measured to you.
Matthew 7:1-2 (NIV)

Bradford eased the SUV out of the underground garage and brought it around to the front door where Adam and Brett were waiting. Even though no one was in sight, Adam sensed someone was watching them from inside the old mansion. As he got into the SUV, Adam turned and caught a shadowy figure at the second-floor window.

Slowly they curved their way along the driveway. Adam had Bradford stop, so he could speak to each guard. He pushed a button and the window rolled down. Bradford noticed a blue glow about each of Adam's hands as he offered them to the dogs. and allow the dogs to sniff him. Adam patted each dog as he spoke to the guard. He had Brett step out of the vehicle and repeat the pattern. Bradford looked at Brett's hands and noted the lack of the blue hue that surrounded Adam's hands.

The last guard posted just inside the massive gate pushed a button and it slowly creaked its way open, just wide enough to allow the SUV to pass.

"Bradford, didn't you say you had fifteen to cook for?" Adam asked.

"Yes, sir. Besides myself, the twelve Brothers, and the two of you. Is there a problem?" Bradford asked.

"I counted seven guards. Are they not a part of the household?" Adam said.

"Yes, sir. They are some of The Brothers. They have been doing this only since your arrival was known."

"And the dogs?"

"They live here. Anything else, sir?"

"No, thank you, Bradford. That's fine." Adam replied.

Soon they were on their way back into the city. Nightlife was just getting started as they cruised by some of the city's well-known clubs and on to an area not quite so upscale. Brett's eyes popped as they passed some of the more liberal areas where he observed many people were openly smoking pot. Prostitutes plied their trade. What surprised him was both female and male prostitutes shared the same area. *I wonder where in hell this Sid's Bar is.*

His question was soon answered as they drove up in front of a three-story faded brick building in an older part of the city. A small neon sign hanging in a window announced they were at Sid's Bar.

Each man had to duck his head as he entered. The doorway was obviously not made for tall people. Dim lights and cigarette smoke mixed with the sweet smell of pot greeted them. Even though there were only a few patrons a blue haze hung heavy throughout the small room. Embedded in the smell of smoke was that of cheap perfume. On the postage size dance floor, two women, oblivious of anyone else slow-danced to a Manilow.

Brett accustomed to his role as a backup, moved to the right side of the room and indicated that Bradford should move to the left. As Bradford moved off, he noted the flash of the Seal's insignia on Brett's holster. His adrenalin went into high gear in anticipation of trouble. His muscles tensed, and his dark eyes became mere slits as he searched the room for any potential threat.

As Adam approached the bar there was no question in his mind that the very attractive young woman serving up drinks was Sydney. He couldn't tell the color of her eyes because the lighting was so poor but there was no mistaking her mouth. The photo Running-water had shown in back at the Mesa showed a slight pout. He still couldn't say it was petulant or come-heather.

"You sure you are in the right place, mister?" Sydney said. Her voice was a sharp no-nonsense voice.

"If you're Sydney, yes I am," Adam smiled.

"That's my name. What can I do for you?"

"I'm here because of Esaugetuh. I'm Adam."

Sydney stopped her busy work, looked directly at the man for the first time, searching his face for some recognition.

"Esaugetuh? What about him?" Sydney said leaning into the bar. "You want a drink?"

"Make it bourbon on the rocks. I was wondering if you would tell me about him." Adam said checking her well-formed breasts and amply exposed by her partially opened green blouse.

"Why do you want to know about him?" Sydney replied noticing Adam's blue eyes for the first time as he held her gaze. *How like Esaugetuh.*

"I'm his adopted son."

"So, that doesn't gain you any privileges here.

Ignoring her tough broad stance, Adam said, "He's missing and I'm trying to find him. I thought maybe you would tell me how you met him and how long ago that was,"

He paused just long enough to let her know he was giving her the once over. Just enough to make sure she noticed his appreciative glances.

"Missing? My god, since when?" Sydney said as her hands went to her mouth in disbelief.

"Over a year now," Adam said.

"Over a year. Have you notified the authorities? I'm so sorry," Sydney said as tears filled her eyes. Wiping her eyes she said, "I'm so sorry. He was such a wonderful man, especially to me"

Sydney leaned over the bar, put her arms around him, and gently kissed him on the forehead and said, "He saved my life, you know."

"Is there someplace where we can talk?" Adam asked returning her hug and enjoying her scent.

"I'll show you talk, buster. Back off. She belongs to me."

Adam found himself on his back with an enormous figure standing over him.

"Stop that, right now T.J.! Do you hear me? Stop it!" Sydney yelled.

"I've told you once, bitch, you belong to me." T.J. Kelly hissed kicking at Adam as he rolled out of the way.

There wasn't a chance for a second try. With a thundering crash, the aggressive hulk landed into the tables on the other side of the dance floor. Struggling to understand what happened T.J. was body-slammed into the floor. Never before had anyone been able to throw him. For the first time in his life, he was paralyzed with fear. Instinct told him that the attacker was preparing a final deathblow. His eyes closed in anticipation.

"I've warned you before," Bradford whispered in the stricken T.J.'s ear; his mouth pushing close.

T.J. felt two ridged fingers clamp down on his throat, ready to rip. Even though he tried, he couldn't make a sound.

"Don't! Release your hold," Adam said to Bradford who maintained his neck hold on the helpless T.J. "I'm okay. No damage done."

Bradford looked at Adam and then slowly eased off. T.J. stricken and still dazed, struggled to get up.

"Adam, are you sure you are all right?" Sydney said, her face flush with anger. "T.J. get out! Never come back here again. If you do, I'll have you arrested. I've had enough of your insane jealous behavior."

Grabbing and overturned chair, T.J. Kelly made a lunge for Adam. Adam felt a bullet whiz by his head as the sound of a Glock echoed in the nearly empty bar. T. J. fell to the floor, screaming with pain. Even so, he tried to hurl the chair. Brett's heavy foot slamming down on T.J.'s outstretched arm stopped that. Brett leaned over; gun pointed to T.J.'s head said, "Just don't. You understand? Just don't!" He paused, shook his head and then said, "My god, Adam, he's a she."

Adam knelt beside T. J. Kelly to check for injuries.

She felt the heat from Adam's hands as they passed over her body. The bullet from Brett's gun had passed through the meaty part of her arm, missing the artery and bones. However, he sensed there was an injury to her ribs.

"I think you have a couple of broken ribs. Don't try to get up."

"Get the fuck away from me you long-haired bastard. And don't think you can cut my time with Sid. She still belongs to me. Just get the hell out of our place!" T.J. said as she grimaced with pain.

Adam held up his right hand, palm facing outward projecting a force field. T.J. felt her body weighted down. She continued to struggle, desperate to get up.

Ignoring her, Adam raised his right hand over her eyes and face, speaking to her in soft quiet tones. Her breathing slowed. She saw his wondrous eyes and as she looked into them all of her anger melted away. Her eyes closed and she slept.

"Is she dead?" Bradford asked.

"No. I simply hypnotized her. The pain will be less for her. Sydney, do you have a first aid kit around?" Adam said.

Adam cleaned the wound, dressed it, and then held the injured arm between his hands. The heat built and began to flow into the wound. It would heal. He held T.J.'s arm for a good fifteen minutes and then released it. He knew the bullet wound would heal, but T.J.'s ribs bothered Adam. He remembered how Running-water had nearly died from bleeding internally. He shuddered at the thought.

"It would be best that we don't move her for now. Have you got a blanket and pillow?" Adam said to Sydney.

While she was gone, two police officers entered the bar. They looked around and then headed toward the dance floor.

"We got a call saying there had been a shooting," Officer O'Malley said.

"We have an injured woman here," Bradford said, pointing to T.J. on the floor.

"Suppose you just stay put, mister. Where's Syd?" O'Malley said as he adjusted his holster strap.

"Well, my employer here was talking to the barmaid and there was this pop, you know, like a campaign bottle being uncorked. Next thing I knew, she was on the floor." Bradford replied.

"Wondered when she was going to get it. She's been trouble for a long time. By the way, why are you men in a lesbian bar?

"I can answer that," Sydney said as she handed the blanket and pillow to Adam. "They are friends of mine. Actually, Adam here is my boss. I only ran this place until he was able to come and claim it."

"Claim it?" asked Officer Lee Chow.

"Yes. He inherited it from his father." Sydney said. "Anything else you need to know?"

"Do you know who shot T.J?" Officer O'Malley asked.

"No, I don't."

"Look here, now Sid, we know you've had problems with this one before. This shooting business could shut you down this time so it's best you level with us. Did you shoot her?" O'Malley said.

Before Syd could answer, Bradford said, "No, she didn't shoot T.J. The shot came from over there." Bradford said pointing to a darkened area of the bar.

"Of course Sid didn't shoot me you stupid asshole. You coppers are all alike." T.J. snarled as she raised herself up on an elbow.

Bending down and glaring at "T.J., O'Malley said, "Watch your mouth! If you know so much suppose you tell me, your high and mighty, who shot you?"

Lee Chow had his pen and pad open and ready to take notes.

"Quiet now," Adam said and T.J. grimaced as she lay back down. Her eyes closed.

"I asked you a question, Miss Kelly," O'Malley said as he exaggerated the Miss until it was almost a complete hiss showing his contempt for her.

"She can't hear you. She's out." Adam said.

"Well suppose you tell me. Where were you when she was shot?"

Ignoring the question, Adam said. "Wouldn't it be a good idea to begin to search for the shooter rather than continuing the questioning of T.J.? After all, she is the one who has been shot. She really should be taken to emergency. You can question her later."

Straightening up, O'Malley's face turned red. He was not accustomed to being told how to do his job and especially not by a foreigner.

"I know my job and I sure as hell don't need an American telling me how to do it." Looking at Adam, he continued, "And what did you say your name was?"

"I didn't," Adam said.

Refusing to be intimidated, O'Malley continued, "Well, just suppose you do that and while you're at it, I want to see some identification."

"And that goes for you other two." Officer Lee Chow chimed in.

Bradford was the first to step forward with his identification. Satisfied, the officers indicated Brett was next. When he pulled out his wallet, it moved the flap of his coat making his holstered gun visible.

"What do we have here?" Lee Chow said, jabbing at the holstered gun with his pen.

"What does it look like? " Brett growled. "It's my gun. And before you get your panties all tight, it's registered."

"Is it now? You yanks are all alike. Suppose you show that registration and keep your hands where I can see both of them."

Brett handed the officer his billfold, flipped open, it showed a badge, Air Marshall. The officer handed it back and said, "Mind explaining what a US Air Marshall is doing here in a lesbian bar?"

"I'm the navigator on Adam's private jet and I'm authorized to carry a sidearm," Brett said pulling the gun from its holster and handing it handle first to the officer.

"Hmm, hasn't been fired," the officer said as he sniffed the barrel and returned it to Brett. "I see you were a US Navy Seal."

Yes, Sir! Of course, I'm no longer in the service."

"It's always the same. Nobody ever sees or hears anything." Officer Lee Chow said. Turning to Brett, he continued, "Don't suppose you saw anything?"

"Well maybe. When we first came in, I noticed a person slumped over on one of the tables. Couldn't tell if it was a man or a woman. Too dark. When the shot was fired I rushed to Adam. When tuned in the direction of the noise. The person at the table was gone. Might be a good idea to bring in some backup and sniffer dogs," Brett replied.

"There you go again, trying to tell us how to do our job. You know, we get calls about 'shots fired' at least once a week. Generally, there are cars or trucks backfiring. Now with Syd, here, there's always a fight or two. Mostly, hair pulling. Once in a rare while a knifing," Lee Chow said.

"We really should call for an aid car and get T.J. to a hospital," Sydney said.

"There's an emergent care a few blocks from here. You can take T.J. Kelly there. They do handle short term emergency situations," O'Malley said. "By the way, do either of you want to press charges against T.J.?

"No, we don't," Adam said.

"Guess we're done here. You going to be in town for a while in case we have some more questions?" Le Chow asked.

"Yes. Sydney will know where we can be located." Adam said. "And officers, thank you for your assistance."

As soon as the door had shut, Adam said, "Brett, how'd you get a clean gun?"

"Easy, I always carry two. I just switched one."

***

Adam had Bradford and Brett take T.J. to a local emergency room. He wanted to talk with Sydney without others being present.

"Before all of this commotion began I was asking you to tell me about Esaugetuh. Are you up to talking?" Adam asked as he began to straighten up a couple of the chairs and a table.

"Sure, no problem but first what are you going to do about T.J.?

"Nothing. That's up to you. Only you can decide not to continue an abusive relationship."

"Yeah, yeah. I've heard all that before. Enough said, okay?" Sydney replied.

"You got a deal," Adam said.

"I met Esaugetuh on a street corner. I was hustling g my ass in those days. He drove up in a stretch limo driven by Bradford."

"Wait a second. Are you saying you know Bradford? Why didn't you recognize him?"

"First, let me get us a fresh drink," Sydney said getting up from the table.

The gentle sway of her hips hypnotized him as he watched her move across the room to the bar.

Sensing he was staring at her, Sydney stopped, turned and said, " He didn't want me to recognize him."

She returned with two glasses of bourbon and a bag of chips.

"I thought it weird that he wanted to do me since I was in a predominately gay neighborhood. But then, I was low on cash and thought what the hell. I could get a few bucks off this guy. So I piled my ass into the back of the limo. He said nothing at first, just handed me ten hundred dollar bills, American. I thought I had died and gone to heaven then I realized the limo was speeding away. My heart nearly stopped beating I was so scared. I was sure I had been picked up by one of those crazies and I was about to end up with my throat slit. That's when I took a good look at him. He was elegantly old. I guess you can say someone is elegantly old. His white hair was pulled back and tied in a braid that fell over one shoulder. He was wrapped in some kind of cape and he had a cane between his legs. All this time he had not said a single word. He just stared at me with those magnificent blue eyes. And you know I felt he was looking into my soul."

"He had that quality about him," Adam said just above a whisper. Her perfume was intoxicating. She was intoxicating and he felt urges he had not felt in a long time. Uncomfortable, he squirmed in his chair. To calm his building heat, he looked away and for a moment focused on a naked light bulb.

"He offered me a job working for him. I thought oh, sure, he probably wants to get off by watching me undress or do some stupid ass dance. He sensed my uneasiness. He said the thousand would be my weekly plus expenses and coverage. I didn't know what he meant by 'coverage' so I said, you want me to stay covered up?"

Adam laughed and it felt good to laugh. And laughing changed his budding focus.

"Just like you did now he burst out laughing and it was a kind laugh. You know, it wasn't mean or mocking me. He was just plumb tickled. I began to laugh and I didn't know why. It just seemed the right thing to do at the time. The limo stopped in front of an old building. Bradford came round, opened the door for me to get out. I was ready to run. It occurred to me that maybe I was to be Bradford's toy and the old man was going to watch.

But that didn't happen, of course. It could have. He went around and helped the old man out of the car. He was bigger than I thought and stood straight but walked with a limp. He unlocked the door to the building and indicated that I should follow. He fumbled around and finally found the lights. It was this bar.

He asked me what my name was. He said it would be a good name for this bar. He then said it was mine to manage."

"Yours to manage? It was my understanding that you were the owner of the bar. So your statement to the police is true. I don't get it." Adam said.

"Simple. He said he had a son named Adam and that he would be coming by and he would decide what to do about the business," Sydney said.

"That's all he said?" Adam questioned.

"Hell no. He described you to a letter. I knew who you were the minute you walked up to the bar. Esaugetuh said you'd be good for me. I guess he thought if I got laid by a real man I'd quit being a lesbian. It wasn't that he was being weird, you know, he just didn't know that you're born the way you are."

"True, people are born the way they are, but they still have choices. I don't think Esaugetuh wanted me to bed you down. I think he wanted me to point out to you that you had made a bad choice with T.J. Kelly. Will you give me honest answers to a couple questions?" Adam said.

"Of course. I don't lie," Sydney said, her eyes flashed building anger.

"I don't mean you lie. I mean you have to be honest with yourself in answering my questions."

"Okay, shoot. What's your question?" Sydney said.

"Do you really want this bar to be successful?"

"Of course I do. What a dumb-ass question," Sydney replied, slapping her hand down on the table.

"Then why haven't you cleaned it up, remodeled, fixed up the outside? You said Esaugetuh gave you a thousand a week plus expenses. Seems to me that included doing something with the place."

"Well, I—,"

"What's on the third floor?" Adam interrupted.

"I don't know. It's boarded up."

"How do I get up there?"

"There's a stairway from my apartment. But its door is nailed shut."

"I want to go up there. One last question. "Do you love T.J.?"

"You sure don't beat around the bush, do you? She does protect me. We do silly things together. When we're in bed she makes me feel good. I suppose you can call that love."

"You can come out of the shadows T.J.," Adam said.

"How long have you been there? Where are Brett and Bradford?" Sydney asked.

"I've been here long enough to hear how your friend here thinks you've made a bad choice. You don't even know who he is and you act like some stupid schoolgirl. I'll show you bad choices, bitch," T.J. said

She lunged for Sydney.

Adam's hand shot up as he stepped in front of Sydney. The flat of his hand caught T.J. under the chin and sent her reeling backward. She hit the floor with a loud thud. She groaned as she tried to get up.

Adam cupped his hands, created a PSI ball, and sent it to circle around the sprawled T.J. She screamed in terror. She tried to crawl away but the fireball followed here. She lay still for a moment, breathing hard from the exertion.

"My God, Adam what the hell was that?" Sydney gasped.

"Stop it. Make it stop. I'll leave." T.J. pleaded.

"All in good time. You *are* to admit yourself to psychiatric care and you are to remain there until you can control your emotions. You are never to come near Sydney, to come into this bar, or to be on this street. If you violate any of these conditions, you will wish you were dead. No matter where you go I can reach you." Adam's voice vibrated throughout the bar, bouncing from wall to wall.

To stress his point, Adam raised his hand, palm facing outward, and drew a circle in the air. With a slight twist of his wrist, the circle rolled on to the floor, glowed for a moment and then broke into hundreds of squirming rattlesnakes.

Screaming, T.J. said, "Stop! Make them go away."

"Where are Brett and Bradford?" Adam's voice boomed.

T.J. covered her ears and said, "I don't know. After my X-ray, I just left."

"Will you do as I say?" Adam's voice boomed even louder.

T.J. was sure it came up from beneath the floor. She could feel it vibrating and that caused the snakes to come closer.

"Yes! Yes! Just take them away. I'll do whatever you want." T.J. wailed as she curled into a fetal position and covered her face with her hands.

Adam felt the swoosh of fresh air as the front door to the bar flew open.

"I see you've got things under control," Brett said as he and Bradford rushed in.

"How'd she get out of the hospital?" Adam demanded.

"She decked the technician and slipped out a side door," Brett said.

"And neither of you did anything to stop her?"

"Sorry, Adam. The docs wouldn't let us in the examination room. The cops should be here shortly. They will be after her for assault. She broke the technician's nose. I'm sure he will press charges," Bret replied.

"I see you have her," Officer O'Malley said as he and Lee Chow walked into the bar. "This getting to be a real pain in the ass. You know what I mean?"

"You don't have to tell us about it. She came in her and again attempted to attack Sydney. I had to put her down," Adam said as he shook hands with Officers O'Malley and Lee Chow.

O'Malley leaned over T.J. to handcuff her.

"She has agreed to get psychiatric help. I believe I own a private psychiatric hospital somewhere in the environs of Toronto. I will make arrangements for her to go there."

"She'll be out in ninety days. Won't do any good. Never does for these types," Lee Chow piped up.

"I don't' think so. I will pay for extensive treatment as long as a year if necessary," Adam said.

He excused himself as he stepped aside to make a couple of phone calls. Arrangements made, he returned to the group. T.J. was not standing and handcuffed with leg irons attached to her ankles.

He had talked to the chief administrator of a nearby sanitarium, made arrangements for the Esaugetuh Society of Benevolence to foot the bill for one year. Adam went to Sydney, spoke to her and she calmed down. Once Bradford brought the SUV to the front T.J. was loaded into the car, situated between Brett and Adam. Sydney sat up front with Bradford.

"Take us to the Kadmon Sanitarium on Macmillan," Adam said.

"Yes, sir. There's GPS in the car," Bradford said as he eased his way into traffic. He noted the two police officers were close behind them.

***

Toronto, like other major western cities, was still very much alive at three in the morning. Thirty-five minutes later the SUV eased its way up a dimly lighted narrow drive. At the top of a crest, they pulled up in front of a Frank Lloyd Wright style building; low slung, fitting the landscape, and having massive glass windows. The grounds had an eerie look with shadowy shrubs and defused blue lighting throughout.

Bradford exited the SUV. At the main entrance, he pushed a button on the side of the door. He waited and then pushed the button again. Finally, he heard a sleepy voice telling him to wait a few minutes. A robed person appeared at the plate-glass door. A hurried conversation brought a second person with a wheelchair.

Once the attendants were at the SUV, Adam got out, spoke to them and helped them load T.J. into the wheelchair. With obvious practice, they strapped her in and then made a couple of adjustments and then wheeled her into the building. Adam, Brett, and Sydney followed the attendants through the open door. It closed with a swoosh.

At the admissions office, T.J. signed the necessary papers. She didn't bother to read them. As the two attendants wheel her away, T.J. closed her eyes. That was the last they saw of T.J.

"Can I go to her room and say goodbye?" Sydney asked.

"Sorry, mam. Visitors are not allowed for the first two weeks."

"Sydney, don't try to come back here and see T.J.," Adam said, indicating she and Bradford should leave.

Brett remained with Adam as he made the final arrangements for T.J.'s treatment. He insisted she have anger management training and to have help with her compulsive possessiveness. He also made sure that the staff would do nothing to try to change her sexual orientation. Her gayness was not to be considered a disease or as something that could be changed.

Once outside, Adam and Brett saw Sydney standing by the side of the SUV. Her arms were folded across her stomach and her right foot was tapping the ground.

"You coming or are you planning on walking back to the bar?" Adam said.

She stood there, stubborn. Reaching into a pocket of her tight-fitting jeans, Sydney pulled out a bag, rolled a joint and lit it. She took two quick hits, checked her watch. *Shit! It's six AM. What the hell.* She took two more quick hits, threw the joint on the ground, stomped it with her foot and walked around the SUV where Bradford had an open door waiting for her. Once seated, she continued her pout. She couldn't make up her mind. *Should I tell Adam to fuck off or wait and see what he has in mind? Admittedly, he is handsome and well endowed.* She felt her cheeks flush. She leaned her head back and closed her eyes. *What a night!*

Once back at Syd's Bar, Adam asked Sydney to show him the way to the third floor. Brett and Bradford followed. Her apartment though tastefully decorated showed signs of a recent tantrum. Adam surmised it was the remnants of a battle with T.J. He said nothing.

Adam pulled on the door of the stairway to the third floor. It didn't budge. He looked at the door and realized it was not only nailed shut but had a least a dozen wood screws embedded in it.

Turning to Sydney Adam said, "We need a crowbar, screwdriver, hammer and maybe a chisel. You got those?"

"I don't know. There's a toolbox downstairs in the storage room," Sydney replied.

Bradford volunteered to go to the lower level and look for the toolbox. Brett decided to go with him and as they descended the stairs, he thought, *I wonder how Bradford knows his way around here?*

***

As soon the door to the stairway closed Adam turned to Sydney and said, " What more can you tell me about Esaugetuh?"

"Well, the third floor he reserved for himself. I used to hear him up there, pacing back and forth.

70

Sometimes I heard him pounding and other times I heard him stab the floor with his cane. I was never up there so I have no idea as to what he was doing."

"Didn't he have to come up through your apartment?" Adam said, raising an eyebrow.

"No! There were a set of stairs out back. One day, and without explanation, a couple of men arrived and tore them down. "

"And that's all?" Adam's disappointment showed as he dropped his voice.

"I'm sorry Adam. I really am. But that's all there is. I do have the contract that appointed me as manager and that's it," Sydney said as she walked over to a red painted cabinet, pulled open a drawer, and brought out a large manila envelope.

She offered it to Adam.

"You keep it. Stay on. Get the place, fixed up and make it worth something." Adam said as Brett and Bradford pushed open the door to Syd's apartment.

"Found some tools. You want us to begin?" Brett said, popping open a large wooden box.

"Yes. We'll probably make a mess, but don't worry Sydney, we'll clean it up," Adam said.

By the time they got the door open mid-morning sunlight filled the apartment. The stairway to the third floor had a single light bulb and it provided just enough illumination for the steep narrow steps. At the top, a second door barred their entry into the apartment. Bradford eased his way past Adam and put his weight into the door. It did not budge. Bradford gave a powerful karate kick that normally would have shattered the door, but not this one.

"It has got to be sealed from the other side," Bradford said. "Stores are open. Want me to go and get some power tools?"

The three men backed down the narrow stairway and as they reach Sydney's apartment they were greeted by a mixture of wonderful smells.

"Breakfast. Montana flapjacks, Canadian bacon, flipped eggs and lots of real maple syrup and hot coffee to slush it down," Sydney said as she handed each man a warmed plate.

Once they had stopped their eating frenzy, Bradford excused himself and left to go buy some power tools. Adam got up from the table, went to the window and watched Bradford drive away. He pulled out his cell phone and punched a number.

As Brett strained to hear what Adam was saying, the old question of a lack of trust began to know at his gut. *Adam's behavior is becoming more and more secretive. Was a time he kept Dutch, Running-water and me in the loop. Not much of that anymore.* He got up from the table and went down to the bar.

The place still smelled of cheap perfume. Brett whipped out his cell phone and called Dutch at the plane. *Damn, no answer.* Next, he called the airport tower, gave the N number of Adam's private jet. The voice on the other end told him the plane had departed. *Enough is enough.* He went back up to Syd's apartment.

"Dutch has flown out. Want to tell me what's going on?" Brett said. His voice betrayed his feelings. A nervous quiver along his lower lip confirmed that.

Twice Adam had called on his cell phone. His conversation was muffled so Brett wasn't able to determine what was going on. The old question of trust began to gnaw at his gut. Adam's behavior,

"Hmm. Don't know about Dutch. Did you try to contact him?" Adam replied.

"Yes, but got no answer. I did call the tower and he flew out before daylight. I thought you had called him since you have been on the phone." Brett said.

"Ah! So that's it." Adam said managing to control a smile. "The phone calls have been about a lecture series I plan to give at the mansion. Specifically, they were about publicity. "

Oh, man! What an ass I have made of myself, Brett thought. He felt his face redden. He opened his mouth to speak, hesitated, and then changed his mind. *No use trying for damage control.*

"Lectures? What lectures?" Brett said.

"A series of lectures on benevolence," Adam said.

There he goes again. Just pulling stuff out of thin air. Never any chance for my input.

Looking at Brett, Adam started to say something but Bradford's clumping up the stairs interrupted that.

Bradford had a gas-powered chain say, a can of gas, and a pair of heavy-duty gloves. A pair of safety goggles sat on top of his chauffeur's cap.

"Let me get my hat and coat off and I'll rip that door open in no time. I brought these masks just in case there's a decaying body in there."

"Believe me, if there was a decaying body up there I would have smelt it," Sydney said, looking up from doing the dishes.

Bradford stomped up the narrow stairway. He barely had room to start the chain saw. With three quick strikes the chain saw had ripped through the door. Four by fours, screwed to the wall prevented the door from being pushed open. Chips flew every which way as Bradford deftly handled the heavy saw. Within a couple of minutes, he had an entry through the 4X4's cut.

Despite opening the windows to her apartment, the smell of sawed wood, and gasoline combined with the dust was everywhere.

Once Bradford cleared the doorway, Adam stepped into the apartment. An occasional small ray of light forced its way through a decaying black shade and broke the penetrating darkness. He found a light switch, flicked it.

Stunned, he stood absolutely still. "My God!" he whispered.

With deliberate slowness, Adam looked around the room, from one wall to another and then back again. Photos covered every inch of all the open wall space.

"Incredible."

Everywhere he looked were photos of himself. Some baby pictures; others were pre-puberty and as a teenager. In some, he was naked and these were life-size. Several of the adult shots were full frontal. He felt his face flush, sure it was bright red, he touched his face. His embarrassment settled into total awe of this photo montage of his life.

"Totally unbelievable and yet here it all is," Adam said. There was a slight quiver in his voice.

There were photos of him on the Baskatong Reserve in Canada, at Mesa Verde, and at the old motel in central Florida.

A smile spread across his mouth when he saw the photo of himself along the Skagit River in the state of Washington. There were even photos of him working at Jedediah Wood's farm in Pennsylvania. There were dozens of photos of Running-water and him. His whole life laid out before him.

Strange there are no photos of Esaugetuh. None of my biological father. Odd, I never used that word before to refer to him, not even after his murder. It's even more strange there were only photos of my mother and always with me or by herself. None with her husband.

Brett's voice finally penetrated. Still, in total disbelief, Adam shook his head.

"You okay, Adam?"

"Yes. Yes, I'm fine," Adam said as he stepped closer to a set of photographs.

One photograph caught Adam's attention and it brought tears to the corner of his eyes. It was a picture of him sitting beside Running-water at the hospital in Pennsylvania. Running-water had nearly died. It was then that the battle for Running-water's soul had begun— a fight with Moon Woman that nearly killed them both. The remembrance of all the deaths brought a shudder to Adam. It didn't go unnoticed.

Another pair of eyes, unseen by those in the room, noticed the shudder, blinked and turned away.

Brett caught Adam's shudder, felt Adam was thinking about past personal hurts. He too remembered the attempt on their lives as they flew over the ocean, the bloody scene at Christopher Saint-Michaels, seven bodies in a bloody heap. Oh, sure, he had helped kill them but even in self-defense, it left an unpleasant feeling. Despite the fact that he and Dutch had both witnessed death as Navy Seals, the deaths they witnessed while employees of Adam sometimes made them wonder if he wasn't Death personified. Yet when you looked at him, you saw only love as unequaled compassion. Even the nude photos of Adam, though naturally sensual, showed that reverence that so marked him as truly unique. He hoped he could control his suspicious mind, no his jealous nature. That thought brought a flush to his face.

Sydney's cussing broke the mausoleum silence. She was struggling to open one of the curtained windows. The more she struggled, the louder she cussed.

Like the doors, the windows had been sealed up. The stuffiness of the place began to bother her.

But she said nothing about it. The light filtering in through the dirty windows didn't reveal a great deal of dust in the place; it was just the stale air. The lack of dust surprised her since no one ever came to clean the place while Esaugetuh lived there. A particular cabinet caught her attention. It was beautifully carved and she liked things like that. As she caressed it, she looked at her hand, no dust.

"Adam," she called, "Don't you think it's strange there's no dust in here?"

There was no answer. She turned her attention back to the curio cabinet. The quaint bottles inside intrigued her. She collected hand-blown glass bottles, especially small ones. She put her hand on the door handle. It didn't budge. She started to pull but Adam's hand stopped her.

"Those are Indian medicines bottles. Some of them may be poisonous. You like this cabinet. You may have it once it's been emptied. There must be a key for it around here someplace. We'll look a little later. Right now, I need some information.

"Information? What about?" Sydney said.

Do you know of a reliable moving company and a company that specializes in reconstruction?" Adam asked.

"I don't know of any, but I sure there are many available ones," Sydney replied. "Are you planning on moving in here?"

"No, I want everything here moved to my house, except the cabinet, of course. I'll need someone to take down all the photographs, to keep them in the exact order in which they are placed on the walls. Do you have a good camera?"

"I have a digital if that will help. You have a house here?" Sydney said.

"Yes. It's on the water."

"You mean out along the lake? Wow! It must be a mansion, 'cause that all that's out there."

"It is. It's called Karuna, a Sanskrit word meaning 'compassion'." Adam said. "It is also the center for The Esaugetuh Society of Benevolence. I'm going to deliver a series of lectures there. Would you like to come?"

"Yes. That would be nice. Thanks for asking me." Sydney replied as she disappeared down the narrow steps to retrieve her camera.

Once Adam had the camera, he began systematically photographing everything in the apartment. Noting the sequence of each photograph in a small notebook. Once he was satisfied with that, he began to go through closets, drawers, and boxes. There were dozens and dozens of boxes neatly stacked in the two large closets. Some contained audio tapes while others contained videos. The videos were neatly labeled; some had his name on them, others had Running-water's name on them. He had his work cut out for him and it would take a long time. It would be a good job for the Brothers to sort and catalog each item.

"Brett," Adam called. "Have Bradford drive you to a place that does billboards. Have five created with the words what is benevolence? printed on them. Be sure they are placed in strategic locations. Let me know the charges and I'll give them a credit card number."

As Brett and Bradford left, Adam walked over to the curio cabinet, slide his hand down its back side.

"Ah, the key," he said.

Adam unlocked the cabinet door, picked up an empty box, and carefully placed the bottles in it, and in the exact order that they were on the shelves.

"See this one," Adam said to Sydney as he held up an opalescent bottle. "It's Senega or Snakeroot and it's poisonous."

"And what is that one in the bright red bottle?" Sydney asked.

"It's used to enhance the sex drive," Adam said as a blush caressed his cheeks.

Even with the Stilettos, Sydney had to stretch to get her arms around Adam's neck. "Thank you," she said barely above a whisper.

"For what?" Adam said. He felt the rub of her nipples against his chest.

"For letting me stay on here and run the bar and—."

"And," Adam said, pulling her up and kissing her.

She held his kiss, eagerly seeking his tongue. She felt his hands slide down her back, her butt tightened as he pulled her closer.

He picked her up, laid her down on cot that must have served as Esaugetuh's bed. Hungrily she sought his thrusts. Rivulets of sweat soaked his long hair as he finally spent himself.

"Mind if I shower?" Adam said as he eased himself up from the cot.

"Yes, unless you let me shower with you," Sydney said.

CHAPTER 4
AT KARUNA HOUSE

Let your actions be in the interest of many and result in the happiness of many.

Bahujan

Darkness once again engulfed Toronto as the three men returned to Karuna House. There Bradford was pleasantly surprised that several of The Brothers were already in the kitchen doing prep-work for the evening meal. He slipped out of his chauffeur's jacket and put on a crisp white bib-apron.

The menu was a rack of lamb. It would take several to feed fifteen men. Bradford busied himself seasoning the lamb. he felt a new ease and comfort. *It's got to be Adam*, he thought as he rubbed selected spices into the lamb. *I feel good about him. Even Brett seems less hostile.*

He placed the lamb in the baking pans and slid those into the brick oven. Closing its door, Bradford set the timer. He turned his attention to the four men in *his* kitchen. The Brothers as they liked to be called, seemed genuinely pleased in their new role of taking care of themselves. *That's different. Course they never counted me as one of them. To them, I was just the hired help.*

Slightly embarrassed, Bradford realized he was staring at them and they were staring back. The one called Timothy broke the silence.

"What do you think about this benevolence business?'

Bradford blinked. "Sounds okay to me," he replied.

"You got any ideas about how we're to be benevolent?"

"Nope. You'll have to check with the boss about that," Bradford said. *Man, this is unreal. I've never been asked my opinion about anything as long as I've worked here.*

"I don't think Joseph knows," Timothy continued.

"Joseph's not the boss. Adam's the boss! Remember that."

Timothy's face colored as he realized Joseph was no longer The Master. *At least that's how is for now.* You want me to check the dining room?"

"No, I'll do that. Thanks for the offer," Bradford replied as he left the kitchen.

He pulled open the huge sliding oak doors. The dining room with its long mahogany table was ablaze with six three feet tall crystal candelabras. Fresh flowers filled ornate silver baskets. Bradford enjoyed their sweet smell as he walked around the long table. He counted fourteen settings of Versace black and gold trimmed porcelain dinnerware. He noted the Wallace gold flatware and the Saint Louis gold water glasses and champagne flutes. He stopped and straightened one linen napkin in its gold ring.

"Well, some things haven't changed. I see I am not included in this dinner," Bradford muttered as he shrugged his shoulders and left the dining room. He quietly closed the doors to the dining room.

Once back in the massive kitchen, Bradford changed from his white apron to a white chef's jacket. He quickly placed food into the warmed serving platters and dishes. His four helpers had disappeared. He knew the routine. Wheel the steaming hot foot in on carts, serve it, and leave. Come back and clear the table, bring in the desert. For tonight, he had prepared a deep rum bread pudding. The first cart contained the racks of lamb and three side dishes.

He pulled the carts to the massive oak doors of the dining room. Stopped, pulled them open and the proceeded to pull in the food carts, one at a time. Closed the doors. Deftly he sat the dishes on the long table. Once everything was on the table Bradford headed for the doors.

"Bradford, come and sit next to me," Adam said.

Bradford stopped, did a double check of the table. There were fifteen place settings. He was sure there had been fourteen. After a brief hesitation, Bradford went to the middle of the table and sat down next to Adam.

Brett, on Adam's right, nodded.

Tonight, with a nod from Adam, the one formally known as The Master, gave thanks for their meal and added a "grateful" for good measure. The only sound during the meal was an occasional clank from a dish being passed around. silence. A rare "ah" escaped someone's lips as some food item brought pleasure.

Once everyone had finished eating, Bradford got up to clear the table. Adam stopped him. "Each person will carry his dishes to the kitchen and bring back his own dessert and coffee. After that, I will address the group," Adam said, as he got up with his dinnerware in his hands.

Once dessert was over, Adam stood up to address the group. Bradford also got up and started to leave.

"I'd like you to remain," Adam said as he indicated Bradford should sit back down.

Adam waited until Bradford had seated himself.

"I am planning a series of lectures and I would like your help in preparing Karuna for a small group of about fifty people. I want to use the third floor. I believe part of it was once a ballroom and that it will make an excellent lecture hall. I will need chairs, valet parking, and security on all floors. And yes, I want refreshments."

"I will take care of security. One of the others can take care of valet parking," Joseph, The Master said, pulling his out from his robe to point at one of The Brothers. Changing his mind, he slipped his and back into his sleeve.

"Brett will take care of security. Joseph, you can handle the valet parking."

"I'll do the refreshments," Bradford offered.

"Good and would you see the others have assignments?" Adam said. "Thank you for your help," Adam continued as he got up and headed for his apartment on the third floor.

Adam had barely left the dining room when Joseph with feigned reproach in his voice said, "Oh, dear. I forgot to tell Adam there were two men waiting for him in his apartment."

"You stupid ass," Brett snarled as he grabbed Joseph and slammed him to the floor.

Racing to the stairs, Brett leaped three steps at a time as he desperately tried to beat the old birdcage elevator. At the top of the third set of stairs, he pulled his gun, shoved a shell into its chamber.

The elevator creaked to a halt and Adam exited.

"That ass Joseph let two men into your apartment," Brett said as he cautiously stepped further into the room.

Adam followed. Both listened and sniffed the air. Voices from one of the hallways floated into the ballroom.

Man, when you fart you stink up the whole damn place. What the hell have you been eating?"

"Don't get your panties in a sweat. Adam should have been back by now. I don't trust that weasel that brought us up here. Maybe we better have a look around."

The two emerged from down the hallway.

"Dutch? Running-water? Suppose you two tell me what you are doing here," Adam demanded.

"You going to shoot us, Brett?" Dutch said, reaching out and giving his navigator a slap aside of the head. Continuing, he said, "Running-water, here, thought you needed some help. Called me to come and get him."

Running-water hung back and said nothing because of the frown on Adam's face.

Sensing a heavy heart, Adam grabbed Running-water around the neck, hugged him, and gave him a slap on the back. Then he said, "Come sit. Have either of you eaten?"

Adam pointed toward four chairs in front of the huge fireplace. He picked up a phone from a marble table, punched in a number for the kitchen and asked Bradford to bring up hot food.

Food was bought up for Dutch and Running-water. Brandy snifters were filled and passed around. The four talked for several hours. Finally, Dutch and Brett drifted off to sleep in their chairs. While Running-water and Adam huddled together in another part of the apartment. Running-water sat with his head held in his hands.

"What troubles, you Brother?" Adam said.

Looking up at Adam, Running-water replied, "My mating has not gone well. I don't understand. I've never had any trouble bedding a woman. Most of the time they were the ones wanting to get into my pants. This woman I am with is different. I asked her to marry me."

"And?" Adam said.

"My god, Adam, she refused. I - - -," Running-water turned his head to hide his tears. "I have never been so ashamed in my life. Not even when you sent me away. Yes, I called Dutch to come and get me. Please don't send me away again."

They sat in silence for a few minutes.

"Tell me, Adam, why was I rejected. Shit man, she was the only woman I've ever asked to marry me."

"Many things I know, my brother, but a woman's heart is not one of them. You feel up to answering a few personal questions?"

"Sure. You mind if I have another brandy. I sure could use another."

"Help yourself. Has that been a problem?"

"No. I seldom drink. Just nervous tonight. I wasn't sure how you would receive me since you sent me away. You know Dutch and Brett think you are getting ready to dump them, too."

"Correction! I didn't dump you. I sent you back to take care of business. In this case to find yourself a woman, marry her, and start a family. That's what you most wanted, is it not? Anyway, back to my questions. First, do you love this woman?"

"I asked her to marry me, didn't' I?"

"That's not my question. People marry for many reasons. I asked if you love her and since you didn't immediately say yes, I suspect she feels you don't love her—that you have simply been using her for your sexual satisfaction. Speaking of sex, how was it with her?" Adam said, raising an eyebrow.

"Man, you sure are direct. I've never had the question asked before. It was great. I couldn't get enough of her.

"You missed the intent of my question. I want to know if you made sex something special for her. Did you concern yourself with her needs, her desires, and her comfort level or was she merely the object for your own release?"

"My god, Adam. You sure lay it out. I told her I loved her. What the hell more should I do?" Running-water said becoming agitated.

"Telling someone that you love them is important, but once said, you must show it, make that person feel it, believe it," Adam replied.

Continuing he said, "You have to give it away, clean, clear, and unencumbered. You need to make her feel that your love for her is unconditional. Do you understand, my brother Do you understand?"

"I don't know, Adam. One thing I do know Is I want to be with her the rest of my life. It's all so confusing. Should I go back and try again?"

"No, it's better that you stay here for a while. Since you are here, there are some things I want you to do. Right now, however, you need to get some rest. There's a bedroom for you down the hall, on the right. I'll see you later in the day. And Running-water, you are loved." Adam said as he got from his chair, walked over to the elevator, entered the cage, pulled the lever, and returned to the ground floor.

Like another in bygone days, Adam too went for a walk in the gardens. But unlike that other Walker, he felt no sense of betrayal. Solitude was a necessary ingredient in his life now, and he often sought its company. \ It was enough to try to locate

The garden at Karuna House was spacious, taking up one whole side of the mansion. He tried to quiet his mind as he walked. Questions about the missing Esaugetuh, the apartment full of photos refused to leave him.

I never saw Esaugetuh with a camera. How would he have gotten photos of me as a newborn, as a toddler, and on into my adulthood? Adam thought. *Maybe Esaugetuh had someone else take the photos. I can't imagine anyone spending years in photographing just* one person. *And then, why wasn't he in any of them? Somewhere in the hundreds of boxes, there has to be an answer.*

As he paced up and down in the garden he did not see the beauty that surrounded him. A fountain with splashing water caught his ear and he looked up. It was a smaller version of the statue of Prometheus that graces Rockefeller Center at New York City.

"I want no need answers," Adam said aloud.

His voice surprised him, and he stepped back from the gushing fountain and looked at it. It reminded him of Esaugetuh's comments on what he called Promethean necessity.

What is the Necessity of Esaugetuh? Of his involvement in this photo montage of my life? In my life, period. There have to be clues but what are they? Questions and more questions. Always the damn questions nagging me.

He sat down on the edge of the fountain. The water's spray fell upon him. Turning to Prometheus he said, "Will I never know the answers to my being? What game is being played?"

"Life? Isn't all life a game? And how we play it determines how well we live it." Joseph the former Master said as he came from the other side of the fountain.

"That's certainly one way of looking at it," Adam said, resentful of the intrusion into his space. He grabbed his side as a sudden pain announced itself. *Haven't felt that for a while. Always the reminder; never the answer.*

Ignoring Adam's tone, Joseph continued, "I come here often to sit, to listen, to look, and to learn."

"To learn?" Adam questioned.

"You'd be surprised at what one can learn in a garden. Notice how the vines intertwine with the other plants, each having space yet sharing space. Even the lowly weed gets to show its flowering head."

The point was made and feeling the sting of Joseph's comment, Adam snapped, "What is it you want, Joseph?"

"We, The Brothers, and I are waiting for you to tell us how we may go about being benevolent— compassionate. They are gathered in the dining room.

"Tell The Brothers I will join them. I will be in shortly."

"You are both wrong, you know." Said a timid voice from behind one of the many large statues that were throughout the garden.

"Who's there?" Joseph demanded. His voice assuming its former authority.

"Thomas, Master."

"Ah, yes— Thomas. Well since *you* have interrupted come forward. And Thomas I'm just Joseph– not the Master anymore– just Joseph."

"What do you mean we are both wrong?" Adam asked ignoring Joseph's effort to elicit sympathy.

"Sir, excuse me for speaking, but in the cosmic sense, life has neither beginning nor end. To see it as if it did is to put artificial limits on it." Thomas continued as he stepped a bit closer.

"Explain," Adam said,

"When life is viewed as having a beginning and an ending, it becomes a mere game, a battle. Then we become concerned with the issue of winners and losers. We end up asking ourselves if we won."

"So! And just what's wrong with that?" Joseph said annoyed at Thomas's continued efforts at being a philosopher.

Feeling self-conscious and intimidated yet somewhat emboldened Thomas continued, "We become so concerned about winning or losing that we fail to live the moment, to realize the potentiality of the day. Even when we have won, we are so wrapped up in the idea of having defeated someone we lose all sight of compassion."

Adam was surprised by the insight and independence shown especially since it was apparent such discussion and independence was not encouraged. He was pleased more by the reminders

91

he had just received. *A garden is a place of learning. Each thing, no matter how small, has its space and time. What Thomas didn't say was that in viewing life as a game with its winners and losers we don't stop and ask what happens to the losers. Like so many things in today's society, we simply throw them away.*

Adam reached out and put his hands on Thomas' shoulders, and said, "You're right Thomas. We fail to ask what happens to the loser. Like so many things in today's world, we tend to throw them away. Come walk back with us."

Quietly they walked back into the house each absorbed in private thoughts. Sensing Joseph's continued annoyance with him, Thomas made sure he walked paces behind yet flushed by his daring, he gave a little hop.

"What was that?" Joseph demanded as he turned back to look at Thomas.

"Uh, I stumbled."

Once back at the front entrance, Joseph opened the massive door with a grand gesture and a bow. Adam ignored that and entered. But when Thomas came up the last step, Joseph rushed on in and slammed the door.

I'll wait for Thomas, " Adam said as he pulled open the door.

An embarrassed flush flooded Joseph's face

In the dining room, ten of The Brothers were waiting for them. They were seated in straight back chairs lined against one wall. Stiffened with hands placed on their knees. Adam noticed their faces as

92

he looked at each man. They looked as if they were waiting for execution. Thomas and Joseph joined them. As he continued looking down the row of twelve seated men, Adam remembered another time from his past. *I chastised Dr. Saint-Michaels for not knowing his people and I had done the same thing with Dutch and Brett when they had first signed on as my pilot and navigator. I will not repeat that mistake.*

He walked down the row of men, asked each his name, shook each man's hand, and made a point of direct eye contact. Adam noted they were still wearing their red robes and he had specifically told them to take them off. He also noted that Joseph had not returned his eye contact.

Turning to Thomas, Adam said, "Why are you and the others still wearing the red robes when I said you were no longer to do so?"

Joseph cringed at the slight. *After I all, I am The Master despite what HE says.*

"Simple. We have nothing else to wear."

Looking at each man, Adam said, "Do you gentlemen prefer to wear robes tied with pieces of rope?"

"Yes!" came the unified reply.

"What does the color red suggest to you, Allen?" Adam asked.

"Blood, courage, bravery."

"Tell me, Samuel, can red also represent anger, danger, and fear?" Adam asked.

"Sure," Samuel replied. Samuel was a very large man and despite his hugeness showed gentleness in his mannerisms.

Adam made a point of asking each man for his view and spoke to them by name. Knowing full well that he was setting the stage for a broader issue, Adam reluctantly asked, "Do you think you could accept a different color? Perhaps one that suggests tranquility, peace, and compassion?"

"Sure. How about blue? I like blue." Samuel said.

"Light blue would be nice," Allen added.

The men nodded in agreement with light blue being chosen as the new color. Turning to Joseph, Adam said, " Order new robes and sandals and have them delivered right away."

A knock on the dining room doors brought Joseph to his feet.

"That will be Bradford."

The door opened, slowly. Bradford was pulling a large cart loaded with teapots, cups, and some kind of small cakes. His appearance changed the tone of the room.

With a swish of his robe, Joseph went over to Adam and whispered, "It's customary that I pour the tea for each member and offer one of the cakes."

"Why don't you go ahead and do that this time," Adam said.

After another and somewhat grander swish of his robe, Joseph bowed to Adam and as he turned, his lower lip curled upward. *This time? Ha! If he thinks he's going to replace me, I've got news for him.*

No one spoke while they ate. Once done, each man got up, placed his empty cup and plate ever so carefully on the tea cart and then returned to his seat. One, the youngest of the group, fell face forward into the teacart. The antique china and accompanying teapots crashed to the marble floor. Shattered pieces flew everywhere.

"You clumsy idiot. How many times do I have to tell you—," Joseph's voice trailed off as he realized Adam was bent over the boy. The look he received from Adam silenced any further comment.

Gently, Adam eased the boy over on to his back and then passed his hands over the limp body. As he did, a blue light hovered around Adam's hands, changing to bright red as slowly grew hot. The Brothers gasped as Adam became nearly transparent.

Leaning close to the boy's right ear, Adam whispered, "Charles what have you done to yourself?"

Charles' mouth opened and closed. No sound emitted from his fevered lips.

"It's okay. Right now, we need to get you healed. You are burning up with a high fever. You have an infection of some kind. Why have you wounded yourself?" Turning to the watchful group, Adam said, "Take Charles up to my apartment."

Two of the men stepped forward, picked up the youth, and waited for Adam's instructions. They put him on the elevator and rode to Adam's apartment.

There, he thanked them and sent them back down for boiling water, soap and heavy towels. Adam pulled open Charles' robe revealing bloodied underwear. He slit those open and pulled them away.

"My god, Charles why have you cut off your testicles?"

"So I can remain pure to serve The Brothers," Charles whispered, his lips parched and his throat sandpaper dry from his high fever. "Am I going to die?"

"No, it's not your time. Quiet now," Adam said as he drew his finger down Charles' nose. He then leaned over and blew into Charles' eyes.

Bradford came in with hot water, soap, and towels. Seeing Charles' bloody body, he said, "May I help?"

"Sure, cut open this role of bandage."

"Man, he must have suffered some real pain cutting his balls off that way."

"As soon as we can get some clothes on him, take him to Kadmon Sanitarium. Use the SUV. Use this credit card if you need it. I want to find out who suggested Charles do this to himself. It outrages my sensibilities. Self-negation and or self-immolation will not be tolerated. Whoever is responsible will be thrown out," Adam said as he turned to go down a long darkened hallway.

With Charles in his arms, Bradford pushed the elevator handle. Slowly it began its creaking downward journey. He actually felt good felt like a human being instead of a lackey to a bunch of weirdos. "Can you believe that? He gave me a credit card. That's a first. He trusts me. More than I can say about The Brothers. I sure as hell don't trust them. What's trust anyway? Just a convenience."

Once down the hallway, Adam stopped at one of the doors, opened it, and walked in. Gently, he placed a finger on Running-water's open mouth. Immediately, he opened his eyes and sat up. Because of their past experiences, Running-water knew he was not to speak. He waited for Adam to mind-talk.

"I need your help, my brother. One of The Brothers urged young Charles to castrate himself under the guise of making himself pure to serve them. I need you to help interrogate them."

"Holy Mother of Jesus! That's totally gross. When do you want to begin?"

"Right away. We'll divide the group."

"Good idea. That way, we can switch groups and check for discrepancies," Running-water said as he pulled on his pants.

"Come, we'll round up The Brothers."

CHAPTER 5
THE INTERROGATION

If you store much away, you are bound to lose a great deal more. Lao Tzu

Adam had decided he would begin the interrogation with Joseph. He sat down in one of the chairs in front of the massive fireplace. Slowly he paged through his experiences with Joseph: The charade of a laser light show, the staged guards, his sudden appearance at the Fountain of Prometheus, and the uncalled for treatment of Bradford and Charles. Long ago he learned to pay attention to the warnings that came like red flags, warnings of trouble and sometimes of danger. He stretched out his long legs, made an adjustment in his crotch. *I wonder what Joseph's game really is. He knew I was coming here to take over.*

Adam picked up the phone, punched a double-digit and waited.

"Yes, this is The Master," Joseph said. Realizing his mistake, he corrected himself. "This is Joseph."

"Come up to my apartment immediately," Adam said.

***

While Adam waited for Joseph to arrive, Running-water talking two steps at a time hurried across the main entrance to what was the communal sleeping quarters. There he made a quick search of Joseph's locker, stored army style, at the base of his cot. He found driver's licenses for both Ontario and Detroit, a checkbook from a Detroit bank, a passbook from a Canadian bank showing a balance of a hundred thousand dollars, and an address book.

"Damn, I bet that little bastard is skimming the monies sent to take care of this menagerie," Running-water said out loud.

He sat down on one of the bunks, turned on his laptop. He checked the Esaugetuh Benevolent Society's bank account against the checks he had written. *No question about it. He's skimming.*

Stuffing the bankbooks and driver's licenses into his pockets he headed up to Adam.

***

Joseph exited the birdcage and as its gate squeaked shut, he looked around and then walked on into the main room.

"Ah, there you are," Joseph said, making a sweeping gesture with his right arm. "You want to see me?"

"Yes, I do. Come and sit down."

As Joseph reluctantly eased himself into the red leather chair next to Adam, Running-water quietly slipped to the back of the room and squatted down.

Adam waited a few minutes without saying anything. Sensing Joseph had prepared himself against hypnotism Adam thought, *Wonder where he got his training and why would he have activated his safety code? Just ask him questions and look for the contradictions.*

Twenty minutes of questioning only brought vague vacuous answers.

"And you have no idea," Adam said as he leaned across the arm of his leather chair and looked directly at Joseph, " why Charles would say he had castrated himself to make himself pure for The Brothers?"

"Absolutely none!" Joseph said as he stood up to leave.

"Where are you going? I still have questions I want to ask you," Adam said.

With total scorn, Joseph said, "It's time for meditation. I always start that."

"Not today, Joseph. Sit down."

Detecting no threat in Adam's voice, Joseph continued walking toward the elevator.

"I said sit down." Adams' voice filling the room seemed to come from everywhere.

Joseph covered his ears with his hands.

"But I must go. They—." Joseph stopped. Stood very still. Turning around to face Adam, he bawled, "What is it you want of me? I've told you everything. My god, you come waltzing in here, take over this place, change my position with the men, throw me out of my private quarters, and give them to a servant. And now you act as if I cut that boy's testicles off. Enough is enough!" Joseph continued to bellow as he threw his hands up in the air.

Ignoring the melodrama, Adam said " First, I want the truth and second, I will tell you I am finished with my questions. And sit down."

Joseph gulped, walked back around the chair and plopped down, With a resigned sigh he continued, "I've told you all I know about him. He generally keeps to himself. That's what monks do in a monastery."

"Correction. This is not a monastery and never will be. You are not a monk. This is not a religious order. I remind you that I own this place, that I am the one who has been providing for you and the rest of the men here."

"But I've. . ."

" Did Charles seem to favor any of the other men? Did he talk more with one than he did the others? Did he seem to gravitate toward one more than the others?" Adam said.

"I just don't know. He slept in the communal room and I in my apartment. I would see him in meditative prayer and at meals only," Joseph replied exasperated.

Running-water still squatting on the floor cleared his throat and, looking directly at Adam sent him a thought message.

Just like the old days and it feels good, good to be home. Running-water thought and then realizing he was transmitting his thoughts to Adam, he closed his eyes to stop his thoughts.

"Come and join us," Adam said as he stood up and waived for Running-water to come over.

"This is Running-water," Adam said to Joseph, "he's my attorney. You saw him last night when you showed him to my apartment. He'll ask you some questions while I attend to some other business. Stay put and answer them."

***

When Adam went to his office on the first floor he found Sydney was waiting for him. She was visibly shaken and crying.

"What's wrong?" Adam asked as he reached out and hugged her. He felt her quiver and pulled her closer. Her smell once again tantalized him and a familiar urge began to show itself. Quickly, he disengaged himself.

Sydney smoother her green blouse. She liked green and felt it flattered her eyes and hair. Wiping her eye, she said, "I've had several threatening phone calls. Even though the voice is disguised, I am sure it's T.J."

"I thought she was your lover. Would she really hurt you?"

"Yes, she would and has. She broke my arm and a couple of ribs once while she was in a jealous rage. She's extremely possessive. Look how she reacted to you," Sydney said, hugging herself in an effort to still her shaking body.

"Okay, move here into Karuna House. I'll have someone go back to the bar with you. Get what you need and return here. Close the bar for a few days and have new locks put on the doors. It would be a good time to have the place repainted. Put a sign up closed for renovation. I need a couple of minutes to make a phone call. "

Adam called the sanitarium's director and was assured T.J. was there and had agreed to cut her telephone privileges and to take her cellphone away from her. He then left his office, went down the hall two doors where The Brothers were meditating.

Interrupting them, he said, Samuel, I'd like a word with you." And to the group, he said, "As of today, there will no longer be a daily meditation."

Samuel heaved his hulk up from his chair and obediently ambled out into the hallway. Adam told him what he wanted him to go to Kadmon Sanitarium and make sure T.J. was still there.

Samuel barely contained his excitement. Frozen in time, he was beside himself that Adam had asked him to run an errand. Furthermore, he was to drive the Lincoln SUV. Only The Master or Bradford ever drove that. *For once, I am not just the fat pig.* He did a little dance as he scooted down the hall to the stairway to the garage. Adam returned to his office and called for Brett.

"Sydney believes T.J. has threatened her. She'll be staying here for a while. Take her back to the bar, get her clothes, and lock the place up. Bradford will drive you. Maybe you should take your friends along."

"No problem," Brett replied as he patted his side pocket.

103

As Sydney and Brett left, Adam joined the remainder of The Brothers who were still seated in their straight-back chairs, too dumbfounded by Adam's announcement ending their meditations. Adam took his time surveying the red-robed men.

Clearing his throat he said, "Those of you who acted as guards and handled the dogs I want to see in my office immediately. We'll be having a young woman living here for a while. Her name is Sydney. She has been threatened and I would like each of you to be on your guard for any intrusion. A guest room needs to be prepared for her."

"I'll take care of the room for you, Adam," Thomas said. "I have sisters so I know a little something of a lady's needs."

"And I'll put the dogs out and electrify the fence," Allen said.

"Thank you," Adam said as he left with seven of The Brothers in tow.

As they walked through the reception room, Adam caught a glimpse of Joseph using a phone located in the hallway at the top of the stairs. *Hmm, wonder who he is calling. Wonder if all the phones are interconnected, especially those in my office and apartment. Must remember to have Brett check that out.*

Dutch was waiting for them. He didn't bother to get up when Adam and his entourage of The Brothers walked in. He stretched his long legs, rubbed his crotch, and yawned.

"Adam."

"Glad you are up. I want you to take over security. The men are to help. We have Sydney moving in, and she is in danger. Set the men up in three-hour shifts, you Running-water, and I will take up the slack."

"Not you, Adam," Running-water said as he walked in. "You may be the real target. It could be revenge."

"Yeah, I agree, Adam. We can't be worrying about you. See you later, " Dutch said as he motioned for The Brothers to follow him.

Running-water shut and locked the door. Turning to Adam, he said, "Joseph has agreed to return the hundred thousand dollars. He asks that you not tell the rest of the group and the will be allowed to stay here at Karuna House."

"I'll have to really think about that. Did you get any inkling that he was behind the castration?"

"None."

"Hmm. I couldn't pick up anything. He's been well trained to block any attempt at hypnotism and mind reading. I find that even more strange. Why would a former street derelict have such training? Anyway, when I was bringing some of The Brothers to my office, I am sure I saw Joseph using the phone. Maybe he was calling the bank to transfer the money. Did you get a signed statement that he would return the money?" Adam asked.

"Yes, and I also got it on tape. I have his bankbooks, and I did make sure he transferred the money over to the Society's account, and I have its checkbook."

"Before I forget, can you check the phones to see if one rings here it can be answered anywhere in the house?"

"Sure, I can run a check for bugs while I'm at it," Running-water said.

"Did you look in Charles' locker?"

"No I go so wrapped up with the Joseph issue, I forget."

"No problem. Let's go and take a look at his locker. We'll bring Joseph with us. If we both watch him we may be able to tune into his reactions."

"Good idea. I'll have to admit he's a damn good actor."

***

Dragging his feet like a schoolboy on his way to the principal's office, Joseph reluctantly joined Adam and Running-water on their way to the communal sleeping quarters. If his bottom lip were any lower, Joseph would have stepped on it.

The communal sleeping quarters was a large barren rectangle arranged like an army barrack, looking like something out of an old 1940's black and white movie. Along one of the windowless walls were a dozen military cots, each neatly made, and each with a military green bunk locker at its foot.

As the trio moved from bunk to bunk, Adam remembered his days as a Boy Scout, and as the came to Charles' bunk, he was tempted to see if a quarter would bounce on the taunt bedding.

Resisting the temptation, Adam opened Charles' footlocker. Inside, he found several religious books, and pamphlets condemning homosexuality and one with the lead-in line of castration as a means of ending homosexual temptation.

"Why in hell would a guy want to cut his balls off?" Running-water blurted.

"He was totally misguided and it's all my fault," Joseph said as he placed the palm of his right hand over his lips.

"Your fault? " Adam said. "How's that so?"

"Well, indirectly anyway. I am supposed to be The Master, the leader, the one to set an example. Instead, I was boss, a regular little Napoleon," Joseph said shaking his head.

"Explain," Adam said.

Lowering his eyes and then gazing upward, Joseph replied, "Had I really been interested in the men who live here I would have tuned into Charles' problems."

"Actually..." Running-water began. Joseph cut him off.

"I am so sorry, Adam. I really am. I can only hope he and you will forgive me."

He struck a pose he thought showed humility and even dabbed his eye with a tissue.

"I really am," Joseph's was barely above a whisper.

"I can forgive, however, trust is another issue. You will have to prove you can be trusted. Are you willing to doing that."

"Yes, I turned the money back to the Society. I'll do whatever else is necessary," Joseph whimpered.

Adam watched the small beads of perspiration form on Joseph's forehead, just below where his hairline would have been.

"Suppose you choose something will show you in a different light. Then we'll begin from there," Adam replied.

Because he detected no sense of conciliation, Joseph continuing with his self-deprecation, grabbed both of Adam's hands, clutched them close to his heart. *I suppose I could have kissed them. No that's really too much even for me.*

"Thank you! I swear I won't disappoint you," Joseph sniffed.

CHAPTER 6
THE GUESTS

You have come into the world for a particular task, and that is your purpose. Rumi

Joseph remained in the communal sleeping quarters while Adam and Running-water returned to the office. Shortly after the arrangements for the hospitalization and treatment for Charles were completed, Within minutes Thomas knocked on the office door and let them know a room across from Adam's had been prepared for Sydney.

Running-water, relieved, said, "That makes security much easier. We won't have to be spread out on so many floors."

A couple of hours later, Bradford returned with Brett and Sydney. Thomas helped her with her luggage as he took her up to her room. Bradford returned to the kitchen.

He hesitated at the entry to the kitchen because of the noise. Slowly, using his foot, he nudged the door open. He was surprised to see three of The Brothers busy prepping for the evening meal. Bradford coughed once to let them know he was present. They didn't look up. As he walked around the large tables he say an elegant looking crème brûlée, a large platter of stuffed butterfly shrimp floating on a bed of finely chopped red cabbage. Three trays of rolls, already plumped, and oven ready. Bradford was so surprised by the selection they had chosen he broke the silence: "How did you know I was going to make these dishes?"

"Easy," Allen said. "We found your "today's menu" pinned on the wall there. We waited for you to prepare the meat."

"Thanks for the help. I will prepare roast suckling pig. Can one of you make the brandied sweet potatoes?" Bradford said has he lit a huge gas grill. *We have a new order and I like it.*

The main dining room was readied. Beautiful Royal Dolton China dinnerware had been put out complimented with Irish crystal stemware. Elegant three-tiered silver candleholders with colorful tall tapers lined the center of the long mahogany table. Fresh flowers in colors matching the tapers filled crystal vases and were appropriately placed at just the right distance from each candleholder. A place card with each guest's name in calligraphy sat in silver lyre-shaped holders. Because there were five additional people to feed, Bradford came to the main dining room to check it out. He was surprised to see twenty place settings. By his count, there were only seventeen people in the house. He counted a second time just to make sure, even walking around the long table and stopping at each place. Twenty was correct. He stopped by one chair and was about to pick up the card when Adam entered the dining room.

"We are having three additional guests this evening, Bradford. I take it the folks in the kitchen didn't tell you," Adam said

"No, sir. But don't worry. There will be enough food."

"Good. We are having three members of the media dine with us this evening. They are here to interview us for my series of lectures," Adam said.

"Us?" Bradford asked.

"Yes. They are free to chat with anyone at the table. I have placed you at the center of the table, next to the man from the press. Joseph will be seated next to the person from the radio station, and Thomas will be seated by the person from the television station."

"Yes sir," Bradford said. He was especially pleased that he was included and placed at the center of the table. *That will give his royal ass a hissy fit.*

"Oh, by the way, since you are the resident chef, I've assigned Samuel to chauffeur this evening. Do you think you'll be ready to serve by nine?"

"Yes, sir," Bradford replied.

"Bradford, call me Adam?"

"Yes, sir. I mean, Adam."

"Good. Would you ask Samuel to come and see me if he's returned from his earlier trip? Ask him to join me in the study."

"Yes S–, uh, Adam."

***

Samuel's report on T.J. Kelly was not glowing. She had been very uncooperative with the staff, smashed some furniture, punched one of the attendants and had to be sedated. She did have a phone in her room and it was removed.

"Mr. Adam the security at the sanitarium is lax. I simply walked in, went directly to T.J.'s room. She was asleep. I walked out. Not once was I asked for identification nor even why I was in the building. No one was at the front desk."

Samuel took a deep breath. "The front door wasn't locked. Did I do good?"

"Yes Samuel, you did. Thank you. I would like you to be doubly cautious this evening. Each time you stop to pick up one of our guests make sure you have the right person. Take one of the other men with you. T.J. is dangerous and if she finds out Sydney is here we may have some problems."

"Don't worry, Sir. We'll be extra careful."

"It's Adam, Samuel. It's Adam."

Adam walked over to the office window and watched as Samuel drove out in the limo. An uneasy feeling took hold of him and refused to let go. *Wonder where Joseph has gotten himself off to.*

Once the limo was out of sight, Adam went to the elevator, turned the brass handle to three and with its usual snail-pace, it slowly brought him to his apartment. It felt good to be alone. He'd have time to have a leisurely shower and time to meditate before dressing for dinner.

He stopped halfway to the shower. Stood very still. His body tensed. The change in the room brought him to rapt attention. For several minutes he made no movement or sound letting his senses search the wide expansive rooms. A strange odor gradually penetrated his being. Something similar to ozone; however, not quite ozone. *I've smelled this before.*

Dismissing throwing a PSI ball or projecting a voice to make the intruder show itself Adam decided to let his nose lead him. Turning to return to the main room, Adam caught a glimpse of a shadow as it shot across the wall nearest the fireplace. *Must have been a bird flying by. The curtains and blinds are all open.*

Shrugging, he turned and went back down the hallway and hit the shower. The warm vibrating water soothed him. He turned off the shower pushed open the heavy glass door and stepped into a dimly lit room.

She was on him, nearly knocking him over and smothering his face with rapid-fire kisses. "Sydney," he said as he slipped his hands down to her buttocks and lifted her up. Slowly he eased her down and he was in up to end of his shaft. Her gyrations brought him to a boiling point.

"Just a quickie," Sydney whispered.

He felt her quiver and thrust upward.

"See you later," Sydney said as she eased herself up from Adam.

As Adam dressed he felt the garage doors open. Their vibrations traveled throughout the old mansion. Samuel had returned.

Once the huge doors closed, Samuel exited the stretch limo, opened its doors for his four passengers to emerge. He escorted them through the underground garage to the stairs and led them to the upper level.

As they stepped through the doorway, they saw Joseph on his hands and knees scrubbing the floor with a small brush. Wearing a torn wet, dirty robe, he pretended not to know the guests.

"Why in the world are you scrubbing the floor on your hands and knees?" Patricia Livingston, the television reporter said.

"Penance," Joseph replied without looking up.

"Punishment? Good lord. How barbaric. Who's responsible for this?" Patricia Livingston demanded.

"I am," Joseph replied as he wiped at an appropriate smudge on his face.

"You are? I don't understand," Patricia Livingston said. Turning to her cameraman, "You getting this? I'll run it on tonight's late news."

She heard a mumbled, "Yeah, yeah."

"I have done something wrong and I am punishing myself. It's a small thing that I do in comparison to what I have done." Joseph said.

"And what is it that is so terribly bad that you have to do this?" Patricia Livingston demanded.

"I betrayed a trust. And I don't have to do this. I want to. Really, I'm not being made to do this. Now if you'll excuse me, there is much to be done," Joseph said. Disliking the woman he wished one of the others had spoken to him. *She spells trouble.*

"I thought we had agreed that there would be no cameras this evening, Ms. Livingston. Or is it your custom to violate your host's requests when you are invited to a dinner party?" Adam said.

Patricia Livingston whirled around ready to blast whoever it was that dared speak to her in such a harsh way. She stopped. Her mouth hung open in total surprise. Before he stood the most drop-dead gorgeous hunk, she had laid eyes on in a long, long time. Unlike the others she had been meeting, this man wore no makeup, hair was natural, and beautiful azure blue eyes that lit up the whole room. *My god, he's to die for! Wonder who the guy is in the red robe?* she thought.

"Not to die for, Ms. Livingston," Adam said.

Patricia Livingston thought of herself as a hardass, a tough broad who'd seen it all, done it all, and had been it all. But this totally blew her away. This man answered her thoughts. She was about to speak but Adam was welcoming the other two members of the media.

"Thomas here will show you around. Please feel free to ask him or anyone else questions. You must excuse me, I will arrange for another setting at the dinner table. I'll see you at dinner in about thirty minutes. And Thomas, offer our guests wine." Adam said.

"Oh, don't bother with Jimmy, my cameraman. He can eat in the kitchen," Patricia Livingston said.

"Not in my house. Here, everyone dines together. And that includes you." Adam said to Joseph who was pretending to scrub the floor.

Patricia Livingston watched Adam walk across the large reception room. He certainly would be a handsome man in street clothes but in the tuxedo, he was more than movie star handsome. *The tux, obviously tailor-made, outlines his muscularity and certainly, she thought, makes his buns so totally yummy.* From her perspective, a man's buns told her if he would be good in bed.

Thomas's 'this way' broke her momentary reverie. He served the three reporters a glass of imported French champagne; however, when he began to pour the fourth glass for Jimmy, the cameraman, Patricia Livingston said, "None for him."

Thomas ignored the bossy woman and handed a glass to the cameraman and then suggested the group should follow him to begin the tour of the first and second floors.

"Look, I was invited here to get a story and part of that story is this beautiful old mansion. I want to see the whole place. What's on the third floor that I can't see?" Patricia Livingston said as she stepped aside to avoid a wet spot on the marble floor. She noted the man identified as Joseph was not around.

The birdcage elevator came down. Sydney stepped out into the reception room. Dressed in a designer gown of emerald-green silk that clung to her body in all the right places, Sydney paused as the elevator slowly creaked its way back up.

Whew! Maybe I should have dressed a bit more. No, what the hell! Patricia Livingston thought as she took a good look at the exquisite emerald necklace gracing Sydney's neck.

Once again the elevator arrived. Brett, Dutch, and Running-water exited. Each dressed in tuxedos. For a moment, Patricia thought she had died and gone to stud heaven. Her attention was drawn to the circular stairway by a slight cough. The Brothers, each dressed in a light blue robe, in single file, eased their way down the stairs. Patricia Livingston noted the one called Joseph was with them as well as the chauffeur that brought her here. *It's got to be a cult.*

Bradford also dressed in a tux, stepped into the room and announced that dinner was ready to be served. Adam offered his arm to Sydney and then led the group into the dining room.

Steaming dishes of food lined the table. Two roasted suckling pigs held the center place. As each guest was seated there was an appreciative 'ah' expressed. Adam joined them but instead of sitting down, he walked around the table, pouring each a glass of vintage wine from a crystal decanter. Once everyone been served, he went to the head of the table and said, "Unto Thee."

As he seated himself, Patricia Livingston replied, "And unto thee." thinking he had toasted them.

No one else raised a glass.

During the course of the meal, Patricia Livingston's voice dominated the group as she regaled story after story about her exploits as a star reporter. The third glass of wine after the champagne had loosed her tongue. At what point she realized no one was paying any attention to her,

117

she couldn't say. She stopped talking. Those around her were engaged in quiet conversation. She began a study of the people at the table.

Sydney was her first point of focus.

She's certainly beautiful. Two of the hunks seem to hover over her and at the same time, Patricia Livingston thought, *she seems a little bit too nervous. It's strange that she's the only other woman here. Wonder which one she sleeps with.*

She shifted her focus. *The longhaired Indian is staying very close to Adam. They often look at one another as if they were talking, yet they do not speak. Strange. Very strange. Holy crap! Maybe they are lovers.*

Patricia Livingston took a long look at the man seated next to her. *This monk or whatever the hell he is\very tense. Maybe he doesn't like women. Wonder what would happen if I squeezed his balls.*

She dropped that thought and brought her attention to the hulk that brought her here. *He's really pumped up.* Wonder what he's on. *The way he's piling the food on his plate you'd think he hadn't eaten in days.*

She looked at the man seated next to Samuel. *This guy is the chef. His eyes tell an entirely different story than his facial expression. What is going on here?. Guess I better start asking some questions. After all, I am a reporter.*

***

A loud crash set off the alarm.

Running-water immediately stood up and stepped in front of Adam, his guns drawn.

"My god, what's that?" she heard herself saying.

The two men with the woman behind them, stood with guns drawn. A hideous maniacal scream filled the room.

Sydney stepped out from behind Brett and Dutch. She knew who it would be. A shot echoed throughout the dining room. She fell to the floor. Adam started for her but Running-water pushed him to the floor.

"God damn it! Stay put. You hear?" Running-water growled.

Patricia Livingston sat stunned.

Gunfire erupted and the doors to the dining room were splintered by the nonstop rapid fire from Dutch and Brett's guns. Each man slammed in another clip into their guns.

The noise combined with the earsplitting alarm and the smell of spent cartridges caused Patricia Livingston's stomach to flip-flop. She was sure she was about to vomit. She didn't get the chance.

A dark figure hurled over the upturned chairs and lunged, animal-like, through the shattered dining room doors. There was a terrible crash so loud it caused the crystal chandelier to sway.

Adam struggled to his feet as he wrested himself free of Running-water's grip. He bent over Sydney. Checked her pulse. There was none. Anger filled him. As he got up from his knees, he heard a loud snap from the reception room. Running-water grabbed him.

"Damn it, man. Let me go." Adam said.

Once in the reception room, Adam saw Bradford sitting on top of a body, its head still in his arm lock.

Seeing Adam, Bradford got up, turned his head so Adam would not see his tears. Adam caught the action.

"Bradford, you okay? What's with T.J.?"

"Yeah. She was my sister. I told her one day I would have to kill her. Today was that day."

"I'm so sorry, man. I didn't know," Adam said as he placed his hand on Bradford's shoulder.

"We wanted it that way."

"I don't understand, " Adam said.

"Sid, as we called her, had been friends with T.J. and me back when were just little kids. I've loved her all these years. T.J. knew I loved her and boasted that she'd get her before I did. It's been a bad thing between us since we were teenagers. It's over now."

Adam turned back toward the dining room to see if anyone else was hurt. He heard a gurgle and a thud. Bradford lay on the floor, trashing in death throes. He had slit open his jugular vein all the way down his neck. *Three more dead. Will it never stop?* Adam thought.

"Yes, it will stop, my brother," Running-water said, grabbing Adam in a bear hug. "It will stop."

Brett and Dutch joined Running-water at Adam's side. They looked like a football huddle.

The Brothers, too stunned, remained at the table. Samuel, oblivious to everyone, continued to eat. Joseph glared at him. *Glutinous pig. I deal with you later. This little mess should take of Mr. Big Shot. Come in here and remove me will he?*

Patricia Livingston's reporter instinct kicked in and she hurried into the reception room.

"Did you call Adam 'brother'?" Patricia Livingston asked Running-water.

"Yes. We are brothers."

"What about the dead woman? Who is she? Jimmy, you got that camera rolling? This one is hot." Patricia Livingston said as she frantically pushed the buttons on her cell phone.

Running-water had the phone and camera before either she or the cameraman knew what had happened.

"How dare you?" Patricia Livingston screamed. "You will show respect!" Running-water growled

Ignoring the obvious disdain shown by Running-water, Patricia Livingston snapped at her cameraman, "Jimmy, give me my note pad.

"Oh, shut the fuck up, Patricia. Just shut the fuck up!" Jimmy said.

He ducked as Patricia Livingston took a swing at him. He was pleased. He finally had the courage to tell the bitch off. *She tired of me some time ago just as she has tired of all her other cameramen. Once she tired of them, she fired them, hired another one. I guess I can go back to being a freelancer.*

Using his cell phone, Adam punched in 999, gave directions to the Toronto police and then headed back to the dining room.

"I've notified the authorities. When they arrive, cooperate with them," Adam said as he looked at The Brothers. A line from Robert Frost's *Out Out* popped into his head: 'And they, since they were not the one dead, turned to their affairs.' Do not clean up, or remove anything. One of you go to the kitchen and make sure there is an ample supply of coffee. It's going to be a very long night."

Patricia Livingston appeared at Adam's side, leaned up, and gave him a kiss on the cheek.

"Oh, Adam, I am so sorry. What a tragedy! Was she your wife?"

"No, Sydney was a family friend."

"Who is the person out in the reception room?"

"A poor soul."

"Really? Why did the man you called Bradford kill himself?"

"I guess you could say it was misdirected love," Adam replied as he stepped away.

The police had arrived and as usual, Running-water took charge. Each of The Brothers were interviewed and sent about their business. Joseph asked one of the inspectors to tarry a moment; whispered something to him and moved on. Dutch, Brett, and Jimmy the cameraman were questioned. Then came Patricia Livingston's turn. And she ran her mouth non-stop.

CHAPTER 7
THE LECTURE

Love is the extra effort we make in our dealings with those whom we do not like and once you understand that, you understand all.

Quentin Crisp

By early morning the investigation began to wind down. Exhausted after a very long and emotional time, Adam opted to go to this apartment. It was nearly dawn. Once the gate of the elevator closed, he looked out at the mess still in the reception room. There he saw Joseph pull aside one of the inspectors and whisper something to him. He was unaware of Adam watching him. When he heard the clank of the elevator, Joseph scurried off.

Exiting the elevator and walking into his apartment, Adam found Running-water slouched in front of the television.

"Man, they are really going ape over this mess. Are you sure you still want to begin this lecture thing?" Running-water said. Looking up from the TV, he continued, "Good god, Adam. You sure look like a piece of shit. Are you okay, my brother?"

"Just tired and saddened by the continued loss of life wherever I go."

"Yeah, I get it. The morning papers are on the table and they are having a field day. Headlines are three inches high."

"I want to know how T.J. got out of the hospital and how she got into this house. Something isn't connecting," Adam said.

"What do you mean?"

"For starters, how did T.J. know Sydney was here?"

"I'll get on it right away. You got any ideas?"

"As I was coming up here I saw Joseph whispering to one of the policemen. Remember, I saw him talking on the phone in the balcony area. I don't trust him. That whole charade of scrubbing the floor with a toothbrush just makes me all the more suspicious."

"Listen, get some rest, will you?"

"I want to get out of this bloody tux, shower down and then I'll head to bed. Thanks."

***

A traffic jam created by the number of people arriving at Karuna House and the slow pace at which they were allowed to enter the estate grounds caused a number of temper flare-ups. Local residents were not happy over the congestion laid on their car horns to show their displeasure. The notoriety because of the murder and suicide furthered the "gawker" traffic.

Inside, patience was insured by an ample supply of champagne and delicate Hors d'oeuvres. The crowd gave the old birdcage elevator a real workout chugging a hundred guests up to the third-floor ballroom. Among these special guests were

Patricia Livingston and her cameraman, a radio talk-show host, and two reporters from local newspapers. Unknown to Adam, two inspectors from the Canadian Mounted Police were also present.

The ballroom with its twenty-foot high mahogany paneled ceiling was aglow with lighted crystal chandeliers, sparkling crystal wall sconces, and newly cleaned mirrors displayed a certain hint of what it once was. A touch of amber incense combined with the soft sounds of First People flutist created a nascent atmosphere.

The Brothers, in their blue robes and sandals, with hands tucked into their sleeves monk-like, entered in single file and seated themselves in their straight back chairs lined up along the fireplace wall. Their entrance quieted the chatty group. Joseph got up and with as much stateliness as a medieval lord, slowly took a few necessary steps to be in front of the group. He cleared his throat and paused.

"Good evening. Ladies and gentlemen, members of the press, and other special guests welcome to Karuna House. I should like to take a moment to tell you a little something about Karuna House and the men who live here.

Karuna is a Sanskrit word meaning compassion. The Esaugetuh Society of Benevolence, named for its founder and benefactor, is composed of a group of men who used to live on the streets. Each man, seated before you, including me, has a personal and private story; each was brought here by the compassion of Esaugetuh, certainly the most powerful and respected shaman about the First People of Canada and the Native Americans of the United States.

Each of us was brought her to promote the compassionate nature of mankind. In addition Karuna House, the Society owns and operates a local sanitarium. Unfortunately last evening one of the patients there, escaped, broke in here, and killed a dinner guest. A member of our security staff killed the perpetrator of that heinous act. Regrettably, none of us knew at the time, that the murderer was the sister of that security guard. Tragedy was not done with us yet."

Joseph paused for dramatic effect.

"That security guard, in an act of total grief for having killed his sister, took his own life. Please join me in a moment of silence as we publicly acknowledge the tragic loss of three lives."

After a deliberate long pause and with what he thought was an appropriate change in facial expression, Joseph again addressed those assembled.

"And now, with me, please welcome, Adam, the son of Esaugetuh, our leader and benefactor."

Polite applause filled the room as people shifted in their seats to get a look at their host as he entered from the back of the room. Adam, in casual black slacks and an "untucked" tan shirt that accentuated his muscular physique, took his time walking to the front of the room. His long black hair shimmered under the crystal lights. Some, expecting to see an earring dangling from an earlobe were surprised to see none. Others noticed the ease with which he walked and others checked his full crotch. All noticed his azure blue eyes.

Adam was followed by Running-water, who in modified Indian attire, created a singular contrast, and that was not wasted on the guests. Once Adam was in front of the group, Running-water moved to the side, sat down on the floor at just the right angle to the mirrors to allow him to check the people in the audience. Every watchful, Dutch and Brett remained at the rear of the room.

Adam stopped in front of the massive fireplace, nodded to The Brothers and then stepped in closer to the audience. Quietly, he looked at each person in the room, going from left to right, row after row. his wondrous blue eyes, magnet-like, drew them in.

"Good evening and welcome. Tonight I wish to discuss two words: Trust and Love. Both seem appropriate in light of recent unfortunate events that occurred here. I have a question for you: Is trust given or is it earned? And a second question, is love given or earned? And since I have two questions I must confess to a third: What is the connection between trust and love?

Once we have answered the first question, we may then say it serves as the pinion for love, the basis, the rock upon which love is built. And there is no doubt, that's what's what the world needs now. So what does it mean to trust? To love? The issue goes back to the beginning of time. In Christianity, the first Adam and my namesake trusted Eve. He had no reason not to trust her when she offered up the fruit from the tree. Sampson had no reason not to trust Delilah. Caesar, though warned, to beware of the Ides of March, had no reason to mistrust Brutus. Each of these people had their trust betrayed. What happens when trust is betrayed?"

Adam paused, looked at Joseph who shifted uncomfortably in his chair. Then he continued.

"Love flies out the window. To love, one must trust that the other is going to promote their well0pbeing and happiness. Violate that trust and love is lost, perhaps never to return. If it should return, it may not be the same, secure footing as before. How do you get it back? Ear it? Yes! You have to make regular installments just as you would in a savings account at your local bank. And then, maybe, when the account is full, trust may return. if it does, it will return in the name of love. It is love that engenders harmony and peace; it is trust that engenders that love that each of you seeks. In today's restless and violent world, we must do all we can to create a love-based reality. In doing so, we must realize it is a 'moment to moment affair'. how does one love? First, let's see if we can arrive at a working definition. I love chocolate ice cream. I love the Toronto Maple Leafs. I love mystery novels. I love my dog. Love, Love, Love. And not one ounce of understanding. The word *love* has been so overused it is now nearly vacuous. How do we take something that has lost its meaning and get it back The question is no different than the one about trust. How do you get it back?"

Adam walked partway down the aisle. He paused, looked directly at Patricia Livingston. A slight flush moved across her face. Had he caught her staring at his crotch?

"Trust is given. Love is given. Do you give trust with conditions? Only if it's violated. Is it necessary to read the fine print to know if you are trusted? Isn't that what prenuptial agreements or pre-assigned responsibilities within a relationship are—fine print conditions? We are told by the musical muses that "love is a many-splendored thing," we are told that love is what makes the world go around," and we are told that "love is the greatest thing since sliced bread." Yet, do we not put restrictions on its natural flow? Do we not have reservations because it is an unconditional commitment? After all, isn't conditional love something that can be turned on and off? A conditioned love requires that one of the partners is to do something that pleases the other.

On the simplest level, a child picks up its toys from the floor and puts them away. Its mother says, how sweet. I love you, honey." The message conveyed by such behavior is that one must earn love People who are perfectionists and those who are people pleasers most likely will have experienced love conditionally and have never really felt loved. They have not experienced that unconditional commitment. How sad!"

Adam walked to the last row. Taking his time to give what he has said the chance to sink in. He stopped and turned facing the front of the room.

Some in the audience turned to see him. His baritone filled the room.

"Dare we ask a commitment to what? To faith, that love will be returned? In Christianity, one is reminded that 'faith to move mountains' is worthless without love. We are told that even philanthropy without love is lacking in spirituality. In love, we give to others. That is the essence of philanthropy; it is the essence of faith, and it should be our basis for interaction with others. When one loves, there has been a choice—an expressed desire made for the happiness of someone else. That we call benevolence. The commitment then is to personal behavior that reflects benevolence.

Do not confuse benevolence with altruism. Altruism dictates that you sacrifice yourself for the benefit of others; that is, their needs claim your actions and behavior and even your life. If I may borrow a term from today's computer jargon, benevolence enables. It enables you to achieve your value from relationships with other people. Benevolence does not rest upon the misfortunes of others whereas; altruism seems to be directed by that fact. The simple act of giving someone the benefit of the doubt creates an avenue for benevolent behavior, the opportunity to demonstrate the value of unconditional love. When that love is a commitment to personal behavior that derives value from life itself, from the interaction with others, and with society as a whole, then you are benevolent. Matthew Fox has said, "Compassion is not a moral commandment but a flow and overflow of the fullest and divine energies." That my friends is benevolence!

If a man wants to build a house, he uses wood. He must also provide hollow space within the house empty of wood. Thus, both wood and the absence of wood are required to build a house. Building a loving relationship is similar. The builder of love must bring values (wood) and time (space) to the relationship. To do otherwise results in a house built of sand. You cannot be as shifting sand if you want a loving, personal, and lasting relationship. If you are, there is no permanence. It will have slipped away between your fingers before you have had a chance to grasp it, to taste it, to savor its delicacy. Syndicated columnist, Jim Bishop wrote an inspiring essay called *Love Something Apart*. In it, he states, "Love is giving. It is the unification of two persons into one. It is possession and being possessed. But it is also jealousy, hostility, insecurity, and despair. It is the only thing which must be resurrected every day." Trust is applied here because one trusts that there will be a resurrection. Love allows us to experience life and to connect in a positive way. Denying the existence and experience of love, choosing not to practice it, denies our divinity and that is *the* sin! Denying your spirituality is the damnation of all that is divine.

Buddhists tell us to pay careful attention to the other person, to listen for what is actually being said so that we can recognize the source of what is being felt. If you do that, you can respond with care and compassio9n and isn't that benevolence? And isn't that love? Of course, it is! At the same time, it is so much more. It is the total and complete recognition of the divine in all life. Swami Vivekananda has written, "real existence, real knowledge, and real love are eternally connected with one another, the three in one: where one of them is, the others must be."

We make the mistake in loving the wrong way. A man, for example, loves his wife. he wants her with him at all times, to sit by him at social functions, to eat with him, to walk with him. He calls her several times a day from his place of work. This makes him a slave to her existence. This is not love. Love would set her free to be all that she could be. And if she in turns loves him, she will help him cut the umbilical cord he has fastened to her. It is, after all, a mutual thing. Every act of love should bring happiness and joy if not a sense of wonderment. In real love, love does not deliberately cause pain or suffering. If it does, there is a corruption.

A friend shared this little piece with me. Its author is unknown. It is titled *The Essence of Compassion.* I will close with that. "Resolve to be tender with the young, compassionate with the aged, sympathetic with the starving, and tolerant of the week and wronged . . . because sometime in your life you will have been all of these."

Adam took a breath. Looked directly at the audience. Nothing. Stunned by the lack of a response, Adam quickly walked to the back of the room and down a hallway.

"Come back," Running-water called after him. "They are waiting for you."

Unable to contain his delight, Running-water grabbed Adam and swung him around.

"You're sure about that? Man, they were so dead!"

"Yes! Yes! I am sure. Come."

Once the audience of a hundred people knew Adam was back in the ballroom, they stood, applauded, and whistled. Running-water followed Adam to the front of the room, once again squatted down so he could see the audience in the mirrors.

Turning to each section of the standing people, Adam caught sight of a figure in the shadows of one of the large velvet grapes that covered the elevator entrance, something The Brothers had put up for the occasion. Adam knew who it was even though they had never met. Leaving the audience still standing, Adam immediately went to her, stopping her flight by touching her shoulder.

She turned, eyes brimming with tears.

"Isha?" Adam said.

"Yes," she whispered.

"You love him very much, don't you?"

Crying softly, Isha Sands replied, "Yes and I don't know what to do."

"Don't know what to do? Let me love you with all my heart," Running-water said grabbing her, enfolding her in his strong arms, and kissing her.

"You two, excuse me while I attend to our other guests," Adam said.

133

"Isha, don't go away. Stay. I'll be right back," Running-water said. "I have to—,"

"Yes, I know. Go. I'll be here."

As the caterers served refreshments and champagne, Adam moved among the guests. He found them agreeable, friendly, and supportive. Some asking probing questions while a few of the women made very open passes.

"So, when's the next lecture? How about sex as a topic?" Patricia Livingston said as she deliberately elongated the word so.

"We'll see. Did you enjoy the lecture?" Adam said.

"Truthfully?"

"Yes, of course."

"Fantastic!" Patricia Livingston gushed as she slipped her arm through Adam's. "Tell me, Adam, who was that woman you were talking to back thee? Another family friend?"

She immediately regretted asking the last question.

"Running-water's wife," Adam replied in a voice so cold that Patricia Livingston let go of his arm and quickly disappeared in the crowd.

Joseph, who had been sitting with the other Brothers, go up and walked to the center of the room, rang a bell until he had everyone's attention. This move by Joseph caught Adam off guard. Quizzically he looked at Joseph. Running-water was on his feet.

Unabashed, Joseph cleared his throat and announced, "Ladies and Gentlemen thank you for coming. The Esaugetuh Society for Benevolence appreciates your interest. We will let you know if there is another such function. Good night."

Instead of waiting for the old and very slow elevator, many guests used the stairway to exit. Once the place was secure and the grounds had been swept by security, the large gate at the entrance creaked its way closed. Adam thanked each member of The Brothers, excused himself and returned to his apartment. There he was greeted by a very animated Running-water.

Grabbing Adam, picking him up, Running-water began to dance him around the floor.

"Isha, come and get this mad man. Have you told him the whole truth?"

"The whole truth?" Running-water. His face turned from joy to concern.

Taking her husband by the arm, and kissing him, Isha whispered, "Twins."

Running-water was beside himself with delight. Isha had trouble calming him down. The strain of the flight and the lateness of the hour forced her to say, "I need to retire. Now!"

In the meantime, Brett and Dutch had divided the night's shift. Experience had dictated that at least one of Adam's team by on guard at all times.

Adam flopped down in one of the large red leather chairs in front of the fireplace. He watched its soft glow and he felt good. *New life has been created; new purposes established for The Esaugetuh Society of Benevolence, and a new course of action for myself. Despite the tragic deaths of Sydney, Bradford and T. J. Kelly, something of value has developed.*

With a jerk, Adam sat straight up. Pensive and listening. He sensed someone watching him. Then he heard the soft footsteps.

"Adan, can we talk?" Isha asked as she approached Adam. Her voice was barely above a whisper.

"Of course. Come sit with me in front of the fire. May I get you something?'

"No, but thank you just the same. I apologize for whispering. I don't want to wake Running-water. He's a light sleeper."

"I know," Adam said.

"Of course you do. Running-water is so totally devoted to you that sometimes I think he loves you more than he does me. And in a way, maybe he does. We are having children and it worries me. He longs to be a father and yet when he is not with you, his soul is sad. It is so heavy he goes into a sulk removing himself from me and for days on end, he does not even speak to me. I want our children to know their father. I can't bear the thought of his not being there. I have made a difficult decision and he does not know this. I wanted to tell you first. I hope you will understand, " Isha said.

"And you really want me to make Running-water understand."

"Well, yes. He'll listen to you," Isha whispered as she adjusted her abdomen.

"I'm not sure he'll approve of your decision. When a man becomes a father his instincts merge to protect his offspring because they are his link to the future."

"You act as if you know my decision," Isha said. She could not hide her disappointment.

"I do and I am not sure that the two of you staying with me is the answer. It might be very dangerous for you and the twin boys."

Isha's eyes grew large.

"Yes, boys. Three people died in this house just last night. Sometimes I feel that death uses me as bait. Running-water nearly died once, " Adam said.

"I know. He told me. He said you were willing to give him one of your kidneys, that you fought the she-devil to save his soul. I know all of this, dear Adam. His sons, our sons, need to know the man their father serves. I will not be dissuaded."

"Ah, there you are. I was worried about you," Running-water said as he ambled into the room. "Did you say, sons? What decision? "

Turning to greet her husband, Isha said, "We are to say with Adam wherever he goes. I want them to know the man who controls your destiny, our destiny."

"Are you sure you want to be on the go all the time, packing up at a minute's notice, never knowing what may happen? Are you sure you want to do this rather than having a permanent home, a place where our children can play and grow?" Running-water said.

Adam interrupted. "Have you shown Isha your log cabin?"

"No, but she knows about it. We could go there and live, but not that she is pregnant I don't want to be far from quality medical facilities," Running-water said.

"I've made up my mind. It's settled. I've already told my parents and your uncle and mother. And they agree with me. My place is with you," Isha said.

Running-water looked at Adam, rolled his eyes upward. Both knew better than to protest.

CHAPTER 8
SIFTING THROUGH THE SAND

Lives of great men all remind us we can make our lives sublime, and departing, leave behind us footprints on the sands of time.
Henry Wadsworth Longfellow.

Even though they were not called to come to Adam's office The Brothers filed in with Joseph in the lead.

"You were not called. Leave. Now!" Dutch's military tone sent them scurrying.

Dutch decided to follow The Brothers to make sure none remained lurking and listening outside of the office door.

The Brothers and Dutch had barely gotten out of Adam's office when two inspectors from the Toronto City Police arrived. They were unnerved by the open display of the guns. If the intent was to intimidate them Adam's staff was successful. Soon Adam arrived and like Dutch and Brett, he was armed.

"Good morning officers. How may we help you?" Adam said cordially as he extended his hand.

"Good morning. I am inspector Jenkins and my colleague is Inspector Lavvy."

Jenkins pulled himself up, stretching his back in an effort to ease the pain. His angular face did not betray his discomfort. The grey around the temples suggested the possibility of a full head of grey hair. The three stars on his epaulets indicated he was a staff inspector.

Clearing his throat, Inspector Jenkins said, "Thank you for seeing us. We'll try not to take up too much of your time. "

"Thank you, we appreciate that courtesy," Adam said.

"We know," Jenkins said nodding toward Lavvy, "that two of the victims were female and both were shot. The one identified as T. J. Kelly did not receive a life-threatening wound from the gunshot. We know she died from having her neck broken. We have the gun that was used to kill the person identified as Sydney Thompson."

"Get to the point, inspector," Adam said.

Lowering his eyelids as if taking aim, Jenkins said "Yes, of course. I note all of you are armed. We'd like to have your weapons for ballistic testing to see which weapon was used to wound Miss Kelly."

"That's easy. I shot the intruder," Brett said.

"Our interview of the monks indicates you were not the only one firing through the doors. How can you be sure it was your shot?" Inspector Lavvy asked as he pulled out a pen and pad, ready to take notes.

He wasn't as large a man as Inspector Jenkins, but what he lacked in height he made up for in bulk. His body build suggested he spent a lot of time at the gym.

Running-water walked in and as he shut the door he said, "Is all of this really necessary, inspector? And by the way, they are not monks."

"Sorry if I misunderstood, To answer your question, yes, identifying the shooter is a necessary part of our investigation. And by the way, I didn't get your name."

"I am Running-water, Adam's attorney."

Before Inspector Lavvy could respond, Dutch returned and interrupted the conversation.

"I understand you are trying to identify who shot T. J. Kelly. No problem. I did, Dutch said as he moved to the center of the room and just slightly to the left and in front of Adam.

"Sir, how do you know that?" Inspector Jenkins said.

"Simple. I'm faster on the draw than my friends here," Dutch said.

"Actually, inspector, neither of them is the shooter. I am," Running-water said.

"Come now, gentlemen, we are not so dumb as to fall for that old movie ruse," Inspector Jenkins scolded. "One or all of you could be charged with attempted murder. We are not playing games."

"Inspector Jenkins please excuse my staff. They are only trying to protect me. We will be happy to give you a test bullet from each of our weapons. However, we would prefer not to be left defenseless. Would you be willing to go down into the basement, set up a drum of water, fire into that, and then retrieve the bullets?" Adam said.

"Excuse us for a moment," Inspector Jenkins said as he motioned for Lavvy to follow him outside of the office.

After some hushed conversation, the inspectors stepped back into Adam's office.

"Agreed. We can do that," Inspector Jenkins said. This time the slight edge in his voice was gone.

"Great!" Running-water said as he began to collect the guns.

"Wait, my brother. Give the guns to Brett," Adam said and then turning to Brett he continued, "Brett, show the inspectors where to go, help them set up, give them our guns, making sure each is correctly identified. Once that is done join me here."

Brett stopped at a desk, pulled out some tags, wrote a name on each, tied a matching name to the trigger owner's gun. He handed the four guns to Inspector Lavvy and ushered them out of the office.

A bellowing voice filled the whole area: "Mr. Adam, Mr. Adam."

"What is it, Samuel?" Adam said.

"There's three trucks out front. A driver said they were to unload here. What do you want me to do?"

"Dutch will be right with you, Samuel. Go and tell the driver's to wait for instructions."

Adam went to the office door with Samuel, waited until he was out of sight, and then stepped back into the office and closed the door.

"Dutch, I want you to supervise the unloading of the trucks. Have they go to the back entrance and have the crew take everything to the third floor, set it up in the ballroom. Don't have them use the elevator. Get the necessary computers, equipment for digital photography, scanning machines, and make sure we have secure satellite connectivity. Call whomever you have to and get immediate delivery."

"No problem, Adam. Anything else?"

"Yes, keep The Brothers away from the trucks and do not allow them on the third floor. They are not to have access to the third floor at any time for any reason."

"Adam, what do you want me to do?" Running-water said.

Adam placed his index finger to his lips and then pointed to an old floor vent that was in the ceiling. It was not uncommon for old homes to have them to help heat the upper floor. Adam stepped over to a corner of the room where a 1930 Philo Console Tube Radio stood. A couple of twists of the dial and music blared.

"Running-water, I am not happy with the way The Brothers are forming themselves into an elitist bunch of wannabe monks. I have told them flat out that this is not a monastery. I gave in on the wearing of robes. I hoped it would lead to some sense of connectivity. It has not. Furthermore, Joseph is especially trying. He's still attempting to be The Master of Karuna House. He knew the media people were coming and deliberately played to them with his feigned floor scrubbing. My gut tells me he's the one who tipped T.J. that Sydney was here and I am quite sure he is the one who suggested the inspectors come back. I saw him whispering to one of them last night."

"You may be right. I'm sure he not going to really give up the hundred grand without a fight," Running-water said.

"Pay each of them enough to keep them going for three months and get them out of the house. Supervise their packing. Then call a locksmith and have all the locks changed and change the alarms. When you have that done, meet me upstairs in the ballroom."

"Will do."

"Running-water—,"

"Yeah,"

"I'm glad you and Isha are staying. Thank you, my brother."

***

Adam sat down at his desk, folded his hands in the Dhyana mudra. He closed his eyes and quieted his breathing. His office door flew open with a loud bang as it slammed in the wall.

"You bastard! You god-damned bastard. Who the hell do you think you are? You can't throw me out. You have no right. I am The Master Here."

Adam said nothing for a moment. He just looked at Joseph. Clearing his throat, Adam said, "My father, Esaugetuh, told me a story he said had been handed down by the Old Ones. It's appropriate now.

A grandfather was talking to his grandson about how he felt about a personal matter. He said to the grandson, 'I feel like I have two wolves fighting in my heart. One wolf is vengeful and angry; the other is loving and compassionate.' Grandfather, said the grandson, which wolf will win the fight in your heart? The grandfather answered. 'The one I feed.'

Joseph, you have fed the first wolf for so long you no longer can behave like a decent human being. You were given a chance to redeem yourself. Instead of accepting that opportunity, you faked cleaning the floor to impress the media people. You assumed the role of leadership at my lecture to press again a public image you do not have. The final act of blatant disregard came when you called the sanitarium and told them to release T. J. Kelly. You are directly responsible for the deaths of three people. Still not satisfied with your nasty doings, you arranged for the inspectors to revisit here in an effort to discredit my staff and me. You again have a choice. Leave here with whatever money Running-water has given you or go to prison for embezzlement and contributing to the death of three people."

"You don't scare me. You can't prove a thing," Joseph hissed.

"Your confession to stealing the hundred thousand dollars from Karuna House is on tape," Adam replied. His voice no longer conciliatory.

Joseph's face flushed with anger.

"You wouldn't dare. Think of the negative publicity. Your little utopia here would be finished," Joseph screamed.

"Oh, but he would," Running-water said grabbing Joseph by the scuff of the neck. He proceeded to drag him down the hall, out the front door, down the long driveway, and out the front gate. Joseph, cussing and kicking all the way, was unceremoniously dropped on the side of the street.

"Make sure I never see you again. If I do, I will turn you over to the local authorities," Running-water growled.

Joseph grabbed the bag containing whatever Running-water had thrown in it. Clutching the bag to his chest, Joseph scurried own the street.

On his way back up the driveway, Running-water passed some of the men, each in street clothes, each carrying a duffel bag. None looked at him as they passed. He counted only eight. He quickened his pace, and by the time he was at Adam's office, he was in a dead run. The office door was open.

Thomas and Samuel were on their knees in front of Adam's desk. Running-water stopped to listen.

'We don't want your money. Just let us stay. We will do whatever you ask of us. Besides, Charles isn't in any shape to be by himself. We can look after him," Thomas said.

"You lost your chauffeur. Let me do that. I know the city even better than Bradford did," Samuel chimed in.

146

"Each of the others can contribute to the household. One is great with flowers, another is a baker, and another is into growing vegetables. Don't judge us by the actions of one," Thomas implored.

"Hmm, maybe you are right. I'll tell you what. Go and fetch the others back. Let's see what they have to say," Adam said.

"And Joseph?" Thomas asked.

"Do you know the mythic story of Psyche and Aphrodite?"

Thomas and Samuel both shook their heads no.

"Psyche was assigned four supposedly impossible tasks by Aphrodite as a punishment for loving her son. The last task required Psyche to descend to the underworld with a small box which was to fill with a beauty ointment. Aphrodite told her that she would encounter pathetic people who would seek her help, her sympathies, and her compassion. If she stopped to aid any of these individuals, she would have to remain in the underworld forever. Psyche had to be able to say *no* to those who would deter her from completing her task. They would suggest inappropriate choices for her to make. Joseph is one of those pathetic people. Joseph will not be allowed back," Adam said.

"Thank you, thank you. He's a bad man," Thomas said on the way out the office door. His tone was not quite sincere.

Perhaps it was the tone that brought Adam's attention to Thomas' limp. He had not noticed it before. He made a note to speak to Thomas about his limp.

147

I have two cripples to deal with; Thomas and Charles. I wonder what handicap each of the others has, physical, emotional, or both. Was this a part of the reason Esaugetuh had me in Toronto? Surely he didn't expect me to change Sydney's sex life even though sex with her was hot; nor could it have been to protect her.

Adam swung around in his desk chair, looked out the window into the garden. For a long moment, he looked at the garden and yet not really seeing it.

If it was to protect Sydney, I have failed and failed miserably. Maybe the real purpose for my being here is to teach me how to deal with failure.

He stood up so quickly he nearly knocked his chair over.

Good god! What a horrible thought! All of the deaths surrounding me are failures. Esaugetuh must know how the loss of these lives haunts me with their intrusion into my dreams and making them uncontrollable nightmares.

He sat back down, immovable at his desk, trance-like and fixated.

***

Samuel was puffed up. He was now the official chauffeur of Karuna House. He eased the limo out into the line of traffic. He hadn't driven far before he spotted The Brothers trudging along, walking in single file like little school children. He guffawed.

Pulling up alongside of the men, Samuel stopped, pushed a button to lower a window.

148

Shouting out of the open window, Samuel said, "Adam says you are to come back. Get in."

Eagerly the eight men piled into the limo, slinging their duffle bags wherever they would land. Samuel waited for the traffic break, one came, and he made a U-turn and headed back to Karuna House. Despite the quietness, there was an intense emotional fighting waiting to explode. Upon some unknown signal, the eight yelled, "Go faster, Samuel. Go faster!"

It was a scrambled egg effort to see who would get out of the limo first. Finally, the last one was out, turned, leaned back into the limo, grabbed his duffle bag and lined up with the other seven. Anxiously they waited for Samuel to open the massive wooden door to the front entrance.

Once inside, The Brothers went directly to Adam's office. There, each man offered to return the check given to them by Running-water. And each asked to be allowed to return to Karuna House.

For Adam, this was Deja vu. During what seemed like another time, almost another lifetime, he had given money to another group of men. They too had said they were grateful for another chance and then they tried to kill him. Sadly, they were the ones who ended up dead. Running-water and Brett had seen to that.

Perhaps I am testing fate or maybe it's my belief in the innate goodness of mankind.

"Keep the money. Bank it for a rainy day," Adam said as he indicated they should leave.

As Jedediah Woods would say 'there's fertile ground to be plowed here.'

"Are you sure about that, Adam?" Running-water said as he walked into the room.

"Ah, practicing reading my mind, are you?" Adam said, smiling.

"No. Your thoughts were so strong they just popped into my head. Sometimes it scares the shit out of me, Adam. It really does."

Before Adam could reply, Brett with the inspectors in tow walked in.

"We have collected the bullets from each gun and properly marked them. Your cooperation is appreciated," Inspector Jenkins said as he extended his hand to Adam.

"You're welcome. Good day to you inspectors," Adam replied.

Brett handed Running-water and Adam their guns and holstered his own. Running-water checked his to make sure it had been re-loaded and Adam followed.

Dutch came down from the third floor just in time for evening meal The Brothers had prepared. Between mouthfuls of pasta and Italian Sweet Sausage, he told Adam the movers had unloaded the trucks and had left.

"I have three men who build stage sets scheduled for tomorrow. All you have to do is to have the photos laid out for them to have a visual," Dutch said.

"What about the computers and other electronics?" Adam asked.

"The computers, cameras, and printers have arrived and a technician has set up the system using satellite.?

"Thanks. Once Esaugetuh's apartment is recreated I can begin the search. There are hundreds of boxes to go through. Hopefully, there is a clue as to where Esaugetuh is or what has happened to him," Adam said.

And maybe answer to a new and just as curious mystery. Why was the apartment a photo gallery of my life? Or was it intended as my memorial?

A cough from Thomas brought Adam back to the dinner table. He realized that during the meal The Brothers had not spoken. Even though he was sure they had been listening to his conversation with Dutch, they had returned to their 'communal meal' behavior—no talking during the evening meal. As if upon some silent command had been given, The Brothers rose from their chairs, picked up their plates and in single file marched off to the kitchen.

Adam and the rest of the diners including Isha followed suit and picked up their empty dishes and started toward the kitchen. Samuel and Thomas rushed in.

"You don't do that," Thomas said. "We take care of that." He reached for their plates.

Adam reached over, touched Thomas on the arm and said, "You are not servants here. We will bring our dishes to the kitchen."

In the massive kitchen, Adam found the men working together harmoniously and with a jocular air. Satisfied with his decision to allow them to return to Karuna House, he retired to his apartment on the third floor. Dutch returned to the plane. Since an earlier attempt to blow it up, either he or Brett stayed with the plane. Brett remained at Karuna House and would take the first watch outside of Adam's bedroom door. To make himself less of a target, he sat on the floor.

Wonder if Running-water will take his turn on watch since his wife is now with him. What the hell, I can stay up all night. Done it enough times during my stretch in the SEALS.

Running-water and Isha had retired to their apartment. Once he was sure Isha was asleep, Running-water slipped out of bed and went up to the third floor to relieve Brett at his watch. He would remain there until morning and hopefully would be back in their apartment before Isha missed him.

He should have known better. Within minutes she was by his side. Because of her pregnancy, she sat with her legs outstretched and not in the Indian fashion. They remained as guards together; their hearts full. She felt the new life she and Running-water had created surge through her and she was content.

Adam found them sitting outside his bedroom. Isha, asleep and curled up next to her husband. Adam leaned down, gently picked her up, and took her to another bedroom. There he tucked her into bed. As he turned to leave, he was met by Running-water.

"She insisted on taking a watch with me. She's stubborn like that," Running-water whispered.

"I figured she would. You're a lucky man, my brother. However, she is not to do this again. She needs her rest. If there should be a problem she and or your unborn sons could be harmed."

"Ha! You talk to her. Maybe she'll listen to you," Running-water said.

A knife whizzed by Adam's head. It was so close he heard it push the air.

"I can handle myself, " Isha said sliding down from the high bed.

Both men laughed and both put their arms around her. Running-water gave her an affectionate pat on the butt. He felt her pistol as she pressed against him.

The three of them picked their way through the mountain of boxes and furniture that now occupied the ballroom. Adam pulled open the massive drapery of the windows. Dawn was breaking and Lake Ontario shimmered with the promise of a beautiful new day. Even the birdcage elevator seemed less inclined to groan as it took its charges to the first floor.

There they were greeted with a good morning from Thomas. Adam stepped aside to let Isha and Running-water move on ahead to the dining room. Turning to Thomas, Adam said, "Tell me, Thomas, how long have you been limping?"

"For a while, why?"

"Yesterday was the first day I had noticed your limp. I may be able to help if you are willing."

153

"What do you mean?" Thomas asked. He was taken aback by the sudden familiarity.

"I would like to do a healing on you. Do you know the cause of your limping?"

"Sure. Joseph beat me with a baseball bat because I refused to do what he said."

"Hmm. Lay down on the floor, and I'll see what I can do," Adam said.

Realizing that Thomas and Adam had not joined them in the dining room, The Brothers filed out to see where they were. Running-water and Isha followed. Allen began to speak but Running-water placed a finger to his lips indicating he should be quiet. In the reception area, they saw Adam moving his hands over Thomas' injured leg.

Adam felt the heat build in his hands as they took on a life of their own. They hovered over the injured knee and hip. A pale blue light encircled Adam as he continued to bring PSI energy to Thomas' injuries.

The Brothers, awed by what they saw, stood with mouths agape. One crossed himself. Once the light around Adam diminished, Running-water stepped forward and helped Thomas to his feet.

"I can't believe it. The pain—it's gone!"

"Good. I'll do another healing on you in a couple of days," Adam said.

Wiping tears from his eyes, Thomas said, "Thank you, thank you." He sniffed once more.

"You're welcome," Adam replied. *Hmm. I feel that Thomas' response was not quite genuine. I just*

154

can't put my finger on it. For a time I have felt a lack of sincerity in him.

I agree, my brother. He bears watching.

Adam looked at Running-water and acknowledged his thought.

"Now all of you know who the real mater of Karuna House is," Running-water said as he took Isha by the arm to escort back to the dining room for breakfast.

As was their custom, The Brothers waited until everyone had finished eating before getting up to leave. That meant waiting for Samuel to stop eating.

Adam stood up, cleared his throat, and looked at each person present.

"From now on there will be no mid-morning snack, afternoon snack or evening snack. You will eat whenever you want. There will be three meals served each day. Each of you will have specific chores to do, tasks to accomplish, and each of you will go through a training program in first aid, cooking for large groups, self-defense, and in counseling skills."

He paused, looked again at each of The Brothers and then continued: "If you want to take courses or even degrees at any of the local colleges or the university, please do so. The Esaugetuh Society of Benevolence will pay for that. You, in turn, will become part of an extensive outreach program for the community. Compassion will be your motivation; love of your fellow human beings will be your strength, and your personal commitment to serve will be your guide."

155

Again, Adam paused, checking to see if the men were tuning into what he was saying. He looked at Running-water, seeking encouragement. He got a thumbs up. Feeling better about his pitch, Adam continued.

"You are free to leave here at any time if you feel you cannot meet these goals. There will be no punitive acts against you if you choose to leave. I would request that you let Running-water know of such a decision. Please tell Isha what it is you would like to do, that is, do you want to be housekeepers, gardeners, cooks, shoppers, guards, or gatekeepers. Whatever it is, set your own schedules, and give them to her in a timely fashion. Any questions?"

Isha reached over and patted Running-water's leg. As she did so, she leaned into him and whispered, "I am family now."

"You always have been," Running-water whispered back.

"What about our daily meditation?" Christian asked waving his hand in a semicircle to include all of The Brothers. "Surely," he continued, " it is worthwhile." He rolled his eyes upward as he pointed skyward with an open palm.

"There will be no daily meditation. If you wish to meditate, do so at the beginning of the day or at the end of the day and in the privacy of your own quarters. I remind you once again, this is not a monastery, nor is this group a religious sect. I want the robes gone. You are to wear street clothes, " Adam said.

"Well for pity sake, just how to you expect people to recognize us as the Esaugetuh Benevolent Society if we look just like everyone else?" Christian gushed. "It would make us just so—so common."

"Good point, Christian. You see to it that each of the men has a couple of blue blazers, blue collarless shirts, and gray slacks, and black shoes. Have the jackets monogrammed with a flying eagle and the words, Esaugetuh Benevolent Society. Running-water will give you a credit card to use to pay for all of this. Samuel drive them into the city to a men's shop and while you are out, stop by an auto paint shop and arrange to have the same log painted on the limo and the SUV. Anything else?"

There were no more questions. Christian, beside himself for having been given such an important assignment. *They'll have to nice to me now.*

CHAPTER 9
RECONSTRUCTING ESAUGETUH'S APARTMENT

Maintain tranquility in the center even though things come forth in great numbers, each one returns to its root.

Lao Tzu

Adam with Running-water and Brett immediately went up to the third floor to prepare for the reconstruction of Esaugetuh's former apartment. As Adam downloaded the photos from Sydney's digital camera a sadness flooded him. He felt the tears form and he shook his head to force himself to concentrate on the task at hand. No matter what, Sydney would always be a part of him.

As the photos were printed, Adam carefully placed them on large sheets of foam-board, making sure they were in the exact sequence in which they were taken. He numbered each photo taking great care to make sure which wall of the apartment they were originally hung.

Two carpenters arrived promptly at nine o'clock. Thomas attempted to escort them to the third floor but was turned back by Running-water who said, "This floor is off limits to The Brothers. In the future, if someone has an appointment to come here I'll notify you and you can show them the elevator."

By midday, the apartment's walls had been constructed, connected, and painted. Heat lamps were used to hasten the drying of the paint. When it was dry Adam took one wall with Brett and Running-water each taking another wall to carefully place the photos in the exact position as they had been originally. The sparse furniture, including the cabinet that had held Sydney's fascination, was placed and identified.

They worked on through the night and by morning Esaugetuh's apartment had been recreated and everything was in the exact location as it had been over Syd's Bar. The three men were admiring their work when Isha arrived with a cart full of hot steaming food. "Breakfast," she announced.

She was malcontent. Running-water had not been in their bed. Resentment over the amount of time he spent with Adam gnawed at her. She knew she was becoming more and more possessive of Running-water, something she attributed to her pregnancy. While the men ate, she took her time to look around. She let out a long low whistle. Her beautiful doe eyes widened as she stared at a life-sized photo of nude Adam.

"No question about it," Isha said, "He's an Indian."

"What are you talking about?" Running-water managed to say as he stuffed the last warm biscuit into his mouth.

"Adam's phot. He's sure hung like an Indian man. Whew! What a stud!" she giggled.

"Behave yourself, woman. I might get jealous," Running-water teased.

Isha giggled again and blew him an exaggerated kiss.

"What's all the giggling about?" Adam said as he stuck his head from around a corner of the construction.

"Isha's admiring your manliness. Better watch out, Adam," Running-water said. His laughter filled the room. *What's so strange about that? In the old days, Indian men shared their women if they had a guest. Sometimes, the women took it upon themselves to slip between the blankets of a young warrior. Hmm, wonder if Isha would like Adam to call on her between the blankets.*

He heard Adam's "It wouldn't do her any good. You remember Moon-woman said you would live a long life as an agamete. You know she was wrong. You are about to be a father."

My god, Adam. you gave yourself for me, didn't you? That's what the real battle was all about, wasn't it? You—you agreed to be the agamete if I would live. It's not fair, Damn it, Adam. It's not fair," Running-water said breaking out of their mind-talk.

"What's not fair?" Isha asked coming back from her stroll along the photo gallery.

"That—,"

160

"That he hasn't found any more photos of himself. And that's odd, don't you think?" Adam interrupted.

"Aren't all of these extra boxes filled with photos?

"Yes," Adam replied.

"Well, I am pretty good at systems. have you labeled each box? If not, I can assign each a box number and then list the content of each on one of the computers. I can even scan their contents so you can cross-reference them. It might turn ups some more photos of jealous pants," Isha said. *Looks like I'm not the only one with feelings issues.*

"Great. If you don't have what you need let that man of yours know and he'll get it for you," Adam said.

Breakfasts and dinners merged into seamless non-time as days began and ended. Photos of Running-water and Adam together began to turn up in box thirty. Their point of reference began toward the end of their first visit to Mesa Verde. A photo of Adam getting ready to punch Running-water brought a demand for an explanation from Isha. Running-water told her it was when he and Adam had become real friends.

Another photograph one that caught Adam's attention was that of a very attractive woman standing on a porch. He knew the woman was his mother but the man's face had been rubbed out.

"I'd like to know how Esaugetuh got all of these photos and who took them. More importantly, why?" Adam said.

"one thing seems very obvious to me," Isha said. "You hold a very special place in someone's heart."

"And how do you figure that?" Running-water pipped up.

"None of the photos that we have seen show Adam in a negative way. Even the one where he is about to hit you, he is not shown as a mean person. So, I think the person who collected all of these most have loved Adam very much. Only a parent would have such a collection, especially if he was an only child," Isha said.

"Good God! Are you saying you think Adam is really Esaugetuh's biological son?" Running-water said. The astonishment showed.

"Well, if I was a gambler, I'd say it's a sure bet."

"Look you two; I have no evidence that Esaugetuh is my biological father. All I know is he adopted me when I was an adult. I remember I thought it was so cool being adopted by a shaman. And what made it even better he was the man I had heard about as a small child. He was the subject of a lot of whispering by the women in the wigwams near our cabin. Because he was a man of mystery I became all the more inquisitive. I asked so many questions my father told me to stop."

"Looking at the photos, Adam, you do have his azure blue eyes. Did your mother or the man you know as your father have azure blue eyes?" Isha said.

"No. My father had brown eyes and my mother's were, hazel. I never considered his eyes or drew any connection to my own. But if I am his biological son why didn't he just come out and tell me?"

"Maybe he would have if he hadn't disappeared and especially if he knew your mother was dead," Running-water added.

"Do you really think the answer is here in all of this stuff, Adam?" Isha said as she tried to push the bottom drawer back into the cabinet that Sydney had wanted.

Running-water moved over a bit to help Isha. Realizing that something was jamming the drawer, he pulled it all the way out. A small box fell from behind the drawer. It was an old wooden pencil box. Running-water opened its beautifully carved lid. Inside was an envelope with *Ikaee Wicasa* written in beautiful calligraphy. Knowing that was Adam's Indian name, he handed him the yellowed envelope.

Carefully Adam pulled out the folded papers. Some appeared to be legal documents. One was a letter addressed to him. Slowly, he begins to read.

Dear Adam,

A battle, no a war, so mind fracturing that it nearly sunders me into a desperate melancholy—a fixated state so strong that I can't shake it loose. I don't know where to begin or what to say; yet, knowing I should, no not should, I must say it. Pretense or putting off until a rainy day won't stop the turmoil going on in my head.

The myriad things I want to say and the things I ought to say fight for my attention. There are so many

163

things I want to share. I know that's impossible. Anyway, Adam, because it's your sixteenth birthday, or because I am just a lonely old man, I've decided to write this letter. And I know beforehand I won't mail it. Where's the discipline in that?

I know you have a penchant for questions. And I guess talking about asking questions will eventually lead me to what it is I feel I ought to say.

First, Adam, there's nothing wrong with asking questions. it shows interest, an eagerness to learn, and a mind that is alive and vibrant. All that is good.

Second, every choice you make, no matter how small or how large must be tested by deliberate questioning. The French philosopher, Rene Descartes is a good beginning source for you.

Third, as you question, ask if your choices would satisfy these attributes: truth, safety, health, happiness, and love. If you find any two missing, you have a strong indication a choice is not the best. In such a situation, look for alternatives.

Fourth, ask whether your choice or choices will cause harm to yourself, to another living being, or to the earth upon which you live. If you answer positively to any of these, then your choice is not a good one.

Fifth, once answered, never be ashamed of your decision; and if it turns out to be an incorrect decision, do not be afraid to admit it, correct it if you can. If the error cannot be corrected, move on. Do not stay focused on the same error. It's counterproductive.

Will that said, you might wonder why I have not made myself known to you— why I haven't come forward and admitted who I am. This letter is an effort to correct a previous choice. You have a right to the answers. As difficult as it was for us, questions were asked and choices were made. At the time, your mother and I felt

164

we had to accept the choices made by others because unlike in your world, we were not allowed the freedom of choice.

Oh, we considered two other alternatives. And these I will share with you to help you understand. Your mother and I could have run away knowing that neither of our families would have accepted us; neither our people would have accepted us. A white woman living with an Indian was taboo. We considered mutual suicide. That would not only end our lives but also yours. We choose life for you no matter what sacrifices we would have to make. You are our legacy or connection to the future.

Our problem as it is often the case with young people who are in heat was our failure to ask the right questions. Had we put our choices to the test things would have been different. Because we were so much in love, we were sure that our love could conquer all problems. We were so wrong. Adam, no matter the hurt your mother and I suffered because we could not be together and the loss of not raising our son together, and the loneliness that became my constant companion, we both are grateful that at least one decision we made was the correct one. You were to be born! And you are worth every second of the dismay we experienced. No father could be more proud of his son.

Wiping away tears Adam said, "It's signed Esaugetuh. Finally! Answers!"

"You okay, Adam?" Running-water asked.

Adam nodded his head as he struggled to regain his composure. He heaved a long sigh.

"At last the truth. The man I knew as my father wasn't and what's more I always felt he wasn't. I now have an explanation for the lack of any real affection from him and the gulf that always seemed to be between us."

I'll be damned. I'm a half-breed. What an ugly concept. And to think I had chastised Running-water for referring to himself that way when he learned his grandfather was a white man. One's ethnic background is not the measure of the man. I better pay closer attention to my own preachments.

Running-water's voice finally caught Adam's attention.

"Part of the mystery has been solved. Now, my brother, hopefully, something in these other papers will give us a clue as to where Esaugetuh is or what has happened to him."

Adam folded the letter and slipped it back in the brown envelope. He then read the remaining papers, he handed them to Running-water.

The papers continued to shed light on Esaugetuh's relationship with Adam's mother and his step-father. The real shocker was Esaugetuh was Adam's step-father's silent business partner.

"How similar this is to that of your grandparents, Running-water. Both lived in an unforgiving society, both had unforgiving parents. However, unlike your grandfather who was unaware he had fathered a child, Esaugetuh knew and evidently had kept a secret watch over me," Adam said.

"That accounts for the photo-biography, doesn't it, Adam?" Isha said. "I wonder if Esaugetuh knew about Running-water's grandparents."

"I suspect he did. After all, he sent us to Jedediah," Adam replied.

"One of the documents you handed over to me is your birth certificate. It lists Esaugetuh as your father. Among the other papers is a record of monthly cash deposits into a trust fund he had set up for you," Running-water said as he returned the documents to Adam.

"I was always told that I had a trust from my grandfather. By the way, you keep those papers but make copies," Adam said as he picked up a photo of Esaugetuh and studied it.

So much finally begins to make sense. Answers to my questions are gradually unfolding. I always wondered why we never went anywhere other than the Canadian "bush" of Quebec Province. It was so my real father, Esaugetuh could see me. The whispering by the women was not just about the powerful shaman who came and went with the wind; they were whispering about me.

Adam chuckled.

"What's so funny?" Running-water asked.

"I was remembering a past time on the Baskatong. I've told you about the carved woman's leg given to me by an old Indian woman and the large pot one of the women always seemed to be stirring. My mother told me the woman was boiling the hair off of a deer's skin. I just now realized that awful smelling stuff [4] was a medicine prepared for me. The woman was not just stirring it around she was actually wafting its fumes over me."

167

"I do remember the story of the woman's leg and of the awful smelling stuff that seemed to be always cooking," Running-water said.

"I was still six years old. It was the summer I would turn seven. Remembering the simmering pot just brought back another image," Adam replied.

"Which was?" Isha said, now fascinated by the story that was unfolding.

"There was an old man squatting against one of the poles of the wigwam every time I made a visit. He never spoke or even acknowledged my presence. He smoked a clay pipe and sometimes I notice he blew rings of smoke into the air. Somehow I now realize he watched every move I made."

"How old was he?" Running-water asked.

"Well at age six going on seven, anybody two years older was old. I really have no idea how old he was. It's totally bizarre. Esaugetuh was there all along."

Adam began to pace the floor. Stopped. Squatted on the floor and began to chant 'Om Mani Padme um.' [5]

Running-water and Isha looked at one another with raised eyebrows. Adam's behavior since their arrival at Karuna House concerned them. His obsessive searching was a cause of concern. He simply didn't seem able to let things go.

They watched as Adam fell silent and his breathing steadied. A soft blue glow slowly engulfed Adam. He opened his mouth and the blue glow turned into a swirling spiral that floated upward and disappeared. Adam continued to sit unaware of his surroundings. Finally, well within thirty minutes, he moved, stood up, stretched, and looked around.

Seeing the bewildered look on Running-water and Isha's faces Adam said, "I had a memory flash and I wanted to capture it so I could understand what it was I was experiencing."

"And did you?" Running-water said.

"Yes. I think I was about twelve years old, maybe closer to thirteen. As soon as I was sure my parents were sound asleep I would sneak out of our cabin and go sit on top of a large boulder at the edge of the lake. There I strained to see a white mountain. The mountain, really a good steep hill, had a top that was white. The first time I saw it, I thought it was snow. It was quartz. Anyway, this one night, the light of the moon played a game on the quartz, giving the area a wondrous mystical quality for a young mind's imagination.

I imagined I saw an Indian dressed in a shiny golden-feathered headdress standing on top of that hill, arms stretched upward. Sometimes I imagined I heard the whistle of an eagle. And I imagined he answered it. Then the eagle would fly across the water towards me, come in low, and circle just above me. I felt the wind from its giant wings. I am now sure I wasn't imaging. It was Esaugetuh praying and sending me a spirit guide to watch over me."

"It stands to reason in light of this photo collection. He had to have been around," Running-water said. "So, now what do we do?"

169

"What do you mean?" Adam replied.

"Do we continue this restoration project or do we go on to something else?"

"I want to finish it. Get one of The Brothers up here to help Isha. She shouldn't be lifting these boxes."

"You're right, Pau. He's a regular old mother hen," Isha laughed.

It wasn't the 'old mother hen' that caught Adam's attention. It was calling Running-water by his Christian name. He chalked it up as another change in his life, albeit a small one. *Small changes when added together become significant. That's what Esaugetuh always said.*

Gradually, Adam realized the transformation he had been undergoing was just the beginning. There was now a Self creating his reality—a Soul-Self—a new consciousness. For him, it was like a lifting of the veil. At times, his new powers frightened him; other times they confused him. His abilities to mind-talk, to teleport visually, to hypnotize, to create energy from with his own being as well as the natural world, and his ability to heal produced a powerful sense of awe. Gratitude seemed such an inadequate word to describe his feelings about the unbelievable wealth that was now his, and the friends who stuck by him. At the same time, the responsibility that came with all of this was overwhelming. Adam stood stunned, immobile and frozen in the moment.

Running-water signaled Isha to remain quiet. He was used to Adam's mental wanderings. She stopped the scanner and its hum no longer intruded in the silence. Isha's back was bothering her, and she welcomed the chance to relax. She felt one of the twins kick her, and she rubbed her stomach to quiet the child. Her movement caught Adam's attention.

He looked at her, studied her, and sensed the discomfort of the child within.

"Isha, would you mind if I did a scan of your abdomen?" Adam asked.

With fear showing in her voice, Isha said, "No. Is there something wrong?"

"One of your twins is complaining and I would like to know why," Adam said as he smiled at Isha.

Adam moved his hands over Isha as she leaned back in her chair. His hands grew warm but not hot. Nor did they turn red; nor did a blue light surround him. Adam stepped back, all smiles, much to the relief of the soon to be parents.

"The right son is unhappy because of you bending over. His twin pushes against him when you bend to pull up things from a box. You will not do that anymore. I'll make other arrangements. Subject closed," Adam said.

"Adam, can you tell me, I mean tell us, something about our babies?" Isha asked.

"They are healthy and will be born healthy. It's time you named them. And you must sing their names in a song many times a day. If you rub one side of your abdomen be sure to rub the other side as well. Do not sing one name song longer than the other. Your instincts will guide you."

171

"Why? Why should I do that? I don't understand," Isha said.

"Yeah, what's the big deal?" Running-water said.

"Both of you need to sing their names. It establishes a distinct connection to each of you wherever you are or wherever your children are. You will always know by singing their name song. More important, it will help you develop their souls and that will, in turn, connect them to the cosmic soul, the universal spiritual consciousness. What names will you sing?"

"We can't agree on names," Running-water replied. He had just a touch of an edge in his voice.

"Have you called upon the traditions of your people? Oops. Sorry about that. I now should say our people."

"You mean I should—?" Running-water said.

"Exactly. There is a beautiful garden here for you to pray in after your cleansing and fasting. Never discredit the grandfathers or the Ancient Ones. Their wisdom is special. Come, Isha has done quite enough for one day."

They picked their way through piled up boxes, discarded boxes and pieces of furniture. Finally, at the elevator, they pulled open the wrought iron gate, stepped inside, and shoved the gate closed. Adam slid the level to number one and slowly ever so slowly the elevator creaked its way down to the first floor.

Once out of the elevator, Adam strode over to a table, picked up the telephone from a marble-topped

172

stand, punched a number and announced The Brothers should meet him in the main dining hall. On his way through the open doors, Allen handed Adam a neatly folded note. The hospital had called to say Charles would be released the next day. Adam shared that information with The Brothers, Samuel blurted out, "I'll go and get him."

"I believe he's to be ready around noon. Take the limo," Adam replied. Continuing Adam said, "I need someone to help sort and arrange files."

"I can do that," Allen said. "I've got an Associate's Degree in computer technology and worked my way through college as a cataloger in the college library."

"Thank you. Isha will show you what is to be done. I have one other announcement. After much thought and soul-searching, I've decided to abolish the Esaugetuh Benevolent Society."

"Well," Christian said as he pushed he chair back from the table and threw his arms up in the air. "Well, my goodness Adam. You kick us out and then bring us back to tell us once again that we are not wanted. Really, Adam, this is just too much."

Adam looked at Christian, held his attention for a moment, and then continued.

"Because the Society doesn't provide the best vehicle for achieving the goals I set out for it, I'm changing it into the Esaugetuh Institute, a training center for people who want to serve the community."

Adam paused to give The Brothers time to absorb what he had said. Christian fiddled with his blazer's cuff.

"As soon as your training is over, you will become the role model for others. My goal is to bring a minimum of twenty people into the program each year. There will have to be follow-up in the field and that's where you will come in."

Adam stopped, and looked directly at Christian. Christian squirmed. He didn't like direct eye contact.

"The Institute," Adam continued, "will not concentrate on the poor, the ghettoes, or the slums. There are dozens of programs, public and private that offer all kinds of assistance to those in need. I am not saying we are not to help someone in need. I am saying they are not the primary focus or concern. I ask who is doing anything for the average person. Who is there to help him or her through a crisis? Where is the money to take care of their immediate needs? We will try to narrow the gap of that great neglected mass. The average man or woman generates the backbone of society. They carry the workload."

"So," Christian said with considerable emphasis on the word *so*, dragging it out unnecessarily. So, now we are to go out into the streets with our tin cups and raise money." Once again he threw his hands up into the air as a show of his exasperation.

"No, Christian. We are not in the business of raising money, or running campaigns for charitable

174

organizations. We are not an animal rights group, or an environmental rights group, nor a political activist group and most certainly, we are not a religious group. Hopefully, we will be able to show the way for a compassionate treatment of all living things, but with an emphasis on the 'common man.' We are going to be teachers. Our task is to teach the *art of compassion.*

The Brothers, stunned by this latest development continued to sit with their hands folded on top of the long table. Christian did not. He continued to fidget.

"Christian, you will need to change the jackets I asked you to order. Samuel, you will need to change the logo on the vehicles. While you are at it, Samuel, if you are going to be our official chauffeur, I'd like you to have an appropriate uniform and cap," Adam said.

"Oh my. Am I to measure his fat head," Christian said as he jabbed a skinny finger at Samuel.

"Listen up, you little weasel. Don't try pulling that hoity-toity crap with me. Come a little closer and I'll show you who has a fat head," Samuel replied as he leaned across the table menacing Christian with a snarled upper lip.

"You don't scare me you over grown ape. Touch me and I'll have your fat ass arrested," Christian hissed.

"Great! Just great. Listen to the two of you. You sure are wonderful examples of benevolence. This type of behavior achieves nothing. Christian, you need to work on that haughty tone in your voice when you speak to others. I know you do not always mean to sound the way you do. Unfortunately, you do come off in a way that makes you less than you really are. Samuel, there is no need for you to be sensitive about your size. You are a big man; not a fat one. Much of the time you stomp around like a disgruntled ape. Take pride in your size. A few lessons in ballroom dancing will help you change that stomp into a less aggressive gait. We'll get a dance teacher. All of you will take dance lessons. I will help you develop a sense of grace and dignity. Anthony, perhaps you would help Christian with his voice. Need I say more about appropriate behavior? I hope not."

Adam looked at each man, making eye contact. His all-knowing azure blue eyes made a couple of The Brothers nervous.

"One final reminder, your classes begin tomorrow morning at nine and will run until noon. They are now a part of my conditions for you to remain here. If you feel this is too inhibitive, you are free to leave Karuna House."

"Does that apply to Running-water and me?" Isha said.

Her question threw Adam. He looked at her, searching for intent.

"Of course, you are both free to leave at any time"

"I meant the courses. Are we to take them?" Isha replied.

"Of course, if you want to. You both are welcome."

Thomas raised his hand and said, "Adam, someone needs to stock the larder."

Continuing in her role as task scheduler, Isha said, "David, would you do the weekly shopping? Samuel will drive you. Maybe you could do that tomorrow when Samuel goes to pick up Charles? Running-water will give you the money. Where is he, by the way?"

Until that moment, she had not been aware that her husband had left the room. She excused herself, and returned to their apartment. He was not there. Revisiting the third floor, she found no sign of him. Coming back down to the first floor, Isha went to Adam's office. Running-water was not there. She hurried back to the main dining room. Adam was just leaving.

"Do you know where Running-water is? I've looked everywhere for him."

"Have you checked the garden?"

"No."

"Come, we'll both go and check," Adam said as he put his arm around her shoulders.

In the garden they found Running-water. He was only dressed in a loincloth; his unbraided hair flowing over his bare shoulders, and he was seated cross-legged in front of a small fire. Its small flame cast dancing shadows on his handsome face. He was softly singing.

177

He was unaware of their presence. Quietly Isha squatted down beside him and picking up the cadence of his song, she began to sing.

Peace filled their hearts as they took jo in each other's presence. They felt the magic and value of the old traditions and in keeping with those traditions, Adam as shaman, joined them in their song. He added medicine to the fire as a gift to the Spirits—a thank you for their continued blessings. The fire, for a brief moment, seeming to know what was expected, hurled itself toward the heavens, carried the message of love from the three figures. Running-water slipped his hand around Isha's, raised it to his lips, gently kissed her fingers and said, "Names will come from the Spirits."

"Pohj-chech," Adam said.

"What does that mean, my brother," Running-water asked.

"Blowing breath with eyes that see. Esaugetuh sometimes would say that. He said it had to do with intent and that intent was an important part of the heart. Naming has to do with the heart. Naming, like blowing breath to help start a fire, sets the pattern for a new life," Adam said.

Adam left them, giving the soon-to-be parents time by themselves.

"Tomorrow, the lessons," he whispered to himself.

CHAPTER 10
THE LESSONS

There are three lessons I would write, three
words as with a burning pen, in tracings of eternal
light upon the hearts of man.
       Joseph Christoph Friedrich Von Schiller
       (Hope, Faith, and Love. C. 1786.S6.1)

Encouraged and yet feeling nervous about their lessons, The Brothers wondered who their teachers were going to be. How would these teachers react to a group of men, salvaged wrecks from past lives?

Adam, mysterious this morning, took his breakfast in his own apartment. The married couple did not join them.

The Brothers, not knowing what to expect, cleared the table, took up their daily chores, and waited for their first lesson. Late morning arrived and no teacher had shown up. They began to prepare for lunch.

Samuel, with David and Christian in tow, left to complete their assigned errands. It was David's stop at the food warehouse that nearly drove Christian out of his mind because the huge order was taking so long to process. He was sure they would be late at the hospital.

When they arrived at the hospital, Charles was waiting for them just inside the main entrance.

179

Because of the huge order, Charles had to squeeze in. Neither Samuel nor David mentioned hospital stay. Christian, true to his uppity nature began to question Charles.

"Really Charles, what a d—,"

David jabbed him in the ribs. Rubbing is ribs, Charles continued, "As I was about to say, Charles, what a delight it is for us to have you back. There have been many changes. You'll be surprised."

Turning toward David, Christian steepled his hands and stuck his tongue out. He was proud of his quick recovery from his intended *dumb* to the word *delight.*

David, rolling his eyes said, "Whatever."

Once the four arrived back at Karuna House, The Brothers made short work of unloading the car. Each man welcomed Charles and even went so far as to call him by his name; something they had not done before. The comradery continued. Each man told something of the changes that had taken place at Karuna House since Charles' hospitalization. The tone was no longer one of pettiness and backbiting. They even took time to reminisce and found laugher in Joseph's 'Hollywood antics' with the laser light and sound show. Some even went so far as to wonder why they ever allowed Joseph to intimidate them. Thomas did not comment about the intimidation. Laughter was still in the air when Adam walked in. He was immediately greeted by silence.

"How did you like your first lesson," Adam asked.

"Our what? Oh, for heaven's sake," Christian then stopped. "I mean, a teacher didn't show up, so we went about our business."

"And what was that business?" Adam asked.

"To teach ourselves," Thomas said laughing.

The rest of The Brothers sat there, mouths agape. Slowly, the realization sunk in. They had indeed learned much and they had done much. And they felt good. And they laughed. Adam laughed with them and it was good.

Running-water and Isha came to find out the cause of all the hilarity. To their inquisitive looks, Adam replied, "Fertile ground being plowed."

As The Brothers filed out, Adam motioned for Charles to stay behind.

"Come, walk with me," Adam said.

Nodding a yes even though he feared what might be going to happen, Charles looked down at his feet rather than looking directly at Adam.

"You have friends here, Charles. There is no need to fear, no need for pretense, nor is there any need for you to feel embarrassed. What you did to yourself was wrong, misguided, and very dangerous. You almost died."

"You don't know what it's like. You just don't. That's all," Charles said, looking directly at Adam for the first time.

"You're absolutely right. I can say I know what it's like to have something gnawing at my gut until I was sure I would go totally crazy. Do you know what it is to live a life?"

"What do you mean a lie? It wasn't her fault. He made her do stuff. I didn't know. I just didn't know," Charles sobbed.

"Didn't know what?"

"I didn't know it was my mother. I swear to God, I didn't know. Do you think I would have screwed my own mother? It wasn't my fault!"

"Is this the real reason you castrated yourself? As punishment?"

"Yes, yes it is. I can't stand the idea of having sex."

"Care to tell me what happened?"

"There were always different men coming and going. One night one of them dragged a giggling drunken woman into my bedroom telling me she would be good for me. I was twelve. She got me excited and it happened. When I woke up the next morning, I found my mother in my bed, totally naked. I puked my guts out. Just how'd you feel if your first time was with your own mother, for God's sake?'

Tears flowed down Charles gaunt face as he sniffed, and wiped his nose on his shirt sleeve.

"Probably puke my guts out. Like Oedipus, you didn't know. Does your mother realize she seduced her own son?" Adam said removing any hint of disapproval in his voice.

"I don't think so. When I ran from the house, I noticed the new uncle wasn't there. If she knew, he would have to tell her."

"And you have not been home since?"

182

"No! I can't go back and face her. I'm so ashamed. I feel so dirty."

"You feel responsible for what happened?"

"Didn't I just tell you it wasn't my fault?" Charles blatted.

"Then why do you blame yourself?" Adam said.

"What? I—I don't know," Charles stammered, stunned by such a revelation.

"Did Joseph know your story and did he suggest you castrate yourself?" Adam said.

"He didn't know about this business with my mother. I did tell him I felt impure. You know, dirty. He said that in the old days, real men *fixed* themselves. He gave me the pamphlet on castration."

"The others do not need to know about this business with your mother. They also do not need any explanation from you. You are welcome to continue to stay here at Karuna House, to take part in the programs, and to be a productive member of the group. Or you can leave. It's your choice," Adam said.

"If it's all the same to you, I'd like to stay," Charles said as they continued to walk.

They walked in silence; each working their own thoughts. Adam broke the silence: "Tell me, Charles, how you and Esaugetuh met?"

"Well, I was living on the street. You know, selling my body. It was a very cold night. The temperature hovered right around zero. I had just about given up finding me a warm place with a

183

high-paying client. A stretch limo pulled up, stopped, and the chauffeur got out."

"And?" Adam prodded.

"This guy asked if I was available. And that his employer wanted to know how much I charged. Seeing it was a fancy from uptown, I told him a hundred or two-fifty for the night."

"What happened?"

"I humped the air, clutched my dick. You know, trying to make myself more appealing," Charles replied.

"And?"

"The chauffeur opened the back door for me to get in. Inside was an old guy, dressed in a long black coat, and leaning on a cane. He had long white hair and really blue eyes. He smiled at me and then handed me ten crisp one-hundred-dollar bills, American. Man, I nearly crapped my pants right there. You know, sometimes these fancies come here and want to do weird stuff but for some reason, I wasn't nervous or afraid. I stuffed the money in my pants and the limo took off. It didn't stop until we got here at Karuna House. The old man said nothing until we were inside. He told some guy to feed me and show me a bed," Charles said.

"Did you and Esaugetuh ever talk?" Adam asked.

"Not really. All he ever said was I no longer had to do what I was doing and that I had a place here to live as long as I wanted. I only saw him once after that. He kept pretty much to himself. So, he's your father. Did you two have a fight? Was that the reason he was here by himself?" Charles said.

"No. He disappeared during my Vision Quest and I have been trying to find him. It's been a couple of years now."

"Whoa, that's pretty heavy," Charles said.

"Remember, I asked if you ever lived a lie. Well, all my life the man I thought was my father wasn't. And all this time I've thought I was someone else, and now I've discovered that Esaugetuh was my father. Strange as it now seems, I always felt something wasn't quite as it should be. Not as strange as all you uncles but strange. You understand?"

"Yeah, I gotcha."

"You hungry? There's some great apple pie in the kitchen. We could make a raid," Adam asked.

"Sounds good to me."

They discovered they were not the only ones making a raid in the kitchen. Running-water and Isha and a couple of The Brothers were already there. Charles immediately noted the twin Glocks Running-water had holstered.

"You always carry those?" Charles asked nodding toward the guns.

"Wherever Isha and or Adam are, they are always at the ready. Have you told him," Running-water said nodding his head toward Charles, "About the new security?"

"No. Will you take care of that for me? Before I forget, give Charles a check equal to the amount you gave the others. I'll be in my quarters. Bring it by when you have it ready," Adam said.

***

Adam didn't join the group for breakfast the following morning. Running-water went to the third floor to check. Adam was not there. He next went back down to the main floor office. It, too, was empty. Running-water went out into the gardens and no Adam.

The hair on the nape of his neck stood up. Taking that as a warning, Running-water drew both of his guns as he entered the long narrow stairway to the underground garage. The SUV was gone. After a sweep of the area, he pulled out his cellphone and called Dutch who was maintaining security on the jet at the airport. Dutch had not heard from Adam nor had he seen him.

"Look, have you checked with Brett?" Dutch said.

"No, he's next," Running-water replied.

"I'll be at Karuna House as soon as I can. Keep me posted."

A quick call to Brett brought a negative. Taking three steps at a time, Running-water bounded back up the stairs to the main floor. Isha met him at the door.

"He's not anywhere. Any of The Brothers missing?" Running-water asked.

"No. Can't you and Adam communicate telepathically?" Isha said.

"Of course I never gave it a thought. Let's go back to the office. I'll try visualization. Maybe I can see where he is and then mind-talk to him."

Running-water stopped. Pulled Isha to him, kissed her. "Thank you," he whispered.

Once in Adam's office, they closed and locked the door. Running-water squatted on the floor, began to a deep breath as he eased himself into meditation. Once he had connected to his inner peace, he thought of Adam behind the wheel of the SUV. Nothing. He cleared his thoughts and then simply thought Adam.

Slowly, an image began to appear, gradually getting clearer. Finally, it reached a sharpness that Running-water could identify physical sites. He saw Adam standing on a street corner talking to a woman. He appeared to be urging her to get into the SUV.

Running-water focused on the street sign, the name of a bar and then he turned his attention to the woman. The image went blank. No matter how hard he tried he could not bring it back into focus.

He quickly buzzed Brett asking him to meet at the front entrance. He called Samuel and asked him to bring the limo around. Too late, he remembered it was in the shop having logos painted on its doors.

Beside himself with anxiety, Running-water paced the floor, grumbled, and cussed. Then he heard it, Adam's voice.

"Don't fret, my brother, I'm on my way home. Have Charles meet me in the office."

"Man, can you believe that?" Running-water said.

"Believe what?" Isha asked.

"Adam just said he was on his way home."

"Okay. What?" Isha replied as she looked at her husband's astonished expression on his face.

"He said *home*. I've never heard him refer to any place as home before."

"Hmm, do you suppose he now intends to remain here?" Isha said.

"Beats me. I have to find Charles. Adam wants to see him here in the office.

While Running-water tracked down Charles, Isha returned to the third floor to check on the cataloging. Neither she nor Running-water heard the screeching tires as Dutch slammed on the brakes, spinning the car around so its side faced the front portico. He jumped out of the car on a full run with guns drawn. Not waiting for someone to come to the door, he shot out the lock, kicked the door open, and dove into the main reception room, rolled once, ending in a squat.

The Brothers who had been assigned security duty flooded into the area, bumping into each other as the scrambled to get to the center of the commotion. Running-water leaped down the stairs with his guns drawn. Brett, behind him, miscalculated and knocked Running-water down.

"What the hell?" Running-water shouted.

"Somebody turn off that damn alarm. Holster your weapons. No danger," Dutch bellowed.

Calm finally conquered the pandemonium. Anthony of The Brothers notified the local police that it was a false alarm. Dutch, Brett began dancing around like crazy men. Backslapping each other and giving high-fives. Running-water, laughing, joined them. Their laughter became infectious as The Brothers joined in. They felt it; the goodness that permeated the group—a unity—that moment in which all time is suspended—all become one.

The group was so embroiled in its own moment no one heard Adam return nor did anyone see the woman with him. Loud voices coming from Adam's office shattered their special moment. It was one hell of a shouting match. The air was blue with obscenities.

Running-water untangled himself from the group and ran to Adam's office. Adam was sitting on the floor beside the closed office door and indicated Running-water should sit.

"What happened to the front door?" Adam whispered.

"Dutch got a little carried away. It will have to be replaced. I'll get it done."

"Listen," Adam said, placing a finger to his lips.

An avalanche of verbal obscenities assaulted their ears. Charles was screaming. All the bitterness and felt humiliation he felt spewed from his mouth.

"You never cared about me. All you ever cared about was your booze, drugs, and the men you brought home. Shit, don't tell me you didn't know I could hear what was going on? Go ahead and lie. That's all you ever did."

He stopped yelling. Burned out, zombie-like, he stood before his mother, no longer knowing what to say.

Julie was crying. Anger flooded her. She screamed at him. "You ingrate! Didn't I go through hell to bring you into this world? I could have aborted you. I could have trashed you somewhere or given you up for adoption. You are an ungrateful bastard. I've lived a life of total hell so I could provide for you. And for what?

All the sexual abuse she suffered at the hands of her own father and the rape by a drunken family friend that culminated in her pregnancy burst in unyielding torrents of sobs. Shaking so hard, she no longer could stand. She collapsed on the floor. As she lay there she thought, *God how I wish I had a drink.*

She struggled to sit up. Charles ignored her.

"You got any booze in this place?" she asked looking at her son.

"There's no alcohol for you," Adam said as he and Running-water entered the office. "My offer still stands if you want it," Adam said, extending his hand to help Julie up from the floor.

"What offer? What's he talking about?" Charles demanded.

"I offered you mother the opportunity to get sober, to change her lifestyle, and to come here and join our family," Adam said.

Turning to his mother, Charles said, "You'd do that? Get sober?"

As Julie began to get up from the floor, Charles extended his hand to her. She grabbed him, hugged him, and cried. Looking at Adam, Julie sobbed, "Yes, yes! I accept your offer. When do you want me to go to your sanitarium?"

"Right now. Samuel will drive you. You must understand this is a long-term deal. There is a life open to you that doesn't require you to be drunk, a life that doesn't require you to be a prostitute. A new life filled with joy and laughter rather than one of fear and disgust. You have to want that or it won't work," Adam said.

"I'm ready. Let's go," Julie said.

"No, you will remain here. You mother has to make this on her own. You have lessons to attend," Adam said.

Adam pushed a button, instructed Samuel to drive Julie to Kadmon Sanitarium.

The word "lessons" prompted Running-water to break his silence. "Seems to me, Adam, there have been lessons already taught. Guess the best lessons come about when there is a choice; freedom to choose is a powerful emotional experience."

"As a kid, did you ever lie on your back, look up at the sky, and watch the clouds? It was possible to imagine all kinds of objects, ships, planes, animals, or faces. Maybe you even created little fantasies to go with the images. When I look at people, I see all kinds of potentialities, futures to be fulfilled, dreams to be lived, and hopes to be savored."

Adam stopped talking. He stood very still and then said "Where's Isha? I sense she needs help."

"Third floor," Running-water said as he ran out of the office.

Not waiting for the birdcage elevator, he raced up the stairs. Bursting through the doors, he found Isha doubled –up on the floor. Panic seized him. He didn't know what to do to. His heart went into overdrive. He fainted.

Adam, having stopped to call for an Aid Car, found them both in a heap. Kneeling down to Isha, Adam slowly moved his hands over her body. He experienced her pain, felt her fear, and sensed her urgency.

Hearing her husband moan, Isha opened her eyes. That was all Adam needed. He placed her in a deep hypnotic state. Her body relaxed, her breathing steadied, and peace came to her face. Running-water roused himself, shook his head, and started to reach out to Isha. Adam pushed his hand away.

"Don't! I've hypnotized her so she is not in pain. She'll be fine, my brother. Don't worry. Your sons are about to arrive," Adam said as he gently slapped Running-water aside of the head.

Exasperated, Running-water said, "Oh, shit! We've not named them."

Trying to reassure Running-water, Adam said, "Name them now. Lean over Isha and whisper their names. That'll work."

Running-water barely finished whispering his sons' names and the med team arrived from the sanitarium. Adam explained that Isha was under hypnosis and that he felt one of the twins was trying to turn around and this was causing Isha extreme pain. As a young medic prepared Isha to be placed on a stretcher and thinking Adam was the husband suggested a C-section might have to be performed and suggested he agree to such a procedure ahead of time in the event it was necessary.

"You are not to cut on her," Running-water said.

"It may be necessary to save your sons as well as Isha," Adam said, his voice lowered as he continued, "It's only if necessary."

"No, Adam, for once I will not take your advice. We have agreed that she is not to be cut open to birth our children. Their birthing is to be natural," Running-water said, his voice rising.

"But, sir," the young medic interrupted, "if a C-section isn't done if it's needed you may lose both your children as well as your wife. We need your advance consent. We can't get it if we are in delivery."

"I said no and I mean it. It's just too dangerous," Running-water shouted.

"Sorry, my brother, you leave me no choice," Adam said as he pressed a spot on Running-water's neck who immediately slumped to the floor, incapable of movement or speech.

Adam nodded to the medical team and with machine precision, they had Isha on a gurney and were on their way down the stairs to a waiting Aid Car.

As Brett and Dutch exited their rooms and upon seeing the medics with Isha, they bolted and ran up to the third floor where they found Adam with Running-water slung over his shoulders. Dutch stayed and helped Adam get Running-water to the elevator and Brett went to see if Samuel had returned. He had. With Dutch's help, they got Running-water into the vehicle. Adam and Brett stayed in the back while Dutch road shotgun with Samuel.

At the sanitarium, Adam continued to impose a hypnotic trance on Running-water. Within an hour, a young doctor came out of the OR. His smiles told the waiting men all was well. Adam released Running-water just in time for him to hear the doctor ask, "Would you like to see your sons?"

"Isha? How is my Isha?"

"She's fine, thanks to your friend's ability to hypnotize her. She lost little blood and experienced minimal discomfort. It'll be a bit longer before you can see her. She's being cleaned and dressed in a fresh gown. Do you want to see your sons?"

"Yes! Yes! All of us do.'"

A nurse brought the twins and gave them to Running-water. He whispered to each, kissed each on the forehead, and raised them up above his head. Slowly, he began to dance, gradually creating a circle synchronized with the universe's rhythm—the life-flow itself. A hum, barely audible, made its presence felt and like the pace of the dance, it grew in intensity. From a far-far-away place came another voice, and deeper, completing the established harmony.

"Stop that infernal racket. Give me those babies. You'll drop them," scolded the young doctor.

"Mercy, this is not a playground. In case you haven't noticed this is a hospital," said the nurse who brought the babies to Running-water. "Give them to me, right now."

Running-water stopped dancing and humming as he wrapped his arms around his sons, pulling them close to his chest. Adam, trance-like, continued his humming.

"Did you hear what I said? Stop that damn humming," yelled the doctor as he stepped forward to shake Adam.

Dutch blindsided the doctor with one punch. Brett jumped on top of him with a gun pointed at the doctor's head.

"Guess you don't know who you're dealing with, jerk. He's your boss. He owns this place. You don't ever tell him what to do. You understand?" Samuel said angling to get into the fracas.

Ignoring the chaos, Adam went to Running-water, opened the babies blankets. He took each tiny food into his hands. A blue light began to glow around Adam, growing in luminosity until it filled the room with its liquid blue radiance.

Shadow-like it flowed up and over each child and gradually encompassed their father. Unlike Isis of old, no one broke the magical moment as Adam will all his wondrous shamanistic powers, blessed the offspring of his friend.

And so the seeds for a new beginning have sprouted, and these will be the first of a new generation.

"Gentlemen," Adam said addressing his friends; I give you Lance and Colt Dakota. Welcome them."

"How'd you know their names? I'm not sure if even Isha knows," Running-water said. He felt his face redden as he realized Adam was, after all, a shaman.

"She knows. That's all that matters," Adam replied

"Let me up!" screamed the young doctor.

Adam nodded to Dutch who immediately let the very irritated doctor up and extended his hand to help the doctor up; it was swatted away.

I don't give a damn who you are; you are a disturbance. As long as I am the doctor in charge, what I say goes. Do all of you understand?"

"Of course, but you are not in charge. Mrs. Dakota is my patient. She's a Native American and I am her shaman. And doctor, if you ever behave this way in front of Native American or First People again you will never practice medicine again. Further, you will show respect for the old way. Do you understand that?" Adam's was chilling.

"I—,"

"Good. Now take Mr. Dakota and his sons to see Isha. Have that nurse report to me immediately," Adam said.

The young doctor, trying to bring sense to what had just transpired, nodded and then gestured for Running-water to follow. As they entered Isha's room, the saw the same nurse who had brought out the twins injecting something into Isha's IV.

"What are you doing? I haven't ordered any medications," the doctor said.

The nurse turned, dropping the syringe, she bolted for the door. She didn't get far. A knife sliced the air and found its intended target. The nurse fell to the floor. The long thin blade had pierced her heart.

Running-water knew it was Isha who had struck. The doctor quickly removed the IV from Isha's arm, examined her, and then began a search for the dropped syringe. He found it, under the bed, squirted a small amount on his finger, sniffed, and tasted.

'Morphine. She was going to overdose your wife. Why?"

"I don't know. I've never seen this woman until today," Running-water said as he cradled his wife and sons.

"I can answer your question, doctor. She is the sister of T. J. Kelley and Bradford. I recognized her when she came with the twins. She knew I had made the connection," Adam said.

Turning to Running-water and Isha, Adam continued, "She was the one who upon Joseph's orders, released T. J. from here. Remember, I spotted him talking to someone on the second-floor balcony telephone? He was giving her the code to Karuna House so T. J. could get in."

"I don't get it. Why would that nurse help Joseph?" Running-water asked.

"Not Joseph. She was helping her brother, T. J. so she could get revenge on Sydney," Adam replied. "By the way, Dr. Bach, yes I know your name, you need to call the police. And yes, I own this sanitarium and I am the one who hired you. If you will recall one of your responsibilities was to clean house here, get this place in shape, and make it a top-notch institution.

Further, I expected you to get this place physically cleaned. There's crap all over the place. Security is totally lacking. One of my people walked in here without a challenge. The doors were not even locked. None of this is acceptable. When was the last time as chief of staff you did a routine inspection?" Adam said.

"Well, I've been getting the O.R. sanitized and updated. I don't have time to deal with minor issues," Dr. Bach said. He was defensive.

"Minor details, Doctor, when neglected become major. I specifically hired you to give you a second chance. I sense you have not learned a lesson from your previous experience," Adam said.

"What about my past experience?" Doctor Bach shot back.

"While you were banging one of the nurses, your patient died from hemorrhaging. You were given the option to resign since there seemed to be some mitigating circumstance."

"Mitigating circumstance? I don't understand. What circumstance?" Dr. Bach asked.

"The electronic monitor attached to your patient failed. The nurses' station didn't have a clue that something was wrong. The hospital saved itself from a multi-million dollar lawsuit by making you the scapegoat. I had hoped you had learned to pay attention to minor details that need to be the focus here."

"I don't get the connection," Dr. Back replied.

"Had you paid attention to minor details you would have discovered the electronic failure of the monitor. My sanitarium was a chance for you to prove to yourself that you are still a top-notch physician. This was not to be your tomb. You failed to seize the day, doctor," Adam said.

"Now what?" Dr. Bach asked.

"Your contract is a limited one. I'll be back in a few days to see what changes you have made," Adam replied. "And make sure Isha and the twins are well cared for. No mess ups. You understand?"

Adam left as Running-water remained with Isha. For Adam, it seemed Irkalla [6] even with her minions of souls, still stalked the playing field. She was Adam's consort. He also knew that his battle was not to become heartless, not to become immune to the death of others. Callousness about the loss of life is not an acceptable alternative.

God, how I wish Esaugetuh was here. Adam thought as he continued to stare out the window of the speeding SUV. He remembered he was supposed to be searching for Esaugetuh. *How easy it is to get sidetracked by little things, minor details.*

His face burned and instinctively, he touched it. *Minor details? Good god, didn't I just chew out Dr. Bach for not paying attention to minor details. Change perspective; change perception. Of course, act out of Necessity. That's exactly what Dr. Bach did. The priority was the OR, not the floor in the lobby. It seems there are lessons yet for me to learn.*

Adam pulled out his cell phone, punched in the number for the sanitarium. He asked for Dr. Bach.

"This is Adam. I just realized it's not your responsibility to keep the building clean. It's the job of the administrator. I will deal with him. I apologize for my abruptness, lack of understanding and for the members of my staff. Sometimes they get a little overly protective."

"Apology accepted," Dr. Bach replied.

"Good. I will have more staff hired and in the meantime, I will send over The Brothers to sanitize the building. I would like you to come to dinner this evening at Karuna House. Say around eight. I'll have Samuel come and get you."

"Thank you. I look forward to it," Dr. Bach replied.

CHAPTER 11
THE VISITORS

Muddy water, when stilled, slowly becomes clear; something settled, when agitated slowly comes to life.

Dao De Jing

As Adam walked through the main reception room toward his office, the doorbell clanged. And it was a loud clang—a very loud clang at that. It was one of those old-fashioned doorbells; the kind you pull a chord out of a poorly sculpted lion's mouth and then release to make it clang. Adam stopped, turned around, and went to the front door.

When he opened the door, he sucked in his breath, an automatic response when he was in the presence of something extraordinary. And she was all of that; beautiful, more beautiful than any woman he could have ever imagined. Like the proverbial teenager, he stood there with his mouth open, totally dumbstruck.

"Hello, I'm Daphne. You must be Adam."

"Yes, of course, you are. No. What I mean is yes, I'm Adam. Come in," Adam stammered, holding the door wide for her to enter. He watched the subtle sway of her hips. Star-struck dumber than a thirteen-year-old, Adam continued to stand there.

"Aren't you going to close the door?"

"Uh, yes of course. Welcome to Karuna House, Daphne. Running-water and Isha will be delighted you have arrived. How was your flight in from DC?"

"No problems."

"As soon as you have had a chance to freshen up, I'll have Samuel drive you to the sanitarium."

"Sanitarium?" Daphne quizzed.

Before Adam could reply, Anthony rushed in. It was his job to welcome guests.

"Sorry, Adam I was on the john," Anthony said. Looking at Daphne, he continued, "It's a private hospital owned by Adam. Come, I'll show you to your room."

Anthony picked up Daphne's suitcases and waited for her to follow him to the third floor.

On the third floor, Daphne stopped and gawked at the nude photos of Adam. She felt a flush come to her cheeks as she mused, *Umm, bet he'd be good in bed. What a hunk!*

The photos of a naked Adam embarrassed Anthony and he wondered how he was going to explain them to this very beautiful young woman. The clanging of the doorbell saved him from giving an explanation. He scurried down the three flights of stairs rather than waiting for the birdcage elevator. Breathless, he opened the door just as the doorbell clanged.

Gordon Rapport, Daphne and Running-water's uncle dropped his suitcase with a loud thump onto the marble floor. Cornelia Dakota, Daphne and

Running-water's mother stood in awe of the massive foyer in which they were standing.

"Welcome to Karuna House. I am Anthony. Wait here. I will notify Adam that you are here."

Adam was warmly greeted, each giving him a hug. As Gordon let go, Adam sensed a subtle change in his Uncle.

"Anthony will show you to your rooms. As soon as Isha's parents arrive, well take you to see the twins. They're really something," Adam said.

Anthony indicated the guests should follow him. He had barely started the "birdcage" when the doorbell clanged again.

Isha's parents had arrived. The greeting Adam received was considerably different than the one from Rapport and Mrs. Dakota. The Sands knew there son-in-law worked from some very wealthy man, but when they saw Adam, they knew who he really was. His long hair and azure blue eyes told them all they needed to know. Out of respect they kept their distance and did not use familial language in his presence or become familiar with him. And just for a moment, Adam thought they were going to bow.

Once the visitors were gathered again in the main foyer, Anthony announced the arrival of the limo and held the door open for them.

The stretch limo with its fancy new logo was impressive. Samuel was more so in his new uniform with the Institute's logo on his breast pocket and his name on a brass pin prominently displayed above the monogram. He gave a snappy two-finger salute from the brim of his cap as he opened the doors for his passengers. Once they were seated, belted in, he made an announcement over the car's intercom.

"Ladies and gentlemen, there's a cold bottle of champagne ready for your pleasure. Simply push the button on the box between the seats."

While the families were rushing off to see the new ones, The Brothers were busy in the large kitchen preparing a lavish meal for the guests. They liked all the activity and if pressed, they really liked not being reclusive hermits or monks. One of them had figured out how to use the huge firebox and was preparing it for roasting two dozen game hens. Exotic vegetable dishes with international flavorings and designed to comingle with the game hens were underway. Pans filled with bread dough waited to rise. Flavored butter was molded into shapes of eagles. Two distinct sauces for the birds made from pomegranates and blended with fresh mustard and honey warmed by one of the stoves. Bottles of wines, both aperitif and digestif were opened and set out to breath.

***

Even though The Brothers were happy about having a fancy dinner party, they did, in small ways, show concern. Raised eyebrows and pursed lips here and there betrayed the cheerfulness of the group. The horror of the last dinner party lingered. For them, the sounds of gunfire shattered glass and screams remained all too real. Some of The

Brothers secretly wore crosses, others wore different amulets, and some repeated the Rosary over and over to ward off any further potential evil. Occasionally, a few cuss words punctuated the tension or a dropped dish or the harsh clank of a heavy pot. When they heard the heavy garage door and felt its subtle vibration, The Brothers knew the guests had returned from the sanitarium.

The grandparents, uncle, and parent emerged from one car. A second car, the SUV, pulled in beside them with Dutch and Brett. And like last time, they were dressed in tuxedos; an announcement the evening was formal. Dr. Bach arrived in his own car. He pulled the rope and the doorbell clanged. Anthony opened the door and ushered the doctor to a small anteroom. The others went to their rooms to dress for dinner.

"Perhaps you should not go down to dinner. I can have something sent up for you. It's only been two days since the twins arrived," Running-water said as he pulled on his pants.

"I'll be fine. Just need to go a bit slow, "Isha replied as she blew Running-water a kiss.

"That's not going to do," Running-water said as he leaned down and kissed his wife. "My bed has been empty too long."

"You'll have to wait . . ."

He cut her off, "I know."

***

Even the American domestic diva would have been proud of the table. It was gleaming, outdone only by the bejeweled women. Daphne was not only the focal point of Dutch, Brett, The Brothers, but also of Adam. He could not keep his eyes away. Once again her beauty dumbed him. She was enjoying the art of tease with Dutch and Brett. Even the good doctor received her coquetry. Her intuition told her to tread carefully when it came to Adam. Returning his gaze, she felt the color come to her face. Yet, yet there was something-something about his eyes. She was not alone in noticing Adam's eyes. Running-water caught their intensity. He had decided to send Adam a mind-thought when one of the babies whimpered.

Isha gave Running-water a wifely nod and stood up to leave.

"It's been a long day. If you will excuse us," Running-water said as he picked up the twins and with his free arm, wrapped it around Isha.

"Good night," he said as they exited the dining room.

Taking that as the appropriate signal, the other diners left. Adam thanks The Brothers, and retired to his apartment on the third floor. Brett went back to the plane to stand guard and Dutch assumed his role as Adam's security guard. Quiet reigned at Karuna House and it was good. Except for one.

Peaceful sleep would not come to Adam. Dreams, lucid dreams floated in and out of his consciousness. He felt himself being dragged, but he was sure from where to where. That unnerved him. Whisperings invaded his hearing, unclear and mysterious. He felt he was the subject of those whisperings.

Anamnesis grabbed its foothold. Adam recalled when he had heard the great trees whispering, when the Spirits threw him down and when during his Vision Quest, he was plummeted into the bowels of the earth, spat out, and shot into the heavens. His body reacting to those memories shuddered as it relived the pain he had endured. He cried out. No one gave a reply.

He knew they were there. He felt their movements and heard their whisperings. He concentrated on the sounds, and as he did so, he saw the shadow of a man; actually sensed it, and it was talking to another whose back was turned to him. He struggled to get a different view but the more he struggled, the more the figure continued to turn from him.

Quieting his thoughts and feelings, Adam waited. He was barely breathing. Then he saw who it was. He was looking at himself. [7] The other figure was his shadow-self. [8] Adam further settled himself so he could listen. Somehow, he knew they were aware he was listening.

"The reason the world endures is that it does not live for itself," the double said.

"How can you say such a thing? You're wrong. The world lives for itself. New stars are born, new mountains are created, and rivers change course for their own benefit; not humankind's. The universe is constantly creating copies of itself, clones. It does this because it is selfish. Don't you see? It has to be that way. Humans are no different—they are selfish," the shadow replied.

"No! A thousand times no! The world is simply accommodating, tolerating," replied the double.

"Don't you mean it's being compassionate—benevolent?" Adam interjected.

The shadow, ignoring Adam, said, "Well, my, my, isn't that Taoist."

"Whatever. But I tell you this, the world, the universe, the cosmos is fecund. Of course, certain people don't understand the principle of fecundity," replied the double.

"Are you saying I don't know anything about reproduction?" said the shadow.

"Well, go ahead, reproduce yourself. Wouldn't that be a wonderful androgynous act?"

"You know very well I exist only because you do. And speaking of existence, you are just as dependent as I am. You don't exist without him," the shadow responded, nodding his head toward Adam. "You don't see him reproducing, do you?"

"That's your fault. You allowed the Witch to plant the idea he was sexless."

"My fault? That's not fair," replied the shadow.

"Make it different," the double challenge.

"Knock it off. I haven't given you permission to discuss my sex life. Besides, you know damn well Sydney and I got it on," Adam growled.

The room quieted. Even they dared not disobey the man of the earth.

"True," whispered the double, "but you have not reproduced."

Adam mind-searched the room. It was empty. He was alone except for his vagaries that began to express themselves anew. He stretched his long legs; enjoying the sensuality he felt building. He rolled over and humped the bed.

He wasn't sure which came first: his sensing her or smelling her or the feel of her touch as he rolled over on to his back. She eased herself down on him and he pushed up to meet her downward thrust. She leaned forward and gently kissed him. The smell of lavender flowed from her being. He was ecstatic!

Throughout the night he filled her with his seed, and she knew he had impregnated her. At breakfast, she announced her mating with a coquettish smile directed toward her mother and sister-in-law. Adam showed an ease not noticed before.

Once his guests had finished eating and then befitting custom, he presented himself to Daphne's mother,

"I ask your blessings, mother," Adam said, his voice barely above a whisper.

He handed Cornelia a beautiful, soft animal skin elaborately decorated with sacred totems painted in vibrant colors. He walked over to Daphne and held out a hand-woven blanket. Tucked inside was his mother's wedding ring.

He stood there, waiting for her to accept. Neither spoke. The room was so quiet it was as though no one was breathing. Since Daphne didn't immediately accept his blanket, Adam turned to walk away.

Daphne jumped up from her chair, grabbed Adam around his neck, kissed him, and then wound the blanket around the two of them. She caught the ring as it tumbled from the blanket. She slipped it on her finger.

Visitors are welcome; especially night visitors, Adam thought.

Unlike in other times gone by, Daphne did not open the blanket to invite others to enjoy their mating.

CHAPTER 12
GENEVIEVE VAN BATTEN

Whatever the wind doth blow, some heart is glad to have it so; so blow it east or blow it west, the wind that blows my way is best.

Anonymous

She was definitely in her mid-eighties and probably didn't weigh more than ninety pounds sopping wet as they say. White thinning hair topped a deeply wrinkled brow. Heavy lines from years of laughter accented thin lips that often parted with a smile showing porcelain teeth. Despite the dry wrinkled body, fire still burned in the old girl.

Living in a one-room cabin along a small rippling brook, she enjoyed its gurgle through the one open window. And she liked it that way. An iron wood-burning stove cook stove sat along the back wall that faces the small stream. It's probably as old as she is and like its owner, it had seen better days; yet, at the same time, like its owner, it was still good for a few more fires.

A small wooden take, one leg shorter than the others, and a matching chair sat next to an ancient icebox—the kind you actually put ice in the top to keep things cool. At the other end of the room was a small army cot, a wingback chair worn by years of use, and a 1930's Emerson Radio situated under the cabin's only window. A small closet with an old faded green curtain covering its doorway housed the toilet.

To bathe, the old woman used the little brook or brought up a bucket of water into the house. That depended on the weather. If it was really a warm day she used the brook; otherwise she brought the water into the house.

She was outside when they drove up. As Adam exited from the car, he heard a low whistle. *A real looker* he heard her say.

"I'll be right with you," she said as she lifted her skirt and gave her pantyhose a yank. With the grace of a dancer, she stepped out of the pantyhose, rolled them up, and tucked them in her blouse.

"Ah, much better," she said as she looked at the handsome young man staring at her with his mouth agape. "So, what may I do for you?"

"I'm looked for Genevieve Van Batten, a friend of a man called Esaugetuh."

"You a relative? Better looking than that dried up old coot." Making note of Adam's facial expression, she continued, "Oh, I know what you're thinking. I'm just as dried up as he is. Well, don't be too sure of that. True, I'm a little overripe, but I'm still firm, tart, and juicy," Genevieve said winking at Adam. "You haven't answered my question, young man."

With a nod of her head, she indicated they should go inside.

"I see you are an artist," Adam said breaking the stillness of the place.

"I prefer a painter, "she said.

212

"Yes, a painter of souls," Adam replied as he looked for a place to sit.

"He tell you that?"

"No, I see it in these your paintings," Adam said as he pointed to three unframed paintings lined up along the floor. "To answer your question, Esaugetuh was my father."

He was about to say something else but the use of the past tense shocked him. He had not referred to Esaugetuh as having lived.

"Who're your friends?" Genevieve's voice broke into his thoughts.

Pointing to Dutch, Adam said, "This is Dutch. He is my pilot. Next to him is Brett, my navigator, and then Running-water, my attorney and best friend," Adam said.

"You have your father's eyes. I didn't know the old coot still had it in him," Genevieve chuckled.

"Beg your pardon," Adam said.

"Thought he was too old to knock one out like you. I noticed you said *was* when he identified yourself as his son. What do you mean *was*?

"He's missing. We've been searching for him," Running-water chimed in.

"Missing you say. Then how'd you know about me?"

"Your name was on a list of seven people," Adam replied.

"Sit," Genevieve said, pointing to the floor.

And like obedient schoolboys, they sat. With the four of them on the floor, there was barely enough room for her to pull out the one lone

213

wooden table chair and sit on it. Looking at Adam she said, "Suppose you begin at the beginning and tell me everything."

"No! You begin. How is it you know Esaugetuh and when was the last time you saw him?" Adam's tone told her she had better comply.

"Well, Esaugetuh and I go back many years. I first met him when I was a young woman. It seems just like yesterday."

Whimsy flooded her memory. For a moment she didn't see the four handsome young men sitting at her feet. She blinked away a tear and continued.

"He was a good twenty years older than me but what a figure he cut. Back then, I was struggling to make ends meet. Few commissions came in. Oh, I'd make a sale at a church social or at a county fair. But I sold nothing to crow about, that is until he showed up at one of the church meetings.

He was the guest speaker for the Wednesday Night Meeting. Some of my paintings were still in the church hall, and he liked them. He bought the whole bunch. I'm telling you right now, I nearly wet my panties."

She stood up from her chair, pulled up on her breasts as she adjusted her bra. She sat back down, spread her legs so her dress fell between them.

Leaning forward toward her captive audience, she continued, "A few months later, he arrived here at my door. He wanted me to do some paintings for a museum out west someplace. He gave me a box of old photographs. I was to pick out seven and paint the people. He paid me in advance and paid me very

214

well. Every few years, after that, he would return and have another project."

"Did you ever—," Adam began.

She cut him off. "Get it on with him? Lordy, you are the nosey one."

Two of Adam's companions barely stifled a smirk. Running-water, however, roared with laughter. Adam had been called a lot of things, but never nosey. A quick look from Adam stopped the laughter.

"What I was about to ask, Ms. Van Batten, was did you ever hear him talk about me or what he was doing?" Adam didn't hide the hint of reproach.

"He came by a couple of years ago. Told me he had a son called Adam and that someday I would meet him," Genevieve said.

"Is that all?" He must have something during those stops he made here. How many times did he come by? Think, damn it! Think!" Adam grumbled.

"It's time for tea," Genevieve said ignoring Adam. "Would you young men join me?"

Ignoring people was always her most successful defensive weapon. It put people in their place when they needed it. *Young upstart. No respect for his elders. If Esaugetuh was here, he'd box his ears but good.*

"That's not true. I have great respect for my elders. I do not have respect for little old ladies who try to play coy," Adam said replying to Genevieve's unspoken thoughts.

She turned from the stove and looked directly at Adam. Holding his gaze, she knew he had come

215

to bury her. She felt a chill and her frail body shuddered. *So he sent his only son. How like another father who had sent his only son.*

"How do you, do?" Running-water called after her.

"How do I do? Why I live, of course," Genevieve replied; not really happy about the interruption of her thought.

"Mam?" Running-water said.

"Young man, I don't spend my time worrying about the number of breaths I suck in. No sir, I just relish those times when something took my breath away. And you, you're a good candidate. You married?" Genevieve snickered. She had a mischievous twinkle in her eyes.

"I beg your pardon," Running-water said.

"Nah, I'm sure you wouldn't want to wake up in the morning with this old lady beside you. Oh, for heaven's sake Adam, I'm just having a little fun. Goodness, it's not every day I have four handsome young studs in my house," Genevieve laughed as she poured the tea into five cups.

Noticing her hands shaking, Adam got up from the floor and handed his companions their tea.

Turning back to Adam, Genevieve said, "You want to know what we talked about? Is that correct?"

"Yes, it may provide a clue as to where he is or what has happened to him," Adam replied.

"So, he's off again. He's good at doing that. It's been a while since he's been here. Fact is, I've been expecting him. It's about the right time. You said I

216

was on a list? What things did the others on the list tell you that lead you to me?"

"Nothing was said about you. We tracked you through a telephone number," Running-water said.

"And what did these people have to say about Esaugetuh?" Genevieve asked.

"Each revealed how they had met him, the kindness he showed them, and for some reason, he told each of them about me," Adam replied.

"What happened to these people?" Genevieve said.

"Four are dead; two are still living and doing well. Is there some connection I should make?" Adam said.

"Hmm, and did these six tell you what Esaugetuh said about you?" Genevieve continued.

"Yes."

"And that has not led you to him?" Genevieve questioned.

"No, it has not," Adam answered.

"And what makes you think I will?"

"Well, he wanted me to have the list of names for some reason," Adam said trying to conceal his agitation. "I was hoping you could tell me something. Please try and think about what you talked about, he said what he said. He liked using metaphors."

"That he did. I'm very tired. It's past my naptime. Come back tomorrow. We'll talk then," Genevieve said as she got up to show them the door.

Stopping for a moment, she looked directly at Adam one more time. "Maybe, just maybe it wasn't about you."

Knife-like her last comment cut deep into Adam.

The drive back into town reflected three preoccupied occupants and one mourner. Adam's gloominess was soon reflected by his companions. It had been quite some time she Adam had been forced into personal introspection. Genevieve Van Batten had clearly done that.

What was there about the seven people that might have revealed something about me? What sin or sins have I committed? Is it the lack of charitableness? Is it being disrespectful of others? Is it intolerance? How about being judgmental?

"Damn it! If she knows, why didn't she just come out and say it?" Adam's voice cracked with building frustration.

"Say what?" Running-water asked knowing full well it was a rhetorical question.

Genevieve. Damn her. She's getting to me and she knows it."

"Well, my brother, for a long time now you have been preaching there is only one sin, the denial of spirituality," Running-water said.

"Of course, that's it. I didn't acknowledge her spirituality and that ticked her off. After I told her she was a painter of souls, she expected me to say more. I didn't."

"What more was there to say?" Running-water said.

"Much, much more. Brett, turn the car around. Take us back," Adam said.

The car had barely stopped and Adam was on his way into the little cottage. He didn't bother to knock. She was slumped over her table.

"Genevieve, I didn't come to bury you. You have many years of work ahead of you," Adam said as he gently lifted her head up from the table.

Her eyes were red from crying and her face was ashen. Holding her face between his warming hands, Adam kissed her on the forehead. *I should have guessed. No, I should have known. I was so engrossed in my quest that I ignored the obvious signs of malnutrition. Shit! I even missed her hint when she said Esaugetuh should have been there by now.*

"Forgive me, Genevieve, for being such so self-involved. How long have you been without food?"

"Real food? Going on three weeks. I've had a few wild greens." Crying she continued, "There just isn't any money. It's better I should die."

"No! It's not your time," Adam replied. "Will you come into town with us? Have dinner with us. That is, if you have no objections being seen with four men," Adam teased.

"Give this old girl a few minutes," Genevieve said as she struggled to get up.

***

She ate with gusto, polishing off steak, baked potato, vegetables, salad, and pie a-la-mode. An after-dinner brandy was the finishing touch for Genevieve. She slept on the way back to her cabin. Adam decided to stay the night. And as was their custom, Running-water stayed. Both took turns at the watch; each sitting Indian style slept. Morning birdcalls brought both men to their feet. Genevieve wasn't in her cabin. How she got past the one on watch was a temporary mystery because she soon appeared.

A door exited from her small toilet room that allowed her access to the little creek below. She had her morning dip and was ready for the day. Today would be different.

A trip back into town for breakfast found Brett and Dutch already at table. As the threesome passed the desk clerk, he deliberately snubbed them. He disapproved of what he viewed as shabbily dressed people who came to the hotel. Jeans and sweats were not his idea of appropriate dress. Adding injury was their non-interested waitress who plopped three additional place settings on the table. During their meal, Adam explained to Genevieve that he had arranged for a mechanic to pick up her old Packard, to have new tires all the way around, a motor overhaul, and a new paint job.

"Find a local contractor; have him go out to Genevieve's cabin and come up with a plan to modernize the inside, add a pole shed large enough to function as a studio, and to have new appliances brought in," Adam said to his three companions.

A quick mind-talk with Running-water, Adam, and Genevieve left the hotel to go on a different kind of shopping trip. At a local women's store, Adam had Genevieve pick out new clothes. The owner was sure she was experiencing a miracle because the bill was over two thousand dollars.

Genevieve insisted she wear one outfit that especially pleased her. It was a pair of bright red leather pants, white silk blouse, a red leather bolero vest, and matching red high heel shoes. A sterling silver and turquoise necklace and matched with a sterling and turquoise belt. She loosened it just enough to hang over one hip. She let her white hair hang down over her shoulders giving her a touch of whimsy. Toulouse-Lautrec would have found her a fitting subject for his artistic palette.

Brett was the first to give a long, low whistle as Genevieve Van Batten stepped from the SUV. Dutch chimed in with a few cat-calls. Once the group made its way into the hotel, the desk clerk dropped his usual nose-in-the-air routine and immediately fawned over Genevieve. His nonstop chatter and behavior incensed her. *Earlier he couldn't be bothered with us.*

"Oh, shut the hell up," Genevieve snapped. "Young man, when we came in for breakfast this morning you couldn't bother to even speak to us. Why should we acknowledge you now? Your feigned interest and attention is disgusting."

Continuing with the chastisement of the clerk, Running-water said, "Boy, bring in the packages from our vehicle parked out front. It's the black extended SUV. And make sure you don't drop anything."

The four men escorted Genevieve to the elevator, took it to the top floor, opened a door to a suite.

"You'll be staying here for a couple of months. When the work is completed at your cabin, you can return there to live, or if you like this place, you can continue to live here. You still would be able to go out to your place during the day. Your car will be in shape for you to drive it."

"Oh, my!" Genevieve whispered as she brought her hands to her lips. Tears formed and slowly found their way through wrinkle created crevices.

Adam put his arm around her. He felt her shudder as he said, "If you stay here you may choose to have your meals served here or go down to the dining room and any combination you wish. It as well as this suite is paid for and will be paid for as long as you live."

Genevieve patted Adam's cheek and tried to speak. Nothing, no sounds came from her.

"I've arranged for your paint, canvases, and easels to be brought here. The light," Adam said pointing to the large windows, should be good, don't you think?" Adam said. "Take your time to think it over. There's no hurry."

"I've been here before. But of course, you knew that, didn't you? This was Esaugetuh's suite," Genevieve said as she struggled to hold back more tears.

"Does it bring back unpleasant memories? If it does, other arrangements can be made," Adam said ignoring her question.

"Oh, my no, it was here—," and her voice trailed off as tears once again flowed down the wrinkled crags in her cheeks. Embarrassed by her perceived weakness, she looked out the window and down at the street below. *Ah! What memories—the wonderful meals, the exquisite wines, the soft music, and the dancing. Gone! All gone now.*

"That's an issue, Genevieve. When a person no longer has dreams, they aren't much of a person anymore. Dreams imply a future. They signify life yet to be lived. Memories only, on the other hand, imply an end of goals to live for, to plan, to give birth to," Adam said.

"You really do read minds," Genevieve said.

"Sometimes when thoughts are very strong, those thoughts come to me. I sense an emptiness in your heart. You loved him very much and now you feel abandoned? Because I have arrived, you know he is dead, don't you?"

"I was sure I'd be gone before him. He was always so strong until these last couple of years. When the checks stopped arriving and he didn't show up, I knew something was wrong. I knew who you were the minute you stepped out of that car and I knew," she sniffled, "I knew then he was gone."

She turned from the window and looking at Adam she said, "You talk about dreams. What happens when your dream dies? I had always hoped we'd go out together. Now I am alone, old, and no dreams to build on. So, what now? What now, Adam?"

223

"You still have the gift that first attracted him to you. Use it as a symbol of your love for him. Paint, Genevieve, paint. Paint your souls. By the way, did you ever paint Esaugetuh?"

"Yes, I did a life-sized portrait of him. I must admit, I think it was my best work," Genevieve replied.

"Do you know where the portrait is?" Adam asked.

"Not really. I know he had a place somewhere in Canada, Quebec Province, I think. It might be there. You should go there if you know where it is. Maybe it is there that you'll find the answer to your questions," Genevieve said.

"Perhaps you are right. I guess I should go there. I've just been putting it off. I do want to know what has happened to him or where he is. "

Turning to look out the window once again, Genevieve said, "He is in you and will always be with you."

Running-water who was squatting on the floor along with Dutch and Brett, spoke up, "Excuse me, but did you say checks stopped coming? How were those checks made out?"

Yes, they stopped coming. That's what the bank told me. They were made out to a trust that Esaugetuh had set up for me. Why do you ask?"

"What was the name of the trust?" Running-water said.

"GVB Trust. Is that important?"

"Yes, I know that a check for five thousand dollars has been sent on a monthly basis to a GVB

Trust in care of a bank in this state. It didn't register it was this city until just now," Running-water replied.

"What are you getting at?" Adam interrupted.

"I think there is a serious problem at that bank. I've not missed a payment to that Trust. I need to know exactly when you were told there was no money left," Running-water said.

"Well, let me think. It's been about a year. I had some money tucked away in a tin at my cabin, sold a couple paintings but as I have said, it just wasn't enough."

"Someone has been getting that money, Adam, and I think we should pay a visit to the Trust Department of Whitney Bank. I can have copies of the canceled checks faxed here in a few minutes from your bank. I believe there has been a major rip off," Running-water said.

"You think you're up to a little show of your own?" Adam asked Genevieve.

Catching an extra wink in Adam's eye, Genevieve replied, "Just watch this old girl!"

Within minutes she had refreshed her make-up, fluffed out her hair, and painted her lips red to match her outfit. She was ready. She felt a new energy, a new purpose, and excitement. *Yes, it is good to be alive.*

They arrived at the bank and Dutch deliberately parked the stretch SUV sideways along the curb to take up three parking spaces. That way, they would exit facing the bank. The five of them made quite a splash as they entered the bank with Genevieve leading the parade. She heard the woman at the teller's window say "Goodness, look at that. The way she's dressed you'd think she was a teenager; disgusting, to say the least."

Genevieve pursed her lips and blew the woman a kiss. *Oh yes! This is going to be a kick-ass day.*

Once the woman had stepped away from the teller's window, Genevieve told her she wanted to speak with the chief trust officer. They were escorted to a small office, barely large enough to hold three of them. Brett and Dutch remained outside the open door.

"Young man," Genevieve said scowling, "I know you have been swindling me for over a year. I figure you have ripped me off about $100,000. I'd like you to meet the man who sends in the monthly checks."

She dumped copies of forged checks on his desk. He bleached out. He was so white you could see the bluish lines of his blood vessels.

"And you, sir," Running-water said, addressing the bank president who had stepped to the door. "You are just a culpable. The bank needs to make immediate restitution to Ms. Van Batten as well as a public apology. Fraud perpetrated against the elderly will certainly make great fodder for the media. I have notified the state authorities."

Beads of sweat dripped down the president's face. Flushed, he leaned against the door casing. The trust officer kept swallowing in an attempt to ward off spilling his guts all over the place.

Running-water punched in 911 and handed his cell phone to Genevieve. "You know what to do," he said.

She did and within a few minutes, two police officers arrived at the bank.

"Officers, arrest these two men. They have been robbing me blind. I have absolute proof that they have forged my monthly checks from my Trust.," Genevieve said loud enough so others in the bank could here.

"This true, George?" Officer Clemens asked the bank president.

"Yes, officer, it's correct. They have swindled Ms. Van Batten out a very large sum of money," Running-water said.

"I wasn't speaking to you. I'll get around to you. I'll ask you once again, George."

A shot echoed throughout the bank. George slumped over in his chair; a small pistol dropped from his hand.

Brett, Dutch, and Running-water instinctively jumped in front of Adam. Genevieve screamed. People rushed out of the bank.

"Oh, shit!" Clemens said," Turning to the other officer, he said, "Call the medic." Then to Running-water, he said, "Who did you say you were?"

"Oh, for heaven's sake. Is that you Tom?" Genevieve said as she stepped back from George's desk.

"Yes, ma'am. Haven seen you since the dedication of my dad's portrait. Been a few years, I think. Nice to see you again."

"This gentleman," she said pointing to Adam, "is the one who provides the living-trust for me. This man, nodding to Running-water, "is my attorney. Because of the serious nature of the crime, I had him call the State Attorney's office and to get the auditors in her. If you need to talk to us, we are at the LeBerry Hotel. I'm in Suite 20."

"Yes, ma'am."

With a flourish becoming any aging maven, Genevieve Van Batten turned and left the bank with her male entourage in tow. Once back at the LeBerry, Running-water opened an account for Genevieve at a different bank.

"I think fifty thousand should tide you over until we can get everything straightened out," Running-water said.

"What do you say now? Still bored with life?" Adam said.

"Whatever the wind doth blow, some heart is glad to have it so; so blow it east or blow it west, the wind that blows my way is the best for me," Genevieve replied.

"Just set your sails, Genevieve, just set your sails," Adam said giving her a kiss on the forehead. We'll stay in touch."

Adam and his three companions left. As he got into the SUV, he looked up at the third-floor windows. She was standing there, looking out. He waived and the car sped off.

She stayed at the window for a time after their departure. She had decided to remain at the hotel.

She felt safe here, knowing that Esaugetuh's spirit lingered there, waiting for her to join him.

"Until then," she said out loud, "I have one more portrait, one of a young man whose soul travels a special path as had another before him Anam Cara [9]."

CHAPTER 13
THE HOUSE THAT ESAUGETUH BUILT

Nothing exists nor happens in the visible sky that is not sensed in some hidden manner by the faculties of Earth and Nature.

Johannes Kepler

As the Gulfstream reached its altitude, Adam leaned back in his leather chair, swiveled it around to look out a window. He was glad he had decided to have Running-water go with him, to make the journey to Quebec Province and to Esaugetuh's home. They had come a long way together, covered thousands of miles, passed through many lifetimes with harrowing battles, and together, had survived.

Whatever it was, Adam no longer felt the hesitation of going to Esaugetuh's house. It was now his and he was going home. Home? That was only the second time in his adult life he had a clear recollection of using that word. Home, he liked the sound of it. It's calm euphoria encased him.

Dutch's voice over the intercom announcing their approach to Montreal-Pierre Elliot Trudeau International Airport brought Adam out of his introspection. He adjusted his seat and checked his seatbelt and waited.

Dutch eased the Gulfstream into its slot and waited for security. Once they had passed the check, they deplaned. Adam rented a truck so he and Running-water could drive into Montreal and then on to the ranch. Dutch and Brett remained with the jet.

Their trip from the airport to the city was easy. Finding the correct bank was another matter. Fortunately, Running-water was fluent in French, and they were able to local the bank where Esaugetuh had accounts. The building was small when compared to other banking behemoths within Montreal.

Once inside, even though Adam's French was not the best, he made the clerk understand what he wanted and presented proper identification. Bank policy prevented Running-water joining Adam who with a bank escort entered a huge vault. He brought out a large vault box and was then taken to a private viewing room. The escort stationed himself outside as he discretely closed the door.

The dread that had plagued Adam in the past about going through Esaugetuh's personal things came back. For several long minutes, he did nothing but stare at the large black box. He started to open it, hesitated, and then caressed it. With a flip of its latch, he had the box open.

Several large brown envelopes, a rolled copy of the blueprints of the house and its outbuildings, a survey of the property all lay on top of a pile of other documents.

Among the documents were the deed to the ranch already in his name, the building in which the bank is located, apartment buildings, and the registration to the Gulfstream. Another envelope contained a set of keys, each identified in a handwritten name tag.

Stunned by all of this, Adam carefully opened the third large manila envelope. It offered up another mystery; Lists of lettered numbers filled two pages, and on a third, a single sequence of numbers. These he assumed might be for a combination lock. Finally, at the bottom of the box were several stacks of one hundred dollar bills, American. Adam carefully placed all the contents in a briefcase and signaled the bank guard he was ready to leave. Together, they returned the empty box to the vault.

As he exited the vault, a young man dressed in a dark suit, approached Adam. "Sir, the manager would be pleased if you stopped in to see him."

The manager, an agreeable man in his mid-fifties simply wanted to meet one of the bank's major stockholders and the owner of the building in which the back was housed. After exchanging pleasantries, Adam asked the manager to close out the safety-deposit box and handed him the set of keys. Leaving the manager's office, Adam was again approached by the same young man who had asked him to meet the bank manager.

"Excuse me, sir, are you going out to your ranch?"

"How do you know I own a ranch?" Adam asked.

"My grandparents are the caretakers out there. They told me they expected you. Please forgive my forwardness but they are getting up in years, and I was hoping you would give them a message for me? I've tried calling them, but I have gotten no answer."

"No problem. I'll wait for you to write your note," Adam said.

"Don't have to write it down. Simply ask them to call me and to tell them the time has come," the young man said.

"And what is it that has come?" Adam asked, holding the man's gaze. He detected nothing.

"Uh, that it's time for them to think about their retirement. They are excited to meet you. They have heard about the 'white shaman'," the young man said, looking away. "Excuse me, I see the manager is giving me the eye."

With that, the young man scurried off as if he were on an important errand.

"What was that all about?" Running-water asked.

"Seems we're expected at the ranch," Adam replied as he handed Running-water the stuffed briefcase. "Check out the contents." He slid in behind the wheel and waited for Running-water to get in on the other side.

It wasn't unusual for Adam to drive. He did so whenever he felt conflicted. Driving calmed him down.

Running-water let out a long low whistle as he examined the contents of the brief. He checked the pages of lettered numbers and then the blueprints of the house.

"I'll be damned," Running-water exclaimed.

"What?"

"Adam, there's a hidden vault in the house. I bet the set of lettered numbers are is a reference to the vault's content and the other sequence of numbers is the combination to the safe."

"Where's the vault located? Unfortunately the blueprints really don't show that."

"Then what makes you think there's a hidden vault?" Adam asked.

"The interior walls do not reflect the exterior walls. It could be just an illusion, but I believe the sets of numbers indicate a vault or safe."

"Sure is strange but then, everything about Esaugetuh is strange," Adam said as he swerved to miss a car backing into traffic.

"Maybe, if there is a vault, it will contain the answers to your lingering questions. What proof do we have that he is dead? What is the source of his vast wealth? What is the source of the power he had and why yours has been so dramatically strengthened?"

Ignoring Running-water's comments asked, "Is there an airstrip at the ranch?"

"Yes," Running-water said, and anticipating Adam's next question added, "It can take a jet. Why"

I've got spooky feelings, and I think it might be a good idea to have Dutch and Brett bring the plane up. What do you think?"

"What's got your hair up?" And what made you think about an airstrip?"

"I don't think Esaugetuh used the public airports. There is not plane registered at the Montreal airport. Second, the young man at the bank knew who we were and where we were going. Do you have any record of payments to caretakers out there?"

"Offhand, no, but let me check when we get somewhere I can connect to the Internet. There's something more, isn't there?"

"The comment he made about the bank manager giving him the eye bothers me. The manager was nowhere in sight. And finally, he left the bank without saying anything to any of the other employees. He was out of there before we were. It just doesn't hang right," Adam said.

"You've not been wrong about your feelings before. See no reason to doubt them now. We better stay alert. I'll call Dutch and have him bring the plane up," Running-water said.

Adam slowed the truck because of heavier traffic and as he braked, Running-water caught the all too familiar red dot of a laser. Immediately, he leaned over, stomped on the gas pedal and as he did so, he smashed Adam's foot. Adam struggled to keep control of the speeding truck as he swerved in and out of traffic. Angry motorists honked their horns, yelled at them, and give them the middle finger.

What's the hell the matter with you? Have you lost your friggin' mind?" Adam yelled as he jerked the steering wheel left.

"Sorry Adam, just keep this baby floored and keep your head down. We've got company," Running-water said, freeing up his Glock 45's.

The rear window of the truck shattered as a bullet pierced the truck, just missing Adam's head. He ducked down further, using the side mirror to drive.

"Slow it down, Adam," Running-water said as he leaned out the window, and looked back. He spotted the shooter. Fired one round.

Brakes squealed. Then the thunder of a crash and the flash of an explosion as Adam eased the truck to the side of the street. Running-water jumped out, went to the rear of the truck to check on the damage. There were several bullet holes but nothing to disable it.

"Guess your instincts were right again, Adam, what do you want to do now," Running-water said as he slid back into the cab of the truck.

"I am not sure the situation at the ranch is on the up and up. Can you ride a horse?"

"Of course, why?"

"Maybe we should arrive after dark and not in a truck. Horses will give us a chance to check it out. Use that laptop of yours to see if you can find a livery around here. Maybe outside of the city?"

"Pull over. I need to locate Wi-Fi.".

Within a few minutes, Running-water found a place that rented horses as well as horse trailers. Three hours later, they abandoned the truck, mounted the horses, and rode into the ranch well after dark. No lights on and no one seemed to be around. Even the caretaker's cottage had no lights on.

"I got the creeps, Adam. According to the grounds' map, there are lights surrounding the immediate buildings. Strange that they are not on."

After corralling their horses, they eased their way up to the main house. The front door was wide open. With their guns drawn, they approached so quietly that not even the ground creatures felt their movements. Inside, Running-water using a small flashlight found the light switch. A flick of the switch lit up what was obviously a great room.

A quick search of the house turned up no one and there were no signs of a struggle or forced entry. They went back to the wide veranda, pushing a bottom that flooded the whole area. Running-water saw the bodies, hit the off button, and brought his Glock with its night scope.

"Two bodies," Running-water said.

"We need to get out there. They may still be alive," Adam said as he hustled off the veranda.

Running-water was right behind Adam. Both men ran across the open area, keeping low and a few feet apart.

Reading the signs, they decided the couple had been dead long enough for rigor mortis to set in. Marks in the earth suggested the old man had crawled to the woman. They were a good twenty feet apart when she was shot. The old man had almost made it to the woman, his arm outstretched toward her, a last heroic effort to be with her.

The old man was still alive. Adam desperately tried to save him, but the old one refused to live. Adam sensed his only desire was to be with the woman and stopped the resuscitation.

Using a small flashlight, Running-water checked the couple's wounds. "Looks like a rifle was used. Probably shot from some distance. Whoever it was, had to have used a scope."

"I agree and from the blood on the ground, I think they were shot here and not inside somewhere," Adam replied as he got up from looking at the bodies. "The couple is First Nation. I have no idea which tribe. Let's check for identification."

Since they found no identification of the bodies, they decided to check the caretakers' cottage. Running-water printed a few feet ahead of Adam, keeping low and in the shadows. Adam followed. They waited at one side of the narrow porch, bringing their breathing under control. With cat-like hearing, they listened for any sound change. Satisfied, they cautiously entered the cottage. They made a quick search, checking the three main rooms, and bath and closets. No one was found.

"Sure is strange," Running-water said. "The place has not been ransacked and that suggests robbery was not the motive. Was it a random killing? I don't think so."

Uneasiness prevailed. Both men remained alert knowing the killer or killers could be somewhere on the 20,000-acre ranch.

Because the dead couple was First People and because he was a shaman, Adam decided it was proper to give them a Native funeral. He and Running-water created a funeral pyre. They changed the couple's blood-stained clothing. Once that was done, Adam cut a lock of hair from each and carefully placed them out of the way. Since the man had made a heroic effort to reach out to his wife, Adam placed them side by side, arms entwined.

In the tradition of their people, Adam took some powder from his medicine bag, sprinkled it over the two bodies, and then set them ablaze. While Running-water played his flute, Adam offered up a prayer.

"I am Ikaee Wicasa. Hear me Spirits. Into the very bowels of the earth, I was dragged and spat out into the cosmos from where I emerged the son of Earth and Heaven. I have walked among the living, and I have walked among the dead. The soul-snatcher held no sway over me. It is true that my powers are great, but when it comes to you, I am nothing; a mere speck. In the name of my father, Esaugetuh, the Master of Breath, I ask you to accept the spirits of our fallen brother and sister."

Running-water played his flute until the fired died out. Adam, in the meantime, had found an earthenware pot with a lid, had cleansed it so it could be used as an Ollas. Next, he scooped up the cremated remains and places them in the pot. He and Running-water then dug a hole, lined it with small stones, and laid in the pot. They gathered rocks and made a cairn to mark the place of burial. A grouse's feather tied to a single pole and driven into the ground completed the grave site.

Picking up the braids of hair from each of the victims, Adam went into the cottage. He tied each braid with a piece of colorful cloth taken from the garments he found in their living quarters. He attached a small delicate pin made from a single seashell to her spirit bundle and included a beaded armband in the spirit bundle of the man. *I'll place these in the main house, near the entrance as a place of respect.*

Speaking to Running-water, Adam said, "When any of their relatives are located, including the mysterious young man at the bank, these spirit bundles as well as the couple's personal belongings should be divided and given to them. I want a proper table of food set out for them once they are located."

The anonymity of the deceased couple bothered Adam. They had no identification on them and they found none in the cottage, not even a checkbook. *Why had they been at the ranch? Why were they gunned down? What had they done? The grandson, if he was their grandson bothers me. Why had he suddenly left the bank in such a hurry and why had he lied about the bank manager?*

"Questions, always the damn questions, " Adam said aloud.

"What was that?" Running-water asked.

"The attempts on our lives were just too coincidental. I have questions and more questions and as usual, no answers."

"Don't you wonder where Dutch and Brett are? They should have been here. You want me to call them?" Running-water said.

Before Adam could answer, the two wayward men arrived. As usual, they were wrangling over some insignificant bit of trivia. Both were covered in dirt and by their smell, they were in need of some serious showering.

"We heard about the shooting back in the city. Sure caused a ruckus; totaled several cars. People said it was just like the gangster movies, bullets flying everywhere. We knew it had to be you two. You okay?" Dutch said.

"Uh huh," Adam said.

"We've camouflaged the plane, and set up a secure parameter," Dutch said.

"Yeah, since we didn't hear from you we decided to come on it. We've got a couple ATV's outside, loaded for whatever action might come along. It took a bit of a doing to get some of the stuff you wanted Running-water. Where do you want us to stash the gear?" Brett asked.

"In the great room up at the main house. Bring in the ATV's inside as well. There's been a double murder here and all of us need to be on guard. Don't know what's going on, but I'm sure we'll find out before long," Adam said.

"Don't see any bodies," Dutch said.

"We've taken care of them," Running-water said.

"Taken care of them?" Brett asked.

"Yes," Adam said and by his tone, they knew it was a closed subject.

At the main house, they busied themselves setting up new security parameters for the interior as well as some several yards from the house. Dutch and Brett's SEAL training served them well. For them, the small lake was a security issue since its far side boarded the road into the ranch. Any approach to the main house required special attention. It would be the first alert that intruders were on their way in.

While Dutch and Brett secured the lake and the road, Running-water explored the interior security system. He noted with satisfaction that the control was in the master suite. *Man, some of the Nevada casinos would envy the visual set up.*

As was now his custom, Adam served a brandy after dinner. Even in early August, the nights cooled enough to warrant a fire in the massive stone fireplace. The four sat quiet and comfortable, each enjoying the warmth of friendship, the warmth of the fire, and the after-warmth of the brandy. Even the large copper-enameled sculpture of a bald eagle in flight reflected the warmth of the place.

Not to be seduced by the ambiance they were enjoying, Running-water said, "Dutch you take the first watch, Brett you follow that, and I'll follow you."

"Don't leave me out," Adam said getting up from his chair.

"Sorry about that Adam, but I am," Running-water replied as he got up, walked over and checked the doors and then climbed the massive staircase to the upstairs.

A pomegranate sky mixed with a splash of Spanish gold streamers announced a new day. The glass-smooth lake slowly gave up its foggy blanket. As the mist floated skyward, a single look gave out its crazy laughing call. It silenced itself and waited for an answer. And since there was none, it called again, hitting a somewhat higher note not much different than a teenage boy whose voice was in flux. After a pause, an answer came floating back on the airwaves. The whirring of wings spoke to the morning as the loon picked up speed for flight. The First People used to say the loons walked on the water and when the fog was heavy, it kept them from taking flight.

Adam lazily rocked in his father's chair. The long veranda gave him an expansive view of the front property, including the small lake.

It's a good time to be alive, a good time to reflect. Why was it necessary for the man and woman to die? What was it about their relationship that made it easy for the man to choose death rather than to continue living alone? What had their lives been worth? Socrates was right: 'A life unexamined isn't worth having lived.'

A bird flew in close, made a pass, and came back and landed not far from Adam's chair. It

243

cocked its head, looking at Adam. For a brief moment, Adam felt it had read his thoughts. He began to rock again and the bird flew away. Adam continued his introspection.

Not hating would surely be of worth. My children, if ever have any, and Running-water's children and all others like them will have that as part of their mission in life; to eliminate hate. They will show a higher consciousness capable of penetrating the veil, capable of removing the shroud of ignorance; thus, bringing about the natural fecundity of the next evolutionary development in human existence.

The rocking chair creaked, then stopped and all was still. A shadow of sadness passed over him as he accepted the fact that his children would never know their grandfather.

His momentary shadow of regret was short lived. A reflection from binoculars or the scope of a rifle caught his attention. He began to rock slowly, and as he did, he moved the rocker behind one of the large pillars that graced the front of the house. A new sense of danger permeated his being as he eased himself out of the rocker, squatted, and waited. He would engage whoever it was in their waiting game. He was used to waiting. Minutes dragged by. Adam decided whoever it was, had backed off, at least for now. Slowly he inched his back up the large pillar until he was standing erect. He stepped from behind the pillar, looked toward the spot where he had seen the reflection. He saw nothing. He turned and walked back into the house.

A commotion coming from the rear of the house spilled out into the great room. Dutch had a man, hogtied and slung over his back. Without ceremony, he dumped his prisoner on the floor and with his foot rolled him over onto his back. He dropped a spotting scope beside the man.

"You want me to cut his balls off?" Dutch said pulling out a large bladed knife from his boot.

Horror-stricken, the young man's eyes watered. The more he struggled the tighter the snare around his neck became. A barely detectable whimper escaped his lips as he sucked in air and waited for the first cut.

Adam recognized him as the young man at the bank.

"What are you doing here?" Adam said.

"I came to warn the Old Ones, my, ah, grandparents, to tell them they should leave here."

"Why should they leave here?"

"Bad trouble is coming. Have you see them?"

"Maybe. What do you mean bad trouble?"

"Uh, could you loosen the rope around my neck?"

Adam nodded to Dutch to remove the rope.

"The bank manager," he said as he rubbed his neck and wrists. "He's been paid big money by a group of men to use the landing strip here at the ranch. Uh, could I have a glass of water? My throat . . ."

Dutch gave him a bottle of water. He took a long drink and then continued, "When you showed up, it complicated several issues for him. I figured he wanted to make sure it was you. Where are the Old Ones?"

"What is your name?" Adam asked ignoring the question.

"Joshua Briggs. Josh for short."

"I'm sorry to tell you. Josh, your grandparents are dead. We found then in the yard; both had been shot," Adam said.

"Oh, uh, whew! I guess I have to well— I mean— I need to make arrangements for a funeral."

"Running-water and I gave them a traditional burial. I'll show you their burial site. Would you like their spirit bundles?' Adam said.

"Their what? Uh, ah, sure. Yeah, I would."

Adam bent down, cut the rest of the rope, and helped Josh to his feet.

"What do you know about the people who have been using my airstrip? Where are they from? What are they doing here?"

"The Canadian government believes they are part of a developing terrorist cell. I work for the investigative branch of the banking industry. My government sent me here to track the laundering of large sums of money. My credentials are in my coat pocket. You can have them checked," Josh said as he gulped more water and then rubbed his neck.

"And your grandparents were aware of these activities?" Running-water said.

Adam interrupted, "Hmm, do you have any idea how many there are and who they represent?"

"According to the Old Ones, there are about two dozen men. We believe they're from one of the

246

Middle Eastern countries. They have been using your landing strip in practicing taking off and landing," Josh said.

"Did your grandparents do anything to stop them? Did they try to contact the authorities or Adam?" Running-water asked.

"Well, yes. I guess you could say they did," Josh replied.

"And," Dutch said as he rubbed a finger along the edge of his knife.

"They ah, reported it to the authorities, and they then received a letter giving two men permission to use the airstrip."

"Where did this letter come from? Did you ever read it? Any idea as to why these two men wanted to use my airstrip?" Adam asked.

"Supposedly, they were doing a geological survey for the government. Shortly after that my—ah—grandparents, you know, heard a plane landing and taking off. They became suspicious when more than one plane began to land. Sometimes the planes were the larger two prop kind," Josh said.

"So, who did you say contacted the authorities and how do you fit into all of this?" Running-water said. The lawyer in him began to take over. *Things are not adding up.*

"I guess they did. I uh, work for the government," Josh replied. He was fidgeting.

"I thought you said you worked for the banking industry," Running-water said.

"The regulatory end of the business is the government," Josh replied He was pleased with

247

himself for his quick response. He brought his hand to his mouth to hide a smirk and feigned a cough to cover it up.

"Dutch you and Brett take care of security. Be sure to give us some breathing space."

Dutch knew Adam meant there should be layers of security put in place. If they needed to escape they would need time to do that. He gave Adam thumbs up.

"Running-water, make sure the generator is working. If I recall the blueprints correctly it should be located at the north end of the house. We may have a need for it. Josh, you are to remain with Running-water. I have a few preparations of my own to make and will be in the master suite," Adam said as he began to climb the stairs to the second floor.

***

Upstairs, in the master suite, Adam located the control panel. It was as shown on the blueprints of the house. He carefully selected a button, gave it a push, and a mirrored wall slowly opened, revealing a closet filled with Indian regalia.

Adam was very particular in his selection: a breechcloth, a headdress with feathers trailing to the floor, and a pair of deerskin moccasins. Pushing a second button brought out a drawer filled with cosmetics. He chose to do a traditional war paint. He was careful in applying the cosmetics to his face as he created a Harlequin Mask. He painted a red strip from his throat to his navel. He stripped off the rest of his clothes, tied the breechcloth around his waist, put on the headdress and moccasins. Not satisfied with his appearance, he selected an armband with an eagle's head in beads. Around his neck, he placed Esaugetuh's medicine bag.

Turning back to the command console, Adam pushed the buttons to close the closet. The mirrored wall slid back into place. He selected another button, pushed it with a finger, and another wall opened revealing an arsenal of Native weaponry. He selected a bow and tested it. Next, he picked out a quiver of arrows and a war club. He closed the closet, stood back and looked at himself in the mirror. Satisfied with his appearance, he went back downstairs.

Josh barely stifled a laugh. Running-water understood. In mind-talk he said, *I'll join you. Do you have an extra bow and arrows? I'll need some paint and clothes. We'll come at them from two different directions, quiet, swift, and final.*

"My, uh, grandparents, you know, said the planes started flying in and out of here around ten o'clock at night. We don't have much time to get ready for them," Josh said.

"Not we. You stay put," Running-water said. Shifting back into mind-talk, he said, *I'm sure they have been tipped off that we are here. They will come for us. The attack on us in the city, the Old Ones being murdered convince me that we are in for a real battle.*

Replying, Adam said, *Well, I have a few surprises for our unwanted visitors. We'll need to keep them close together. Make sure none get away.*

Riding the horse they came in on, the two of them quietly worked their way out to the airstrip. Adam noticed his plane, now turned around with its nose pointed off the runway. In that way, it could fire its chafe if necessary; thus stopping a plane.

As he dismounted Adam remembered another incident in which the chafe from his jet had saved their lives. They had been flying over the ocean on their way to see Dr. Michael Saint-Christopher at his Institute. Another plane tried to knock them down by hitting their plane on the roof. Dutch had accelerated and ejected the chafe. It caught in the engines of the attacking plane and blew it up. Adam shuddered as he changed his focus.

Adam sat down on the tarmac, a short distance from his jet, crossed his legs and with back straight, he began to meditate. His body rhythms slowly changed, and a bluish aura formed around his body and by all appearances, it began to ascend. Slowly, Adam's legs uncrossed and he eased himself up. He was a warrior.

Running-water watched this magical transformation with total awe. The hum of a plane's engines slowly worked its way into his consciousness. He decided by its sound that it was a twin prop probably with a ten passenger capacity. He understood that timing would be everything. Anticipation tightened his muscles. He struggled to relax but he could not take his eyes away from

Adam who was now a giant bluish figure floating in mid-air. *Someday I'll ask Adam how he did that.*

As the plane eased along, the pilot was so surprised at seeing a giant Indian in full warrior stance he instinctively swerved the plane and it nosed off the runway. Adam waited.

Six heavily armed men jumped out of the plane. They stopped unable to believe what they were seeing. A giant Indian swinging a war club towered over them. They hit the ground.

"Now!"

Arrows came from two directions. The men didn't know what hit them. Quickly, Running-water and Adam dragged the bodies to the side of the runway and returned to their hiding places and waited.

Rapid gunfire and explosions rocked the night. Dutch and Brett were meeting an assault along the main road. A second set of explosions told them another group was trying to get across the lake. Dutch's death trap caught them.

The sound of the second plane penetrated the gunfire. Instead of waiting for them on the tarmac, Adam used the first plane to be the distraction. And it was. To avoid clipping its tail, the pilot hit the brakes and the plan ended up with its nose down.

As the armed men clambered out of the plane, Adam counted six. One man seemed to be giving the orders filled with barrages of obscenities. That was short lived. An arrow flying out of the darkness pierced his throat. The remaining five men opened fire, blindly shooting into the darkness. A volley of arrows silenced them.

Another volley of rapid fire from the area closer to the house filtered out to them. Then all was quiet. Adam and Running-water remained hidden as they waited for a call from Dutch. Fast approaching helicopters broke the night's new silence. Flares from the choppers lit up the night sky. As the lead swooped down over the ranch a voice barked over a loudspeaker, "Lay down your weapons."

Adam and Running-water remained where they were. Using mind-talk Adam asked, *I got a couple of arrows left. How about you?*

I have a couple also, and of course, I have my twin Glocks.

I have one special arrow and my guns. Stay out of sight, my brother.

Three of the four choppers had landed. The fourth remained airborne and continued to circle the area with its searchlights on. When it came over the airstrip, Adam let an arrow fly. Its attached rope tangled in the blades of the chopper and it came down with a loud thud. Four men ran from the smoldering wreckage and right into the waiting Adam and Running-water. The men were so taken aback by the appearance of two men in war paint they surrendered immediately. Once Running-water had identified them as the Canadian military, he returned their weapons.

***

Josh ran from the house toward the choppers even before their blades had stopped. Immediately, he began speaking to one of the men. Shot-gun words, rapid and sharp filled the air. The arrival of Dutch and Brett in their ATV stopped any further conversation. Next Adam and Running-water still dressed in their Indian regalia rode in on their horses. They slid off their horses with such ease the shoulders for a moment thought they were in another time.

Josh with his incessant annoying chatter destroyed the illusion. He made the introductions. Adam was asking the Captain and his men to come into the house when one of the soldiers broke rank and swiftly moved toward Adam. Brett slammed the ATV into gear, floored the pedal and drove in in front of Adam, grabbed the soldier by his neck, and dragging him, sped off at full speed. Instinctively, Running-water knocked Adam to the ground and jumped on top of him. A flash of light and an explosion filled the air.

Instantly, Dutch had the Captain in a death grip while pointing his Uzi at one of the choppers. His voice boomed even over the noisy chopper. "Back off, all of you. Do it now!"

"Let me up. Get off of me," Adam growled.

Running-water rolled over, came up in a squat with guns drawn.

Adam ran to the smoldering ATV. Body parts were everywhere. He turned from the tangled mess, tears streamed down his face as he walked back to the group. Running-water and Dutch were both standing together, each with an Uzi, and each ready to die as they held a Canadian military unit at bay.

Speaking to the Captain, Adam said, "Tell your men to stand down."

The Captain obeyed and his men lowered their weapons. Despite the apparent calming, Dutch held his grip on the Captain and applied just a bit of pressure with his knife to the Captain's throat.

From the darkness came a familiar voice. "Shit! I rolled in goddamned horse shit."

"Man, I thought you were dead," Adam said, grabbing Brett and giving him a bear hug.

They both smelled so bad that Dutch let go of the Captain, picked up a hose and began hosing them down. With much yelling and laughter, the two men danced around trying to avoid the hosing. Adam stopped, lunged at Dutch, and knocked him to the ground, both rolled around on the wet muddy ground. Jumping up, Adam grabbed the hose and turned it on Dutch. Still laughing, Adam picked up the wet headdress, shook himself, and then finished inviting the Captain and his men into the house.

Once inside, the Captain said, "I am sorry we didn't get here sooner. We got tied up arresting three men and the banker back in Montreal. Sorry, we missed all the action. My men will guard the two planes and supervise their removal. I'll have a separate team come in to remove the bodies." Looking directly at Dutch, he continued, "Would you have slit my throat and blown up the chopper?"

"Believe it," Dutch replied.

"We are done here. The forensics team is on its way. You need a lift?" The Captain said to Josh.

"No, thanks for the offer. I'll stick around here. Let Command know about the infiltration. There'll be an investigation and some heads are going to roll," Josh said in a tone that belied his former wimpy persona.

Once the Captain boarded the chopper, he leaned out the doorway and gave Josh a salute. Adam caught that action. *Strange that a military man would salute a civilian.*

In a deliberately measured tone Adam said, "Josh, you are more than you have lead us to believe. Suppose you fill us in, now."

"So, it's okay that I hang around? Great!"

"I did not imply you can stay here. Answer my question."

"Well, uh, I'm sort like your FBI or CIA type operative. I work for the Canadian Government, as did the old couple. They, uh, weren't my grandparents. They were hired to report on the activities here at the ranch," Josh explained.

"Do you know who they were? We should notify their next of kin," Running-water said.

"No relatives. They- uh-you know, volunteered for this assignment. Came out of retirement to do this job. Actually, I can't say anymore. Classified, you know. They understood there would be risks," Josh said. He was defensive.

"And you just arbitrarily placed two spies on private property without notifying the owner?" Running-water said.

"The Department, you know, tried to find Mr. Esaugetuh, but when it had no success it took a different tactic," Josh said. "Mr. Esaugetuh," he continued addressing Adam, "I had heard, you know, that you were a powerful shaman. From the display at the airstrip, you are quite the magician."

Running-water was steaming. He didn't like this guy and made no bones about his feelings. "First, his name is not Esaugetuh. That's his father. Second, his name is Adam Kadmon. Third, he is not a 'magician' as you suggested and finally, he is more powerful than you can imagine and you may experience his *display* sooner than you think."

"I meant no offense, Sir. It's, you know, obvious that Mr. Kadmon commands great respect. You knocked him to the ground and covered him with your own body. Few men are so blessed to have others so willing to die for them, you know," Josh said.

Irritated by the idiotic repletion of 'you know,' Running-water was ready to shove his fist into Josh's bird-like mouth. Sensing Running-water's building agitation, Adam sent him a mind-talk message. *Easy my friend.*

"Maybe you had better retire. It's been a long day for all of us," Running-water said.

Misunderstanding the implied suggestion he should retire, Josh said, "No hurry. Later, I'll bunk down in the caretakers' cottage. I know the ay."

"No, you are to remain in the main house. It's safer. Follow me and I'll show you to a room," Running-water said.

The coldness in Running-water's voice told Josh it was not in his best interest to arouse further displeasure, so he dutifully followed Running-water to the upper level.

Once he was sure Josh was battened down for the rest of the night, he returned to the great room. He found Adam sitting on the edge of his chair, leaning forward with his hands folded up under his chin.

Looking up at Running-water, Adam removed his hands from under his chin and signaled that he was not to speak.

Hmm, wonder why Adam is not mind-talking. For once, I am glad I took the time to learn American Sign Language. It has become a useful tool.

Adam quickly signed that he was concerned the place might be bugged. Silence was to be the mode of operation until the house had been secured. Running-water stepped out onto the veranda; saw Dutch and Brett resetting their security defenses. He explained Adam's concern. Immediately, the three went inside.

Dutch rummaged around in the baggage on the one remaining ATV sitting in the great room. He found what he wanted. He soon had an electric device made to check the house. All verbal communication ceased until the sweep of the house was completed.

Satisfied that there were no electronic eavesdropping devices, Adam with Running-water returned to Esaugetuh's bedroom. Actually, it was a four-room master suite.

From the hallway, double solid oak doors opened into a large bedroom with a massive bed. A red leather chair with table and lamp sat near a small stone fireplace. Adam ran a finger along the top of the chair. *Esaugetuh probably sat here, sipped a glass of his favorite brandy while reading a book.*

Beautiful walnut wood paneling surrounded the fireplace, complementing the stonework. The oak floor had bearskin rugs scattered on them. To the left of the bedroom was a library.

Adam stopped at one of the bookcases. Its shelves contained books on herbs, plants, and folk medicine. He fingered several, lingered over some, particularly those that seemed well used. He moved on into the office. It was on the right side of the bedroom and contained a computer, telephone, a second red leather chair, a table; the twin of the one in the bedroom contained a matching lamp.

A large bathroom with mirrored closeted walls made an L from the office. In the center of the marble floor was an inlaid brass bald eagle. Windows were noticeably absent as were wall decorations.

The ceiling throughout the apartment was of defused light and it quietly unified the four rooms.

He and Running-water returned the bedroom. There, Adam picked up a control pad from a built-in shelf that was part of the headboard. He pushed a numbered button. The walnut-paneled wall in front of the bed slowly opened revealing a bank of monitors and recording devices. Adam selected camera one. It showed the front yard. He pushed a button on the console and a video began to play.

"Watch this," Adam said to Running-water.

"Okay."

"Look at Josh's actions just before the suicide bomber approached," Adam said.

"I don't see anything unusual."

"Watch his hand as the bomber begins his approach," Adam replied as he replayed the tape.

"I'll be damned! That little bastard is one of them. I'll nail his ass for good," Running-water said.

"Don't be in such a hurry. Let's see what he's up to. We have an even bigger question. Were the men on the choppers Canadian military?" Adam said as he flicked to another camera.

"There's another chopper still out at the airstrip. It might be a good idea to check it out. Dutch can take care of that. There's a possibility the two planes were sent to check if the ranch was ready for occupancy. Make they plan to take over and use this place as a training base," Adam said.

"Man, you might be right. I'll give Dutch a call. No, better yet, I'll go get him."

"No, stay here. There is more for you to do. I'll call Dutch and Brett. Get out your laptop and do some research on our uninvited guest."

Adam punched in a couple of numbers on his cell phone and then hung up. Within minutes, Dutch and Brett were at the bedroom door.

Running-water got busy at his laptop searching Adam's account while Adam gave Dutch and Brett their marching orders. He found what he was looking for; rather what he did not find that further aroused his ire. There was no Joshua Briggs listed as an employee at the bank where Adam had an account. There was, however, a Joshua Langford listed who had been at the bank only three months. *Well Joshua whoever you are, you have some explaining to do.* He put down his computer, stepped out of the bedroom onto the balcony overlooking the great room and called out.

"Hey, Dutch, you got any connections in the military that might shed some light on this mess?" He spoke loud enough so Josh could hear.

Looking up from the TV, Dutch said, "Yeah, give me a second."

Dutch made a call to a military buddy assigned to the Pentagon's OSI. Long ago, he had learned not to ask a lot of questions. He got right to the point. *So we are dealing with a terrorist cell.*

***

Brett had gone to check out the cottage that had been used by the caretakers. The front door was partly open. Sure that it had been closed up when he and Dutch set the new security boundaries, he quietly inched his way to a side window and peered in.

Josh was rifling the place, pulling stuff from the bookcase, turning chairs upside down, and looking behind pictures that hung on the walls. *He sure doesn't seem to have any concern about how he leaves the place.*

Josh moved into the kitchen area, dumped the contents of drawers on the floor, searching as he kicked stuff around. He was so intense in his search, he didn't sense Brett's presence. Brett returned to the front of the cottage, slipped in and fired one round. Josh fell to the floor screaming in agony. The bullet shattered bones as it went through his thigh.

"Don't do as I say, you die. Get up, slow and easy. Keep your hands folded behind your head," Brett growled. "Man, I'd sure like it if you tried something. I'm just itching to blow your head off. You are one son of a bitch."

As Brett shoved Josh out the door, he gave him a quick kick in the ass to hurry him along as he herded him back to the main house. Dutch met them at the front door and Adam who was on his way down the stairs joined them.

Brett slammed Josh into a chair. Adam drew a circle around Josh's head with his right hand, bringing a finger down his nose. He then gently blew into Josh's eyes.

The response was a complete surprise. Josh began singing "Mary had a little lamb."

"He's been preprogrammed to resist hypnotism," Adam said.

Instead of trying to elicit information from Josh, Adam decided on a different tactic; he would implant information using his every growing Psionic ability. He decided to use the same tactic he had used with T. J. Kelley back in Toronto. Adam placed both hands on Josh's head. A barely audible hum filled the air. Then all was quiet. Adam removed his hands, went to a table picked up an Indian rattle, and began to shake it. Josh went ballistic.

His eyes bulged with wild terror; salvia dripped from the corners of his mouth, and urine soaked his pants. Rapid convulsions seized him, and he slid to the floor. He spewed vomit on the floor and trashed around. *My God! Why won't they help me? Can't they see I have been by that large rattlesnake?*

Adam created a PSI ball to throw but the main alarm signaled an intruder. He looked out the window and saw a fast-moving military vehicle speeding toward the main house. Dutch, Brett, and Running-water prepared for another possible assault. The vehicle slammed to halt causing dust to fly. Two men exited the vehicle.

"State your business," Dutch growled over the intercom.

"I'm Captain Lance, of the Guardia di Finanza, that is the Canadian Military Police. Is Josh Langford still with you?"

"What if he is? What's it to you?" Dutch snarled.

"We are here to arrest him," Captain Lance replied.

Playing dumb, Dutch asked, "Arrest him? What for?"

"He's a member of a radical terrorist group and a traitor to our country. May we come in?"

Slowly, Dutch opened the massive oak door. "Show me your credentials."

The two men complied, standing back from the door just enough to be apparently respectful.

Satisfied, Dutch, making sure they saw his guns as well as his SEAL's insignia, opened the door for the men to enter.

Captain Lance and his aide were surprised to see Josh thrashing around on the floor and screaming. Adam released the PSI ball terrorizing Josh as it rolled around him.

"Will you tell me what I want to know?" Adam said.

"Yes, yes. Please help me," Josh sobbed.

"Are there others involved and how many," Adam said as he tossed a second PSI ball for effect.

Instead of answering Adam's question, Josh began speaking in a foreign language. His voice inflected a sing-song intonation. Neither Adam, his associates, nor Captain Lance understood what was being said.

Adam fought to control his frustration over his lack of success. Captain Lance's aide saved the day. Jameson understood the language Josh was speaking.

"Sir, he's reciting nursery rhymes," Jameson said.

"He's what?" Captain Lance replied.

"Nursery rhymes, Sir. He's saying, 'Little Miss Muffet sat on a tuffet eating her curds and whey. Along came a spider and sat down beside her and frightened Little Miss Muffet away.'"

"You getting all of this down? This could be a coded message," Captain Lance said.

"No need to worry. We have everything being recorded by video and audio," Adam said. Turning back to Josh, he continued, "Who did the old couple work for and why were they killed?"

No response. Dutch picked Josh up from the floor, held him while the Captain handcuffed him. Running-water had excused himself and returned with a copy of the video and audio tapes and gave them to Captain Lance.

"Another copy has been emailed to the Royal Canadian Mounted Police," Running-water said.

He did not mention that another copy had been emailed to Dutch's friend in the Pentagon. With prisoner in tow, Captain Lance and Jameson both thanked Adam and left.

Quiet finally came to the ranch; something that had been denied since their arrival. And in that quiet moment, the four of them had the same realization: they had not eaten and simultaneously announced they were starving. Piranha couldn't have eaten the food any quicker.

Once their hunger was appeased, Dutch and Brett moved the remaining ATV out of the great room, hopped on and drove out to check on the jet, to redefine their security parameters, to change several, and to add new ones. Both men were masters at making booby traps. Some would be set with explosives while others were made from things in the natural surroundings, quiet and just as deadly as a bomb. Some would serve as alarms.

When they arrived at the airstrip, they faced a new reality. The whole area was cordoned off, a half dozen heavily armed soldiers were on patrol. One in typical military fashion told them to leave. Dutch responded with, "Soldier, get your commander."

After a quick radio call, another soldier arrived. Once Dutch and Brett showed their credentials, they were allowed to check out their plane. Satisfied, that there were no bullet holes and the tires were intact, they got back on their ATV and head back to the ranch.

"My god, I didn't realize those two were so deadly," Dutch said.

"Who you talking about?" Brett asked.

"Adam and Running-water. That's who. Who the hell else used a bow and arrows?"

"Well, aren't you the grump one. You still pissed because you didn't get laid while we were in Montreal?" Brett said.

"Just shut the fuck up!"

***

Adam and Running-water decided it was time to make a thorough inspection of the house. As Adam looked around the great room, his eyes focused on the bank of windows gracing the front of the house. They rose from the floor to the top of the thirty-foot ceiling and were bulletproof as evidenced by their construction. *I wonder why*

Esaugetuh felt the need for such windows. He continued to examine the room.

He guessed the great room was a good sixty by forty feet in size. It had beautiful hand-pegged oak flooring. Three well placed stained glass skylights set at perfect angles allowed the moonlight to flood the area in a spiritual serenity. *Bet the sun really makes this room a color wheel.*

As he continued to look around, he noted seven large multi-bulb lights hanging along a massive I-beam. From the I-beam, the open rafters made of large split logs stretched rib-like across the high ceiling. The enormous log stairs leading to the upper balcony of the second floor belied their massiveness by seeming to float.

Continuing his visual tour of the room, Adam's attention turned to the enormous fireplace occupying a whole wall from floor to ceiling. Two-man boulders were the choice of construction. Its gaping mouth was large enough to hold logs six feet in length.

"Good God!" Adam gasped.

"What ?" Running-water asked without looking up from the blueprints of the house.

"How could I, no we, have missed it? I can't believe I didn't notice it when we first came in. Did you see it when we came in the first time?"

"See what?" Running-water asked.

"I thought there was a large copper-enameled sculpture of a bald eagle hanging above the fireplace."

"Was?"

"It's gone. Genevieve's portrait of Esaugetuh is now there," Adam said. "Look for yourself."

"I'll be damned. So life-like. She really captured him," Running-water replied.

"So, when and how did that portrait get up there? " Adam said.

"I think I saw an eagle up there, but it could have been an illusion created by the sun shining through the stained glass skylights."

"I am sure the eagle was hanging up there. It was a three-dimensional sculpture and must have weighed several hundred pounds. It even had its own spotlight. It could not have disappeared without some help. We better check more closely. There still could be someone else in the house. I think the blueprints indicated there were interior passageways. If so, then we could have any number of people moving in and out undetected."

Running-water spread the blueprints out on the floor as Adam sat down on the large couch. While Running-water was getting the numerous sheets of paper in order, Adam noticed two remote controls on a nearby table. He punched one and a large TV flickered on. It showed a 360 degree interior of the room they were in.

"There," Adam shouted. "See it. There's the eagle."

"Clever. It rotates with the painting. But what causes it to change?"

"No idea. Let me play it back. There! See that shadow? "

"Still could be the sun creating shadows. Hand me those two ashtrays, will you? I need them to keep the blueprints from rolling up."

Once the blueprints were flattened out, Running-water said, "The way the walls seem to be constructed would suggest open areas between them. There is definitely a passageway from the master suite to an underground bunker."

"Not pinpointing them certainly is in keeping with Esaugetuh's secretive nature," Adam replied. "Let's go back up to the master suite and begin there."

Once inside, Adam got another surprise. The fireplace had been replaced by a large cherry wardrobe. The ever curious Running-water picked up the control pad and systematically began pushing the buttons. The large wardrobe slowly rotated three quarters the way open. It revealed a hidden passageway.

The passageway was so narrow that they had to walk sideways. Passage was further complicated by the low ceiling which forced them to scrunch their six-foot frames into a squat. As usual, Running-water went first. He had taken a sacred oath to always protect Adam, a source of heated discussions between them on several occasions. Adam no longer argued with him. Running-water was grateful for that.

With his hand pressed flat against the narrow outer wall, Running-water slowly inched his way along. Then he disappeared.

All Adam heard was Running-water's typical exclamation, "Oh, shit!"

Adam didn't have a chance to ask if Running-water was hurt. He plummeted downward and landed on top of a bed made of stretched animal skins. He bounced a couple of times, rolled off the homemade trampoline, and landed on his feet. The room was well lighted and ventilated. It was also heated.

A small two-man tank with mounted turret cannon and machine gun faced them. Shocked by its presence, Adam said, "It's hard to believe Esaugetuh was that concerned about his safety. "

"Good god, look at those walls. There's a regular arsenal," Running-water said.

"You sure that tank is real? Maybe it's a toy replica. It has to be fake. There isn't any way out of here," Adam said.

"Yes, it's very real, brother. Because of the way it is set up and directed, I suspect it would go right through the wall it faces."

"Don't think we better try that. Wonder if there is another way out?" Adam said.

Running-water removed a small round cylinder from around his neck, opened its top and pulled out a match.

"I see you still carry matches," Adam said.

"You bet, got three. Remind me to replace the one I am going to use to check for a draft."

"Good idea. It might lead us to an exit," Adam replied.

"I think we are at the back of the house and I think we made a left turn coming down the chute. If that's true, then there should be an exit on our left. Was Esaugetuh a southpaw?"

"Come to think of it, I never noticed. He very well could have been," Adam said.

Running-water lit the match, held its flame an inch from the left wall. The flame flickered. He immediately pressed his hand on the wall. A small door slid open revealing a set of narrow lighted stairs. Running-water, followed by Adam began the climb. They came out on the balcony overlooking the great room. Esaugetuh's portrait was gone and the flying eagle sculpture was back in its place. Both men stood with their mouths open in disbelief.

"There's got to be a space behind the fireplace wall. The question is what is switching the portrait and the eagle," Running-water said.

"I agree, my brother," Adam replied.

"When you were checking through some of the papers didn't you say you thought they indicated there was a vault here?"

"Yes, but I found no indication as to where it may be located. Let's check out the fireplace," Adam said as he started down the wide staircase. Running-water was beside him, looking at the ceiling surrounding the fireplace.

They heard the click. It was too late. The stairs folded and down they went, sliding on their butts and hitting the floor with a loud thud. Once they got their legs untangled, and realizing they were not hurt, they began to laugh.

"Maybe I pushed a button that activated the switching, or maybe it's an alarm, a silent alarm to warn Esaugetuh that someone had been in the house while he was away," Running-water said.

"You might be right. But what started it before you began playing with the remote? I'll go back upstairs, check the master control while you look for another hidden panel," Adam replied.

***

Back in the master suite, Adam discovered the large wardrobe was again missing and the fireplace was back. He examined the controls. None of the buttons seemed to be stuck.

Opening the monitors, Adam scanned the grounds. Dutch and Brett were at work on ground's security. Nothing unusual appeared. He did a scan of the interior, going from room to room. He paused to watch Running-water checking the fireplace wall. He rewound the tape back one day. It showed Josh entering his bedroom and then exiting from the master suite without first exiting from his bedroom. Adam notice Josh had a remote control in his right hand and he was pointing it at various locations along the wall as he hurried back to his assigned room.

Leaving the master suite, Adam went to the room assigned to Josh. He knocked on the door and then entered. Josh was not there. He began to search the room for the remote. It was not insight so he lifted up the mattress and there it was. Two buttons were still depressed one for the eagle and one for the wardrobe in the master suite. He pushed each to their original position. He left Josh's room, went to the balcony, looked down into the great room where Running-water was still checking the fireplace wall.

"Found the key," Adam yelled. "Another remote hidden in Josh's room. Watch this."

Adam pushed one button and the eagle appeared. Pushed it again and the portrait of Esaugetuh appeared

"Better step back. I don't know what part of the wall may move when I push another button. I'm sure the vault is behind that fireplace," Adam said

Adam pushed a button. The fireplace wall did not move. Then he heard it; a slow rumble. The firebox itself began to sink into the floor. Once it was out of sight, the floor closed above it and a back panel slowly slid open. As Running-water bent down to crawl through the opening a second panel above him opened and he could stand erect. Above him hung the eagle.

Adam ran down the stairs, taking two at a time and joined Running-water. The vault was 10 X 20 with rows of built-in steel boxes lining three of the walls. A small table with a chair sat beside the entrance wall. In the center of the vault was a round marble column, the kind that a great grandmother would keep for a fern stand, Victorian. On top of the column was a golden box with a jewel encased lid.

"Don't touch that box or its pedestal until we know more about its purpose," Adam warned. "It still could be booby-trapped."

Adam looked at the rows of steel boxes lining the walls. He remembered the odd lists of letters and numbers he had gotten from the bank.

"I have to go back and get that list I got from the bank. Don't touch anything, don't even move. You got that?" Adam said.

"Got it," Running-water replied.

In the great room, Adam grabbed the blueprints and all the other paperwork from the bank and hurried back into the vault. He pulled out the pages of letters and numbers. Beginning with the letter "A" and the first series of numbers beginning with one-hundred, Adam entered the numbers in the lock. A click announced the box had opened. Carefully, he removed the box and placed it on the small table. When he opened it, both men gasped. Thousands of cut diamonds, the smallest not less than two carats in size, filled the box.

Adam pulled a different box. This time it was M100. It was a larger box than the first and when opened, it contained stacks of U.S. hundred-dollar bills.

"Man, from the width and depth of this box, I'd guess it contains a least a million dollars," Running-water said as he emitted a long low whistle.

As Adam read the long list, he realized that some of the letters were in bold print and that those letters spelled his name. He selected box D100 and opened it. It held rare gold coins. Then he opened

A100 and that box contained certificates of stock in the world major corporations. The wealth was staggering.

"My god, Adam, it's just unbelievable. I knew you were wealthy but this—this is—,"

"Unreal!" Adam interrupted.

"You got that right, unreal, for sure. What do you think is in the gold box?" Running-water asked as he bent down to get a closer look.

"We'll come back to that later. Right now, we need to continue our search of the house, the guest house, and other out-buildings," Adam said signaling that they should leave the vault.

Once they were back in the great room and the vault was closed and Esaugetuh's portrait back in its place, Running-water said, "You suppose there's another remote control and that's what Josh was looking for in the Old One's quarters? Maybe he thought it would open other places in the house, even the vault."

"I don't know. He sure was looking for something and his intensity made him careless. Come on, let's take a look," Adam said.

A short walk put them at the Old One's cottage. Inside, Adam and Running-water began a systematic search. They laid out the space of each room much in the same way archaeologists would do during a dig. Dividing the space into sections allowed them to be more thorough. There had to be something tangible, something that revealed information, and something that Josh desperately wanted.

The search of the living room and the small bathroom turned up nothing. Remembering how his mother's husband had a secret safe behind a toilet, Adam checked that. Again, he found nothing. That memory led to another. When you want to hide something freeze it.

In the freezer compartment of the small refrigerator were several small packages. Among them was an even smaller bag filled with water and a small fish filet. Adam almost missed it. A small dark spot about the size of a quarter caught his attention. He ran the bag under cold water and then the fish. It thawed just enough for him to pry the out the object. He held it under the water just long enough to get the lid open. Inside was a roll of microfilm, the answer to what Josh was looking for. Fearing the frozen film might break into pieces, Adam was careful not to touch it. Carefully, he closed the lid of the little box.

"Found it," Adam shouted out to Running-water. "Microfilm. The old couple knew a thing or two about microfilm."

"What do you mean?" Running-water asked.

"They knew enough to seal it in an airtight leak-proof container and that storing it at a reduced temperature would help assure its preservation."

"That means there must be a camera around and there might be more film," Running-water said as he began examining several belts hanging in the bedroom closet. Adam took up the search by checking the two pairs of shoes, especially paying attention to the heels.

275

"Of course, the camera is probably in their clothing," Adam said. "Come on, back to the house. I saved their clothes and whatever else they had on them before we performed the burial ceremony and set their cremation fire. There's one box for each. I put them aside for the next of kin."

They locked the door to the cottage and hurried back to the main house. There Adam retrieved the two boxes and slowly began to their contents. He found a small box of matches. It was the camera and it appeared to still have a film in it. Adam was unsure about how much of the film had been used.

Running-water called the officials in Quebec, apprised them of the film, and asked if they would bring a microfiche reader to the ranch. It was agreed. They would have one come out from Montreal.

As soon as he hung up Adam said, "I wonder if the film shows Esaugetuh? Do you suppose he discovered the terrorists using his property? My god, maybe they are holding him somewhere, or maybe he is hiding somewhere until this mess is cleaned up?"

"Anything is possible, my brother."

"Maybe I should try communicating with him again. I haven't tried in quite some time. Maybe being here in his house might help," Adam said.

"Give it a shot," Running-water said.\

Adam sat down on the floor, legs in a yoga seated position, forefinger and thumb on each hand gently touching, palms turned upward. He slowly began deep Ujjayi breathing. His broad shoulders relaxed as he softly chanted Om Mani Padme Hum. Slowly his soul-energy floated throughout the house sensing for any remnants of Esaugetuh's presence. Adam sensed nothing. The place had been sanitized. He let his soul-energy float out over the ranch. Nothing! In desperation he cried out, "You said you would always be with me. Where are you?"

Stifling emptiness was his only response. Adam raised himself up from the floor. A sad disappointment showed in his eyes.

"Might just as well make a pot of coffee. It'll be a while before they get here from Montreal," Adam said as he went into the large kitchen.

The wait dragged on. Even Running-water was pacing the floor. He stopped, cocked his head.

"You hear that, Adam?"

"Yeah, the rumbling of a helicopter. Strange they would send the reader by chopper. I think there's more than one," Adam replied.

Adam's cellphone vibrated. It was Dutch.

"Two military choppers have arrived. They're here to remove the bodies and their planes. You want Brett and me to stay put? Hold it, a jeep at high speed is headed your way."

"Stay put. Keep your phone open," Adam replied.

The jeep with its horn blaring at full blast brought Adam to his front door. It was Captain Lance. With him were two armed guards who took up posts a few feet from the large veranda. The fourth man was from the Royal Canadian Mounted Police.

That's unusual for an RCMP to be present since they did not have a contract with Quebec Province.

Instead of questioning Captain Lance, Adam decided to wait and see. He sent Running-water a mind-thought to be on guard. Adam made no effort to cover his twin Glocks that rode easy in their shoulder holsters.

The RCMP, a handsome man with a small scar on his lower right jaw, introduced himself as Major Bolt.

"Our government felt that under the Security of Information Act and with the special request of the officials in the Province du Québec, it was appropriate for me to be present. The government has agreed to let Mr. Adam view the microfiche to see if his father is in them. Further, you must agree to not communicate any of the information on the film. If you do, it is a violation of Section4 of the Security of Information Act," Major Bolt said.

"You understand that Adam? There must be total adherence to the intent of the law. There can be no leaks of any sort regarding the operation going on here. These are dangerous times. Caution is the rule. We also do not wish another media frenzy like we had over the last terrorist episode. I have the reader and I'm ready any time you are," Captain Lance said.

"We can use the study. Follow me," Adam said.

"Sir, excuse me, but only you, the Captain, and I are allowed to view the film," Major Bolt said.

"Running-waters goes with me," Adam said.

Bolt, heeding Adam's tone, politely agreed. On their way to the study, Adam asked if either of them knew of the Old Ones who were murdered.

Major Bolt, momentarily thrown off guard by Adam's question, asked, "How do know the old couple was murdered?"

"We found them in the yard. The man was still alive when I got to him, but he didn't want to live. He wanted his spirit to go with his wife's. Because they were First people, I performed a burial ceremony for them and sent their spirits on their way," Adam said.

"Sent their spirits on their way?" Captain Lance asked.

"Yes. They were cremated. I would like to know who they were so I may give their relatives their spirit bundles," Adam said.

"They had no relatives, no children. It is good the old man went with his wife," Captain Lance said answering Adam's question.

"So you do know who they are? How is it that they were here and why were they murdered?" Running-water said.

"They worked for the Department of Internal Security and were sent here to get the details of the terrorist activities going on here. I suspect Langford's responsible for their deaths," Captain Lance replied.

"Perhaps the film will provide both of us some needed answers," Adam said.

The microfiche reader was set up and Adam handed over the film. He made no mention of the camera or the film it contained.

Each frame of the film was carefully examined. Bolt took copious notes. Joshua Langford was seen with the group of terrorists. There were several close-up shots and this pleased Captain Lance. Joshua Langford was shown digging a grave and shoving a body in. The image was not good enough for any clear identification.

"I want to locate that grave site. That body might be my father," Adam said as he shut down the machine.

"Why in hell did you do that? I'm not through," Captain Lance yelled.

"Don't raise your voice in Adam's presence," Running-water bristled as he got into the officer's face.

Stunned by Running-water's fierceness, the young Captain stumbled back nearly knocking the microfiche reader over.

"Perhaps you would like us to bring in our dogs to help locate the grave. They are specifically trained to locate cadavers," Major Bolt said. If you do, I will have a pair brought in."

"Why not use a plane? There are infrared cameras that can detect decaying bodies. More territory could be covered that way. The ranch consists of 20,000 acres," Adam said ignoring the offer to use dogs.

"I think we can work something out. Allow me to see what can be done," Major Bolt replied as he left the study.

The lights lining the entrance road to the house and its immediate area began to glow as they announced the night was lowering its shade. Glowing coach lamps, moon-like, flooded the area with their silvery luminescence. Adam, standing at a window and looking out did not offer the hospitality of the house sent a mind-talk message to Running-water to escort them out.

"I apologize for not being more forthcoming," Captain Lance said as he extended his hand.

Adam was not there to receive it. Running-water opened the huge oak doors and waited for the Captain and Major to leave.

Adam had returned to the study where he tried to visualize the grave site he had seen in the film. He desperately wanted to find it, to see it, to get a sense of who was buried there. His efforts at visualization failed and further frustrated him. *Crap. Now I'll have to wait until morning to begin the search.*

Disgusted, he left the study and as he walked along, he realized he was thumbing something in his pocket. It took it out. It was the undeveloped roll of film from the camera. His sense of distrust returned. *I better have the film developed elsewhere. I can't be sure of any of these so-called government and banking people. Running-water's uncle in New Mexico can get it developed. I'll have Dutch and*

Brett fly it there. They can stop in Toronto and take care of some unfinished business for me.

CHAPTER 14
THE SEARCH

There is nothing covered that shall not be revealed; neither hid, that shall not be known
Luke 12:2 (KJV)

Once the military and the Royal Canadian Mounted Police Officer were gone, Dutch and Brett rejoined Adam and Running-water at the house. As they approached the house both were surprised to find Adam and Running-water waiting for them. Like Adam and Running-water, they were amazed the remains of the suicide bomber and the shattered pieces of the ATV lay where the explosion occurred.

One thing puzzled Dutch. A frown slowly formed across his broad face and his dark brown eyes narrowed to mere slits. Slowly, he walked around the remains of the ATV. With a flashlight, he bent his six-foot frame to get a closer look. He took his time to study the point of impact. The explosive device that was used was not powerful enough to blow them all up. He shook his head. *Strange. Was Adam or Josh Langford the target? If it was Langford that would account for the small explosive charge and that would make it an assassination and not a terrorist act.*

To try and answer his suspicions, Dutch took extra time in checking the mangled ATV. The impact of the explosion would tell him a good deal. The young soldier, in Brett's headlock, was dragged along as the ATV sped away. The front of his body was pointing away from the vehicle and the scuff marks in the dirt suggested the soldier tried to stop the vehicle. That most like turned his body slightly away from the right front seat and helped save Brett's life.

"Fast approaching vehicles coming along the road," Brett shouted.

Dutch stopped his investigation and joined those standing on the veranda. Instinct claimed them as they made ready for another battle. A military ambulance followed by a canvas covered truck stopped a few feet from the veranda. Dutch brought his Uzi up. A young corpsman jumped out of the ambulance.

"Gentlemen, I am Corporal Jason Brown. We are here to retrieve physical human remains as well as the ATV wreckage." Turning around to face the two vehicles, he snapped a couple of orders.

Floodlights were brought out from the canvas covered truck and set up. Two other soldiers were dressed in hazmat outerwear and systematically began picking up body parts while others picked up parts from the ATV.

Speaking Corporal Brown, Running-water asked for a receipt for the ATV. He waited for the Corporal to write it out and then went back into the house.

"Didn't you set an alarm at the entrance to the ranch?" Running-water asked Dutch.

"Yes, why?" Dutch replied.

"It sure didn't warn us about the approaching ambulance and truck. Both vehicles could have been loaded with dynamite and driven right into the house. What the hell kind of warning system did you put out there," Running-water demanded.

"Hey, don't get your panties all in a sweat. Shit, how in the hell do I know why the damn flares didn't go off? I won't know until I go out there and check," Dutch shot back.

"Maybe you just better do that," Running-water snapped.

"It's not a big deal. You can check them in the morning," Adam interrupted.

"It is a big deal, Adam. That solder almost got you," Running-water said.

"I'm not sure Adam was the intended target," Dutch said.

"What?" Running-water said. "Are you out of your friggin' mind?"

"I think Josh Langford was the intended target. The explosive wasn't powerful enough to take us all out. I think he was a suicide bomber, and he was to knock off Josh," Dutch explained.

"How so?" Brett asked.

"He was approaching Josh, not Adam. Josh recognized him; his hands in the surveillance video suggested that recognition. Had he been after Adam, Josh would have stepped out of the way. And since he didn't, I am sure he didn't' know the soldier was a suicide bomber. Had he suspected something, he would have taken off," Dutch replied.

"You might be right," Brett piped up.

"I think the cell found out that Josh might be double-dealing, or that he was a weak link and decided to remove him. Hell, maybe they decided they just didn't like him anymore. Live has no meaning to these people. Anyway, maybe we'll find more answers in that grave we're going to look for," Dutch said.

"You might be right. And that reminds me. I have a camera with film still in it. Dutch, I want you to take it to Running-water's uncle in New Mexico. Have he get it developed and then email me the photos. I'm not comfortable with having it developed here," Adam said.

"No problem, I can leave real early in the morning," Dutch said suppressing his delight at getting away from the ranch.

"One other thing, go via Toronto and go to Karuna House and tell Samuel to come here. Tell the others to pack up and prepare to move out," Adam said.

"A new location for The Brothers? What's going on Adam?" Running-water said.

"I didn't really want to surprise you, my brother, but I want to unload Karuna House, the sanitarium and Syd's Bar. They don't fit into our future," Adam replied.

Stunned, Running-water stammered, "Why?

"I believe we will be better off in the United States. Put the properties in Toronto up for sale. I'll let you know when to put the ranch up for sale."

"What about all of Esaugetuh's stuff you had moved to Karuna House? Your photos?"

"Have all of that packed up and made ready for shipping. Do not have The Brothers do that. Hire a professional company."

"You have a place in the United States in mind?"

"No, anybody hungry," Adam said heading to the kitchen.

"Food would be good about now. I'll help," Running-water said as he followed Adam.

Brett and Dutch knew that was the end of that conversation. Each looked at one another. Astonished by Adam's sudden pronouncements they felt their relationship strained.

"Man, he's just too much. You know what I mean?" Dutch whispered, knowing that Adam could tune in if he so chose.

"He sure doesn't ask for any input from us in any decisions he makes," Brett said. "Even granting the emotional upheaval caused by the deaths at Karuna House that sure doesn't account for Adam's behavior."

"Yeah, it's like we don't exist. We need to ready the plane," Dutch replied as he leaned back in the chair and rubbed his crotch.

***

In the kitchen, Running-water and Adam busied themselves with food preparation. Running-water watched every move Adam made, looking for some hint; some clue as to what was really eating at his friend.

Adam's whole demeanor, short very much like the strokes he made in cutting the meat. With each slice of the knife, the agitated frown on Adam's brow deepened.

"Okay, spill it. What's gnawing at your gut? Spit it out," Running-water said as he placed his hand on Adam's arm forcing him to stop slicing the meat.

"You're a father. My son is about to be born. What kind of life will our wives and children have if we continue to be on the go as we have been doing? Are you not missing the pleasure of your wife, the joy of your sons? Daphne's on my mind. I miss her very much. We need a home," Adam said.

"I'll be damned. You're feeling horny. The city's not that far from here. Go in and get laid. You'll feel better," Running-water said stifling a laugh.

"Don't be so damn gleeful. I won't go to Montreal. Daphne is the only woman for me. That's that," Adam said.

"Yeah, I do know how you feel. I belong only to Isha and I do miss her and the twins. But Adam, aren't all young husbands away from home a good deal of the time and don't they miss their wives and children?"

"Probably, but we, you and I, aren't must husbands. We don't have to be away. We can stop this impossible search for Esaugetuh. There's enough money to keep us, our children, and their children for several lifetimes. Your sons need you; they need to smell you, to feel you, to know your masculine sexuality. How can that be if we are always on the go? It's not right. I should be there when my son is born," Adam said. "I need to finish cutting the meat."

Running-water turned to his task. How like our ancestors. They were migratory, following the great herds of buffalo, moving with the changing seasons. Fleeing the never-ending encroachment of the Europeans. What demons does he flee? What tortures drive him?

Breaking his thought, Running-water looked up at Adam and said, "What is in your heart, Adam? Let your heart speak the truth."

"So, it's the truth in my heart you want to hear, is it? All in good time, but right now, I am not sure you would understand, my brother. Powerful forces are at work—forces that we must turn from. There may be great danger. One of us must survive to care for the others—."

"Family," Running-water interrupted. "There has never been a question in my mind about it, Adam. I know you will. Take good care of Isha and my sons. I know my destined fate. It is finished. Say no more about it."

"You," Adam began to say.

Cutting him off, Running-water said, "I mean it Adam. That subject is closed. I would ask a favor, though."

He placed last of the meat on a super sandwich for Dutch, poured a whole back of chips in a dish, pulled out cups for coffee.

"There are still secrets here to be discovered. After we finish the vault, there will be time for your favor," Adam replied.

"Hey, are you two going to take all night with that food. Man, bring it on," Brett yelled from the great room.

"Here you go," Running-water said as he sat down a huge tray of food. Hot coffee coming up.

The food was sucked down faster than any maelstrom could suck down a ship at sea. Continuing their after dinner custom, they sat quietly enjoying an aged brandy. Each man keeping his thoughts to himself, old men, young in years; each waiting for whatever destiny had in store for them. One among them knew and like his namesake who had fathered all humanity, he would begin their next step, one etched deep within his soul.

As the dawn awakened, a police van arrived at the front of the house with Major Bolt, three dogs and their handler. A second vehicle arrived with a forensic team. Introductions were barely made when a helicopter began a systematic sweep over the 20,000 acre ranch and even over part of the joining parcel.

After a quiet conversation with the dogs' handler, Running-water had them search the house as well as the guest house. Nothing was found. The dogs were searching the property in every-widening circles when the people in the chopper reported they had located an area of interest. The handler whistled and the dogs returned. He, Major Bolt, and the dogs took off in their van. The forensic team followed with Adam and Running-water close behind on horseback.

"It's a grave, no question about it," said one of the forensic team members.

Several hours later, they had uncovered two bodies, hands tied behind their backs, and bullet wounds in their heads. The bodies were carefully extracted.

"It will be hours before the site is cleared and then days maybe weeks before we know who they are," Major Bolt said.

"Thank you for your help, Major. It is appreciated. The man isn't my father. He's not big enough. I would like to know who they are any relatives," Adam said.

"Another disappointment but that leaves us with hope that your father is still alive, Adam," Running-water said.

"True, my brother. It—,"

The crackle of the Major's phone interrupted Adam.

"We have another possible grave."

"Let's go," Running-water said.

Once they reached the new site, the dogs were let lose. Within minutes they had sniffed out the grave. The forensic team went to work. Like the dirt in their sieves, the day had slipped by.

"I think the dogs may have made a mistake," Major Bolt said.

"Got it," shouted one of the forensic team members.

With meticulous care the body was removed. Even though the decaying process had begun, the body was still identifiable as that of a small man, fully clothed.

"Suppose this is the original Josh Langford?" Running-water said.

"Could be," Adam said as he shook his head.

"What?" Running-water said.

"When will it ever end; the killing?

Running-water said nothing as he put his arm around Adam and then mounted his horse. Adam followed and they returned to the main house.

The night was a restless one for Adam. Images faded in and out; images of the dead in his past, of the grave sites, their corpses, and of Esaugetuh, Sleep was denied. He got up and paced the floor. A tingling sensation slowly enveloped his taut body. His breathing quickened and small beads of perspiration formed along his hairline. His heart displayed its anxiety by loudly pounding in his ears. Every nerve in his muscular body screamed.

Images of the ashes of Moon-woman flashed before him. Thoughts of her spontaneous human combustion flooded his mind. *I'm going to burst into flames.* He tried to call out. No sound escaped his open mouth. He stood very still. A distinct smell filled the room. Ozone was everywhere. Its presence made the hair on the nape of his neck and arms stand up. Its memory was burned into his soul. Like past experiences, he was sure it signaled either the arrival or departure of Esaugetuh. He waited. *Am I in a lucid dream or am I hallucinating?*

"Esaugetuh if you are here, for god's sake, speak to me. You know I hate these damn cat and mouse games," Adam grumbled.

He heard it.

"What is you most desire, Adam?"

It seemed to Adam that the voice was raspy, almost wheezy than it was in other conversations. Maybe it just sounded older. He couldn't quite identify what was different but it was.

"Desire or want? Adam growled; his grouchy mood returned. "I'm don't have time to play your silly ten and twenty questions. What the hell difference does it make anyway?"

"Considerable. And mind your manners."

I'll be damned. There's a puff of smoke spiraling up into the air just like it should be when Esaugetuh got disgusted with me. So much, so terribly much has transpired since then. How innocent I was.

"If you are not going to answer my question, I am out of here," Esaugetuh said. "You like putting things off, don't you?"

"What do you mean by that?" Adam demanded.

"Well, for one thing, you sure put off Running-water's request for a favor," Esaugetuh said.

293

"As I have already said, I don't know what you mean by desire. I can't answer your question and why should I? You sure as hell don't answer mine," Adam said.

He was in a real pout and was not about to be tricked out of it by some damn heavy-minded discussion. He felt the sweat dripping down his face as the old weakness made itself all too painfully known. Adam slumped down in the red leather chair by the bed.

"Guess there's no reason for me to hang around," Esaugetuh said, his voice fading.

"No, don't go. I—,"

"Then answer my question."

"I told you I don't know what you mean by desire. I desire my wife," Adam blurted.

"Hmm, I had something more in mind, something less, excuse my words here—but less ordinary," Esaugetuh said.

He cleared his throat. "I sense a deep melancholy, a need for that something more. You have wealth beyond most people's imaginations, and you have power most never dreamed existed. You have a beautiful woman who is pregnant with your child. You have devoted friends. You had a Society for doing good works; you changed its purpose and now you are abandoning it. You own seaside estates, mansions, office buildings, and this ranch. And none of these bring you happiness and joy. This, above all else, is my failure."

"Don't even go there! I will not have you placing a guilt trip on me with this crap of, 'I have failed.'"

"Guilt trip, humph! You sure haven't learned much, have you? No one can make another person feel guilty unless they allow it. All these years I never thought you would be such a wimp, incapable of decision, awash when it comes to your friends. Each time I have had to prod you. Oh, you are generous with your money. You hand it out but ignore the reason for its need. And again, I ask you, Adam, what is it you desire? What is it, you want? Now is the time for decision making," Esaugetuh fumed.

"I have made decisions and you've been critical of those decisions. The question is, what is it YOU want of me?" Adam yelled. His face reddened with his building anger. "I've taken care of the seven people you had me find. I've done whatever you have wanted. You shroud yourself in mystery, not ever explicitly saying what it is you want of me. And another thing, this damn cat and mouse game of hide and seek is to stop. And it is to stop now! Because I say so!" How's that for a decision?"

A thunderous roar filled the room and blue lightning filled the room as it bounced off the wall and ceiling. Adam fell to the floor.

"So you challenge this old man, do you?" Esaugetuh said. Like the lightning, his voice came from everywhere, bouncing from wall to wall.

The loud noise and voices brought Running-water to his feet. Without hesitation, he threw upon the bedroom door, his guns drawn. The blue light was so intense it blinded him. Squinting, he gradually brought things into focus. A swirling mass of light filled the center of the room. It was so intense he covered his eyes with his hand.

Dutch and Brett, hearing all the commotion ran up the stairs and in their haste nearly knocked Running-water down. They placed their hands over their eyes and looking through the slits of their fingers, they were stunned at the spectacle in front of them. Running-water was beside himself; not knowing what to do, he watched his friend begin to dissolve in front of him. The hair on his head and arms stood straight up creating a grotesque troll frozen in time.

With a tremendous effort, forcing every muscle in his body to move, Running-water dove into the center of the swirling firestorm. The scream was so shrill Dutch and Brett cupped their hands over their ears. Blood dripped from their noses, and their eyes filled with burning tears. Wildly, they stumbled back from the master suite entrance, groping the wall as they desperately trying to escape the earsplitting noise.

It was over in an instant. They collapsed on the floor unable to move. None of their SEAL's training or their experiences on the battlefield prepared them for this. They had heard of strange powers while they were involved in several clandestine and highly secretive missions. They did not talk about it; not even to each other. Some of the stuff they had witnessed in the jungle, as unbelievable as it was, was nothing compared to they had just experienced.

With extreme effort, Dutch finally moved his head enough to see Brett. Brett's mouth was eschewed intro a grotesque shape; his lips curled back from his teeth, eyes rolled back in his head, and his blonde hair singed. His long legs, eagle spread with his feet turned sideways made him into a marionette.

"Shit! What the hell happened?" Brett groaned as he heaved himself forward to get up. He fell back, nausea overpowering him.

"Damned if I know. We better try to find out what happened to Adam and that foolhardy, Running-water. Man, can you get that guy's balls? Whew! He's sure as hell is something else," Dutch said. His voice was raspy. He rubbed his throat because it hurt.

Slowly and painfully, they struggled to get up on their fee. The whole area was swimming as nausea gripped them both. Clinging to the way, they inched their way around the corner and peered into the bedroom. A lingering pale light, an ignis fatuus, filled the room. The stinging smell of ozone assaulted their nostrils. Coughing caught their attention. I was Running-water in a heap on the floor.

"Damn it, man. Get off of me," Adam said.

"Don't be such a mother hen. You okay?"

"You could have been fried, you know," Adam said shaking himself loose from their entanglement.

"I warned you there were powerful forces. You sure you're okay?"

"Glad to see you two are still among the living, what the hell just happened in here?" Dutch said.

"A little family disagreement," Adam replied.

"Promise me you'll never get me involved in any of your family disagreements," Brett said. "By the way, who won the argument?"

"I am that I am," Adam said.

"What about Esaugetuh?" Running-water asked. Do you know where he is? Is he alive?"

Adam's voice echoed the heaviness he felt in his heart. "I have a feeling he is gone. I don't think I'll hear from him again and I don't think I will ever see him."

"What was the argument about, if you don't mind saying," Dutch asked

"My failure or I should say my failures," Adam said.

Running-water, still shaken, got up from the floor, gave their two friends a sign they should leave. Turning to Adam, he said, "We will talk now, my brother."

CHAPTER 15
THE TALK

A friend is someone who knows the song in your heart and can sing it back to you when you have forgotten the words.

Anon

Both men sat in the moment; both needing time to compose themselves after their ordeal. Each wondered if they had melded into one another. Each wondered what happened to Esaugetuh. Each fearful of what had been and was yet to come. Both knew the unknown always strikes a discordant chord.

Adam had experienced wondrous and fearful symmetries. Animals had communicated with him; great and powerful spirits had made themselves know to him; he had traveled among the living as well as the dead, but nothing—nothing in his young life had prepared him for what had just transpired. It was a total physical experience in another world in which he engaged in a fight with his father—one in which one destroyed the other.

Hot tears tumbled down his handsome face. Shame hurt, and love clashed. Deep within, Adam knew he would not find his father or see him again. One of Esaugetuh's favorite secrets of shamanism popped into his head. *All shamans are one living in many different forms. Not as the multi-headed*

hydra, nor as the head of Medusa with its squirming
snakes, but as human beings.

The hot tears continued to spill from his azure blue eyes as he looked into another time. He was just a kid, maybe twelve, or thirteen. His hair was long and flowed down his back. Except for his loincloth, he was naked. There were other young men, seated as he was in a circle. Frantically, he searched their faces for his brother, Running-water. He couldn't see to the other side of the circle. As hard as he tried he could not see beyond the huge crackling fire. Between the tongues of flames that reached up to kiss the night sky, he caught glimpses of young women dancing. He looked to his left and then to his right. Running-water was nowhere to be seen.

Throbbing drums beat in his ears. He was sure his head was going to explode. The young women, in an ever-widening circle that extended out from the huge crackling fire, quickened their pace. He felt the wind against his face as they whirled by him. Suddenly the cadence of the drums stopped. The young virgins suddenly bolted and ran off into the woods.

With a loud whoop, the young men took up the chase. Adam rose to join the mating but a wave of dizziness laid its hold on him. He felt a hand on his shoulder. It was so forceful he was compelled to sit back down.

"Esaugetuh!" Adam gasped.

"Not yet, my son. You know so little of the reality in which you live, of the different

300

dimensions existing in multi-verses. It is not your time to experience a woman's pleasures. You first must experience that other Self who creates your inner being; your personal Self—your soul!"

Adam struggled to get up but the hand held him down. It was too strong. Dizziness swallowed him and he fell forward.

"Easy Adam. Just be still and don't try to move."

Adam thought it was Running-water's voice. It was light years away and seemed to echo. Desperate, he tried to focus. Slowly, a hazy image formed.

"Man, you look like a piece of cow dung," Running-water said.

Still struggling for reality, Adam whispered, "Is that really you, my brother?"

"Yeah,"

"You okay" Adam stammered.

"Yeah, what the hell happened?"

Ignoring the question, Adam said, "It just occurred to me, once again, that this thing we call *Self* is a made self. It has to be. The choices we make at any given time affect all other choices before we even make them. Our failure, if it can be called that, is we don't consciously question those choices before we make them. A good rule to follow is to see if those choices meet five necessary attributes: truth, beauty, health, happiness, and compassion. "

He took a deep breath and then continued. "Crap, here I go again, not answering your question.

I'll try to explain what happened later. I'd like to come back to an earlier question. What is the favor you want to ask of me?"

"It is of the utmost importance to me, Adam. It is so important that I give you my word I will never ask for anything else," Running-water said.

"Take a moment and apply the five attributes I just mentioned to your quest. Do any not apply to your choice?"

"Actually, I've not considered any of them. I think your checklist is woefully shortsighted. And I suppose you'll argue with me about that."

'In what ways are these five attributes short?"

"You don't have to curl your lip up at me. There's nothing with any of your proposed attributes. It is your list that is short. You have not accounted for *peace,* the peace in one's soul," Running-water said.

Getting up from the floor, he extended his hand to Adam. He caught him just before he hit the floor. Gently, he picked Adam up and placed his limp body on the bed. Looking closely at his friend, Running-water noticed small rivulets of sweat trickling down the side of his colorless face and that his lips were twitching. Adam suddenly opened his eyes. They were blood red and their intensity frightened Running-water. With a blink, Adam was as he was.

"What favor do you want of me?" Adam said as though nothing had happened, nothing at all.

'Man you scare the shit out of me. What the hell just happened?"

"I'll try to answer this question before we get to the favor you want. Because we move through time as participators, often as initiators, there are three basic directions for our travel: We may move forward into future time, go back into past time, or we go into vertical time. In vertical time, the most interesting phenomenon happens. For every instance, for every precise moment of our existence, there is a reproduction of those exact moments occurring simultaneously. Most people are not aware of them. Sometimes strange events get entangled and cross through those vertical layers. It is there we can see all time past, present and future are one and the same. Esaugetuh and I met in one of those layers, argued, and in our anger, we jump-crossed those layers. That's what caused the tremendous thunder and flashes of light. Just at the precise moment of the flash, you jumped into that time layer. You are lucky you weren't fried. The energy there is pure energy not dissimilar to the energy of Zeus when he showed himself to Semele. She was immediately cremated."

Running-water loudly exhaled.'

"Now then, what is this favor you want from me?" Adam said.

"For some, my brother, I have felt uneasiness in you, troublesome and nagging. It's like you have been deliberately putting distance between us. I think- I feel, I know why and because I do, I ask that you take Isha as your woman and protect her. Take my sons as your own. I am destined to leave this realm before you do. Give me your word,

303

Adam. Promise me," Running-water said, his voice breaking.

"You're partially right. I have been and am bothered. I can't put my finger on it. Whatever it is, it nags at my soul. I have no sense of your imminent death. As far as I am concerned you are not about to die; nor will you necessarily die before I am called to another time. Have no fear, my brother; I will honor your request. You have to realize I service only one woman, your sister. Is that enough to give you peace?"

"I am at peace."

"It's settled, then," Adam said.

Dutch stuck his head into the room. "You two okay?"

"Yeah, we're fine," Running-water replied.

"Okay, I'm going to hit the hay. Brett will take the first watch, I'll come on second. Running-water, you take the third if this is okay with you," Dutch said.

"Fine with me. And, Dutch, thanks," Running-water said.

CHAPTER 16
THE VAULT

To enjoy the rainbow, you must accept the storm that brings it.

Esaugetuh

Morning brought a promise of a beautiful day as the sun began its rise in the eastern sky. Its golden-orange rays stretched out over the 20,000 acres bringing a diamond-like sparkle to the fresh dew. Its warmth, mixed with the wonderful smell of cedars brought a refreshed energy.

Dutch and Brett, up early, boarded the Gulfstream and prepared for takeoff. Both barely controlled their excitement at getting back to civilization, to a city and some much needed female companionship. Both had agreed ranch life would not be for them, particularly one so isolated as the one they were leaving. They were city men and craved the excitement of a large cosmopolitan city. Toronto nicely filled that bill.

Running-water was also up early. He called Thomas at Karuna House, explained to him that Dutch and Brett were flying in, that he was to go to the airport and bring them to Karuna House.

"And Thomas, movers will be arriving to pack all of Esaugetuh's furnishing on the third floor. Brett will be supervising that. Adam is selling

Karuna House so tell The Brothers they have to move out."

"Yes sir," Thomas replied.

"Thomas there is one more thing. Have Samuel come to the phone," Running-water said.

Samuel was told to rent a flatbed, load the limo on that, hitch it to the SUV and drive to the ranch in Quebec Province.

"Samuel, you understand you are to leave immediately. That means right now. Throw some clothes in the SUV. Use the Karuna House credit card to pay for your expenses."

"Yes sir, I will. Tell Adam —," Samuel said as he paused.

"Tell him what, Samuel?" Running-water said.

"That, well, it's just not the same without him here."

When his phone call was finished Running-water found Adam sitting on the veranda. Thunder clouds had begun to roll in and spoiled the promise of a beautiful day by the earlier sunrise. He also noted the change in Adam. Moodiness was now the operative word. He could almost feel Adam grumbling just as he could feel the thunder building.

"Sure hope Dutch and Brett got above this incoming storm," Running-water said.

"Uh huh," was the reply.

"Do you want to open the vault and continue examining its contents?" Running-water said. *Maybe that will help his mood.*

For the second time, they opened the vault. As before, they were awed by the wealth stored there.

Each labeled box brought renewed amazement. Care was taken to inventory every item in each box. As they continued going through the alphabetized list of numbers, Adam again noticed his Indian name, Ikaee Wicasa spelled out. As he continued to look at the letters, Adam realized they created a complete sentence.

"I'll be damned! Look at this," Adam said to Running-water. "Another mystery.

Running-water looked at the words and then read them out loud. "Esaugetuh and Adam are one."

"Have no idea what that means," Adam said as he opened yet another box filled with what appeared to packets of legal papers, each tied with a red string.

Adam put them aside. Time slipped by; morning turned into noon; noon into the late afternoon before they realized it. Adam went over to the pedestal and began to open the golden jeweled box when very loud banging on the front door finally penetrated their senses. Immediately, they left the vault, put its closure into motion, and went to the front door.

"I didn't hear any alarms going off," Adam said. "Did you?"

"Come to think about it, no," Running-water said as he checked the security cameras. Two men were standing at the door. Out of habit, he checked his twin Glocks and then slowly opened the door.

"We're from the Canadian Department of Aviation," one said showing his credentials.

The older of the two then said, "We are saddened to inform you that a Gulfstream jet registered to an Adam Esaugetuh has apparently crashed. Are you a relative?

Shocked by this news, Running-water stammered, "No, I'm his attorney. Adam is here. Come in."

Adam stepped forward and said, "I'm Adam. I'm sorry but I didn't get your names."

"I'm Alex and my partner is Jim," said the older man.

"You are saying my jet crashed?" Adam said.

"Yes sir; seems there was a midair explosion a few miles out from the airport at Toronto airport.

"And survivors? Have any survivors been located?" Adam said as his voice cracked.

"We've found no one at this time. How many people were on board?" Jim asked.

"Two, my pilot, and his navigator," Adam replied.'

"What was the nature of their trip to Toronto?" Alex asked.

"They were going there to take care of some of my business interests," Adam replied.

"How do you two know the plane exploded?" Running-water said.

Unruffled by Running-water's curt tone, Alex said, "Eyewitnesses."

"What about the ground?" Adam said.

"There were no deaths or injuries reported," replied as he shifted his weight from one foot to another.

"And the black box? Has that been found?" Running-water said

"No sir, not yet. Not much of the plane has been found. It'll take some time to locate it," Jim said. Switching subjects, he continued, "What were their names and what was the nature of your business interests?

"They were not married. The pilot has a child. The navigator has no family, Adam said" Excuse me a moment, I'll be right back."

Adam started up the wide oak stairs that led to the second-floor balcony. Stopping on the fourth step, he turned and said, "Dutch Masters and Brett Montana," and then continued his climb.

Jim had only gotten as far as the second step when a shot rang out. He fell backward, screaming in agony.

"Move and you're dead," Running-water growled.

Alex made a quick move and that was a mistake. Running-water's second shot tore into his knee, shattering it.

"My god, Running-water have you gone crazy?" Adam yelled.

"No! The alarms didn't go off. Second have these two jerks been from law enforcement or from civilian aviation, they would have known Dutch and Brett's names as well as basic information about them. They would have been in contact with Dutch's ex-wife before they came here," Running-water said.

Looking at the two wounded men, he said, "Suppose you assholes talk. Never mind. I'll just let you lay there and slowly bleed to death."

Running-water sat down in a chair and waited.

Adam had noticed this callousness in Running-water before. Suddenly, it struck a raw nerve. *I'm witnessing my own behavior reflected back to him. Have I become so accustomed to death that I've turned into an unfeeling and callous thing? Dare I even call myself human?*

A quotation from the Book of Thomas, The Contender [10] came to his mind: "He who has not known himself has known nothing, but he who has known himself has at the same time already achieved knowledge about the depth of the *All*."

Adam turned to continue up the stairs to the second-floor balcony. He stopped midway, turned back around, stopped, and looked beyond the two men on the floor, unseeing. *Like a screaming banshee, it tortures me night after night. And now it devils me during the day. Esaugetuh was right. I am a failure. Or, sure, he'd say there's potentiality. And that brings me back to that terrible argument we had over my desire in contract to my wants. What do I desire? My god, how I wish I knew.*

His thoughts were disrupted by a voice in the great room.

"Please, mister, don't just stand there and let us bleed to death. Do something," Jim pleaded.

Adam shook his head and ran back down the steps. He went to each man, laid his hands on them. Each felt the heat build and each saw a blue light radiate from Adam and they became afraid. Quietly speaking to Alex and Jim, Adam brought calm to each. The bleeding stopped, the pain lessened, and they talked; telling Adam everything.

Running-water called the authorities to come and pick the men up. He had been correct in his initial assessment of Alex and Jim. They were a part of the terrorist cell that had exploited the ranch and both confessed to planting altitude bombs on the Gulfstream. They also said they had been ordered to come to the ranch, find out who was there and to kill them.

Adam and Running-water's cell phones buzzed at almost the same time. Daphne and Isha had heard about the plane on the news and were worried. Even though they were reassured both men were okay, they were not happy about their continual absence. Yet, being strong women, they said nothing.

"Why didn't you tell my sister that you were selling out and returning?" Running-water asked.

"Avoiding the question, Adam said, "Did you say anything to Isha?"

"Hell no. Client privilege of confidentiality prevents that. You know that," Running-water said.

"Yeah, I know. Just wanted to hear you say it. The amount of explosive to take the jet down suggests Dutch and Brett never knew what hit them," Adam said as he looked out the massive windows.

The storm had abated. A rainbow spread its glorious arch across the sky. *Esaugetuh was right. To enjoy the rainbow, you must accept the storm that brings it. I never thought of it before, you that also applies to life itself. To enjoy life, you have to accept its tragedies and sorrows that come and go like the passing of a storm. You go on. That what you do. You go on!*

Running-water's voice penetrated his thoughts.

"Too bad they didn't have time to get in the escape pod and launch it."

"They knew about it. Maybe they did use it and that's why their bodies haven't been found, Adam said.

CHAPTER 17
THE PORTRAIT

Within some humans resides a spark of the divine that needs to be liberated in order to return to its real home.
Bart D. Ehrman in the Lost Christianities.

Once the authorities had Alex and Jim in custody, quiet returned to the ranch. Yet, there was hollowness about it. Something had gone out of it. The spirit of place they had originally felt was gone. Perhaps it wasn't so much the place as it was Adam's reflection on it.

He had avoided coming here from the very beginning. He now knew why. It was a harbinger of death! He fought the land swell of emotions that had begun to dominate him. No matter where he lived, death had sought him out and destroyed those around him. His battle over the implications of desire and want has ended. Actually, they had come together. Adam knew, finally. His desire; his want was actually his need. He needed to be about his father's business. *And that business is in that gold box.*

Adam turned from the massive windows and went over to the wall to open the vault. Running-water's outburst stopped him.

"My god, Adam. Look!"

"What are you yelling about?" Adam said.

"You. You are Esaugetuh! There's your answer to the message in the letters and numbers in the vault."

He dashed across the room to where a large mirror was hung and took it down. "Take a good look, Adam. Then look at your father's portrait. You look exactly like him; just a younger version.

Twins, yes they could have been changing the age just a bit. Since Adam had let his hair grow long and his skin had darkened from being out of doors, the likeness became more pronounced. Even Adam's azure blue eyes held the same quality of mystery so noticeable in Esaugetuh. The subtleness of skin hues gave a quality of sheerness; not transparent but something otherworldly. Perhaps it was more of an aura than a physical reality. Whatever it was, Genevieve Van Batten had captured it in her portrait. Adam reflected those same hues.

"There you finally have it, Adam," Running-water said. "Esaugetuh and you are one. And you are one and the same. Esaugetuh has been found!"

CHAPTER 18
THE MESSAGE

I must bear my destiny as best I can, knowing well that there is no resisting the strength of Necessity.

Aeschylus
Prometheus Bound

Once the jeweled and gold inlaid canopic chest was open, an old piece of rolled deer skin tied with two leather thongs. Adam thought it was deer hide because of its subtleness and because it was lighter in weight than buffalo hide, for example.

Carefully, Adam placed the rolled animal skin on the small table next to the vault door. With extreme care, he untied the two straps, and gently unrolled it. He estimated the scroll was about 24 inches long and about 14 inches wide. The entire surface of the skin was covered with strange figures. Neither man knew what they meant.

"I think we better photograph this," Adam said. "I'll be right back. I have a camera in my backpack."

Adam stepped out of the vault, located his backpack, and returned. As he took several photos, he said, "I'll send them off to a cryptologist."

One of the issues was the way the symbols should be read; left to right or vice versa. The way they were arranged suggested they were not to be read downward. The marks did remind him of Egyptian Hieroglyphics and at the same time something from Ancient Greek. Some of the letters looked like animals while others could be human forms and then there were sets of straight lines not unlike in *The I Ching,* Actually, the stick figures looked like something a very young child would draw; yet, some notable detail in the eyes. The figures were in color, and Adam was amazed by their vividness.

"My god, Adam, do you supposed this dates back to the Ancient Ones, the Anasazi?" Running-water said. He didn't make any attempt to conceal his excitement. "There have been rumors among my people for years and years an ancient document existed."

"Excuse me! Your people?" Adam teased, his mood had changed.

"Guess I still not used to you being half Indian," Running-water rolling his eyes upward. "Well, do you think it's Anasazi?"

"I don't know. Let's finish checking the boxes. There might be documentation in one of those."

Running—water picked up the gold box, turned it over. To Adam's quizzical look, he replied, "Remember the bottom drawer of the cabinet Syd wanted."

He found nothing and gently replaced the box on its stand. By they finished their inventory night had slipped in. Their search produced no clues as to the significance of the animal skin and its strange

316

markings. One thing was sure and was the fact it was stored in an elaborate box in a climatically controlled vault and therefore must be of great value. If it dates back to the Ancient Ones, it would set the Native American community on fire.

Adam's busy mind was already working on the possibilities. "Suppose this goes back further than 12,000 years? What if it came from some other time, some other place? Out there." Adam pointed to the night sky, now ablaze with a mass of blinking stars.

"You mean this could be the missing link? The one that once and for all tells mankind where it came from?"

Running-water let out a low whistle as he exhaled.

The possibility stabbed at their brain cells. Both had heard of the Fibonacci series, and neither of them could detect a repeating pattern that would equal the sum of each preceding item in the sequence of the numbers they had been working within the vault. Nor was the animal skin document similar to the famous Voynich Manuscript [11] touted as the most mysterious manuscript in the world.

"Adam, I really think this is from the Ancient Ones and—,"

He stopped short realizing Adam was not listening and was off somewhere just like he was once at Mesa Verde. Quietly he went into the kitchen to prepare their evening meal.

Adam continued to stare at his father's portrait. *I know Old One that you were the revered keeper of the Seven Pipes. I also know that you were a powerful shaman; one whose powers seemed supernatural. For some, that created fear. I also know that you moved in different realms, displayed powers beyond the understanding of most human beings. I also know that during such times you were not much different from a particle moving through the Higgs Field. And I know that once through the field, you gained mass or form. I remember you told it was actually transmigration of spirit.*

Adam eased up out of a chair and went over the fireplace to look more closely at Esaugetuh's portrait.

I have not tried traveling to another realm since my attempt in which I used hypnotic-channeling with Christine Lilith Conduit. And maybe, father, it has been since then that I have been harboring the idea that may the real reason many of these attempts on my life is to stop the continuation of the knowledge and power that you passed on to me. Damn, maybe Daphne and our unborn son are in danger.

A shudder passed through him and he shook himself to get rid of it. Misunderstanding the shudder, Running-water who had come in from the kitchen said, "You've had a rough day, Adam. Come and having something to eat. We can examine the deerskin afterward."

"Now who is being the mother hen," Adam said as he gave Running-water a playful cuff aside of his head. I "I am hungry. Are you?"

"You bet," Running-water replied, sensing an improvement in Adam's attitude.

Adam lit a fire in the massive fireplace and turned down the lights to allow the evening sky to illuminate the large room. Running-water brought out his flute and began to play. Adam nodded his head in approval.

"It's been a while since you played, my brother. It is a good time," Adam said as he went into the kitchen.

It wasn't a sad song, rather it was one filled with a special joyfulness commemorating their lost comrades.

Adam listened as he began the preparation for their evening meal. He caught the subtle change as the flute's song swept up to the rafters of the huge great room, bounced off the paneled walls, and floated in a three-dimensional harmonic vibration. The melodic notes announced the mourning for another lost one and Adam knew it was for Esaugetuh. A shudder passed through him as he brought two plates of steaming food to a kitchen table, gave a whistle that Running-water should come to the kitchen. They ate in silence.

As was their custom, they had a glass of aged brandy after their evening meal. Tonight, as they sat in front of the fireplace and its dancing flames that cast shadows around the room in the house that Esaugetuh built, Adam broke the silence.

"Do you recall seeing a Calvin and Hobbes? [12] Calvin, in one of the cartoons, has asked Hobbes if he thinks it's "better to live in stupefying security or to takes risks and live life on the edge. Even though the question is interesting, Hobbes' answer is significant. He says it is better to accept danger and live life to the fullest. He shows a value judgment; one that reveals the essence of character. Both Dutch and Brett took life to the edge and therein, showed their *anima mundi*, their souls of the world in all their purest and ethereal spirituality. You and I have been so privileged."

After a brief pause, Running-water said, "Amen to that, my brother. We certainly are. You feel up to taking another look at that skin? We might find something of help in the library. I noticed it was crammed with old books."

At a large oak table in the library, Adam once again carefully unrolled the scroll. He pulled his Kodak from his pocket and took several more pictures. Then he recounted the seven circles of painted figures. Running-water looked for similar figures and counted the number of times they were repeated.

Rummaging through one of the draws in the table, Adam found a large magnifying glass, paper, and pens. He systematically copied the larger figures, and the counted the number times they appeared in a circle while Running-water concentrated on the direction the figures were pointing.

Dawn found them no closer to discovering the meaning of the images on the scroll. And as it was designed to irate them more, the sunrise foretold a hot day. True to its prediction, the heat began an unmerciful assault on the land. The ranch house became insufferable and oppressive.

Adam stripped off his clothes, threw them on the floor, and rushed out the front door. Running at full speed, he dove into the cooling waters of the lake. His noisy splash startled the ducks that had sought its shelter. Adam's strong arms brought him to the other side of the lake near some shade trees. Clambering out of the water, he wrung the water from his long brown hair and then flopped down on the grassy bank. The trees shaded him from the sun. The large leafy maples created shadows up and down his naked body. Sleep, sweet sleep conquered him.

Midday brought a cooling shower that turned into a thundering downpour. It brought Adam to an upright position. Blinking his eyes to clear the rain, he was surprised to see Running-water squatting next to him. Sensing Running-water's seriousness was just too much; Adam tackled him, rolled them both into the lake, and dunked him. When Running-water came back to the surface, Adam began splashing him with water. The two, like teenage gladiators, jostled one another, throwing one another over, tossing each into the air.

Running-water scrambled up the slippery bank, stripped off his wet clothes, dropped them in a pile, and broke into a gallop around the lake. Slipping and sloshing in the heavy rain, Adam took up the chase. In a dead heat, the jumped the gage and sprinted to the veranda. Both, gasping for air, collapsed, laughing and yelling, and feeling alive.

The rain stopped. The sun came back out and a beautiful full circled rainbow with its promise filled the whole area, and they felt good, really good for the first time in a long, long time.

CHAPTER 19
THE INTRUDER

Investigate not mythical creatures, but myself, to know whether I am a monster more complicated and more furious than 'Typhon' or a gentler and simpler creature, to whom a divine and quiet lot is given by nature.

Plato
Phaedrus

Adam's laughter stopped. A tall dark-skinned figure with unkempt hair and shaggy beard suddenly appeared in front of them. Rumpled clothing accentuated his strange thinness. Adam reached for his gun he had left on the back of the chair when he stripped down to go swimming.

Waving the pistol at Adam and Running-water who were still naked, the stranger said, "Ya looking' for this?"

"Easy with that gun. It's got a hair trigger," Adam said. Still speaking quietly, Adam asked, "What do you want?"

"T'aint for you to ask. It's—,"

Before the man could complete his sentence, Adam raised his right hand, opened his clenched fist, palm outward. The stranger was slammed against the wall of the house. He was held there by a power he knew all too well. Horror drew across the man's skeletal face making it grotesque. His eyes rolled back into his head. He fell to the floor; his gaping mouth showed yellowed teeth.

Running-water jumped up and tried to extract the gun from the man's grip.

"My god, Adam, you've killed him. I can't dislodge the gun. Rigor mortis has already set in. But how can that be? Doesn't it take a least a couple of hours?"

Adam, kneeling by the stricken man, placed a finger on his neck, and then pulled back an eyelid. It remained open. Slowly, Adam pried open the man's fingers and retrieved his gun.

The man heard them and with the one open eye could see the man's face kneeling beside him. Yet, he could not move; nor could he open his other eye. He knew the naked man beside him controlled the power holding him. Desperately he tried to cry out but his words were lost deep within his dry throat. They rattled there, and then faded into the depths of his chest cavity. Panic seized him. His heart pounded wildly. He was sure it was about to explode and he could do nothing; absolutely nothing and he will have failed his mission.

He sensed the naked man passing a hand over him. It was over in an instant. The release was spontaneous and his gravelly voice spate out, "It's for the shaman to hear."

"I am that I am that," Adam said as he helped the disheveled figure to its feet. "Come inside. Talk to me while I fix you something to eat. You need water."

Before he let the man pass between them, Running-water frisked him to make sure he had no weapons. Each pat brought a wince to the man's face. Running-water felt the lack of real flesh and quickly withdrew his hands. Once inside, Adam stepped into a bathroom, grabbed a towel, and wrapped it around himself. He tossed one to Running-water as he went into the kitchen. There, while he sliced some meat, Adam gave the stranger a glass of water.

The man gulped the water down and wiped his thin lips on the sleeve of his shabby coat.

"Who are you and what is it you want of me?" Adam said.

"I come from a very long line, going all the way back to the Old Ones. I am ancient. I have met your father, Esaugetuh, the Master of Breath. He told me I should come here when you opened the golden box."

"How do you know my father? When was the last time you saw him? Do you know where he is?" Adam came alive; his voice full of excitement.

It's a long story and I am very old and I do not have a lot of time before I close my eyes for the last time," the stranger said. His voice cracked.

Alarmed, Adam did an immediate check on the stranger's life force. It was not strong. Sensing Adam's alarm, the stranger said, "It's nothing. I've lived a long, long life. I have this one last task to complete. You want to know when I met Esaugetuh. Very well. Do you think it would be acceptable for me to sit down?"

"Of course, Come along. I'll bring your sandwich."

In the living room, Running-water poked the fire to life and then poured each of them a glass of aged brandy. The sandwich was gone with two bites and the brandy in one gulp. The old man, smacked his lips as he wiped them on the sleeve of his coat. For a long moment, he looked at Adam. *Yes, I will tell this one much. There is still time before I pass over to the other side one last time. It's just as it has been foretold.* He looked up at the portrait, and then looked directly at Adam. *Yes, they are of the same seed. When the fire dies so too will I.*

"So let me begin. I am Howahkan [13] I have traveled far; many moons have risen and faded since my journey began."

"Please tell me of my father," Adam interrupted.

"Not your father as you knew him. It was during Dreamtime that he came to me and extracted a favor from me. I have not met the man you call your father in his time," Howahkan said. His voice, sinking into a barely audible whisper seemed to vibrate as in a hollow chamber. It was hoarser and lacking in compassion.

"Are you a medicine man? Running-water said.

"No, I am a wisdom keeper," Howahkan replied.

"What is this favor my father asked of you in your Dreamtime?" Adam said.

He and Running-water both had a deep abiding appreciation of one's Dreamtime. It was during such a time that Adam had called for Running-water to come to his aid during his battle with Moon-woman.

"I was asked to come to you when you opened a golden box. You are to lay your hands on me to make my going easier. For that, I am to tell you the meaning of the message written on the animal skin."

"You will not have to leave for a while yet. There is no hurry in my laying my hands on you. We both will now the time for that," Adam said.

Stunned by this revelation, Running-water said, "My god, are you saying Howahkan is dying?"

"Yes. As he has said, he's traveled far. What he meant was he is from another time. He dies only in this time," Adam replied.

"Only in this time? What does that mean?" Running-water said.

"Death means he leaves this world and goes back to the one from which he came. He is not of this world," Adam's voice showed his irritation at Running-water's persistent question.

He relaxed, took a deep breath, and said, "It's okay, my brother, ask your questions. There's time."

"You know much. There is more for you to learn. The message in the golden box tells you what you need to know. It's up to you to—,"

The silent alarm was flashing, a warning that someone had entered the property.

"Damn, evidently Dutch did not reset the explosive charges along the entrance," Running-water said as he checked his guns.

Through the massive bulletproof plate glass windows, Adam and Running-water saw two vehicles speeding toward the main house. Running-water immediately made his weapons ready. He added an Uzi. Adam followed suit.

"Howahkan lie face down on the floor and don't get up until I tell you to," Adam ordered as he and Running-water headed out to the veranda. Adam took one side and Running-water took the other. Whoever was coming at them at full speed would be caught in a deadly cross-fire. Escape would be impossible. Death patiently waited.

Blaring horns echoed across the lake as the two vehicles got close enough for Adam and Running-water to get a clear shot. Cat-like they waited.

"Holy shit! It's Samuel," Running-water shouted as he recognized the SUV.

The two vehicles nearly slammed into the wide veranda as they careened to a halt. Samuel, the first out of the SUV, yelled at the top of his lungs, "Adam, I am here!"

Emerging from the shadows, Adam said, "So you are."

Samuel, so excited nearly messed his pants. The rest of The Brothers emerged from the SUV and limo. They rushed Adam and began hugging him, patting him, shaking his hand, and all talking loudly at the same time. Julie held back for a moment and then leaned forward and kissed Adam on the cheek and hugged him.

"How is it, that all of you are here with the exception of Samuel whom I asked to come?

"An old man who stopped at Karuna House said you would need us. He said Esaugetuh had sent him. So, I brought everyone," Samuel said. "Did I do wrong, Adam?"

Before Adam could respond, Charles piped up, "Besides, we didn't know what else to do."

"Well, it just seemed right for us to come since the terrible deaths of Dutch and Brett. It's just horrible. Have you heard anything more?" Julie asked.

"Glad to see you are staying strong, Adam said. He shook his head and said, "No, nothing new."

Running-water said, "You better come inside. It's not a good idea to stay out in the open."

"Damn! I forgot about our guest," Adam said as he held the door open for Julie to enter.

Once everyone was inside, Adam turned on the lights. The fire had burned out. Adam bent down and he knew. Howahkan said he would die when the fire died. *Damn, damn! Now we may never know.*

Bitterness flooded him and that boiled over into anger. Adam felt cheated. The disappointment overshadowed all of his other emotions, especially at seeing how well Julie was doing. So absorbed with his feelings, he didn't notice a slight movement from Howahkan.

"It seems I was more tired than I realized," Howahkan said as he struggled to rise up from the floor. "Who are all these people?"

"Thank god! You're alive," Adam said extending his hand to help the strange man.

Howahkan saw the mark on Adam's wrist; the eagle's feather with a lightning bolt through it. His eyes widened as his lower draw dropped. He reached out, took hold of the arm, and pressed his hand on the mark.

A yellow flash filled the room. Adam stood motionless, dazed by the sudden blinding light. The Brothers covered their faces and Julie screamed. Ozone filled the air causing some to cough. At Adam's feet was a small pile of charred powder with a thin line of smoke slowly spiraling upward. A few inches from the smoldering ashes laid an amulet, one that Howahkan had worn around his neck.

"Adam!" Running-water called as he shook his friend. "Are you okay?"

"What?" Oh, yes. Help me sweep up what's left of Howahkan. We need to prepare a proper burial," Adam said bending down and picking up the amulet. Will you play your flute for him?"

"Of course, I'll go and prepare the fire for him," Running-water replied.

"Let me help," Samuel said.

"No! You are to guard Adam. You are always to guard him. Never leave him," Running-water was adamant.

"Yes, of course, whatever you say," Samuel stammered, totally taken aback by the urgency and command in Running-water's voice.

As Running-water left to get a broom, he noticed The Brothers cowering behind Julie. Instinctively, he didn't trust them and there was something about Thomas. Soon, he had a large bonfire going and while Julie and The Brothers gathered around the fire, he and Adam changed into full Indian regalia.

Adam was dressed in a beaded white leather vest that showed off his well-defined pectorals. A line of dark hair traveled down the center of his chest and disappeared beneath a pair of white leather pants that continued the muscular definition. A single white feather with a black tip emerged from his black headband. He stood before them, silent and waiting.

Running-water, dressed in tan buckskins and moccasins, sat Indian style, his blue-black hair hung over his left shoulder in a single braid. A black band was on his right arm. Showing no emotion, he carefully unwrapped his flute from its velvet cloth, put it to his lips, and began to play his goodbye song for Howahkan, the Wisdom Keeper.

The Brothers had formed a circle around the fire. With their shaved heads bowed, they made quite an impression dressed in their blazers with the Esaugetuh Institute insignias. If Howahkan was looking down on them, he would have seen a shining rose-colored orb reflected back at him. Julie had stepped to one side. She was dressed in a simple black dress, her hair pulled back, and a silver pin at her left shoulder.

Adam, standing tall, looked out over the group. He was proud of Julie and pleased he was able to help her turn her life around. Her son, Charles was still a question mark. Shifting his azure-blue eyes up

331

to the sky, he began to sing. A deep baritone rose slowly from his throat. It was a sound rooted in ancient traditions, passed on from the earliest of times when humankind looked out from its cave and cried out to the spirits of sanctity.

Gradually its cadence increased. Even though they didn't know the language or its meaning, The Brothers picked it up with perfect pitch and created a beautiful harmony—a spiritual harmony. Unknown to the ceremony makers, hundreds of eyes watched from the darkness. They had heard; they had come. That's the way it was done. That was the calling of the old ways.

The song ended, and Adam began to speak.

"From the day we are conceived we begin to die. All life is a preamble to death; the first a fleeting speck in quantum time; the other, an eternity for that which houses the soul. For the human body, there is no life without death. A scoop of dust in the hand of the Creator is given breath and a soul is born. It has its assigned time to carry out its assigned tasks. On occasion, some souls return to finish tasks while others return to foretell things yet unlearned by those of us who remain here at this moment in the everlasting now. Our visitor, Howahkan of the 'mysterious voice,' is a Wisdom Keeper. We have been privileged to know him albeit a too short a time. His journey, dangerous and costly, brought us a renewed promise of hope— hope that we can change our destructive ways. For that hope we are grateful; without it, we are lost.

Thank you Howahkan. May the spirits guide you on your journey."

Soul-sounds from Running-water's flute gradually filled the air, mingled there with the night people, and then floated upwards to join the stars. From the darkness came *hu-hu-hu* complimented by the beat of a skin drum and the synchronized movement of feat. The Brothers felt the vibration and it alarmed them, yet they remained where they were. As the song intensified, the dancing feet brought the crowd into the firelight. The dancers, some in *dress*, others in street clothes, formed a large circle around The Brothers, terrified now and unable to move.

The song of the flute stopped. The chanting stopped, and the dancing stopped. All was quiet. Not even the night birds sang a single note. In that frozen moment, a star shot across the sky. And like Eta Carinae, [14] winked, spent its moment, and disappeared; a reminder that, that is all we have, a moment when it comes to the nature of things. And then it was gone.

Adam took Howahkan's remains and tossed them into the flames. There was a momentary flare-up. And like the song of the flute, the chanting, and dancing, too passed into the night.

"Welcome!" Adam said to the visitors. "Come. Refresh yourselves." He moved off into the darkness.

The Brothers, hands clasped, heads bowed, walking in single file lead the gathering in solemn procession back to the house. Running-water remained by the fire. As he watched the fire continue to quiet itself, he thought, *So close; yet, so far. An answer so near. Now we'll never know what the inscription on the animal skin means.*

"I know much of the secret, my brother. The Wisdom Keeper passed it to me when he grabbed my arm. We have much to learn. He completed his task and that is why he died," Adam said as he walked into the remaining light of the fire.

"Do not speak of this in front of The Brothers. They are yet to be tested. Come, we can talk as we go back to the house."

I hadn't noticed the Wisdom Keeper's amulet around your neck. It's glowing," Running-water said.

"The black obsidian began to glow at the exact moment a star shot across the horizon," Adam replied.

"Then you have truly become a Meshkini," [15] Running-water said.

"The funeral pyre is to burn for seven days and seven nights. We'll have The Brothers do that," Adam said.

It had become Adam's custom to do things that referenced the number seven. Finally, he understood. His father, Esaugetuh, The Mater of Breath, was the seventh son of the seventh son. The chain had to be broken so it could be renewed and begun again. New blood, so to speak. *That's what my father meant when he said 'there can be only one.' I am that I am!*

"Of course you are, Adam.," Running-water said.

"Listening to my thoughts, are you," Adam said as he gave Running-water a playful cuff. "So many things have happened that I sometimes have difficulty trying to make any sense out of it all. Do you ever feel that we are out of control?"

"Hell, yes. In fact, I feel that way a lot lately. Have you been reading my thoughts?"

"No, but because we are of a certain mindset, it would be possible for you to pick up my unease and translate it as your own. Often, I do worry that I may have lost your soul and you have become a mirror of mine; that somehow, in my battle with Moon-Woman, part of me split and was transmitted to you."

"Hadn't better be true, my brother. It wouldn't do to have part of you in bed with Isha and me while we're having sex," Running-water howled with laughter. "Are you going to tell me what Howahkan released to you?"

CHAPTER 20
THE WISDOM KEEPER'S WORDS

The one teacher of virtue and freedom in all humanity is Nature.

Menander

"He said much and it requires long and serious thought," Adam replied. "I'll tell you when we can be totally private. Right now, don't even mention it. Okay, my brother?"

Once inside the house, Adam found The Brothers busy in the kitchen. Julie was very involved in supervising. Someone among the guest softly played a drum and another began to sing.

"I agree, Adam. Let's take a walk to the lake It's quiet there. I know at some point you will need to make your presence known," Running-water said.

They stopped at the south end of the lake so the northern night sky would be visible to them. On cue, the Northern Lights turned on giving them a fabulous display; one that complimented the ceremony offered up for Howahkan.

Adam cupped his one hand, brought it to his eye, and peered at the sky's personal show. For a moment, he was looking through a rotating crystal prism.

"It's beautiful, isn't it," Running-water said.

After an extended pause, Adam replied, "Please do not take offense by what I am about to say to you. I do not mean it in a hurtful way. When you asked if the Aurora Borealis was beautiful you broke the ecstasy, the sheer joy of a living moment. You stepped out of the experience to analyze it; something that is not necessary When you and Isha are being intimate, do you stop and ask if it's wonderful? Of course, you don't This is the first lesson of Howahkan, the Wisdom Keeper. Analysis is not always required; acceptance often is. We live with the Spirit, which finds expression in the Self as it reflects that which is Natural. I just used the word acceptance. It is the second lesson written on the animal skin."

Puzzled, Running-water asked, "The Old One told you how to read the message on the animal skin but when did you go back to read it?"

"In that moment of the flash, he revealed all to me. It was a last-ditch effort to complete his assignment. It is beautiful and powerful, my brother."

Esaugetuh's last will and testament flashed before Adam's eyes. He now understood the implication of fiduciary. He now realized that he had been given a trust, a message to be delivered to his people. *But I am half-breed. Who then, are my people?* Then he heard. No, he felt it. The word ALL came roaring across the Aurora Borealis—a thunderous revelation. *Of course. We are one race, the human race.* Tears formed, welled up, and

337

tumbled down along the ridge of his nose. *At last, I know, I know my destiny.*

Stillness reigned between them; each deep in his own private world, each accepting the spirit of the moment. And it was good. Adam began to head back to the ranch. Running-water took hold of his arm to stop him.

"There is not hurt felt, Adam, because none was given. I do understand and I'll be more aware from now on."

Adam nodded. As they continued to their walk back to the house, a helicopter buzzed the compound. Coming in lower, it circled the place again. Adam and Running-water broke into a run. Neither was armed. Out in the open, as they were, they were sitting ducks. Running-water let loose with a barrage of cuss words as anger filled him. Heavy breathing from in front of them stopped them. They prepared to fight.

"Down, get down. For god's sake lay down. I'm coming," Samuel yelled. "I will get it."

Running-water tackled Adam, knocking him to the ground., and jumped on top of him. A barrage from an Uzi filled the air as the chopper came back into view. It sputtered, flamed out, and plummeted to the ground. Two figures ran from the burning debris. Nether got far. A large fishing net, expertly thrown by one of The Brothers, trapped them. Immediately six others piled on the two men, pinning them to the ground.

"Get the hell off of us. Have you lost your freaking minds?"

"You're supposed to be dead. Is that really you, Mr. Dutch?" Thomas said as he pulled himself up from the top of the heap.

"You were expecting Santa Clause? Not get off of us and let us up. Brett just farted. Jesus, what a stink!"

"Move and you're dead," Samuel said puffing his lips in and out as he gasped for air. *I'll have to get in shape now that I have new responsibilities.*

"Go easy with that gun, Samuel. Dutch said. "By the way where did you learn to shoot like that? Man, you ripped off the rear blade."

"What's going on at the house? Having a powwow?" Brett asked.

The Brothers waited in silence for Thomas to reply. He was their surrogate leader and deferred to his leadership. Stepping forward as they expected him to do, Thomas replied, "We've been here but a short time. Much has transpired since we were all together. I'm sure Adam will fill you in."

"And that I will," Adam said as he grabbed his two friends and gave them a bear hug. *Strange that Thomas answered for me.*

Happy to see him, they glad-handed Adam. With Dutch on one side and Brett on the other side of Adam, they walked arm and arm back to the house. Samuel was right behind them still clutching the Uzi. They, including The Brothers, left Running-water behind.

For a moment, Running-water stood still. His cheeks burned as the flush of being snubbed hit him. *It's odd that one of them didn't call to say they had survived the explosion and to say they were on their way back. Wonder where they got the chopper from?* He turned, looked for the N number on the remains of the chopper. He saw enough to check on later. He hustled to catch up with the group.

At the main house, some of The Brothers had several fire pits going and food preparation well underway and under control.

The First Nation People had gathered along the path to the caretaker's cottage. Some were softly talking. Adam's approach brought total silence, anticipatory, and unsure of this powerful new shaman they had heard about; the one who could throw lightning, the one who walked between many worlds. True, they had come to pay respect to the Wisdom Keeper but they had really come to see for themselves this man who fought the soul-snatcher and had won.

Three of them, clearly people of importance, sat to one side of the larger group. To test their position, Adam deliberately walked in front of them. One he was just past the third one, Adam turned and said, "Mistake." That was what was expected of him.

The Elders nodded and Adam continued to the center of the group. Unsure of what they expected of him, he knew they had already heard him speak, and ruled that out. As he struggled with what to do, he walked around the inner part of the large circle, looked at each person, deliberately making eye contact. And they, they, in turn, turned their eyes downward. As Adam came back to the center it came to him what he should do. *The snake in the sack is too well known as a trick of shaman for me to do. Perhaps some smoke and disappearance will satisfy them.*

Adam held out his hands, palm up, showing them to the gathered group. Then he closed his hand as one would around a baseball, and threw a pitch into the air. A small glowing orb floated above the crowd. Adam then drew a circle around his body and with his right hand and then threw the floating PSI ball to the ground. Smoke engulfed him. When it had cleared, he was gone. It was an old ruse, distract the audience. The three elders got up and walked to the center of the astonished onlookers. They looked up at the sky and then down at the ground where Adam had stood. They shook their heads in unison as they returned to their places.

Adam stepped out of the shadows and stood the three elders and made a low growl of a bear. The elders scrambled and this brought a roar from the group as Adam stepped into the firelight.

The Brothers passed hot food around to the large circle of guests. Thomas passed food to Dutch and Brett and Running-water and ignored the now always present Samuel. Adam, busy talking with one of the elders, had not noticed the deliberate slight. Running-water immediately passed his food to Samuel and said, "Don't ever do that again, Thomas. Do you understand?"

Thomas cringed and managed to say, "I was going to bring him a larger plate." He scurried off.

341

After they had finished eating, one of the three elders stood, waved for the group to be quiet. It was story time. In perfect diction, the elder thanked Adam for the respectful ceremony for Howahkan, the Wisdom Keeper, for the plentiful food, and for the magic trick.

Adam, with Running-water and Samuel seated next to him, nodded in recognition of the thanks. Then the elder, speaking directly to Adam said, "It is customary for the host to begin the story time. We would like to hear your story, Ikaee Wicasa."

The use of his Sioux name surprised Adam. It also was the sign of official acceptance by the First Nation People gathered.

Adam stood up, turning to take in the crowd said, "Thank you Old One, but I must decline. There are those among you who have real stories to tell, stories full of wisdom. The young among you would lose much if you did not tell their stories."

Adam's eyes told the Old One more than his words. No insult was given. He understood the command. With a nod of his head, he selected the first speaker.

While the Old Ones' told their stories, Adam, Running-water, and Samuel returned to the main house. There they found Dutch and Brett finishing their food. They had not told their story. The Wisdom Keeper's words would have to wait.

CHAPTER 21
THE STORY

Rule of survival: Pack your own parachute.
T. L. Hakala

The five of them, Adam, Running-water, Dutch, Brett, and Samuel sat in front of the massive stone fireplace. Its warm fire was welcome. As was their tradition, Adam opened a bottle of aged brandy and poured each a glass.

Samuel, very much aware of his new responsibility as guardian, declined. With the Uzi at the ready, he took a position directly in front of the front door. He could still hear and waited for Dutch and Brett to tell their story.

Sitting back on his haunches in one of the large red leather chairs, Dutch stretched his long legs out in front of him. With his thick black hair and in his black leather jacket, open just enough to reveal his broad chest with its patch of black curly hair up to his throat line, he was Travolta-like and right out of Grease. Older though, being in his late twenties, he had just enough tough-guy about him to turn women's heads. He was the first to speak.

"As you know when we left here darkening skies surrounded the ranch and we climbed above the incoming storm. We were cruising about 25,000 feet. There, the sky was clear blue, the kind of blue that makes you feel you can see forever. I put the plane on auto and settled in for a relaxing trip to Toronto. You can imagine what I was thinking about, a big city, and big city women. It happened while Brett was back in the galley making some coffee. The damndest thing happened. I still have trouble believing it."

Dutch paused, took a sip of the aged brandy, licked his lips, and continued.

"So, there I was sitting in my pilot's chair, looking out at a couple of large white clouds. The blue of the sky enhanced their Clorox whiteness. As I continued to sit there, waiting for coffee, I wondered would it felt like being a cloud. Wondering was so unlike me and just for a moment I thought I had reverted to my childhood."

He took another sip of his brandy. He nursed it knowing Adam seldom offered a second.

"One of the clouds took on the shape of a human head. Suddenly, its mouth began to move. I kid you not. I can't read lips so I cupped my ear as a signal that didn't get what it was saying. The head grew larger and came closer to the Gulf Stream. I considered taking the plane off autopilot and taking evasive action, but before I could we were in the mouth of that damn cloud. Now I have flown in all kinds of weather and through millions of clouds, but nothing—nothing has ever even come close to this. Man! And I mean nothing."

"What's your take on this, Brett?" Adam interrupted.

"It's Dutch's story. I wasn't up front. Mine comes later," Brett replied.

"As I was saying, nothing I have experienced has equaled this. Once inside this cavernous cloud-mouth, everything changed. The colors were atomic. Four of July sparklers exploded everywhere. Time stopped. The plane stopped, suspended in space. Blue lightning was everywhere. Everything went quiet, so quiet I could not hear my own heartbeat or hear myself breathing. The colors, as well as the lightning, vanished. All animation stopped. I was sure we were caught in one of the time-warps you see in the SF movies."

"Wow! How'd you feel?" Samuel called out from his post.

"For some reason, Samuel, I felt warm and safe, comfortable. I was thinking it would be nice to have a sweet chick snuggled against me and just as I was feeling nicely wrapped in my reverie I heard it."

"Heard what?" Running-water said.

"One word! And that damn word changed everything. It changed my life right then and there. It was totally unbelievable. It vibrated into every living cell of my body, echoing, and reverberating. It blasted into my consciousness, shattering it beyond belief. I felt I sat there for an eternity, frozen and incapable of any movement."

"Come on Dutch, spill it. What was the word?" Running-water said impatiently. He then got up and defying what had been their tradition of just one drink he went to the liquor cabinet and brought back the bottle of brandy and refilled their glasses. He set aside a second glass for Samuel.

For the first time, Running-water noticed that Dutch held the brandy snifter with both hands. Dutch turned, looked out the window to take attention away from the tremors in his hands and the quiver that played along his lower lip. Adam also caught the move and said nothing.

"One god damned word destroyed my whole wonderful word. Can you believe that? One friggin' word. I couldn't believe my ears. Then it struck at me again, hammering until it consumed me, and finally, it spit itself out into my reality."

"What? What?" Samuel called out.

"Bomb!"

"Bomb? You mean the cloud told you there was a bomb on board? You've got to be kidding," Running-water said.

"What's so extraordinary about that? Esaugetuh talks to Adam, Adam talks to you using Psionic Telepathy, animals talk to both of you," Dutch replied.

"True, but a cloud? So, what did you do then?" Running-water said.

"I hustled my butt to the galley to tell Brett."

"Yeah, you should have seen him. I thought he was hallucinating, you know, out of his friggin' mind," Brett interjected.

"I started screaming, bomb on board. We've got a bomb on board. Help me find it."

A frantic search of seats, cushions, and overhead compartments, the heads, bedroom, and the bar turned up nothing. We were so busy searching for the god damn bomb we hadn't notice that the plane had begun to climb. We both rushed back to the cockpit. The plane had climbed another thousand feet. To bail out at that altitude we'd need oxygen tanks, and if we had them, it would be risky, Brett said.

"At that point, I said what the hell. Let's just get drunk and let it happened. We returned to the main cabin, got out two bottles of hooch," Dutch said.

"We'd been through some shit together, but this we knew would be our last," Brett added.

"We fastened ourselves into our seats which was a dumb thing to do, settled back to get totally wasted. Before had taken a second draw on our bottles there was a whirring sound and a loud clank. Brett still thinks it was more of a ripping sound," Dutch said as he used both hands to set his snifter down on a nearby table.

"All hell broke loose. We were catapulted right out of the side of the plane. We thought the bomb had exploded and had ripped us out of the main cabin," Brett continued.

"It took us few minutes to realize we were in an escape pod, a glider. I thought those were just on the drawing board of some engineer's desk, you know, something out of Sci-Fi," Dutch said.

"Dutch realized the controls were the arms of his seat and took command. A small screen popped up from my table revealing a miniature navigation system. I went to work," Brett said.

"Some distance above us there was a bright flash. Within seconds the glider rocked with the shock waves from an explosion. We bounced around hard, and I was sure we weren't going to make it in one piece. We were riding a roller coaster with a chunk out of its wheel. We were tossed up and then thrown down. I still believe we did a loop at least once. Finally, Brett got the glider on track and we prepared for a landing.

"We thought we were in for a splashdown. Instead, we landed in a farmer's field on a little island in James Bay. The glider traveled a good thousand feet or more. High stalks of corn whizzed by our window as we continued to plow up the field.

As we crawled out of the glider we came face to face with a guy holding a double-barrel shotgun, and man, he was really pissed. He thought we were aliens from outer space despite the fact we tried to tell him who we were. One of his sons came roaring up in an old army surplus jeep and tied us up. We were put in an old milk shed, the kind that had a deep well to keep the place cool. Old milk cans lay around on the rotting floor." Brett said.

"Man, it was so cold in there we nearly froze our balls off. On the third day, at least I think it was the third day, the old coot decided to feed us. I think I drank a gallon of water. He retied our one free hand behind our backs and as he bent down to check the shackles on our feet, he suddenly stopped, undid the shackles and cut our the ropes from our wrists."

"So what made him change his mind?" Running-water asked.

"Yeah, what did?" Samuel pipped up.

"Dutch's belt," Brett said.

"His belt? Explain," Adam said.

"The old man recognized the Navy SEALS insignia. Dutch then convinced the old man to check his wallet. When he saw Dutch was a certified air marshal he agreed to let us go on one condition," Brett replied.

"And what was that condition?" Adam asked.

"He made me promise that you'd pay him top dollar for his corn crop," Dutch replied.

"Nice of you to offer my money. Running-water, deduct the cost of the cornfield, as well as the plane from both of their yearly salaries. That should take a few years to pay it back. Maybe next time you will check the plane as you are supposed to do," Adam said.

Blown away by Adam's comment, Dutch and Brett got quiet. After an awkward pause, Brett said, "You're kidding, of course."

"No, I am not. You nearly lost your lives because of your carelessness. What would have happened if either Running-water or I were also on board? And to top it off, I am now without a plane. I suppose you rented the chopper and that will have to be paid for. And all because you were so eager to get away from here, to get away from us. I should fire your sorry asses."

Adam stood up, walked over in front of Dutch and Brett. For a long minute he looked at them; first one and then the other.

"I'd like the microfiche back. You still have it don't you?"

"Well, yes and no," Dutch replied.

"Damn it, Dutch, you know that film is very important. Where the hell is it? Don't tell me it went down with the plane," Running-water said.

"No. I forgot to take it with me. It's still in my room," Dutch said. "I didn't realize it until just before all the shit happened on the plane."

Brett stood up, put his glass down and as he left the room he said, "Guess there's nothing to toast here, after all."

"So, Adam what are you going to do?" Running-water asked.

He then sent a thought message to Adam: *Don't you think it strange that neither Dutch nor Brett indicated any suggestions on how the bomb got on board your plane?*

Adam ignored the question. He motioned for Samuel to join him.

"Samuel, it will soon be daylight. Make sure the SUV and the limo are gassed. You will be having some passengers to take to Montreal. You will be driving the limo."

"Yes, Adam. I will do it right now."

"Got the film, Adam," Dutch said as he came down the stairs.

"Good. You are to go to Montreal, lease a Lear or Gulfstream. On second thought, you better make that two. Can Brett fly kind of plane?"

"Someone say something about my flying? Name it and I can fly it as well as navigate," Brett surprised by what he heard as he returned from the second floor.

Adam paced back and forth as he clicked off a list of what he wanted to be done.

"Good, I want you to fly the microfiche to Albuquerque and get it to Running-water's uncle. Once developed bring it back to me. Any questions?"

"When do I leave?" Brett said.

"Within the hour. Dutch, I want you to fly to Toronto, take The Brothers and Running-water with you.

"Running-water, while you are in Toronto, oversee the sale of the sanitarium, of Syd's Bar, and Karuna House. Have the stuff from Esaugetuh's apartment packed up and ready to ship out. When that's done, put this place up for sale."

Adam turned to Samuel who was standing at attention with the Uzi leaning on his shoulder.

"Samuel, once you airport put the limo in storage, "Yes, Adam," Samuel said he turned to leave.

"Uh, Sam, find Thomas and have him come in here."

Within minutes Thomas scurried into the great room. Breathless, he said, "You want to see me?"

"Yes, have The Brothers pack and ready to leave. All of you are to go back to Karuna House. You are to supervise the packing of everything on the third floor. Make sure it is packed and labeled just as it is."

"How am I to get there?" Thomas asked.

351

"All of you will fly back with Dutch," Adam replied.

"Is that all?" Running-water exploded. "Good god, Adam you are firing off orders faster than an automatic assault weapon. It would be nice if you let me in on what the hell you are doing."

Before he could answer, Adam's cell phone rang.

"This is Adam. " Uh-huh. Good. Let me know when the modifications are complete. Are the trucks on their way? Okay. Thanks."

Turning back to Running-water Adam said, "Back to your question. It has come to me during dream time that we should change our method of transportation. I just bought a train with sleepers, cook and dining cars, two flatbeds, and three boxcars. I've hired the necessary staff to operate and maintain the train, to feed us, and to keep the sleeping cars clean. The modifications I mentioned on the cell phone are security changes. The train, a leftover relic from the Cold War Era, was built to withstand an atomic attack so the government could continue to function."

Running-water was hot. The veins in his neck bulged. "That's just great, Adam. You've managed to get rid of everyone who protects you; Dutch, Brett, Samuel and me. You've been barking orders like a drill sergeant growling at his squad. And now you plan to be living on a Cold War relic. What the hell are you going to do; travel from one end of the country to the other and back? For once, Adam, you will not have your way. Don't even consider to

352

force the issue by using your powers on me. You know damn well I have taken a sacred vow. I stay with you, and that's that."

He slouched further down in his chair; frustrated, angry, and ill-at-ease. Adam's new secretiveness coupled with the appearance of a sense of superiority. *I've never known him to present himself as superior to others. This has developed since meeting Howahkan.* He suddenly sat straight up in his chair. He looked at Adam and then his eyes fixed on the amulet around Adam's neck; the one left by Howahkan. I'll be damned it's glowing and if I'm not mistaken it's keeping time with Adam's heartbeat. *I wonder what it does.* He got up from the chair.

"Adam, do you have any idea where you are going?"

"No, but I will know when I get there."

Running-water, dumbfounded, just stood there. *There he goes again with his exclusiveness. Just 'I' and no 'we.'* "Adam, with four eighteen wheelers, two other vehicles, two jets, a mile-long train, you've made the decision that everyone wants to go wherever it is you want them to. What the hell is this? You are not making any sense."

Immediately, he regretted what he had said. His tone was hurtful and he had meant it to hurt. Adam's eyes told him it had.

"I assume you are referring to The Brothers. They came here on their own accord and because they did, I feel safe in saying they wish to continue being in my company. Dutch and Brett are employees and as such, they are free to explore other avenues."

"And me, Adam?"

"Have I not told you on many occasions that you are free, that you are under no obligation to remain with me?"

"Well, yes," Running-water sheepishly admitted.

"Further, if you choose not to continue as my attorney and as manager of my financial affairs you are free to change that as well. Free! Do you understand? Free!"

Adam's words tore into Running-water, cutting deep into his soul. He could feel the icy grip they had on his heart making it difficult for him to breathe

"I'm sure that you must realize the choices have always been yours. You made the first one when you accepted the assignment from my father to find me. You are the one who inserted yourself into my affairs. At Mesa Verde, did I not send you away to lead your own life? And yet, here you are. Have I not called you brother? Have I ever asked you for an accounting of your spending from my money? Actually, have I ever asked you to account for anything? Well—have I?"

"No. No, you have not, "Running-water managed to whisper. He felt he was being strangled. Wiping the back of his hand across his forehead, he felt its wetness.

"And yet you chastise me for making an assumption based on an observable fact? How is it,

354

you have reproached me in such a mean spirit fashion? What is the wrong that I have committed? If I am ignorant of my crime, how then, can I make amends for it? Tell me what it is," Adam said.

"It's true," Running-water said as he took a deep breath. "You have called me brother and because you have, and because you haven't asked for an accounting of my spending, and because you have said I am free to be my own person, I resent it when your decisions are arbitrary. I resent you when you not consider my feelings. I resent it when you do not recognize me as a person, and I resent it when your decisions are vague and understated. The most recent example of your saying 'we're moving on.' For Christ's sake, Adam moving on to where, to what, and for what purpose?"

"I want to go home," Adam said his voice flat.

"Home? You mean back to your parents' place. You sold that, remember. And you just told me to sell Karuna House and this ranch."

"Back to my own country," Adam said.

"You as well as I lost our home country a few centuries ago or have you forgotten our heritage?"

"I meant to the United States and that is our country."

"Okay, fine but where in the US? You gave me the log cabin. It's not big enough to house The Brothers."

"I said I would know when I got there. If that's good enough for me, it should be good enough for you."

"Well, it's not! I have a family. I'd like them to know where they are to come. This is not like you Adam and you know it and I know it. And I resent it," Running-water said.

His face still flushed with anger, Running-water blurted, "You have a wife with a child on the way or have you forgotten."

"What would you have me do? This place, so many others, reeks of death: Saint Christopher's mansion on the island, Marrie Copa's, my mother's place, the suicide of the banker, the senseless slaughter at Karuna House, and how here."

Running-water caught the change from parents' house to mother's house.

"This place, this ranch is a virtual fortress and yet it was penetrated. The attempts on my life have increased. There just doesn't seem to be an end to it. Those who are around me are at risk. I feel obligated to find all of you a place that is safe. And that includes your family. As I said, you and Samuel will leave here. You will know where to end your journey. I have decided the best way to ensure your safety is to separate from you. I have already said my goodbye to Daphne and my unborn child. I simply will not put them in danger. You can protest all you want. It will gain you nothing. The limo is coming around. Take The Brothers and leave."

One of The Brothers drove up in the SUV and parked it, got out and handed the keys to Adam. Samuel following in the limo jumped out and yelled, "Adam I am here."

"And so you are," Adam replied.

The Brothers, in a single line, systematically loaded baggage into the trunk of the limo. Julie, Charles and one of The Brothers squeezed into the front seat with Samuel back at the wheel. The rest forced themselves in the back two rows of seats. Dutch and Brett sat on the floor and were still bickering.

"Get your damn foot out of my crotch," Dutch growled.

"Just shut the fuck up!" Running-water said as the limo moved out.

As Samuel eased the limo around the end of the lake he saw two tandems trucks entering the ranch. He wondered what Adam was moving, but kept the thought to himself.

***

Adam greeted the truck drivers and their helpers and escorted them into the house, showed them what he wanted packed. He went to the library, picked up the scroll. He opened the vault, placed the scroll in its golden box, and locked it. He then gave specific instructions to one of the packers as to how he wanted the vault boxes packed. A second packer went with Adam to the master suite where he, like the first, was told how all of the Indian regalia, armaments, and books were to be packed.

Two days, later, the packing was done and the trucks were on their way to Montreal to wait to be loaded on the train.

357

Adam secured the house, picked up his backpack, tossed it into the SUV, drove over to the stable, released the horses into the pasture, called the rental place to come and pick them. and took off.

CHAPTER 22
A PRIVATE TIME

He who has two ears should listen with both, keeping mouth shut. Much wisdom is learned that way.

Esaugetuh

The Lake, as his parents used to call it, was a pristine woodland-water area inhabited by First People, great bears, wolves, elk, moose, and a profusion of fish, water and land fowl. Technically, it was a man-made lake to prevent flooding in the other areas of Quebec. The Baskatong Reserve, its real name, was a good two and a half hour drive north-west from the ranch.

As he drove along, Adam wondered about the recreational development of the area he had read about in the Canadian papers. Evidently, hotels, lodges, campgrounds have been built since his time there. It saddened him that there was such a commercial development of this beautiful wonderland. The nomadic people used to come here in spring, stay through early fall before moving on. *I wonder if the cabin we used to live in is still there.*

Instead of continuing on the main road, Adam turned off on a side dirt road, drove along on for a while. He felt the hunger pangs in his gut and realized he had not eaten since the day before. He stopped, grabbed his backpack, and ambled over to a large cedar tree. It was a perfect place to spend the night.

He walked around the area, found a strong stick, some dandelions and using his stick, dug them up. He was careful to get the roots. Using the same stick, he dug a shallow fire pit, laid in a couple of stones in its bottom, and then gathered some dried leaves and twigs. He laid in a lair of leaves followed by a few small twigs around the edge of the stones. Adam opened his backpack and pulled out a fire stick and following the old way his father taught him, he soon had a nice fire going. From his backpack, Adam retrieved a small pan, and a bottle of water. He poured about a half a cup of water into the pan, and then placed the pan directly upon the stones.

While he waited for the water to boil, Adam chewed on a small stick of dried beef jerky. Once the water had come to a boil, he reached into his backpack, retrieved a metal cup, used some of the boiling water to rinse the dandelions, and then placed them in the cup, poured in the rest of the water, and waited for the tea to brew.

Ten minutes later, Adam leaning against the cedar tree, sipped his tea and munched on a hardtack biscuit he had made several days ago He felt at peace. In the morning, he would look for some fresh berries and nuts to have for breakfast. *I better get myself set for the night. I see the sun is beginning to set.* Adam got up, went to the SUV, turned it around so it pointed outward, locked it and then began gathering up moss and other dried matter. He went back to the cedar tree, laid the moss, and dried vegetation down to make a bed. He placed his backpack in such a way that it would be his pillow. He made sure it flap was open so he would have easy access to his guns.

Using an old trick Esaugetuh taught him, Adam created a secure perimeter, stoked his small fire, and rearranged his bed so the fire was about two feet directly in front of him. Not quite ready to call it quits for the night, Adam propped himself up against the base of the giant cedar tree. Its smell combined with the night shadows and the appearance of stars refreshed him. The hoot of an owl and a response some distance away added to the luxury of the private time his soul needed.

I have much to sort out. My decision to remove Dutch, Brett, and my devoted Running-water wasn't an easy decision to make. I hope someday, Running-water will understand and not resent me. The Brothers are a whole different situation. I choose to take on the responsibility of their training and keep. Being placed in physical danger is not what they signed up for. None of these people would be in danger if it weren't for me. They have on their own interfered with and prevented my death. I owe them, especially Running-water, so much. How does a man say thank you for all of that?

"He says thank you."

"Who's there? Show yourself," Adam said as he reached for his gun.

"A simple thank you is always acceptable."

The voice came from the glowing embers in the fire pit.

Adam's head nodded as sleep, deep sleep overtook him. He dreamed of another man, in another time, in another mythology. The great Sumerian King, Gilgamesh was denied that which he most wanted, immortality. And like Adam, he had a best friend, Enkidu, who died because of his actions. Adam groaned as thoughts of Running-water's death flood him.

Bird song and the warmth of the morning sun woke him. Stiffness was his reward for his return to simpler ways. A hardtack biscuit and the remains of the leftover tea to slosh it down was his breakfast. He decided he could pick up some moved on. Taking pains to make sure his campfire was out and the site was left clean. He stepped behind the cedar and relieved himself. The stick he had used for digging came in handy once again.

Adam picked up an animal trail and headed northwest. As he padded along at a leisurely pace, he grabbed a few berries. He kept his ears tuned for the sound of water. He knew at some point along the trail there would be a water source and he would need to refill his canteen.

As he jogged along, he thought of the first settlers, particularly the Algonquin, who had traveled this wooded paths. How different it must have been. And then came the fur traders who slaughtered huge numbers of animals for their skins, often leaving animals in their traps to suffer an agonizing death. They were a different kind of human. They didn't take the animals for food and clothing; they took them out of greed.

Several times, Adam stopped to listen. His presence in the woods caused a stillness. People sing 'On a clear day you can see forever.' In a forest, if one is still, one can hear everything. He stopped, stripped off his clothes, and buried them. He unrolled his deerskin shirt, britches, and moccasins. They offered better protection against briars, thorns, and cold nights. He double checked his gun, making sure there was a bullet in its chamber and then strapped it on. He fished out an extra clip from his backpack and stuffed it in his shirt pocket.

He adjusted Esaugetuh's medicine bag around his neck, tucking it back under his shirt. It comforted him. Remembering Howahkan's amulet, he decided to remove it to look at it more closely. When he did, the golden cord on which it hung drew tighter around his neck, resisting his efforts to remove it. Startled, Adam tried to rip it off. It grew tighter and made it difficult for him to breathe. He sat down, cross-legged, and began to meditate. As he calmed himself, the golden cord relaxed its hold. It was now long enough for Adam to slip it over his head.

He began to examine it in much the same way a jeweler would a fine gem. Slowly rotating it, he carefully studied it. Its edges were sharp to the touch, yet smooth. Despite its endless blackness, the stone gave off an aura that beat in time with his heart rhythm. Adam continued to turn the amulet

363

between his fingers. Feeling its life-force, he realized, no—understood—the fire with the heart of the Earth created the obsidian.

Its story is an old story, and it needed to be changed. He had been trying to go back to an earlier time; even now, his outward appearance was of a past time He had fallen for the illusion for past reality was better. Burying his street clothes was a deliberate act of rebellion against the truth. The obsidian cut to the heart of the matter. It is indeed the revealer of truth, and as truth does some times, it offends.

"Okay, so what, I can't be a shaman as they were in the past. At least not in the way I imagined them to be. These clothes I am wearing are just metaphors for something I thought existed—the pure and noble savage. He never existed!" Adam realized he was speaking out loud.

The obsidian amulet heated to a new intensity; its colors brilliantly beautiful mated with a new vibration, slowly at first, gradually increasing until exquisite deep baritone tones filled the air. Adam caught up in the moment, was unaware that he was thumbing the obsidian-like it was one of those executive pacifier stones that had had their moment of popularity.

Adam felt all negativity drain from him. Lightheartedness replaced all former doubts. He replaced the obsidian around his neck, picked up his backpack and sat a fast pace along the trail he had been following.

Morning became afternoon, and he still had not come on a water source. His stomach complained that it was long past the time for nourishment. His leg muscles took up the complaint next forcing him to stop and rest.

The strenuous pace he had set coupled with the heat of the afternoon reminded him of how out of shape he really was. He opened his canteen but resisted splashing the water on his face. Instead, he dipped a finger in the water and moistened his lips. The heat of the day had quieted the birds and the chatter of the squirrels. Adam bent down to rum his aching legs, dropping his canteen. Its water splashed out onto the ground.

"Damn!" Adam said out loud. "Great! Just great!"

Even though it might be some time before he found a water source, he knew he could rely on berries to provide necessary fluid. He slowed his pace to a stroll and began taking rest stops. He faced the sun, held up his right hand with its palm facing him and his fingers parallel with the horizon. Next, he positioned his index finger so it rested just below the sun and his little finger was parallel to the edge of the horizon. Slowly he counted out the number of fingers it took to reach from the sun to the horizon. With each finger representing about fifteen minutes, he calculated he had about 45 minutes of daylight left. He decided to make camp. He found some wild elderberries and Iroquois greens. Since he had no water to make tea or to cook the greens, Adam decided not to build a fire. He chewed the elderberries and greens very slowly to extract the fluids. He cut a few pine boughs and wove those together to make a blanket to cover him.

"Tomorrow, I will listen for the hum of the bee. It will tell me water is close by," Adam said as he lay down.

Morning did not bring the hum of bees or the buzz of flies. He looked for animal tracks and found none as he walked along, pushing aside the underbrush, and marking his direction by the sun. He realized he had to make some radical changes. The jerky and hardtack were now gone.

He'd been walking for three or four hours. Actually, he wasn't sure how long he had been walking. He knew he didn't feel well. He dismissed it as a lack of proper nourishment and not used to living off the land. Dizziness forced him to stop and sit down.

Adam's eyes fluttered and he saw a beautiful fiery display of dancing blue balls. He marveled at their different sizes and the speed they spun around and then shooting off in many different directions. For a moment, he felt he could reach out and catch them. He tried to get up. Instinct told him he had to get up and keep going. He fell to his knees. Adam shook his head in an effort to clear it. That was a bad move. A sharp pain struck his temples. He cried out.

Determined to keep moving, he walked along like a staggering drunk, bumping into trees, clutching at shrubs in a desperate effort to steady himself. He had to stop to rest. He fell asleep.

Several times, he moaned. With a sudden jerk, he was awake. His heart was racing and he felt sick on his stomach. Nausea came in short harsh waves. Spasm after spasm wracked his body as he vomited. A sense of hopelessness engulfed him. Realizing he was lost, any semblance of his survival skills vanished.

Speaking to the trees, Adam said, "Survival for what purpose? What is it that I have accomplished? What contribution have I made? Keeping a rag-tail band of misfits together achieved nothing. Man, now that what I call important! What about Running-water? Oh, sure I've set him free. What a joke that is. All I've done is make him feel unworthy; thus, enslaving him all the more. Am I not the catalyst for many deaths? A tally of those dead far outnumbers those whom I have saved or helped. The first syllable of the word shaman fits me like the proverbial leather love—sham. That's what I am, a sham. A fake who can't even find his way out of the woods. Ha! And I am supposed to be a healer. Just look at me, wallowing around the ground crying like a baby and puking my guts out."

He tried using his cell phone. The effort to get it out of his backpack exhausted him. No service was available. *Well, that's that. Why make any further effort? It's so much easier to just sit. I'll sit a while longer and then decide what to do.*

"Haven't learned much have you? And to think, I thought you were one of the smart ones. Guess I was wrong."

Adam shook his head.

"Who's there?" Adam said.

"I am," came the terse reply. "You are really stupid. You know that don't you? You don't even pay attention to what's around you. Look at you, laying there and feeling sorry for yourself. You sure are a miserable excuse of a man. You definitely can't be an Indian. No Brave would go around pissin' and moanin' the way you are—not a real one anyway."

"You are saying I'm a real man? Watch your tongue, whoever you are. I am Ikaee Wicasa!" Adam grumbled.

"Ha! What a joke. You're not much of a man.' If you were, you'd not be sitting there," the laughter faded.

"You dare to criticize Adam Kadmon," Adam snarled.

"You're certainly not much in the way of flesh and your Spirit is definitely questionable," the voice mocked.

"Who are you? Are you Meshkana, the Spirit Master?" Adam managed to say as another wave of nausea hit him.

At that, the whole wooded area was filled with loud raucous laughter. Adam was sure everyone in the world heard. His anger surfaced.

"How dare you mock me?

He was seething. Anger burned deep within him. He was sure he had stumbled upon the earthly lair of the mysterious Mishtapeau. [16] Instinctively, he reached for his Nimapan, Esaugetuh's medicine bag. *Oh, man! I am losing it.*

I'm delirious. Maybe I got some snakeroot and didn't realize it. Or maybe someone slipped poison in my food or drink. Yes, in my canteen. That has to be it.

The voice continued, "So you think you are henos Anthropos, the one man, the Adam? Ha! He's the one who let sin into the world. Or have you forgotten that, too?"

"Oh, no you don't! You can't blame the sins of the father on the son. Besides, this henos Anthropos, as you call it, is an old story of nature; one that implied that all classes of things have a single nature. If there is only one standard, then that implies all others are inferior. Doesn't that make for judgmental reasoning? And you, whoever you are, are surely judgmental. The Christ showed man has more than one nature. And isn't His compassion? Isn't His, love?"

"Ah yes. I was wondering when you were going to get around to that. How can you talk about love when you don't love yourself enough to survive? What have you to say about that?"

Adam struggled to get up. Hanging on to a tree, he waited to catch his breath. The effort winded him. Once his breathing has stilled he heard—water!

CHAPTER 23
REALIZATION

With the dawn of realization comes understanding.

Esaugetuh

Using all the energy he could muster, Adam forced one foot to move in front of the other. He staggered and stumbled his way toward the sound. Reaching out to grab a tree branch to steady himself, he missed and fell face down. Panting from the exertion, he struggled to get up. He could not. He began to snake his way along. Sharp rocks and pieces of wood cut into his skin. The underbrush tangled his dirty matted long hair. When he brushed his hair from his unshaven face, he was sure it was falling out.

After what seemed like years and miles of crawling he came upon a small brook; its water sparkled as it cascaded over a rock-strewn bed. Its invitation to quench his thirst and to replace much needed lost body fluid nearly overcame him. His inner voice told him the water could be contaminated. If so, it would finish him off. Inching his way over to the edge, he used the pan he had been dragging with him, to scoop up some water.

With utmost care, Adam placed the pan and its precious contents on the ground. He pulled some dried leaves and twigs from beside him, dug a hollow in the soft earth, and then placed the tinder around its outer rim. Cautiously, he put the pan in the center of the fire pit, making sure not to spill any of it. He pulled the medicine pouch from his neck, took out one match, and lit the dried debris. He watched the water come to a boil as he added more twigs. He knew that it would take at least ten minutes of boiling to kill any potential contaminants.

As he waited, Adam counted to 60 and drew a line in the soft earth. Since he no longer had a watch, this gave him a good estimate of long the water boiled. He was sure it was the longest ten minutes in history. Snail-like he inched his way to the edge of the small brook. Rolling over on to his belly, Adam reached for the pan of water and placed it the water to cool it. He fought the urge to splash the gurgling water all over him. As he continued to lay on his belly and holding the pan of water, his patience found a new ally. Adam imagined the reflected light from the water was a water nymph winking at him. It passed the time until the water was cool enough for him to have a drink.

Correct survival behaviors penetrated his fogged brain. He took just a small sip, sloshed it around in his mouth, and then let it trickle down his throat.

Adam breathed a sigh as a bitter smile broke across his parched and swollen lips.

"Guess that shows you, whoever you are. I am a survivor. What do you have to say for yourself now?" Adam said.

"Humph!" the voice said.

Adam, too busy, didn't hear. Scooping up handfuls of dirt, letting it sift through his fingers as he searched for grubs and mealworms. Once he had found several, he popped them into his mouth, chomped down, and swallowed. He swished his mouth with some water. He slowly began to look at his surroundings. He spotted a cluster of white birch trees and crawled over to them. He cut away the outer bark, stripped some pieces of the inner bark, and began to chew a few pieces, one piece at a time. He crawled over to a fir tree, inched his way up its trunk, pulled off some of its needles, and then crawled back to his pan of boiled water. Breaking a few of the needles into pieces, he dropped them into the remaining water. The fir needles would add more nutrients to his starving body.

Deciding to say put until he regained some of his strength, Adam slowly sipped his tea. He edged his way over the bank of the brook, dipped his pan, and set on the fire pit. He rebuilt the fire, gathered up some more twigs and dry leaves to keep the fire going until the water had boiled for at least ten minutes.

Sleep, however, had its way with him. The fire went out and was replaced by night sweats followed by fits of chills. His peace, frittered away, was replaced by the thief, nausea. Finally, he settled down but only to be awakened by a loud noise nearby. He reached for his gun in his backpack and took it off safety.

"Have you learned anything? What is it you have finally realized?"

"Well, I've learned how to stay alive and that's something isn't it?"

"Asking me says you aren't sure. Did you learn how to say alive or did you already know that?"

Adam's eyes slowly closed.

"Stay awake! You must stay awake," the voice bellowed.

The trees and shrubs furiously shook their branches.

"Leave me alone. I'm tired," Adam groaned.

"You really are stupid! With all your training, with all your knowledge, and will all your powers don't you think it's strange you have spent nearly two weeks wandering in a circle? And what's worse, you didn't even know it. Explain that."

The word betrayal screamed at him. He instantly straightened up. "Who?" Adam said.

To drive the point home an owl repeated, "Who, Who."

CHAPTER 24
JUDAS INCARNATE REVEALED

In facing the drama of his own soul, a man is always alone.

Isha Schwaller De Lubicz

Drugged sleep battled his struggle to remain conscious. At some point, he reached for his canteen to have a drink. It was empty. Its emptiness snapped him fully awake. He had filled it the night before he had everyone leave the ranch. Was its water drugged? He swallowed trying to remember the taste of the water. There had been a slight bitterness. He recalled dismissing the taste as simply canteen taste.

Adam's mind raced through the events at the house. Who was in the house? Who had access to my bedroom? The Brothers? The visitors? Howahkan? Dutch and Brett both had been upstairs. He dismissed that notion. Running-water was not even considered. *No one knew of my plants to leave the group and no one knew of his intent to hike to the Baskatong. I'll be damned.*

It suddenly occurred to him that he had called Daphne to tell her goodbye. Someone was listening in on that conversation. Desperately, Adam tried to remember the details of the group's departure. Who did what? What was the motive? Who had a motive? *Damn! Here I am back with the questions*

374

again and as usual, no answers. Now what? Oops, not so fast, hotshot. All of The Brothers were in a tizzy about the sudden move back to Toronto. All but one, that is. Thomas.

Adam leaning against the base of a tree, he slowly inched his way up until he was fully standing. He looked up, searching the heavens; he looked for a particular star.

"Shit! I'm going the wrong way," Adam said out loud.

He turned himself around. He now was facing northwest. That was the direction he should have been traveling. Relief expressed itself as a deep sigh. *I haven't lost it after all.*

To make sure he knew where the correction direction was, he cut an X into the tree. It was a precaution. He would check it again in the morning. He slowly lowered himself to the ground, and began counting as he crawled back to the stream. He turned around and crawled back to the marked tree. Because his self-confidence had been badly damaged, he marked the tree with four slash marks. It would remind him he had moved his right arm forward four times each way as he crawled from the tree and back again. He leaned against the base of the tree, legs stretched out in front of him, and hands tucked behind his head. *I did tell Running-water The Brothers were yet to be tested. Had that been a warning? What other signs did I miss?*

The thought of Running-water brought an immediate alarm. *Running-water is in danger!*

In his weakened condition, Adam wasn't sure he could telecommunicate with Running-water. He realized he had to build his energy and to do so quickly. The question was with what. Almost on cue, Adam heard it, the familiar buzzing of bees. Looking up, Adam watched for bee activity. He cupped his hands behind his ears to help focus the sound. He saw it, in a tree nearby, and not that high up. *How could I have missed this? I knew bees require water to make honey. And honey is a quick energy food.*

Looking around, Adam spotted a fallen tree limb, about six inches in diameter. Crawling on his hands and knees, he retrieved the limb, cut off a few side branches, and smoothed it out. He then propped the limb against the tree, just below the hollow spot that housed the bees. He didn't immediately make use of the pole because he didn't want to stir up the bees. Being in his weakened condition multiple bee stings could be fatal. He crawled over to the brook, leaned down, pulled up a handful of wet mud. He smeared that over his face. Another handful went around the back of his head; a third went to his neck and a fourth to the back of his hands. Once back at the tree and the pole, Adam double check the pole to see if it would hold his weight. He began an agonizing and slow shimmy up the pole.

Good thing no one is around to see me like this. They would definitely agree that I had lost my mind.

But unseen eyes did.

Many minutes later he had reached the hive without being stung. Gingerly, he reached into the hive. Waited. For what seemed an eternity, he waited and then very slowly grabbed a handful of honey. Again he didn't move. His legs, wrapped around the pole, screamed for release. Yet, he did not move his hand. At a snail's pace, Adam moved his hand until it was out of the hive. Like a salamander, he remained attached to the pole. His gut begged for the honey. Inch by inch he came down the pole. Once on the ground, he flicked off a couple of bees and stuffed the honeycomb into his mouth, dirt, and all. He remembered Esaugetuh said, "You'll eat a peck of dirt before you die. A little now won't hurt you."

Man, I am so observant. I am sitting in a bunch of cornflowers. Great for tea.

Adam pulled out his knife, cut off several small pieces of the white birch bark he had cut from the tree. At the brook's edge, he again filled his pan with water, restarted his fire, and waited for the water to boil. He added the cornflowers to the boiling water. He ate the bark and drank some of the tea. He waited a bit; felt better, and decided to try to communicate with Running-water. He leaned over to straighten his back and he vomited. He began saying a mantra over and over to calm himself and as he did, he regulated his breathing.

Unconsciously, as he sat there propped up against the base of the tree, he began to thumb Howahkan's amulet hanging around his neck. It began to hum; its tone sharp like its edges. Both sensations penetrated his whole being. His body took on a light blue glow, making him appear nearly transparent. He called Running-water's name; waited, and then repeated it.

"Great danger! Go Home! Go Alone!" Adam's voice cracked.

"Where are you? My god, Adam are you okay?" Running-water replied.

"Danger! Get away. Now!"

"From whom? From what? Why?" Running-water's voice vibrated through space-time.

There was no reply. Exhausted, Adam passed out.

A young deer, licking Adam's hand and face woke him. It was enjoying the last bit of honey that remained. Adam's movements startled the deer and it bolted. Adam managed to get off one shot; the deer fell in its tracks. He made short work of skinning and cutting up the meat. He cut enough to eat now, and some for breakfast, and some to take with him. He wrapped the rest in its skin and buried it. And remembering the ways of his father, after the burial, and before he ate, Adam gave thanks. He liked the way Jedediah Woods, Running-water's late grandfather gave thanks. Simple and to the point.

"Unto Thee."

After a quick light meal, Adam set about making a small birch bark basket and taking great care to fold the seams inside. Pulling some fringe from his shirt, Adam stitched the sides together. Next, he cut a hole in an evergreen tree, collected the pitch, and sealed the seams. Next, he got another pan of water and set it on the fire to boil. While that was being done, he made a lid for the basket. Once the water reached its boiling point, Adam poured a small quantity into his basket. Cautiously, he checked for leaks. Satisfied there were none, he filled it with the rest of the boiled water, and then placed the lid on and sealed it with pine pitch. He whittled a small wooden plug. Later, when he needed water, he would punch a small hole in his basket, take a drink, and insert the plug.

Adam decided the best thing to would be to return to the ranch. He walked around the tree he had marked. He felt relieved. He had not been out of his mind. He headed southeast. He knew where he was going and why. Thomas be hanged. As he walked along he noticed the evidence of his wandering circles. He shook his head to clear the image of what nearly had been. If he kept his current pace and followed true to his direction he figured it would take him most of three days to get back to where he had hidden the SUV.

Images of Daphne and his unborn son floated in and out as he trotted along. *Damn! My absence may have placed them in greater danger. Fool that I am.*

That thought quickened his pace, but it soon because too much. He had to slow down. He stopped once to take some water. Night came all too soon. He was forced to stop and make camp. Only once during the night did he wake up and was to vomit.

Morning sunrise found him trotting along, nibbling on his allotted ration for the morning. He had broken camp before daybreak to get a head start. It also would help him conserve his strength and cut down on his need for fluids. The swinging canteen attached to his belt reminded him of the urgency to get to the ranch. He played out various scenarios of how Thomas had poisoned his canteen. He tried to think. He wondered what kind of poison it was. And then he turned to motive.

Why would Thomas want me dead? What would he gain from my death? All of my assets are in a trust fund. With my death, neither he nor The Brothers receive any monies from my estate. Thomas moved into the titular head of The Brothers. I raised no objections. He has enjoyed my respect and acceptance. What then? Revenge? Revenge for what?

His second night out, Adam's questions haunted his already restless sleep. Images of Samuel shooting down the helicopter floated in and out of memory. Several times he woke up moaning. He wondered why Samuel was so quick to shoot it down before he knew what the intent was. Did he know it was Dutch and Brett? Then he couldn't remember if Samuel was behind the wheel of the limo. He woke with a start and became acutely alert. Nothing. He got up. Listened. The sun was waking up. He decided that if he kept up his current pace he would reach the SUV in less than two hours. He relieved himself, had a drink of water, and checked his directions. He headed south by southwest. By mid-morning he was busy clearing away the branches that hid the SUV. His hand shook as he fumbled for the key hid under the fender. Hurriedly, he unlocked the vehicle, got in, started it up, and backed it out into the open field. Even though he knew better, he traveled at a high speed for the rough terrain he was driving over. A couple of times he had to swerve, to miss large outcropping of rocks. During one such sudden swerve, he had overcompensated and to avoid hitting a large tree stump, he stomped on the brakes.

The SUV did not slow down. Adam pumped the brakes. It had no effect. He grabbed the emergency brake. It snapped in his hand. The SUV lunged forward. Adam checked the speedometer. He was moving at 70 miles per hour. He hit the tree stump at full speed. The SUV rolled over several times, spun around a couple of time before stopping with the driver's side partially buried in the dirt. Gasoline fumes surrounded him.

Sensing immediate danger, he quickly slashed his seat belt, reached up to the door above him, and got it unlocked. His arms gave way before he could push the door all the way open. The door slammed shut. He pushed on the handle, the door opened a crack as Adam crouched, firmly planting his feet on the door, he pushed. The door flew open. Adam held his breath as the door teetered. Jumping out of the driver's side, and clutching his backpack, Adam ran for the old tree stump and hit the ground. The SUV burst into flames. He waited. The explosion came.

Once he felt safe, Adam got up, looked over at the burning vehicle, and then headed toward the ranch. It was early evening when he arrived at the ranch. Caution, now his guide, he circled the ranch, a couple of times to check it out, No lights were on. Remembering the underground connecting passageway from the caretaker's house to the main house, Adam picked up a long stick and tapped each step, and then the door to the cottage. Nothing happened. Slowly he turned the nob of the front door, and using the stick, pushed it open. He picked up a chair from the porch and shoved it through the door. Nothing.

He turned on the lights, looked around, found a flashlight, and then opened the hidden door to the underground. Cautiously, he eased himself into the tunnel. The air inside was stale and that told him no one had been in the tunnel or operated the air system. He was soon in the hidden chamber with the tank and back in his master suite on the second floor. Adam quickly checked the security system. After doing a visual survey inside the house he did a sweep of the parameters of the property. He could see a faint glow from the still burning SUV. The lack of transportation struck home enforcing his isolation. *Good god! The horses!*

Reaching for his backpack, Adam removed his two Glocks and two extra clips. He adjusted their shoulder holsters and then headed out the door. He stopped, went back into the room, fished around in his backpack and retrieved his knife, strapped that on his hip and then left. He paused at the controls, shut off the alarm system, and then headed for corral. No horses. He whistled. No reply. Straining to see if there were any dark mounds in the pasture,

Adam could detect none. Even if wolves or bears had gotten the horses, part of their carcasses would be visible.

Adam whistled again and from far off in the distance came a distinct whinny. He whistled again. And again received an answer. He went into the barn and filled two buckets with oats. He checked to make sure water was still running in the trough. Once they had their fill, Adam led into the barn, put them in their separate stalls, tossed in some fresh straw, and then brushed each down. He locked them in and as he was leaving he remembered the truck. It was parked in one of the stalls. He picked up the keys that were hanging nearby on a peg. He climbed in, turned the ignition; the engine fired. He eased the truck out of the barn and drove it up to the house. Being in the truck brought back the whole panorama of events that had taken place since his arrival at the ranch. He shuddered at the memory of all the deaths.

That thought put Adam on edge as he re-entered the house. Hunger made itself know and he immediately went to the kitchen. He ate a light meal, and as was custom, he went into the great room to sip an after dinner brandy. He slouched on the remaining couch. He had had the red leather chairs packed. Memories again took hold of him; unpleasant as they were, Adam finally drifted off into a deep sleep.

It was either the morning sun or the growling in his stomach that woke him. After a quick breakfast, Adam opened the vault. No eagle sculpture and no portrait of Esaugetuh showed up. The room was empty. He sniffed the air. It was foul.

"Man, something sure stinks in here," Adam said out loud.

Realizing he was smelling himself, Adam returned to the master suite, stripped off his overly ripe deerskins, shaved off his beard, and jumped into a very much need shower. After enjoying a luxurious shower, he stepped out and stood in front of the wall of mirrors. He took his time toweling down, letting his towel glide over his private parts. *Well, you don't look too bad from all the crap you've been through. Not bad at all.* He let his fingers linger beneath his towel as he enjoyed his sensuality. It had been too long since he had—that thought was cut off when he noticed the blinker on the telephone. He pushed the button to play the message. It was Running-water pleading with him to make contact. It brought Adam's personal inner despair to the surface. He wept, long deep gut wrenching sobs, spasms shook him. *Why me? What have I done to deserve this constant inner pain, this damnable demonic torture?*

From the wellsprings of his tormented soul came his answer: Because you are man!

That answer brought Adam clear focus. The old saw, 'no use crying over spilled milk' had new meaning. What was and what has been is over. Time to move on. After all, reality is neither right nor wrong. It just is! And that reality brought a new decision. Once dressed, he went out, got in the truck, and drove out to the airstrip. He sat there for a while, examining what had gone on there. *At what point was the bomb planted on the jet?* An answer was not made known. He started the truck, backed it up, and headed back to the ranch.

Adam had gone only a short distance when he spotted movement in the brush. Thinking it might be a bear, he slowed the truck. He heard the most god-awful bellowing. Out of the bushes lumbered a wild-looking figure. It hobbled, lunged, and then fell down, still yelling at the top of its lungs. The forlorn figure jumped up, wildly waving its arms. Adam stopped the truck. He couldn't believe his eyes. The once rotund Samuel, now half his former size, clothes tattered flapped around his skinny body.

Out of breath, and quite beside himself, Samuel, still bellowing, said, "I'm so sorry, Adam. I know I've failed you. Forgive me, please. I beg you."

Tears streamed down his once round face.

"Where have you been? Climb in," Adam said as he reached across the seat and opened the door.

"Thank god you are alright. I've been searching for you. Running-water said I was to stick with you and that's what I was trying to do," Samuel said.

"What happened?"

"I lost your trail. I found it again, but it just kept going around and around in circles. Then it suddenly veered off. And here I am," Samuel said gasping for air.

"And so you are," Adam replied as he headed back to the ranch.

Once Samuel had something to eat, he showered and much to his dismay realized he didn't have any clothes to put on. He began hollering, "Adam, I'm naked. No clothes."

Adam went upstairs, found a pair of pants and a shirt. Samuel was happy to have them. Adam had to stifle a laugh. Standing in front of him was the best clown he'd ever seen. Actually, a living vision of an old Laurel and Hardy silent movie. Baggy pants, shirtsleeves hanging below his fingertips, and a belt wrapped around him a couple of times created a wonderful child-like image in a grown-up body. "Yes, Adam thought, "a living cartoon."

Adam took the mirror down from the wall; the same one Running-water used to make him look at himself.

"Look at yourself. Go ahead, take a good long look."

Samuel began to laugh. They both laughed. The place needed laughter to cleanse it of the horror that had taken place there; a humor sanitation. And it worked. Adam pushed a button and all the lights in the house came on making the place warm, inviting, and glowing.

"Go back upstairs to either Dutch or Brett's room and see if they left some clothes that might fit you," Adam said as he replaced the mirror.

Samuel did as he was told. Went to Dutch's room and found some clothes that almost fit him. He did a double take in the mirror. It was true; he was almost handsome. He was pleased. *Man, I have never looked so good. All my life I have been overweight. When people were nice to me they called me 'the hulk' but when they were mean, which was most of the time, they called out 'oink oink'.* He remembered trying out for the football team. The coach told not to bother. He had hoped The Brothers would provide him the family he never had, always wanted; at least accept him. *Man that would have been something had my old man accepted me. He was too drunk most of the time to I even existed.* Joseph was especially cruel making him do the dirtiest of jobs.

Samuel tilted his head just a bit and then began to hum "There's been a change in me." And there had.

"Samuel, come join me in a brandy," Adam said patting a cushion next to him on the couch he was sitting. The place looked really naked without all the other furniture. *Strange this couch wasn't taken.* Handing Samuel his drink, Adam continued, "Why didn't you go with the others? I'm sure I saw you behind the wheel of the limo?"

"There was a lot of whispering going on among The Brothers as we were loading the limo. Thomas was giving a lot of orders. You know they never liked me; always made fun of me," Samuel said.

"You have any idea what they were whispering about?"

"No. Every time I would get near them, they shut up."

"Did you ever notice any of The Brothers handling a canteen in the kitchen?"

"A canteen? No. Why?"

"I believe my canteen of water was poisoned," Adam said. He had decided to completely trust Samuel. "I think it was Thomas but I don't know why he would do such a thing. I've treated him with respect and kindness."

"You don't know? Thomas and Joseph are real brothers. Joseph was always the boss, and Thomas would do whatever he was told. I think Joseph is trying to get even with you for tossing him out on his ear."

"I didn't know. That explains much," Adam said.

"I'll go back to Toronto. I know where Joseph is. I will get both of them and ring their necks. Just leave them to me," Samuel said, deepening his voice.

"All in good time, Samuel. All in good time. Right now, we have other things to do," Adam replied.

"We do!" Samuel loved it, especially the *we* part.

The aged brandy worked its magic on both men. Neither being in the best of shape, went to sleep where they were. Morning sunrise found them still asleep. It was the sound of a jet, flying low, that woke them.

Adam rushed to the veranda, Samuel with a gun, hobbled along; his feet still sore from all the miles he had walked. He was ready to shoot. The jet came back, tipped its wing and heading for the landing strip. Adam with Samuel drove the truck to the airstrip. As the plane taxied to a halt, Adam saw Brett wave.

Once out of the plane, both Dutch and Brett exclaimed, "What the hell happened to you, Adam? Who's that with you?"

"It's me, Samuel."

"I'll be damned," Brett said as he scratched his head.

"How'd it go in Albuquerque?" Adam asked.

"Great. Running-water's uncle is a neat guy. Even though he hired Dutch and me, it was my first time meeting him. It took him some time getting your film developed because he thought you wanted prints made," Brett said handing Adam an envelope.

"Thanks," Adam said as he shuffled the photos.

He sighed in relief. None showed Esaugetuh. One did show Josh Langford giving orders.

"We were right about Langford," Adam said.

"Yeah, he was one smooth character," Brett said.

We still don't know what has happened to my father or where he might be. Anyway, tomorrow we will fly back to Toronto. We have an issue there that needs our attention," Adam said.

CHAPTER 25
THE TRAP

With the proper bait and hook, patience becomes the line to make the catch.

Esaugetuh

Unannounced, the trio, Dutch, Brett, and Running-water arrived a Karuna House. Their unexpected arrival threw The Brothers into a quandary. Thomas, now ensconced on the third floor of the mansion, was beside himself. He paced up and down the floor, muttering and sometimes swearing.

"Why have these bastards come here, especially now? I'm sure Adam has sent them off in different directions. Ah, Adam is dead. That's it. They've come here to tell me Adam is dead. Now we'll see who's the Master of Karuna House."

Gulping in air, Thomas struggled to control his inward excitement over the prospective news. Shaking himself before he emerged from the creaky elevator, he paused, took a deep breath, and emerged. He was dressed in a flowing white robe with a large medallion hung on a rope around his neck. Sole-thin white leather sandals were on his feet. He was sure his outfit would impress.

Dutch's loud laughter roared up to the top of the mansion and echoed back as he looked at the pathetic figure standing in front of him. All it lacked was a crown of laurel on its head. Julius Caesar, it wasn't.

"Well, well what the hell are you supposed to be? Didn't Adam tell you to get rid of the robes?

"I am Master of Karuna House now, and I'll dress any way I please. And don't get unpleasant with me. There are ways to deal with your kind. Why are you here? Aren't you supposed to be doing something somewhere else?"

"You are laboring under a grand delusion. You, Thomas, are master of nothing, let along Karuna House. As Adam's attorney and trustee, I know of nothing that even mentions you or The Brothers. If I recall, he ordered you to leave here. You were each given a nice sum of money and told to put it away for a rainy day. Well, Thomas, the rain has come," Running-water said.

"Yeah, and while you are at it toga boy, round up the rest of the crew and have them meet me in the main dining room. I've got work assignments for them," Brett said. "And Thomas, for your sake, I hope you haven't moved into Adam's private quarters. Adam's wife will live there once she gets here."

"Well, why is she coming here?" Thomas replied with a petulant look. He never could stand up to men bigger than he was.

"Why? This is her home, that's why. I sure she'll want to do some redecorating, even remodeling the place and I am just as sure she will not want a bunch of misfits getting in her way," Running-water said.

"Misfits? How dare—,"

"Didn't I just tell you to do something? Do it!" Brett said as he stepped toward the cowering Thomas.

Picking up his robe as if it were a long skirt, Thomas hurried off. On his way, he stopped and made a phone call. *Joseph will know what to do. He always does.*

A loud banging rumbled up from the main gate. Two of The Brothers were tearing down the sign that said The Esaugetuh Institute. They would have removed the name Karuna house if it hadn't been carved into one of the cement pillars that held the massive gate.

Inside, Running-water finally answered the ringing phone. As he listened to his wife, Isha, pretending to be Daphne he heard a click. She continued giving orders for work to be done; the listener heard it all just as it had been planned.

A beehive of workers and their activities began early the next morning. Dutch and Brett had chores for The Brothers in preparation for Isha's arrival.

Refusing to come to breakfast, the sulking Thomas stayed in a small apartment. His patience was evaporating as he waited for the call from his brother, Joseph. Then it struck him. *Oh shit! If I could listen in when the phone rang so could someone listen when I called out.*

Totally dumbed, he stood there. Then anger flooded him. Frantically, he searched for a cell phone Joseph had given him. He didn't like new gadgets and had put it somewhere out of sight. He had classified it as a nuisance. *Yes, it's in one of my suitcases.*

Thomas yanked one of the heavy cases from his closet, dragged it out into the room, and hurriedly opened it. The cell phone was not there. Panic seized him. He dragged out two more suitcases. He dumped everything on the floor. No phone. Beads of sweat formed along with his shaved head. He felt them trickle down its sides. He wiped his head. Then it came to him. *My blazer! Of course; what an idiot. Joseph had insisted I carry it with me.*

Throwing clothes out of his closet, he found the blue blazer. He found the phone and quickly punched the number his brother had preset.

"Hello," Joseph said.

"Why have you called me back. I've been waiting. They are here. What do you want me to do? She's arriving soon. What? No, nothing has been said about Adam's death. No, I don't think they are suspicious. No, nothing has been said about remodeling the garage area. You should have called me. You know I get nervous," Thomas whine.

He listened to the screaming voice on the other end. He was so nervous he hadn't noticed he had wet his pants. Once the screaming stopped, Thomas punched 'end'. He dropped his robe and changed his boxers. He slipped into a pair of gray slacks, white collar-less shirt, and the blue blazer with the monogram on the right breast pocket. *No robes. Okay, I'll give them no robes but the sandals stay.*

Once he had returned to the main part of the mansion, Thomas found everyone busy. No one

393

stopped and looked up. He felt left out. He went into what was 'their' dining room. It was empty. Two of The Brothers were scrubbing the floor. Thomas cleared his throat to draw attention to himself.

"You still here? You missed breakfast. Too bad, 'cause it was good. Well, just don't stand there. Grab a brush and start scrubbing. This whole place has to be disinfected," Charles said without stopping his rhythm of circular strokes on the marble floor.

Ignoring the curtness, Thomas said, "You seen that high-and-mighty lawyer?"

"I'm right behind you," Running-water said.

Thomas froze.

"Since you are nearly dressed suppose you get ready to greet the mistress of the house. And Thomas, the sandals, a bit girlish, don't you think?"

"No actually—,"

Running-water was gone.

"Damn you. Just you wait Mr. Smart ass lawyer, Just you wait," Thomas said.

"What did you say?" Charles said.

"Shut up, freak," Thomas said as he swirled around and left the room.

The clanging of the doorbell brought Dutch to the door as he unsnapped the strap to his holster. Running-water was right behind him.

"What do you want"? Dutch growled.

"It's me, Samuel."

"Good god, man."

"Here. This is all I found," Samuel said.

"What this? Running-water asked.

"Adam's leather backpack," Samuel said.

"Better come on into the office," Running-water said.

At the office, Samuel took great pains to speak loud enough for the eavesdropping Thomas to hear every word.

"Found the SUV. Burnt to a crisp. Nothing but a frame left. He's dead. At least I think he's dead," Thomas said.

"What do you mean you think he's dead? Running-water asked.

"Well, it's sort of strange. I suppose it could have been my imagination. Probably was.

"What was strange? Get to the point," Brett said as he joined the group.

"Well, at the ranch, I heard this noise. I was in the main room. I looked up and I swear to god there was this shadow along the wall of the upper balcony. It scared the life out of me. Didn't sleep all night."

"That's all, a shadow and a noise?" Dutch asked.

"Well, not exactly. You see, at the same time, I saw the shadow the fire flared up," Samuel said enjoying every delicious embellishment.

"Big deal, The fire flared up," Running-water said.

"I hadn't built a fire," Samuel said.

"Now that weird, actually off the wall weird," Brett said.

"Yeah, it was like his spirit or ghost was there. I don't think I've been the same since," Samuel said as he turned to leave the office.

"Where are you going?" Dutch asked.

"I'm not staying here. He may come here."

"Who might come here?" Brett asked.

"Adam. Ghosts can travel. He may have followed me," Samuel said.

"Come on now. Surely you don't believe in such things?" Running-water said.

"He was a shaman. Anything is possible. I'll be staying in town," Samuel said as he winked at his three interrogators.

Thomas barely ducked out of sight when Samuel stepped into the hallway and headed toward the main reception room. He stopped in the middle of the room, looked at himself in one of the mirrors. *Yes! There's been a change in me.* He clicked his heels together and then went into the room where Charles was scrubbing the floor.

"Give your mother a call at the sanitarium for me, will you. Tell her Samuel is coming to call on her."

Shocked, all Charles could do was nod. Julie was working nights and would be even more shocked.

Thomas scurried back to his apartment. Stunned to see his personal belongings sitting out in the hallway, he tried the door. It was locked. He fumbled around in his blazer trying to find his key. It didn't work. Anger swelled up and choked him. His temples pounded in a rage, and his face turned a deep red. He began to hyperventilate. He sat down and desperately tried to relax. His mind was in a race with itself. *I should have known there'd be trouble. Relax. I've got to relax. Joseph, all me. What am I to do? Where am I to go? Oh, God! I think I'm dying.*

Thomas became aware of someone standing over him.

"Ah, here you are. There's a cot for you in the garage. You might ask one of The Brothers to help you with your belongings," Running-water said. "Watch the steps, Thomas. There's not much light there and they are narrow. Might even have a rat or two sitting on them. You could fall and hurt yourself."

The word 'rats' brought a new terror to Thomas. He was sure he was going to pass out, fall the full length of the narrow stairs, and then the rats would eat him alive. He shuddered at the thought as he tried to pick up one of the heavy suitcases. *Hmm, wonder where the pig is. He can carry these down there. He sure looked different. Charles, yes, Charles can do this.*

Charles was nowhere to be found. Thomas dragged the suitcases and his other belongs down the stairs. Off in a corner, he found a cot with his footlocker. He sat down and bawled. *They are going to get theirs.* He sniffed, got up, and inches his way back upstairs.

Unbeknown to The Brothers, Adam had slipped into the house when Samuel had arrived. Revising the Dickens' "A Christmas Carol" Adam made use of the sound system Joseph had used to scare him away, add a different dialogue. Two Toronto Police officers had also slipped into the mansion and helped Adam set up additional hidden speakers. Once he was sure Thomas was back upstairs, Running-water joined them. Turning Thomas' cot over, Running-water made some adjustments which included a small motor that would tip the cot over. Projectors were in place to flash images of a ghost-like Adam meandering around the basement. Satisfied that the stage was properly set, Running-water returned to the first floor. He went directly to the office and called the police. He emailed them the evidence of Joseph's embezzlement of the Esaugetuh Benevolent Society and requested Joseph be arrested. He heard the clang of the doorbell. It would be Isha pretending to be Daphne. He waited a moment for Thomas to go to the door.

Thomas slowly opened the door. His lower jaw dropped. Standing before him was a woman dressed in a silk black dress, black stilettos, and a string of black pearls, black gloves, and a wide-brimmed black hat. As Running-water approached he hugged the woman and said, "Daphne."

Turning to Thomas, he said, "Show Adam's wife to her apartment. Also, have our evening meal sent up. I will be staying with my sister."

Dinner that evening was later than usual. Thomas was in a pout and ate little. Dutch and Brett ate and excused themselves to go back into the city. All were amazed at how little Samuel ate. Conversation did not exist; each man keeping his thoughts to himself. Once finished, The Brothers took their plates into the kitchen. Samuel left to go and call on Julie. Thomas returned to the basement garage.

Not bothering to undress, he lay down on the cot and tried to mediate. The single ceiling light flickered. He unfolded his hands from their prayer position and folded them as he imagined they would be, on his chest, in his coffin. The light's continual flickering began to annoy him. He considered turning it off but changed his mind. *The rats might come out.*

He sat up, straining to hear. He was sure he heard someone groan. He held his breath. He heard it again.

"Who's there?"

No answer. He tried to calm his breathing. He heard the groan again and this time he was sure it came from behind the new wall they had put up. *Yes, I'm sure of it. It's coming from that room.* He rolled over and covered his head with his pillow.

At some point after midnight, Running-water joined Adam and the two Toronto Police Officers in the basement. Adam was dressed in a ghoulish looking costume that glowed in dim light. Running-water pressed a button and the groaning began. He pressed a second button and Thomas' cot began to shake and eventually turned up on one side, rolling him onto the cement floor.

At first, Thomas thought he had been having a nightmare and fell off the cot. Moaning from the darker corners of the garage quickly changed his mind. He shivered as he tried to cover his eyes with shaking hands. He saw it. It was moving toward him. Large and terrifying it stopped right in front of him. Thomas wet his pants as the ghastly thing raised its long boney finger and pointed it at him. Bloody eyes stared at him. Thomas tried to scream. No sound came from his mouth.

"Why did you do it? Tell me why," a growly voice echoed throughout the garage.

"Who, who-who are you? What do you want?" Thomas whispered.

"Why did you do it? Tell me why," boomed the voice as the ghoul leaned over the sprawled Thomas.

Thomas felt his bowels give way. The smell made him sick to his stomach. He leaned over and vomited.

"Tell me why or you will die. Why did you do it?"

Moaning filled the garage as a canteen flew across the floor and stopped inches from Thomas.

He screamed. "Joseph, Joseph made me do it. He made me poison you."

"Why? Tell me why?"

"He killed your father and made me help him. He wanted you out of the way so he could return as Master of Karuna House. Oh, god, please, please don't hurt me," Thomas sobbed.

At that, Adam grabbed Thomas by the throat and began to shake him. "What did you just say? Speak up you miserable excuse for a man."

"Your father is dead. Joseph killed him. He's behind that wall."

Adam released his hold on Thomas. He dragged a finger down Thomas' nose and blew into his eyes, and whispered, "Fear is now your companion."

Thomas collapsed, whimpering.

The two Toronto Police Officers stepped out of the shadows, cuffed Thomas, and let him out to a waiting police car.

A phone call from Running-water brought a half dozen police cars. One officer, using a jackhammer, tore through the wall. The smell was nauseating. Their floodlights revealed a lump on the floor. Two officers, with their faces masked, entered the small room.

Ignoring orders to not enter the six by four-foot room, bent down to look at the figure on the floor. He saw some strands of long white hair, a medicine bag, and something shiny beneath what appeared to be fingers. He was about to take it when an officers yelled at him to not touch anything.

"You must wait outside, sir. I'm sorry, but I must insist."

"A moment, please, a short prayer," Adam said.

In respect, the officer waited. Quickly, Adam picked up the shiny object. It was a ring.

"Thank you," Adam said. "We'll be upstairs if you need us."

In his office, Adam looked at the ring. Inside were his mother and Esaugetuh's names. Tears flowed as he showed the ring to Running-water.

"At last I've found my father," Adam said as Running-water hugged him.

"So you have, my brother. So you have."

THE END

End Notes

1) The Anasazi are often referred to as The Ancient Ones. It's a Navajo word originally meaning "ancestral enemies" but has now been accepted as appropriate archaeological terminology and connotes nothing derogatory.
2) Metate is a stone with a hollow area in its center and is used as a grinding basin. The mano is a smooth stone used to grind corn or other edible vegetation.
3) Wilder, Thornton. The Bridge of San Luis Rey. Washington Square Press, Inc. New York. 1959. Pp 116-117.
4) Actually it was asafetida, an herb used for protection. Highly pungent.
5) Means "If mind and heart become one, nothing is impossible."
6) Sumerian Queen of the Underworld. Also spelled Eriskegal.
7) In Ancient Egypt, this was called the Ka; a double that existed independent of the body and capable of eating, drinking, and moving at will.
8) In Ancient Egypt, this was called the Khabit, and like the Ka, it could travel at will.
9) A Gaelic word meaning soul friend.
10) 2,138,14-18

11) Wilfred M. Voynich, an American antique book dealer who discovered the manuscript in 1912.
12) Calvin and Hobbes are character created by world renowned cartoonist, Bill Watterson.
13) Sioux name meaning 'one of the mysterious voice.'
14) A star that disappears and is often linked to Zeus, The Titans, and or Dionysus.
15) Spirit Master
16) Giants are often a topic in the ancient mythologies. They also appear in Samuel, Genesis, Deuteronomy, and Joshua of the Christian Bible. They are referenced in The Book of Enoch.